Gansett After Dark

The McCarthys of Gansett Island Book 11

Marie Force

Gansett After Dark
McCarthys of Gansett Island Series, Book 11
By: Marie Force

Published by HTJB, Inc.

Cover by Kristina Brinton
Interior Layout: Isabel Sullivan
ISBN: 978-0991418237

marieforce.com

The McCarthys of Gansett Island Series

McCarthys of Gansett Island Boxed Set

Book 1: Maid for Love

Book 2: Fool for Love

Book 3: Ready for Love

Book 4: Falling for Love

Book 5: Hoping for Love

Book 6: Season for Love

Book 7: Longing for Love

Book 8: Waiting for Love

Book 9: Time for Love

Book 10: Meant for Love

Book 10.5: Chance for Love,

A Gansett Island Novella

Book 11: Gansett After Dark

AUTHOR'S NOTE

Welcome to *Gansett After Dark*, book 11 in the McCarthys of Gansett Island Series! When I first wrote *Maid for Love* back in 2010, I couldn't imagine a time when I'd be talking about the eleventh book in the series that began with that first story, but here we are! Three years after *Maid for Love* hit the e-book shelves, readers are still clamoring for more of the McCarthys, and I still look forward to every minute I get to spend on Gansett Island. It's a match made in writer's heaven!

In the McCarthy Reader Group on Facebook, we spent a lot of time talking about *Gansett After Dark* and batting around ideas for everything from sexy nights with each couple to a sex toy party hosted by Tiffany, which is something I'd still like to do sometime. While many of the ideas were amusing and fun to think about, when it came time to write the book, Owen's story was the one that called to me the most. He's come so far from his old life and is happily settled with Laura. Now he must confront the past before he can move on to the happy future he deserves. Putting his father's trial at the center of this book also gave me the opportunity to move several other stories forward, namely that of Charlie and Sarah, a couple that has interested me from the day they first met.

Rest assured, you can count on plenty of sizzle between some of our favorite couples and a glimpse at what everyone is up to as we move forward into the next phase in this series. Oh and did I mention you might get more than just one wedding in this book?! And look for a blockbuster development in the lives of Big Mac and Linda McCarthy that will ricochet through their entire family. As always, thank you for coming along on this ride with me. I'm so happy to be continuing to write this series we've all come to love so much.

xoxo

Marie

CHAPTER 1

The creak of the rocking chair on the new wooden deck, the warm afternoon breeze off the ocean, the heat of the baby asleep on his chest and the bustle of the town he now called home soothed and calmed Owen Lawry. Along the newly painted white porch rail were flower boxes containing the pink, lavender and white impatiens Laura had nurtured all summer.

Every square inch of the Sand & Surf Hotel had been renovated in the last year, leaving the scents of sawdust and fresh paint behind. They'd been operating at full capacity since Memorial Day, and it was indeed thrilling to see the hotel open and once again full of happy visitors.

Almost a year ago, Owen had stood on this same deck and watched the last ferry depart on Columbus Day. It had felt symbolic then. With that ferry went his old life as a footloose and fancy-free troubadour, traveling from gig to gig, following the seasons and the work.

He'd stayed that day. He'd stayed because of Laura. He'd stayed because he could no longer imagine a day—hell, an *hour*—without her. And he'd never regretted it. Not for one second. Her son, Holden, the child they were raising together even though another man had fathered him, was now as much Owen's as he was Laura's. Earlier in the summer, they'd been surprised to learn they were expecting twins together. He who had never wanted the constraints of commitment or marriage or family was now as committed as any man could be, and he'd never been happier as their wedding date got closer with every passing day.

Just one thing stood between him and the future he wanted so desperately with Laura, Holden and the twins—his father's trial. The thought of seeing his father again for the first time in more than a decade made Owen feel sick and anxious and fearful, as if he were still a five-year-old who couldn't figure out what he'd done to stir his father's wrath.

In a few days, he and Laura, his mother and Laura's father, along with several friends who would be testifying, would depart Gansett on the ferry and travel to Virginia for the trial. Frank was coming to help out with Holden while they were in court. Owen didn't want Laura to come, but she insisted on being there for him. He hated the thought of her sitting in the courtroom listening to the nightmare that had been his life in vivid detail that would shock and horrify her.

But he would've done the same for her. He would've insisted on being there, even if she didn't want him to come.

The screen door opened, and Owen glanced over his shoulder as his mother came toward him.

"I was wondering where you guys had gotten off to," Sarah Lawry said as she sat in the rocker next to them. She tucked her chin-length blonde hair behind her ear. "Is he asleep?"

"Out cold."

"You could put him in his crib, you know," she said in a teasing tone.

"I much prefer this." Holden's wispy dark hair brushed against Owen's chin, so soft it felt like an angel's wings.

"I always did, too."

Owen looked over at her. "Are you going to talk to Charlie before we leave?"

"I'm having dinner with him tonight."

"Will you tell him where we're going and why?"

"I want to. I need to. I know I do. It's just… It's hard to talk about."

"He deserves to know, Mom. He's been an amazing friend to you for months now." Owen directed his gaze toward the ferry coming toward the breakwater, bringing another group of tourists to the island. This time of year, the ferries came and went all day and well into the night. "Think of it this way. You'll be talking about it a lot in the next week or so. May as well get it all over with at once so you never have to talk about it again."

"You make good points, and I'm going to try tonight. That's the best I can do."

"I'll tell him if you want me to."

"That's very generous of you, but it needs to come from me. I owe him that much."

"I'm still trying to figure out a way to talk Laura out of coming with us."

"I don't think that's going to happen. She's quite determined."

"I know."

His mother reached over to put her hand on his arm. "She loves you, Owen. She wants to support you through this. You have to let her."

"I know that, too. What will you say when Charlie tells you he loves you and wants to support you through it?"

"That's different. We aren't engaged or having children together, and he doesn't love me. Not like Laura loves you."

"If that's what you think, you haven't been paying attention to the way he looks at you. Love is love, Mom. You need to be prepared for him to want to come."

Out of the corner of his eye, Owen saw his mother shudder at the thought of Charlie coming with them to Virginia.

"I talked to John today," he said of his brother who worked as a police officer in Tennessee. "He can't make it next week or to the wedding. They have two guys out on medical leave, so he can't get the time off. He said to tell you he's sorry."

"So… That leaves just us, huh?"

All of Owen's six siblings had called in the last week to tell him they couldn't make it to the trial for one reason or another. For most of them it had come down to a choice—go to the trial or come to Gansett for his wedding. Not surprisingly, most of them had chosen option B.

"It's all right. Between the two of us, we'll get the job done." The only thing that mattered at the end of the day was seeing his father put away for a long time for the abuse he'd inflicted on his wife and children for decades, culminating in the vicious beating that had brought Sarah to Gansett last fall to recover. She'd stayed ever since and had been instrumental in helping him and Laura run the Sand & Surf Hotel and care for Holden, too.

"I don't know what I'd ever do without you, Owen. You and I… We've traveled a long road together."

"I was just thinking how Laura and I never would've gotten through the last year without you here to help us."

The comment drew a smile from his mother. He'd never seen her so happy or so at peace and hated the thought of the trial disrupting the hard-won peace for either of them. "Despite everything that brought me here, this year has been one of the best of my life. With some time and perspective, I can't believe I ever lived the way I did for as long as I did."

"That's over now. One more hurdle to clear and you're free."

"Two hurdles. Still waiting on the divorce, too. Naturally, your father is stonewalling the entire process."

"Of course he is."

"I wish I could've been there when his lawyer informed him that he has to pay half his pension to me every month."

Owen grunted out a laugh. "You earned every dime of it and then some. Besides, he'll be getting his three hots and a cot from the Commonwealth of Virginia for the foreseeable future. He won't have much need for his pension."

"What if he's not convicted?" Sarah asked, her brows furrowing with worry.

"He will be. There's no way he's going to walk with all the evidence we have piled up against him. David, Blaine and Slim will all be there to testify about your condition and injuries when you got here last October. It's a slam dunk."

"Except none of them can testify to the fact that they saw your father beat me."

"That's where I come in. I'll testify that I saw him repeatedly beat you. We'll get him, Mom. Try not to worry."

"What I really worry about is what'll happen if we don't get him. He'll come after me, and we'll all be in danger."

"He won't come near you. No matter what happens in the trial, you'll still have a restraining order that keeps him far away from you."

"I hate the idea of seeing him again. I know you must feel the same way. It's been a long time."

"Not long enough, but I'll do whatever it takes to make sure he can never lay a hand on you or anyone else ever again." Despite his intense desire to keep his emotions out of the equation, his voice wavered on those last words.

"Owen…"

"I look at him, you know?" Gazing down at the baby he loved with everything he had, Owen ran his hand over Holden's back. "He trusts me implicitly. He trusts me enough to fall asleep in my arms because he already knows I'd never let anything happen to him. How does anyone violate that kind of trust and hurt a child who depends on them for everything? How does a man become that kind of monster?"

"I don't know," Sarah said with a weary sigh. "I'll never understand how that happens. And you'll never know how much I regret the way you grew up, the sacrifices you made for all of us."

"I have no regrets, because everything that happened led me to exactly where I belong—and it led you to where you belong, too."

Holden squirmed in his arms but didn't wake up.

"I'm going to walk him upstairs." Owen stood, balancing the baby carefully. "Talk to Charlie, Mom. Let him in. You won't be sorry you did."

"Even if he insists on coming with us?"

"Especially then."

She smiled up at him. "You're a son any mother would be proud to call her own."

"It's all thanks to you. We don't give the sperm donor any credit."

Sarah laughed the way he hoped she would. "No, we don't."

"Have a good time tonight. I'll see you later."

"See you."

Owen left his mother rocking on the front porch and stepped into the cool lobby, where one of the young women they'd hired to help during the summer managed the front desk. She smiled at him as he went by with Holden.

He went up the stairs to the third-floor apartment he shared with Laura and Holden. They were going to have to find a bigger place before the two new babies arrived early next year, but for now, their rooms at the hotel suited them. In truth, Owen would be sad to move out of the apartment where he'd fallen in love with Laura and lived so happily with her and Holden.

He used his key in the door and moved quietly inside the apartment, where Laura was enjoying an afternoon nap. She'd been so tired during her first trimester with the twins. As with Holden, she'd also suffered from horrible morning sickness that tended to go on for most of the day. That was another reason Owen wanted her to stay home when he went to Virginia.

Owen deposited Holden into his crib and pulled the lightweight blanket over him that his mother had crocheted. Sarah fussed over the baby like a proud grandmother. It didn't matter to her, any more than it mattered to Owen, that another man had fathered him. Holden was his, and he was Sarah's, too. There was nothing either of them wouldn't do for him.

Before he left the baby to sleep, Owen bent over the crib to kiss his soft head. Closing the door behind him, he went into the bedroom he shared with Laura, who was curled up on her side, her blonde hair spread out on the pillow. Moving slowly so he wouldn't disturb her, he stretched out next to her on the bed and tried to force himself to relax. However, relaxation of any kind would be all but impossible until they got through the trial that had been hanging over them for almost a year now.

He tried not to think about the worst-case scenario—that his father might actually be acquitted. But even if that unlikely outcome occurred, at least his mother had finally left him once and for all. Owen and his siblings had spent years pleading with her to leave, but she had always gone back—until this most recent blowup, after which she had finally ended the marriage for good. His father was now out of all their lives, or he would be before much longer.

Without opening her eyes, Laura reached out to him, her hand landing on his chest. "What's on your mind?"

"Nothing much. Just taking a break next to my favorite girl."

Her lips curved into a small smile. "I'm a ball of laughs lately. If I'm not puking, I'm sleeping."

Since she was awake, he reached for her and brought her into his embrace, her head resting on his chest. "I'll take you any way I can get you."

"Love truly is blind."

"I love you so much, Laura. You can't possibly know how much."

Her eyes opened and zeroed in on his face. "What's wrong?"

"You think something's wrong because I told you how much I love you?"

"It's more the way you said it, as if you're worried I don't know. So tell me what's wrong."

Owen knew it was probably pointless to try to talk her out of coming with them, but he felt he needed to try again anyway. "I wish you weren't coming to Virginia." He paused before he added, "That didn't come out the way I intended it to. You know I want you with me no matter where I am. It's just this time... The thought of you hearing all that..."

Laura raised herself up so she could see his face. "Are you afraid it might change how I feel about you if I hear the dirty details about your father?"

"Maybe."

"It won't." She kissed him and gazed down at him with love in her eyes. "Please don't ask me to let you go through this by yourself. You did it alone for thirty-four years. You're not alone anymore."

Her sweet words brought tears to his eyes. In his wildest imagination, he never could've dreamed of the life or the love he'd found with her. Trying to contain the flood of emotion that wanted out, he closed his eyes tightly. He didn't want to be this guy—the one who was laid low by childhood demons he should've conquered long ago.

Determined to power through it the way he always did, he settled her gently back on her pillow and sat up. "My mom's going out with Charlie tonight. Why don't we take dinner down to the beach and let Holden get dirty?"

Laura looked at him intently before she nodded in agreement. "Sure, that sounds like fun."

He leaned over to kiss her. "I'll go to the store and get something for dinner. Be right back." Owen left the apartment feeling like he'd dodged an emotional bullet. He knew she was only trying to help him, but her sweetness and desire to help made him feel raw and unable to face the firestorm that lay ahead of him. Somehow he had to find a way to talk her out of coming with them, and he only had a few days left in which to do it.

Chapter 2

For a long time after Owen left, Laura lay on the bed, thinking about what he'd said. He really didn't want her to go with him, and she understood why. However, she couldn't imagine letting him face such an upsetting and difficult thing on his own, which left her truly torn by what he said he wanted and what she thought he needed.

A light tap on the door jarred her out of her thoughts. "Come in."

"Just me," her brother Shane said.

"I'm in here."

He appeared in the bedroom doorway, tall, handsome and deeply tanned from working outdoors all summer. In addition to helping her and Owen at the hotel, he'd been overseeing the building of affordable housing on property left to the town by the late Mrs. Chesterfield.

"You're home early," Laura said.

"It's so freaking hot out. I couldn't take any more."

"Grab something to drink. There's water and soda in the fridge, and I think Owen's got some beer, too."

"I'd die for a Coke." Shane went to the tiny galley kitchen and returned with his soda and a cold bottle of water for her that Laura accepted gratefully.

"Have a seat," she said, gesturing toward the end of the bed. He was lean but muscular, too. His light brown hair had bleached to blond in the summer sun.

"I'm too dirty." He leaned against the doorway and guzzled his drink, sighing with pleasure as he ran the can over his face. The time on the island had been good for her younger brother. He'd recovered—as much as one ever did—from the bitter disappointment of his failed marriage to Courtney, who'd hidden an addiction to pain medication from him. "Where's my nephew?"

"Taking a nap."

"I was going to ask if I could take him down to play in the sand."

"We're going down there for dinner." She reached for her phone and sent Owen a text, telling him to add a sandwich for Shane. "You're coming with us."

"I am?"

"You are. I just told Owen to get you something for dinner."

His bright blue eyes were filled with amusement. "You're as bossy as you were when we were kids. You know that, don't you?"

"You like it when I take care of you. You may as well admit it."

"Yeah, I do. Old habits are hard to break. I keep thinking it's probably time I got out of your hair around here. You could be making money on my room."

"You're not going anywhere, and we're making plenty of money on the other rooms in this place, so get that thought right out of your head. We love having you here with us."

"Still… I probably need to figure things out and get a life of my own rather than piggybacking on yours."

"That's not what you're doing. You've been a huge help to us with the baby and the hotel. You're part of our family, Shane. We *like* having you here. I really don't want you to go."

"Owen probably doesn't like having your brother around all the time."

"That's also not true. He loves you—almost as much as I do. Watching you two become good friends has been such a pleasure for me. "

"If that ever changes, you'll tell me, right?"

"It's not going to change."

"Laura…"

"Fine, I'll tell you, but I'm not going to change my mind and neither is Owen. This is your home now. Relax and enjoy it."

"I do like being with you guys, and having the rest of the family nearby is cool, too."

"It sure does beat sitting alone in your dark apartment."

His smile faded at the reminder of how he'd spent a year after his marriage imploded. "It certainly does."

"Can I ask your advice on something?"

"*You* want *my* advice? Wow, this is quite a moment for the little brother."

"Seriously."

His smile faded. "What's wrong?"

"The trial."

"What about it?"

"Owen doesn't want me to go."

"He came right out and said that?"

"Yes."

"Did he say why?"

"The first time he brought it up, he made it about the travel and the baby and all that. But we just talked about it again, and he's ashamed of airing his family's dirty laundry in front of me. I've already heard a lot of it, but there's got to be so much more I haven't heard."

"You can't blame him for wanting to protect you from that."

"I don't blame him, but who will protect *him?* How do I let him go through that alone?"

"Maybe he needs to do this alone, Laura."

"He's been so there for me, you know? From the very beginning. Before there was even anything romantic between us, he was taking care of me. I want to take care of him, but he won't let me."

"Have you talked to Sarah about it?"

"Not yet, but I probably should."

"It's so hard to believe—when I see the way he is with Holden and with you—that he was fathered by a man like that."

"I know," Laura said with a sigh. "He doesn't say so, but he worries his father's character is lurking inside of him. I've never seen any sign of that kind of rage. Well, except for the night his mother arrived here last fall after his father had beaten her up. He wanted blood that night."

"That's a natural reaction any decent man would feel after seeing his mother abused."

"What should I do about the trip?"

"You've got a couple of days to figure it out, but I can see why you want to go—and I can see why he doesn't want you there. He's trying to protect you."

"And I love him for that, but I want to protect *him*. I want to be there with him through all of this. He'd never let me go through something like this by myself. Remember the night I went to Providence to have it out with Justin when he was refusing to sign the divorce papers?"

Shane nodded.

"Owen went with me and sat at a different table so he could be right there if I needed him. He couldn't bear the thought of me going alone, and that's how I feel about him going to the trial without me."

"Perhaps you should remind him of that incident and how important it was to him to be there for you."

"You're right. I should. Thanks, Shane. I appreciate you listening."

"Happy to do something for you for a change."

Holden let out a squeak from his crib.

"I was hoping if I hung out long enough, he'd wake up." Shane swallowed the last of his soda. "I'll get him."

"He's probably got a thirty-pound diaper."

"I can handle it. Relax for a few more minutes while you can."

"Thanks." Laura lay back on the pillows, smiling as she listened to the delightful chatter between Shane and Holden. The two of them shared a beautiful bond, and Holden lit up at the sight of Shane, which thrilled her brother. Being here with them had been good for him. It had given him time and space to heal but had kept him engaged with the people who loved him while he worked his way through the awful pain that followed Courtney's descent into addiction. He'd stood by her through rehab only to hear at the end that his marriage was over.

Laura and their dad, Frank, had wondered more than once if Shane would ever get past the pain of his divorce. Since he'd been on the island, however, she'd seen a noticeable improvement, and being around Holden had definitely helped. Having Frank here for the summer had also been great for her and Shane, and Laura was hoping her dad would stay after the summer ended.

Everything was falling into place for them. She just had to get Owen through the next few weeks, and then they could look forward to their wedding and the life they'd have together. She appreciated Shane's suggestion that she talk to Sarah about the trial and how best to help Owen through it. She'd do that in the morning.

For now, it was time to soldier through the ever-present exhaustion and enjoy this evening with three of her favorite guys.

*

It had been months since Sarah had felt nervous about going out with Charlie. They'd spent a lot of time together, going to dinner and to the movies. They'd spent many an evening at his place, watching TV, playing board games and cooking meals together. She had no reason at all to be nervous about spending time with the man who had become her closest friend.

He'd never put any pressure on her. He'd never even tried to kiss her. When she shied away from a simple hug, he didn't ask questions. In short, he'd been a perfect gentleman, even though she knew he wanted more from her than what she'd been capable of giving.

Tonight she would tell him about Mark. She'd tell him about her violent marriage and the upcoming trial. She'd tell him why she couldn't bear his touch even though she knew with bone-deep certainty that he'd never harm her the way her husband had. She would tell him everything because he deserved to know and because she was tired of running from the past.

For the first time in her adult life, Sarah looked forward to each new day. She got up with a sense of purpose and enjoyed her work at the hotel her parents had run for decades before they retired and moved to Florida. She loved being with Owen, Laura and baby Holden, whom she doted on the way any first-time grandmother would.

And then there was Charlie, who'd worked his way under her skin one evening at a time over months of evenings together. If you'd asked her last October when she'd fled from her husband after another vicious beating if she'd ever again have feelings for a man, she would've said no. Emphatically. Now she found herself deeply into something with Charlie she couldn't easily explain. Although they'd never even kissed, she felt a stronger bond with him than she ever had with the monster she'd married.

That was why she planned to tell him everything tonight. If it was too much for him to handle, she'd understand. He'd been through his own struggles, spending fourteen years in jail for a crime he didn't commit, earning his freedom after a protracted battle waged by his stepdaughter, Stephanie.

The thought of him turning away from her after all they'd shared made her sad, but she wouldn't blame him. Bringing someone who'd been through his own nightmare into hers wasn't something she did lightly. But she'd been aware for some time now that they were marching in place, unable to move forward with a real relationship because of the demons that haunted her.

He deserved to know the truth, and she would give him that. What he did with it would be entirely up to him.

As always, he insisted on picking her up at her door, and as always, he was right on time. A light tap on the door indicated his arrival.

Sarah took a deep breath and let it out slowly, determined to do the right thing tonight and to accept the outcome, whatever it may be. She opened the door to his handsome, smiling face and couldn't contain her own smile. Being with him always made her happy.

He had an intense, thorough way of looking at her that made her skin tingle with awareness of the fact that he wanted her, even if he never said so. "You look fantastic."

"So do you." He wore a button-down dress shirt rolled up to reveal the tattoos on his forearms. His tall, muscular frame filled the doorway. At first, his size had intimidated her, but she'd quickly learned she had nothing to fear from him. He wore his gray hair in a buzz cut and had piercing blue eyes that didn't miss a thing that went on around him. He'd told her once that his shrewd observation skills had kept him safe in prison.

"Ready to go?"

Sarah reached for the sweater she'd put on the bed and picked up her purse. "Ready."

He closed her door and followed her down the stairs.

She said good night to the college girl working at the reception desk and went out to the porch.

Charlie was right behind her. "Everything okay?"

Sarah wasn't surprised that he'd tuned into her unusual nervousness. He paid attention. It was a quality she'd grown to appreciate after being treated as an insignificant detail for her entire married life. "I know you made reservations at Domenic's, but I wondered if we might get a pizza and go to your place. I'd like to talk to you in private."

His brows furrowed with concern. "Whatever you'd like to do." With efficiency she'd grown to appreciate, he called in their pizza order to Mario's and was driving them to his place within half an hour. When they arrived, he carried the pizza and came around to her side of his truck to help her out. All this was done silently, which wasn't out of character for him. But still, she sensed his concern over what she might have to tell him.

"Charlie?"

"Yeah?"

"It has nothing to do with you. What I want to tell you."

"Oh. Okay." He glanced at her as he held the screen door for her to proceed ahead of him into the house. "I thought you might want to break up with me."

"No. Nothing like that."

"Good."

"Although you might want to break up with me when you hear what I've been keeping from you for all this time."

"No chance of that."

"You should wait to hear what I have to say before you decide anything."

"Sarah."

She turned to face him. "Yes?"

"No. Chance. Of. That."

Smiling, she released a deep breath and relaxed. It was going to be okay. He cared about her. He would still care after he heard her story.

CHAPTER 3

Sarah followed him into the kitchen, where he dished up the pizza and placed the plates on the table. Without having to ask, he poured a glass of the chardonnay he kept on hand for her, grabbed a beer for himself and joined her at the table.

Most men would've prodded her to start talking, but Charlie wasn't most men. He waited on her, giving her the space she needed to collect her thoughts. As usual, the mushroom-and-sausage pizza they both loved was delicious and gave her something else to focus on for a few minutes.

She wiped her mouth and took a sip of her wine. "You've been very patient with me. I hope you know how much I appreciate that."

"It's certainly been no hardship to spend time with you."

"That's sweet of you to say, but still… I know you must have questions that you've never asked."

"I figured you'd get around to telling me—or you wouldn't. Either way was fine with me."

"Even if it meant that our…friendship…never progressed any further?"

Charlie pushed his plate away and took a sip from his beer. "Let me tell you something about fourteen years in prison. It makes you appreciate every damned second you're not in prison. If all you were ever able to give me is what we've already had, I'd be happier than I've been in longer than I can remember."

Sarah's eyes filled with tears. "You deserve so much more than what I've been able to give you."

He covered her hand with his much larger one, and Sarah made a conscious effort not to flinch. It had taken months of casual affection for her to accept it without the dreaded flinch. She was proud of her progress in that regard.

"You have no idea how much I enjoy the time we spend together," he said. "I look forward to it. For so long, I had nothing at all to look forward to, and now I have this. I have you. I'm not going anywhere, Sarah. No matter what you tell me tonight, I'm not going anywhere."

When she heard that, the tears she'd tried to contain came spilling down her cheeks. "Could I…"

"What, honey?"

"Could I maybe hug you?" In all the time they'd known each other, she'd never let him touch her like that.

"I wish you would." Keeping his hand wrapped around hers, he got up. "Let's do this right, though." He led her to the sofa in his cozy living room and sat, patting the seat next to his.

Sarah sat next to him, but out-of-control nerves kept her from reaching for what she wanted so badly.

He held out his arms to her. "Come here."

She was so tired of being afraid, of living in the past, of trying to outrun the demons. Putting her fear aside, she moved closer to him and into his embrace.

He looped his arms around her loosely, which made her feel safe rather than confined. "Often when you hug someone, you put your arms around him, too," he said in a teasing tone.

Her hands were trembling, but she put her arms around him anyway, resting her head against his chest and closing her eyes.

"There," he said softly when she was settled. "Doesn't that feel good?"

She nodded because she didn't trust herself to speak.

"It feels great for me, too," he said. "You always smell so incredible. It's been hard for me to resist the temptation to get close enough to breathe you in."

"Charlie..."

"What, honey?"

"He beat me and my children. He beat me so badly last October that I knew if I stayed, he was going to kill me, so I finally left. It took me way too long to leave. My children grew up in a nightmare, and there was nothing I could do to protect them." The words, once she let them out, spilled forth in a great rush, almost as though she feared if she didn't say it right now, she never would. "He was a general in the air force, and everyone was afraid of him—no one more so than his wife and children. He goes on trial next week in Virginia. That's where I'm going. Owen is going, too. We both have to testify."

"What day are we leaving?"

She raised her head off his chest to find his deep blue eyes staring at her fiercely. "No... You can't..."

"Try and stop me." He paused and looked away from her for a second, seeming to rein in his anger. "That might not be the right way to put it in light of what you've been through. I want to be with you and support you through the trial. I hope you'll let me do that for you."

"It's nice of you to want to do that, but my son will be there. I'll be okay."

"I won't."

"You won't what?"

"I won't be okay sitting here worrying about you. I'll be going out of my mind with worry for you and Owen, who I've come to care for, too. It would be so much easier, for me, if I were there with you rather than here going crazy by myself."

Sarah smiled at the way he'd turned the whole thing around on her.

"You wouldn't want that for me, would you?"

"No, I wouldn't. But I also wouldn't want you to see—or hear—what's going to come out during that trial. I'd be..." She swallowed hard. "Ashamed...for you to know what I tolerated for so many years. He hurt my babies, Charlie. I let that happen because I felt I had no choice, but I had choices. I could've left."

"Shhh. If I know you, and I know you pretty damned well, you must've thought you had no options at all. I knew guys like your husband in prison. They're psychological terrorists. They prey on people who are less able to defend themselves because it makes them feel powerful."

"Yes," she whispered, astounded by his astute assessment. "That was Mark. He ran our home like a squadron. If anyone stepped one inch out of line, they felt his wrath—no one more so than me, although Owen was a close second. He was our oldest and went out of his way to protect his siblings at his own expense. The things he endured... His father once broke his arm in a fit of rage. Another time he turned things around so Owen was charged with assaulting *him* when he'd been protecting himself and his siblings."

Charlie didn't say anything. Rather, he let her talk as he stroked her hair and made her feel safe in a way she'd never felt before with a man.

"I look at Owen now, and I'm so proud of who he became all on his own with no thanks to his father or me. He's a wonderful partner to Laura and an incredible father to Holden. He hasn't seen his own father in more than ten years. And now he has to testify against him just before the wedding." She shook her head with dismay. "I hate that he has to go through this."

"I hate that all of you had to go through it and are still going through it, but I don't agree with one thing you said."

"What don't you agree with?"

"The part about Owen being the man he is no thanks to you. I doubt he'd agree with that. I'm sure he credits you with more than you give yourself credit for."

"I should've left. I blame myself for not packing up my kids and coming here to my parents."

"I would never presume to blame you for anything you did when you felt you had no choices, but why didn't you do that?"

"I was afraid of him," she said with a sigh. "I was afraid of what he'd do to me, the children and my parents if I ever actually left him. So I stayed, and what happened was worse than anything I could've imagined. It was only after I left for good that I've been able to see what a huge mistake I made by staying."

"I don't believe in regrets. I did what I did for Stephanie and paid an awful price for it, but she's alive and well and thriving in her business and so in love with Grant. Every time I see her happy and smiling, I realize everything that happened was worth it. Of all your kids, I only know Owen, and from what I see of him, the same could be said. He's thrilled with the life he has with Laura, and your other kids are living productive lives despite their upbringing. You all survived, honey. That's what really matters."

His sweet words and the gentle tone in which they were delivered touched her deeply, stirring feelings she would've denied she had for him before now, before tonight. "I'm sorry I waited so long to tell you this. I've wanted to. For some time now."

"You have nothing to be sorry about." With his finger on her chin, he compelled her to look at him. "I swear to you, Sarah, you'll never be afraid again—not as long as I'm around. You have nothing at all to fear from me. I'd never touch you with anything other than love on my mind."

"Oh… You… You…"

"Love you. Yes, I do, and I have for a very long time. So please don't ask me to let you go through something so difficult alone. Let me be there with you the way I think you'd want to be there for me."

"You love me." Sarah couldn't get her head—or her heart—to accept words she hadn't heard from a man in longer than she cared to admit. The word "love" wasn't part of her marriage to Mark, at least not after the first month, when he'd pretended to love and respect her. It hadn't taken long for her to see him for what he really was.

"I do. Is that okay?"

"Yes," she said, laughing as tears rolled down her cheeks. "It's okay."

"Then why are you crying?"

"Because you surprised me, and you made me happy."

"And that made you cry?"

She nodded.

He wiped away her tears with the light brush of his fingertips on her face. "What would happen if I kissed you?"

"I…I don't know."

"May I try?"

"Yes. Please."

His smile lit up his face, making his eyes crinkle at the corners. "Always such a lady." He placed his hands on her face and kissed her cheeks and the end of her nose. "Always so polite."

Sarah's heart beat quickly and erratically. She'd spent many a sleepless night wondering if she'd ever be close to him this way, if she'd ever have the courage to try again. But hearing he loved her… Well, that changed everything.

"Is this okay?" he asked softly as he continued to place kisses strategically on her face.

She nodded because that was all she could do. The anticipation reminded her of a long-ago time when she'd looked upon a young air force officer with stars in her eyes, thinking the sun and the moon rose and set on him. For a while, they had. For a short while, everything had been perfect.

"Don't think about the past, Sarah," Charlie whispered. "Think about the future we'll have together." His lips skimmed over hers in a caress so fleeting she almost missed it. "Think about how great it's going to be once we get you free of the past. Can you do that?"

She wanted to so badly. She'd never wanted anything more than to grab hold of the life he envisioned for them. "I want to try."

"I want to help. In any way I can. You're stuck with me now, sweet Sarah."

Stuck with him. She expected to feel trapped and imprisoned the way she had before, but she was well aware that in this case, all the choices were hers to make. "I like being stuck with you."

"Good," he said with a small grin. He leaned in closer, moving slowly so as not to startle her.

She appreciated the care he took to ensure her comfort, even if some parts of her were very uncomfortable. The heat of desire that zinged through her veins was a revelation. It'd been so long since she'd felt anything resembling true desire that it took a moment to recognize the sensation for what it was.

With only a half inch separating his lips from hers, he seemed to be waiting for something. He was waiting for her.

Summoning the courage that had eluded her for so much of her life, she shifted ever so slightly, closing the remaining distance until her lips pressed to his.

A noise that might've been a groan came from inside him, but he didn't move or react or do anything else that might scare her away. Rather, he let her decide how this first, most significant kiss would happen by remaining perfectly still and giving her full control.

Sarah placed her hand on his face and slid her lips over his. "Charlie..."

"What, honey?"

"Kiss me back."

"Are you sure?"

She nodded as her heart beat erratically.

He placed his hands on her face and kept his eyes open, probably gauging her reaction, before he laid his lips lightly on hers.

Sarah wrapped her hand around his wrist and tried to remember how to do this. She wanted so badly to give him what he wanted, what he'd waited so long to have from her.

His lips moved slowly over hers.

Sarah whimpered, and the slight noise had him pulling back.

"Are you okay?"

She nodded. "Don't stop."

He smiled at her and resumed the sweet, slick slide of his lips over hers.

"Charlie..."

"What, honey?"

She loved when he called her that. "It's okay if you want to, you know... Do more."

"Hmmm, *more*. Like this maybe?" He ran the tip of his tongue over her bottom lip, back and forth until Sarah thought she would explode from the desire his kisses stirred in her. "You're trembling."

"Not because I'm nervous."

"No?"

She shook her head.

He reclined on the sofa and patted the spot next to him.

Sarah eyed the cushion and then shifted her gaze to his face. He looked at her with love and affection and amusement. Then she zeroed in on his lips.

"Sarah..." He reached out to slide her hair through his fingers. "Let me hold you."

Because she wanted that so badly and trusted him so totally, she stretched out next to him, appreciating that he'd thought to give her the outside so there was no fear of feeling trapped.

He put one arm around her and encouraged her to use the other as a pillow—a rather muscular pillow. "There. How's that?"

"Good. Really good." She couldn't stop staring at his lips. Now that she'd had a taste of him, she wanted much more, but she had no idea how to tell him that. Her needs, her desires had never been considered in her marriage. "Could we, maybe..."

"Kiss some more?"

"Yes," she said with a sigh, relieved that he'd said the words for her.

"I'd love to. Thought you'd never ask."

She laughed and allowed him to bring her even closer to him. As he slid his leg between hers and drew her into yet another kiss, Sarah relaxed against his muscular body and gave in to the desire that had simmered between them during months of platonic friendship. Kissing him was every bit as wonderful as she'd suspected it would be. And knowing he loved her only made it that much better.

CHAPTER 4

"Would you guys mind if I took Holden up to give him his bath?" Shane asked as the sun headed for the horizon.

"Would we mind that, Owen?" Laura asked playfully. "Hmm, we would not mind at all."

"What she said," Owen replied.

Shane scooped his nephew out of the sand and wrapped a towel around him.

At the word "bath," Holden squealed and chortled. It was his favorite time of day.

"Come on, my little sugar doughnut," Shane said. "Let's get you cleaned up."

"Make sure you rinse all the cracks and crevices," Laura said.

"We got this, don't we?" Shane asked Holden, who clapped with glee.

Shane laughed and headed for the stairs with his bundle.

"They're so cute together," Owen said as he watched them go.

"I was thinking the same thing earlier. Shane is crazy about him."

"And vice versa."

"Shane seems better, don't you think?" Laura asked.

"A thousand times better than he was. Gansett has worked its magic on him the way it does for everyone."

Laura leaned her head against Owen's shoulder and watched the sunset explode into deep magentas and oranges and purples that cast a warm glow upon the flat, calm water. "It certainly worked its magic on me."

He took her hand and linked their fingers. "And me."

He'd been unusually quiet all evening, allowing her and Shane to carry the conversation and Holden to entertain them.

"Are you okay?" She needed to know but was almost afraid of his answer.

"Yeah."

"O?" she asked, shortening his name the way Evan often did.

"Hmm?"

"I know it's your way to go quiet and keep to yourself when you're troubled, and that's okay if it's what you need to do. But I hope you know I'm right here, and I want to help if I can."

"I know you do, and I'm trying to let you in. It's just… It's hard."

The pain she heard in his voice killed her and made her wish there was something—anything—she could do to spare him the awful ordeal that loomed so large for him. Though she wanted to encourage him to talk to her, instead she gave him the silence he seemed to need. As darkness encroached upon their slice of paradise, Laura reluctantly withdrew her hand from his grasp.

"I should go feed Holden and put him down."

"I'll clean up down here and be right along."

She kissed his cheek. "Don't take too long."

"I won't."

Sensing he needed some time to himself, Laura left him staring out at the water and walked up the stairs that led to the deck. At the landing, she used the hose to wash the sand off her feet and then stepped on the towel she'd carried from the beach to dry them. The sound of happy voices, the clatter of dishes and the tinkle of crystal stemware coming from Stephanie's Bistro in the lobby followed her up the stairs to the third floor.

In the apartment, Shane was stretched out on the floor next to Holden, who was playing with his stuffed animals. He was dressed in his zebra pajamas, and his hair was still damp from the bath. His face lit up with delight at the sight of his mother. "Mmmam."

"Oh, that's so close to mama," Shane said. "Come on, buddy. You can do it. Mama."

"Mmm."

"He'll probably say dada first," Laura said. "They always do."

"That's really not fair."

"Right?" She bent to retrieve Holden from the floor, gasping when her back protested.

"Careful!" Shane jumped up to relieve her of the baby, who got heavier by the day.

Laura rubbed her lower back. "That was weird."

"He's too heavy for you to lift him off the floor that way."

"Yes, Dr. McCarthy."

"I'm serious, Laura. He's not a lightweight anymore, and you've got my other niece and nephew to think about."

"What makes you think I'm having one of each?"

"Just a guess."

"That would be nice, since we're all done having babies after these guys. I've puked enough to last me two lifetimes."

"Can't say I blame you." He kissed Holden's chubby face and handed him over to her. "Thanks for a great time tonight."

"It was fun."

"Owen was kind of quiet."

"I know."

"Are you guys going to Seamus and Carolina's clambake tomorrow?"

"I think we are. I guess it'll depend on whether Owen's in the mood for a party."

Shane kissed her cheek. "Hang in there. It'll be over soon, and you guys can focus on the future rather than the past." At the doorway, he turned back to her. "I'm here if you need me for anything at all."

"You're already doing me a huge favor covering for me here while we're gone. I appreciate it."

"Least I can do," he said with a smile and a wave as he closed the door behind him.

The two of them had been through a lot together, first with the loss of their mother as young children and then two painful divorces, all of which had made them the best of friends in addition to being siblings. She loved having Shane close by and back in her daily life—as well as her son's daily life.

As she sat in the rocker in Holden's room to nurse him, her thoughts turned once again to Owen and the difficult question that weighed heavily on her mind. Should she cede to his wishes and stay home from the trip, or should she insist on going with him? She was no closer to an answer half an hour later when she tucked her sleeping baby into bed and drew the light blanket up and over him.

As she looked down at Holden, so perfect in every way, her heart broke for another perfect little boy who'd had the misfortune to be born to a violent, unpredictable man who would never know what a strong, capable, loving man that boy had grown up to be. Tears filled her eyes when she thought of the deep pain Owen carried with him, despite his carefree exterior. She'd do anything to relieve him of even a fraction of that pain, if only she knew how.

Laura took a shower and changed into a nightgown before sliding into bed. She was beginning to worry about Owen when she finally heard him come into the apartment and head right to the shower. Though her eyes were heavy with the ever-present exhaustion, she forced herself to stay awake until he came to bed.

She let him know she was still awake by putting her hand on his chest.

He covered her hand with his own and then turned to her.

In complete and unusual silence, he snuggled up to her, clinging to her in a way he seldom did. For once, he was taking rather than giving, and she was more than happy to give him whatever he needed.

Laura ran her hand up and down his back and raised her face to try to see him in the faint glow of the streetlights. As he looked down at her, she kissed him.

He turned his face away. "I can't."

Confounded by his unprecedented rejection, she said, "What can't you do?"

"I can't make love to you tonight. I'm wound up, and I'm afraid I'll hurt you."

"Owen, you could never hurt me."

"I can't take that chance."

"Then allow me."

"Wait. Allow you to do what?"

Her exhaustion forgotten in the face of his obvious need, she rose to her knees and pushed on his shoulder until he was lying on his back.

"Laura…"

"Shhh. You take care of me every day in a thousand different ways. And yet you find it so very difficult to allow me to take care of you." She leaned over him, kissing his chest while her hand caressed his stomach. "I love you as much as you love me. You know that, right?"

"Yes, I know, but—"

"No buts about it. Let me love you. Let me take care of you."

"You're tired, and you need your rest."

"I'll get plenty of rest, but right now I need you."

He stopped protesting, but his muscles remained rigid and tense.

She slowly kissed her way down the front of him while caressing his chest and stomach. The only sign he gave that she was getting to him was the restless movement of his legs under the covers. "Relax," she whispered. "Close your eyes and just enjoy it."

"I can't do that."

"Yes, you can. You can do it for me."

He blew out a deep breath that sounded frustrated, but his body seemed to lose some of the tension.

Encouraged by his partial capitulation, she continued downward, uncovering the erection that stretched past his belly button. She took him in hand and stroked him the way she knew he liked it.

Sucking in a sharp breath, he lifted his hips off the bed.

Laura bent her head and fitted her lips around the broad crown while continuing to stroke him.

He gasped and fisted her hair, seeming to give in to the inevitable now.

She opened her mouth wider and took more of him, using her tongue as well as her hand and the heat of her mouth to pleasure him. "So much more than your share," she teased when she came up for air.

The comment, as usual, made him laugh. "Come up here."

"In a minute. I'm not done yet."

"We'll be all done in less than ten seconds if you keep that up."

Since she yearned for the connection with him, to show him in every way she could that she loved him, she yielded to his wishes but didn't surrender control. Rather, she straddled him and leaned over to kiss his lips. "How's this?"

"Amazing as always." Running his hands from her thighs to her waist, he eased her nightgown up and over her head.

Laura hated how big and ungainly her breasts were getting with this pregnancy, but Owen said he loved them—almost as much as he loved teasing her about them. Tonight there was no indication of amusement. Tonight he was all about reverence as he filled his hands to overflowing.

He sat up to gain access to her and drew her left nipple into his mouth.

Laura wrapped her arms around him and held on as he aroused her the way no one else ever had or ever could. His touch set her on fire. She raised her hips until she hovered above his erection and took him in slowly, giving herself time to adjust to his considerable size.

"Easy, baby," he whispered as he kissed her. "Nice and easy."

She had no choice but to take it easy where he was concerned. The thought made her laugh.

"What's so funny?"

"The usual thing."

"That's not funny."

"Yes, it is," she said, delighted by the amusement she heard in his tone. "It's hilarious."

"You didn't let me pull out all the stops to prepare you."

"Because you said you didn't want me tonight."

"I never said that. I would never say that." As he spoke, he leaned forward, forcing her onto her back. He followed her, never losing their tenuous connection. "I said I was afraid I might hurt you because I was wound up."

"And I said you could never hurt me, because I believe that's true."

"I'd never hurt you on purpose." He withdrew from her and leaned over to kiss the small baby bump. "Or our babies."

Aching for him, Laura combed her fingers through his shaggy blond hair. "I heard something about pulling out all the stops to prepare me?" Despite the ache, she kept her tone lighthearted, hoping it would have the desired effect on him.

"I might've mentioned something about that." He never touched her with anything other than supreme tenderness, but tonight he took the tenderness to a whole new level, perhaps trying to compensate for his fear of losing control. Settling between her legs, which were propped on his broad shoulders, he opened her to his tongue.

Laura arched into the heat of his mouth, grasping handfuls of the sheet to anchor her to the bed. Encouraged by her moans of pleasure, he slid a finger into her as he sucked on her clit. The combination detonated her release, forcing her to muffle her cries with her hands so she wouldn't wake the baby. As she came down from the incredible high, he moved over her but kept her legs propped open on his thighs.

"I think you might be more ready now," he said, testing his theory with his fingers.

"I think you might be right," she said between deep breaths.

"Let's see, shall we?"

Laura reached for him, bringing him in for a kiss as he pressed his cock into her, his entry stretching and burning despite the preparation.

"So hot and so tight," he whispered against her lips as he moved her legs from his thighs to wrap them around his hips. "It's all I can do to hold on until you let me in. Every damned time."

"I'm sorry it takes so long."

"I'm not. It feels better than anything ever has."

"For me, too."

"I don't know if I believe that. I get an awful lot of complaints."

His teasing was a huge relief to her. Underneath all the worry and heartache he was dealing with, her Owen was still in there and hopefully still would be after the showdown with his father.

"They're not complaints, per se, but rather commentary on the fact that you did, in fact, get more than your share."

His laughter went a long way toward easing the knot she'd carried in her belly all day as she worried about the trial causing a rift between them. She couldn't let that happen. No matter how difficult it got, she had to be the one to keep them on an even keel. He deserved nothing less after all he'd given her.

He kissed and touched and cajoled until he was fully embedded in her, which caused them both to tremble and cling to each other. Owen was always careful not to put too much weight on her abdomen, and tonight was no exception. He took her on an exquisitely erotic journey without causing her a moment of pain or uncertainty over how much he loved her.

He told her so every time he looked at her or touched her or spoke to her. As he made slow, sweet love to her, his gentle strokes igniting her all over again, Laura wished she could make him see that there wasn't one bit of his father in the man he'd grown up to be.

"Owen."

"What?"

"I love you so much. I love you more than I'll ever love anyone."

"You're allowed to love our babies more than you love me."

She shook her head. "I love them as much as I love you. Not more."

His forehead landed on hers. His hands curled around her shoulders as he pressed deeper into her.

Laura tightened her legs around him and lifted her hips to meet him stroke for stroke until they both cried out from the incredible pleasure that overtook them. Still buried deep inside her, he moved to his side, taking her with him. He pulled her leg up and over his hip as he continued to throb and pulse with aftershocks.

Touching her lips to his chest, Laura closed her eyes and breathed in the familiar scent of him. "If you really don't want me to go with you, I'll stay home. If that's what you need, I'll do it."

"I was down on the beach before, thinking about how badly I want to spare you the trip, the trial, all of it. If I had my way, you'd never lay eyes on Mark Lawry. But since I made my stand about you not going, I've begun to worry that I won't be able to handle it if you aren't there. And that makes me the most selfish bastard on earth, because I know you'd be so much better off if you stayed home."

"You're not selfish, Owen. You're the opposite of selfish. If you asked me your biggest flaw, I'd say that you think of everyone else before yourself. And that goes right back to your father and the way you were raised and how you looked out for everyone at your own expense. You're still doing it, and all I'm trying to tell you is you don't have to anymore."

He tightened his arms around her and kissed her. "Keep reminding me, okay? It might take me a while to get the message."

"We've got the rest of our lives to work on it."

"The rest of our lives," he said with a sigh. "That sounds so good to me."

She kissed him and caressed the stubble on his jaw. "It sounds like paradise to me."

"While I was at the beach, I tried to imagine what it would be like if this trial was happening before I had you and Holden in my life. I'd be going insane—much more so than I am now."

"I'm glad that having us around helps you."

"It does help me, Laura. I hear you tell people all the time about how much I do for you, but you've given me my first taste of normal. You can't possibly know how much that means to me."

"I want you to remember that over the next few weeks. I want you to focus on what you have now and not on what used to be. Those days are over, and they don't matter anymore. You're no longer the helpless kid who didn't have any options or any way to protect the people he loved. You're a big, strong man who takes care of everyone in his life with love and kindness."

"Will you keep telling me that, too? And will you ignore me if I'm a total asshole over the next few weeks—at a time when we're supposed to be blissfully happy and looking forward to our wedding?"

"I'll keep telling you, and I'll never ignore you no matter what you say or do. It's not your fault the timing worked out this way. The trial was supposed to be long over by now, so don't add the delays to the list of things you feel the need to be sorry about. None of this is your fault."

He smoothed her tangled hair back from her face with the gentle caress of his big hand. "The day after Janey's wedding, when I found you outside the hotel in the rain, looking up at the place… That was the day my real life began. Everything before that… Well, it doesn't matter now that I have you."

"It matters because it made you who you are, and I love who you are. But it has nothing to do with the life we've made together—unless we let it."

Owen toyed with the engagement ring on her finger, spinning it around and touching it as if he needed the reminder of their connection. "I'd never let that happen."

Though he spoke emphatically, Laura was still afraid of what the trial might do to undercut his hard-won freedom from a painful past.

CHAPTER 5

"I can't believe we're really doing this," Carolina Cantrell said to her fiancé, Seamus O'Grady, late on Saturday afternoon as they took a break in the preparations for the party they were hosting later in the day. They'd hired their pilot friend, Slim, to oversee the preparation of an authentic New England clambake, which was currently simmering in a seaweed-filled pit in the backyard.

"Still time to chicken out," he said in the charming Irish accent that had worked its magic on her for close to a year now.

"I'm not going to chicken out, because that's exactly what you expect me to do."

"So that's the only reason you're going through with it? To save face with me?"

"Yep. That's the only reason."

His green eyes narrowed with displeasure that made her laugh.

"You're so easy to rile." Inciting him—in all ways possible to incite a man—had become her favorite pastime, especially since she'd stopped trying to fight the tsunami known as Seamus O'Grady. He'd pursued her with relentless determination and managed to wear her down until her concerns about their eighteen-year age difference seemed silly and insignificant when stacked against the overwhelming love she felt for him.

"I don't find you funny today," he said, sounding grumpy. "Not one bit funny."

"Yes, you do. You always think I'm funny."

"Normally, I do. Today—not so much."

Carolina took an assessing look at her handsome fiancé and came to a startling conclusion. "Are you *nervous*?"

"What? No. Of course I'm not nervous. What in the world do I have to be nervous about?"

"Um, well, I could state the obvious…"

"I'm not nervous, Carolina, so get that right out of your pretty head and get back to work."

"Not until you tell me what's wrong. If you're not nervous, then what is it?"

"Nothing is wrong except for you poking at me when we've got so much to do to get ready."

The comment normally would've made her mad. Poking at him? She was not *poking* at him. Although… She crossed the kitchen to where he was sorting plastic utensils and wrapped her arms around him from behind. "Tell me what's wrong."

"I swear to you, love, nothing is wrong. Not one single thing."

"Then why aren't you yourself today?"

"How am I not myself?"

"You're prickly, which is usually my thing."

"Perhaps you've rubbed off on me in more ways than one." The sexual innuendo was much more in keeping with what she expected from him.

"So you're not going to tell me?" She encouraged him to turn and face her.

He sighed and pushed his fingers through his rich auburn hair, making a mess of it. "I guess you could say I'm feeling a tad bit…" He made an up-and-down motion with his hand. "Over what we're about to do."

"Emotional. You're feeling emotional."

"Except saying that makes me a first-rate pussy."

Carolina burst out laughing. Her man had a way with words. "It does not make you a first-rate pussy." Her mouth twisted around the dreaded word. "It makes you a first-time groom with a perfectly natural case of jitters." She took him by the hand and led him into the living room, where they sat together on the sofa.

"I don't have the slightest doubt about us or what we're about to do," he said. "You have to know that."

"I do know that. Because if I thought you were having doubts after the campaign you waged to get to this day, I'd have no choice but to kill you."

His face lifted into the impish half grin she adored. "And I'd have no choice but to let you."

"Fortunately, there will be no killing today. Only loving."

He leaned over to kiss her. "Today and every day."

Carolina curled her hand around his nape and kept him there for another kiss. She shifted ever so slightly until she was pressed against him.

He responded to her the way he always did—passionately.

They stayed that way, wrapped up in each other, until Carolina heard a door close in the driveway. She drew back from him. "That'll be Joe and Janey. Are you ready for this?"

"I was born ready, my love."

Smiling, she fixed his hair and left her hand to rest on his cheek for a moment. "Thank you for not giving up on me."

"Aw, Christ, Caro. Don't say that. You'll make a mess of me."

Touched by the fact that his emotions were hovering close to the surface, she said, "I mean it. You've made me so happy—happier than I ever expected to be, and I want you to know that before anything else happens today. I know I gave you a run for your money—"

He grunted out a laugh. "That's one way to put it."

"I just want you to know I'm so glad you were relentless. So very, very glad."

Reaching out to run a finger over her face, he said, "I love you, Caro."

"I love you, too." She kissed him again, lingering until she heard the screen door open. Leaving him with a smile, she got up to meet her son and his family.

"We heard something about a party here today," Joe said. He carried his newborn son, P.J., in an infant car seat that he put on the kitchen table.

"Are we the first ones here?" Janey asked.

"You are." Caro greeted them both with hugs before she turned her full attention to her adorable grandson. Born by emergency C-section several weeks premature, he'd spent more than a month in the hospital until he'd finally been released to come home to Gansett. "How's my baby today?"

"He's doing great." Joe unbuckled the straps and freed the baby, handing him right over to his grandmother. "He's eating well and sleeping a lot."

Carolina gazed down at the tiny face, the feathery brows, the miniature lips, the light dusting of blond hair. He was the most gorgeous thing she'd seen since she held his father in her arms. "That's exactly what he should be doing."

Seamus appeared at her shoulder, leaning in to kiss P.J.'s forehead. "There's my new best mate." The lilting tone of Ireland in his voice had become music to her ears over the last ten months.

"Is there anything we can do to help get ready for the party?" Janey asked, helping herself to a pickle from an open jar on the counter.

Carolina exchanged glances with Seamus. He nodded, encouraging her to share their news with the two most important people in their lives. "There is one thing you could do for us today."

"What's that?" Joe asked, still focused almost entirely on the baby.

"You could stand up for us."

That got her son's attention. "Stand up for you?" Joe's gaze shifted from his mother to Seamus and then back to her. "You wanna run that by me one more time?"

"The party today," Seamus said, "is actually a wedding. We didn't want to make a big thing of it—"

Janey let out a shriek that startled her son. "Oh my God! Are you *serious*? You're getting *married*?"

"We're getting married," Carolina said. "And we'd like the two of you to be our witnesses. If you're willing, that is."

Joe and Janey looked at each other, and for a brief moment, Carolina couldn't tell what they were thinking. Waiting for them to say something made her feel nervous for the first time that day. Then she felt Seamus's hand on her back, and the simple gesture calmed and centered her. No matter what, he was right there with her, and they were in this together.

"Of course we'll be your witnesses," Joe said as Janey nodded in agreement.

"We'd love to." Janey hugged them both. "Thank you so much for asking us."

Seamus shook hands with Joe. "Who else would we ask?"

"Wow, I can't believe this," Joe said. "A surprise wedding. Everyone will be blown away."

"We didn't want the fuss and the gifts and the months of planning," Seamus said. "We just want to be married."

"What about your family?" Janey asked.

"Shannon will represent them," Seamus said of his cousin who'd come to Gansett earlier in the summer with Seamus's mother and then decided to stay for a while. "We talked to my parents in Ireland yesterday, and they're over the moon. My mum loves Caro and couldn't be happier for us. And speaking of my family, I could use a week off at the end of the season so I can take my new wife home to meet them."

"Done," Joe said. "I'm jealous. I'd love to go to Ireland someday."

"I'd be happy to take you," Seamus replied. "If we can find someone to cover the ferries for both of us."

Joe glanced at P.J. "I'm going to be a little busy for the next few years, but I'll take you up on that at some point."

"Any time."

"There's one other thing," Seamus said to Joe. "I've been trying to convince your mum to sign a piece of paper that Dan Torrington drew up for me."

"Seamus," Carolina said.

"What kind of paper?" Joe asked.

"A prenuptial agreement," Seamus said.

"Which I told him is completely unnecessary," Carolina said with a glower for her fiancé. "And it's borderline insulting that he would think about money at a time like this."

"I'm an Irish immigrant who makes a decent living, love, but I don't have what you have. I want you protected."

"Are you planning to leave me and run off with my money?"

"Of course not, but—"

"Then why are we ruining this day having a conversation I thought we put to rest weeks ago?"

"We're not ruining anything, and you put it to rest. I didn't." He turned his attention to Joe. "What do you think?"

Joe thought about it for a moment. "I think you should sign it, Mom."

"Joe!" Janey said.

Joe held up a hand to stop her protest and his mother's. "I think you should sign it, but not because I believe you'll ever need it."

"Then why?" Carolina asked.

"Because it seems important to Seamus."

"It is," Seamus said. "It's very important to me."

He and Carolina engaged in a visual standoff that ended when she blinked. "Fine. If it's that big of a deal to you, I'll sign it. But let it be said that I'm doing this for you. Not for me."

"So noted, love." He went to retrieve the form in the other room.

When he returned, Carolina took it from him, signed it and gave it back to him. "I don't want to talk about it ever again."

As he hugged her, some of the starch seemed to leave her spine. "I can't imagine there'll ever come a day when we'll need to discuss that paper or what it says, but it makes me feel better to know you're protected."

"From you? Now you care about protecting me? Who was protecting me when you were pursuing me like a madman and chasing me around the kitchen table?"

"*Oh my God*," Joe said with a groan as Janey giggled madly. "I so don't need that visual in my mind."

"Not in front of the children, love," Seamus said with a smile and a kiss.

She shook her head with amusement and love and dismay.

"Now I'd like a turn with my grandson," Seamus said, reaching for P.J.

While Seamus held the baby, Caro turned to her son, who was only two years younger than the man she was about to marry. "I'm sorry about him. I keep hoping he's going to learn to behave himself, but I'm beginning to give up on that."

Laughing, Joe hugged her. "I'm happy for you, Mom. How could I not be when I see how happy he makes you and how great you guys are together?"

Carolina closed her eyes against the flood of tears that filled them. It had been just the two of them for a long lonely time after his father died in an accident when Joe was only seven. Now they were both happily in love and had so much to look forward to. "Thank you, Joseph."

He kissed her temple. "Do I get to give away the bride, too?"

"Absolutely."

*

By five o'clock, Seamus and Carolina's yard was full of friends enjoying the chowder and clam cakes Slim had made. Everyone was teasing the dashing pilot about keeping his other talents hidden from them.

"You should see what else I can do," he said to laughter.

Seamus approached Carolina. "Is everyone here?"

"Except for Mac and Linda. I can't imagine what's keeping them."

"Did you ask Janey?"

"I was just about to do that."

"I'll go with you."

They found Janey inside the house, nursing P.J. in the living room. "Hey, guys. Is it time?"

"Not quite yet," Caro said. "Your parents aren't here yet."

"I wonder what's keeping them."

"Do you mind giving them a call?"

"Of course not. My phone is in my purse in the kitchen."

"I'll get it." Seamus was thankful to have something to do with the energy zinging around inside of him. They were so close… So damned close to having what he'd wanted for what felt like forever, even if it was only a couple of years. He could still recall the first time he saw Carolina, shortly after he started working for Joe. She'd come to take her son to lunch and left him completely bowled over.

Right away he'd realized he faced an uphill battle in winning her heart. First of all, he worked for her son. Second of all, he was only a couple of years older than Joe. The third challenge had turned out to be the most complex, though—convincing her she had a right to be happy and to hell with what anyone else thought of them or the years that separated them. He didn't care about any of that, and he'd finally gotten her to the point where she didn't either.

He found Janey's phone and brought it to her, waiting alongside Caro while she made the call. His lovely bride had worn a gorgeous yellow dress that showed off her late-summer tan. A week or so ago, she'd had her hair cut and colored, and to look at her, you'd never know she was a day over forty.

"That's weird," Janey said. "Neither of them is answering."

"I swear to God," Caro said, "if I find out they were getting busy when I want to be getting married, they'll never hear the end of it."

"Thank you for that visual," Janey said. "Brain scrub commencing." Her phone rang. "It's my mom."

"Thank goodness," Caro said.

"Where are you guys?" Janey paused to listen. "Caro is waiting on you to serve dinner. Okay. See you soon." She ended the call and looked up at them. "They're 'running late' but on the way. She did sound somewhat out of breath."

"I knew it!"

Seamus cracked up laughing. "You've no room to talk about spending too much time in bed, love."

"I heard that," Joe said as he joined them. "And I never want to hear it again."

"My apologies," Seamus said with a grin. "Not in front of the children."

"That's right," Joe said, "and don't forget it. Are we doing this or what?"

"We're waiting on your in-laws," Janey said, "who apparently got sidetracked on their way out of the house."

"You don't say," Joe said with a smile. "The old guy's still got it, huh?"

"Eww," Janey said. "Please make it stop."

"And who are you calling old?" Caro asked her son.

The comical exchange went a long way toward ridding Seamus of the last of the nerves that had plagued him all day. These people would soon be his new family, and he couldn't wait.

Frank McCarthy came into the house, looking rested and relaxed after spending much of the summer on Gansett. "What's the holdup, kids?" the judge asked.

"Waiting on your brother and his wife to get out of bed and come to our party," Carolina said.

Frank's eyes widened with surprise.

"I know, Uncle Frank," Janey said. "It's extremely gross."

Frank laughed at his niece's distress. "I don't know if gross is the word I'd use. I was going to go with surprising."

"They're like a couple of teenagers lately," Caro said.

"Good for them," Seamus said. "That's the way we're going to be, too, love, so you'd better get ready."

"Oh Jesus," Joe muttered. "I so didn't need to hear that either."

"I'm sorry, honey." Caro patted Joe's arm. "I've tried to get him under control, but I'm afraid there's no controlling him."

"And she likes me that way, not that she wants you to know it," Seamus said to Joe's profound mortification.

"If you don't stop talking right now, there isn't going to be a wedding," Carolina said.

Seamus smiled at her. Nothing could get him down on the day he was set to marry the love of his life.

Twenty minutes later, Mac and Linda McCarthy came rushing into the house, looking red-faced and flustered.

"So sorry to be late," Linda said. "We had an appointment that ran late and…"

"The jig is up, Mom," Janey said. "We know what you've been doing."

Big Mac snorted, which earned him an elbow to the midsection from his wife.

"Let's get this show on the road now that everyone is here," Frank said.

"What show?" Linda asked.

"Shall I tell them, Mom?" Joe asked.

"Please do."

"The Carolina and Seamus show," Joe said. "They're getting married today."

Linda let out a piercing shriek. "*What*?"

"You heard him," Caro said, clearly amused by her longtime friend's reaction to their news.

"You sneaky devils!" Linda hugged Carolina and then him. "Congratulations! What a fun idea—a surprise wedding." Linda's face turned bright red. "Sorry if we held things up."

"No problem," Caro said with a warm smile for the woman who had been family to her since Joe met Linda's son Mac in kindergarten. "You're here now, so…" She looked at him. "Shall we do this?"

"Oh yes, please, love."

"Excellent," Frank said. "You two get ready, and leave the rest to me. Mac, come help me get everyone where they need to be."

As he followed his brother to the sliding door that led to the deck and yard, Big Mac stopped to shake hands with Seamus. "You're marrying one of the finest women I know. Take good care of her."

"I will. You have my word on it."

Big Mac nodded in approval and continued to the yard.

Seamus stood with Carolina, Joe, Janey and Linda and listened to the McCarthy brothers corral their friends and family into a group.

"Folks," Frank said, "we have a bit of a surprise for you today. Where's Seamus?"

"That'd be my cue." Seamus kissed and hugged Carolina. Whispering in her ear, he said, "You and me forever, love. We got this."

She sniffled as she nodded.

"See you out there. Don't get lost on the way."

"I won't," she said with a laugh as she mopped up her tears with tissues that Linda provided.

Seamus emerged into the yard, where a buzz of curiosity had their guests riveted to what was going on. They'd decided to let their actions speak for them, so he walked over to Frank and shook his hand as everyone watched him with puzzled looks on their faces.

Janey, carrying P.J., walked with her mother to the front of the group that stood around them.

"Give it up, Janey," her brother Mac said. "What's going on?"

"Shush," she said. "You'll see in a minute."

After a long pause that had everyone straining for a better view of the house, Carolina emerged on the arm of her son. She carried a bouquet of daisies that Seamus had picked for her from their garden.

"Oh my God," Adam McCarthy said. "They're getting married!"

CHAPTER 6

Seamus laughed at the startled reactions that followed Adam's announcement. When Carolina and Joe reached the spot they'd decided on earlier, she turned and hugged her son. After a few whispered words, both were dabbing at their eyes.

Seamus held out his hand to Caro, who wrapped her fingers around his. He gave her a reassuring squeeze and let out a deep breath he hadn't even realized he was holding as he waited for disaster to strike. For days after they hatched this plan, he'd expected her to tell him she'd changed her mind. But that hadn't happened, and now they were exactly where he'd wanted to be for almost as long as he'd known her.

"Friends, on behalf of Seamus and Carolina, I'm pleased to welcome you to their clambake-slash-wedding," Frank said to enthusiastic cheers from the gathering. "It's been an enormous pleasure to spend time with them in the last couple of weeks as they prepared for today. More than anything, they wanted their wedding to be casual and fun, and they wanted to include the people who mean the most to them. Seamus and Carolina have chosen to write their own vows, so I'll let them take it from here. Seamus?"

Carolina handed her bouquet to Linda and turned to him.

Holding both her hands, he looked down at her, hoping he could get through this without making a fool of himself. "From the day I first met my new boss's mum, I knew I was in for a world of trouble."

Carolina and everyone else laughed at his opening line, as he'd hoped they would.

"You have led me on a merry chase, my love, and there was many a day when I thought we'd never get to this day. And before I pledge my eternal love and devotion to you, I want to say to your beloved son, Joe, that I thank him for welcoming me into his family and for trusting me with his mother's heart. I promise I'll be careful with it. I might be only a couple of years older than you, Joseph, but that doesn't mean I won't do my best to be a fine stepfather to you."

"Ah jeez," Joe laughed and muttered as he dealt with a flood of tears he clearly hadn't been expecting. "Crazy Irishman."

Carolina smiled brightly at him, seeming pleased with what he'd said to Joe.

"My beautiful Carolina, there are no words to adequately tell you what you mean to me, how much I love you or how much I'm looking forward to spending the rest of my life with you. So I'll simply vow to love, honor and cherish you all the days of my life and thank you for taking this journey with me. There's no one else I'd rather travel with."

Caro had tears on her cheeks by the time he finished, so he leaned in and kissed them away.

"Not yet," Frank said, making everyone laugh. "Caro?"

She took a deep breath and gave Seamus's hands a squeeze. "You, Seamus O'Grady, have been the source of my greatest vexation as well as my greatest love. You drive me crazy most of the time, which I think is deliberate on your part."

Grinning, Seamus shrugged. "You'll never get me to confess to that."

"I had no idea how empty and bereft my life really was until you came swooping in and forced me out of my comfort zone in every possible way. You won me over with the force of your belief that we absolutely belong together and nothing, not even a few years between friends, could keep us apart when we were meant to be. It took me a while to come around to your way of thinking, but once I finally gave in to you, I've been happier than I ever imagined I could be. So thank you for not giving up when the going got tough. Thank you for making me laugh and for sticking around long enough for me to figure out that since I can't murder you, I should probably marry you."

"Is that the first time the word 'murder' has been used in wedding vows?" Seamus asked Frank.

"Definitely a first for me," Frank said with obvious amusement.

"Excellent." Seamus beamed at his bride, pleased with every word she'd said to him, because he had no doubt whatsoever that she loved him with everything she had to give.

"I love you," she said, "and I will honor and cherish you and what we have together for the rest of my life. And when you do finally drive me crazy, I'll go happily, knowing I was fully and completely loved by the most amazing man."

Damn if she didn't reduce him to tears with her heartfelt words. He leaned his forehead against hers, dying for the moment when Frank would tell him she was his wife and he could kiss her.

"Rings?" Frank asked.

Seamus reluctantly released one of Carolina's hands and withdrew the rings from the pocket of the khaki pants he'd ironed for the occasion. They'd gone to the mainland two weeks ago to buy the matching platinum rings. He held them out in the palm of his hand, and Carolina took his.

He slid hers onto her finger, and then she returned the favor, the cool metal wrapping around his finger, the awareness of what it represented humbling him like nothing else ever had.

"By the power vested in me by the State of Rhode Island and Providence Plantations," Frank said, "I'm pleased to pronounce you husband and wife. Seamus, you may kiss your bride."

Seamus wrapped his arms around her and planted a deep wet one on her as their friends and family cheered.

She held on to him for a long moment that belonged only to them, and when he reluctantly ended the kiss, they were both in tears as the magnitude of what they'd just done seemed to register all at once.

"Mrs. O'Grady."

"Mr. O'Grady."

"We have a party to get to."

"So we do."

"Thank you for this, Caro. You have no idea how happy you've made me."

"I think I know."

Seamus hugged her again, holding on for as long as he could before others demanded their attention. He let her go reluctantly, counting the hours until he could be alone with his new wife.

*

"What a fantastic surprise this was," Maddie McCarthy said to the group of friends and family sharing four picnic tables pushed together as they enjoyed lobsters and clam chowder.

Under normal circumstances, these were Laura's favorite times—surrounded by her cousins, their significant others and the friends who'd become like family to her since she moved to the island. But there was nothing normal about a day when Owen was sitting next to her but a million miles away, lost in his own troubled thoughts.

To her sister-in-law Janey, Maddie said, "Did you guys know about it?"

"We found out an hour before you all did."

"Such a cool way to do it," Grant McCarthy said, glancing at his fiancée, Stephanie. "Don't you think, hon? No muss, no fuss. Just get married."

Stephanie shrugged. "I guess."

"There's a lot to be said for no muss or fuss," Laura said.

"Funny," Owen said, "I was thinking the same thing, although ours will be pretty low fuss."

"That's all I'm capable of at the moment," Laura said with a wry grin for him as she rested a hand on her belly. She was relieved to see him making an effort to engage with their friends.

"Still sick every day?" Abby Callahan asked.

"Every single day without fail," Laura replied. "It took five full months with Holden, so three months to go."

"Ugh," Laura's cousin Adam McCarthy said. "That's gotta be awful."

"It's not the most fun I've ever had. That's for sure."

"So I guess our destination wedding is the exact opposite of no muss, no fuss," Evan McCarthy said.

"Your destination wedding is going to get us all out of here in the dead of winter," Blaine Taylor said. "I'm all for it."

"Absolutely," his wife, Tiffany, said. "Bring it on."

"Until today, you guys had the record for the lowest-fuss wedding," Evan's fiancée, Grace Ryan, said. "I think Seamus and Caro have your three-day engagement beat, though."

"Wouldn't change a thing about the way we got married," Blaine said with a smile for his wife. "It was just what we wanted."

"I'm all for eloping and skipping the whole production," Grant said.

"Mom would kill you if you did that," his brother Evan replied. "Like she did when you forgot to tell her you were engaged."

Grant winced. "She was pretty pissed."

"Mom believes she has an inalienable right to see us all get married," Mac said. "As the oldest and wisest, I firmly recommend against elopement."

His comment led to paper napkins from his three unmarried brothers flying through the air, hitting him squarely in the face. Laughing, Mac batted them away.

"You're such a windbag," Adam said.

"He does get a little windy at times," Maddie said of her husband, who glowered at her playfully. "What? You do! It's Mac's way or the highway."

Sydney Donovan and her husband, Luke Harris, carried their plates to the table.

"Push over and let us in," Syd said.

"You're just in time to join the conversation about what a windbag Mac is," Grant said to Luke.

"Oh, I'm in," Luke said. "What's he pontificating about now?"

"The perils of eloping when Linda McCarthy is your mother," Maddie said.

"Yikes, I hate to ever agree with Mac," Luke said. "However, in this case, I'm afraid I might have to."

"Gee, thanks," Mac said to his longtime friend and business partner. "How painful was that for you?"

"Excruciating," Luke said with an engaging grin. "So who's eloping?"

"I'd love to," Grant said. "How great would that be? Just me and Steph and an Elvis impersonator in Vegas?"

"I'm going to get another glass of wine," Stephanie said as she got up from the table. "Anyone need anything?"

The others declined, and she walked away.

"Was it something I said?" Grant asked.

"Call me crazy," Abby said, smiling at the man she'd spent ten years with before realizing her true love was his brother Adam, "but most women don't grow up dreaming about the day they say 'I do' in front of an Elvis impersonator."

"Call *me* crazy," Grant said, his gaze firmly locked on Stephanie, "but I may be the only one in this twosome who actually wants to get married."

"That's not true," Grace said gently. "She's totally in love with you. Everyone can see that."

"Maybe so, but she's in absolutely no rush to get married."

"Have you talked to her about it?" Laura asked her cousin.

"I've tried to bring it up a few times to no avail." Grant pushed his plate aside, apparently no longer interested in his lobster. "Anyway, I shouldn't be airing the dirty laundry in public."

"This is hardly public," Janey said to her brother.

"Still. She wouldn't appreciate it."

"Do you want us to talk to her?" Grace asked. "Laura and I could try to pin her down a bit. Maybe she'd talk to us about things she wouldn't want to say to you."

"Well, shit," Grant said, "if there's stuff she doesn't want to say to me, maybe we shouldn't be talking about getting married."

"Don't say that, man," Evan said.

"Making it an all-or-nothing proposition won't get you anywhere," Mac added.

"I hate when he makes sense," Adam said, "but I gotta agree with him. Don't lay down ultimatums or anything you might later regret."

"If you guys want to talk to her," Grant said to Grace, "that's fine with me. At this point, I'm not really sure what to do. I don't want to push her, but I'm sort of at a loss over how best to proceed."

"We'll talk to her," Laura said. "Try not to worry. She loves you."

"I know," Grant said, but he didn't seem entirely convinced.

*

"When you asked me to be your date to a clambake, I had no idea I'd get to see you do your judge thing, too."

Frank McCarthy chuckled at Betsy Jacobson's dry comment. They had brought plates laden with seafood to a table for two in the corner of Seamus and Carolina's yard. "I'm full of surprises."

"Yes, you are. It was a lovely ceremony." Tall and willowy, she had curly dark hair that usually fell to her shoulders. Today it was contained in a ponytail that showed off her strikingly pretty face.

"Officiating at weddings has always been one of my favorite parts of the job."

"I can see why. So have you known for a while they were going to do this?"

"They asked me two weeks ago."

"Good to know you're so adept at keeping secrets."

Frank laughed. "Only when absolutely necessary. Otherwise, I'm a fairly open book."

"Retirement is looking good on you, Your Honor. You seem very relaxed."

"I love it. Laura told me I'm so tanned that my colleagues at the court wouldn't recognize me. I guess I've been rather pasty-faced for the last thirty or so years."

"You've worked hard and have earned your free time."

"It still feels strange to have nothing much to do when I get up in the morning except go have coffee and doughnuts with my brother and the guys at the marina."

"I bet Mac loves having you there."

"He does, and it's great to be able to see him every day. He's helping me learn how to relax. Had me out fishing in the middle of the day on Tuesday like it was no big deal to run off for a few hours."

She leaned in a little closer to him and said in a conspiratorial whisper, "It is no big deal, Frank."

"Keep reminding me."

"Happy to."

"Have you decided yet what you're going to do at the end of the summer?" he asked, hoping the question sounded casual when his feelings for her had become anything but during the time they'd spent together over the summer. So far that time had consisted of lots of dinners, days at the beach, cookouts with his family and babysitting his new grandson. He was hoping what had begun as a promising friendship might turn into something more, which was a first for him since he lost his wife so long ago.

Betsy was still fragile after the tragic loss of her son in a boating accident earlier in the summer, so he was proceeding with caution where she was concerned.

"I'm still trying to decide my next move," she said. "Ned has been very kind about allowing me to rent month-to-month, which has really helped. Being here has helped. All of you have helped."

"Good," Frank said tentatively. He honestly didn't want to hear that she was planning to leave. The time they'd spent together had been good for both of them, and he was hoping for much more of it.

"At some point, I should probably go back to work."

"Do you have to work?" he asked before backtracking. "Not that it's any of my business. Sorry."

"It is your business, Frank," she said softly. "You've been such an amazing and supportive friend. I don't know how I would've gotten through the last few months without you and your family. My friends at home are all so heartbroken over Steve, which was hard for me to be around. They're wonderful. Don't get me wrong. They all want to help, but they don't know how. Here, most of you didn't know him, so while you're sad for me, it's not nonstop grief everywhere I go. I've needed that."

"I'm glad we were able to help."

"And no, I don't need to work. I received a very generous settlement from my husband when our marriage ended, and I invested it wisely. The office where I work has held my job for me. I suppose I owe them the courtesy of letting them know if I'm not going to be back."

"You don't have to decide anything right away."

"I can't stay in limbo forever. At work or with you."

He was surprised by her unusually blunt assessment of their friendship. "Is that where we've been? In limbo?"

She graced him with the shy smile that had been bowling him over all summer. "I'm aware of the fact that you would like to be more than friends." She paused and then blushed. "Unless I've read this terribly wrong. In that case, I'm beyond embarrassed."

Frank reached across the table for her hand. "You haven't read anything wrong. I'm very interested in you. And in us."

Eyeing him with equal parts interest and curiosity, she turned her hand up and linked their fingers. "Would you have told me that if I hadn't brought it up?"

"I was sort of hoping you might come around to being ready for something more in your own time. I didn't want to rush you. I know how difficult the grief process can be, although I can't imagine what it would be like to lose my only child. That's a whole other level of heartbreak."

"It's been so incredibly devastating, but I've decided I would rather have had the time I had with Steve and lost him too soon than never to have known him or loved him."

"That's a very nice way of looking at it. I didn't know him, and I'll always be sorry for that, but I bet he'd be damned proud of the way you've handled yourself since he died. I know I am. For what it's worth."

"It's worth a lot. Thank you."

He squeezed her hand and winked at her, hoping to lighten the mood. "So does this mean you want to be my girlfriend?"

"Aren't I a little old to be considered someone's girlfriend?"

"You're not even fifty yet, and probably far too young for an old dude like me." He was fourteen years older than her forty-eight years, but the age difference had never been an issue between them.

"You're not old. You're young and vital and..."

"And what?" he asked, delighted by the flush that occupied her cheeks. Since they were sitting in the shade, it couldn't be attributed to the warm sunshine.

"You're very handsome, which you already knew."

"No one has told me that in a very long time."

"Then all the women in Providence must be blind and dumb."

Her indignant reply made Frank laugh out loud, which drew the attention of his kids across the yard, both of whom seemed intrigued to see him holding Betsy's hand. Not that they should be surprised. She'd spent a lot of time with him and his family during the summer, and they'd all become fond of her.

"It's been a long time since I was anyone's girlfriend. I may not be very good at it anymore."

"Oh I think you'll be great at it." He rolled their joined hands back and forth in a cajoling manner. "What do you say?"

"Your kids are looking at us."

"My kids are not kids anymore, and they like you almost as much as I do, so don't worry about them."

"Are you sure they don't mind me taking up so much of your time?"

"I'm sure."

"Did you actually ask them?"

"I don't have to ask them. I know them well enough to state without hesitation if they had issues with me seeing you, they would've said so by now. All they've ever said, without reservation, is how much they enjoy your company. If they didn't, we probably wouldn't be sitting here having this conversation because, as you know by now, they're my world. That doesn't mean, however, there isn't room in my world for other people, too."

"People plural?"

She amused him. She challenged him. And at times like this, she delighted him. He'd been falling for her almost since the day they met, shortly after the tragedy that had claimed her son, and this conversation had been coming for a while now.

"One person. Only you, sweetheart."

"Why, yes, Frank. I think I'd very much like to be your girlfriend."

His heart did a weird little happy dance that made him feel breathless over a woman for the first time since he lost his wife half a lifetime ago. "Does this mean you might be sticking around to see what autumn is like on our fair island?"

"This means I might be very tempted to consider it."

"I'll have to see what I can do to convince you."

CHAPTER 7

Joe waited until everyone had eaten before he stood and let out a sharp whistle to get their attention. His mother and Seamus sat to his right. Janey, holding their son, was to his left. Sharing the day with them were all the other people they loved.

"I was asked to be Seamus's best man about five minutes before the wedding, so I didn't have much time to prepare anything eloquent."

"Time wouldn't have helped," Mac said, which made Joe laugh.

"True. I just wanted to say to my mom and Seamus that this was a really great surprise. And… Well, if I'm being honest, at first I didn't know what to make of you guys together, but over time, I've come to see that the two of you make perfect sense. My mom and I were by ourselves for a long time. Now we're part of a family of five, and it's a pleasure to welcome Seamus today. You've been a great friend and colleague since I had the good sense to hire you to run our business. Of course I never pictured you married to my mother, but I'm glad it all worked out the way it did." He raised his beer bottle in tribute to his mother and her new husband. "To Seamus and Carolina. May you have many, many happy years together, and if he does drive you to commit murder, Mom, I've got you covered with bail money and a shovel."

Everyone laughed and clapped as Carolina wiped away tears and kissed her husband.

Janey reached out to him, and Joe took her hand as he sat back down.

"I'm proud of you," she whispered so only he would hear her.

"Is that right?"

"Uh-huh. This wasn't easy for you at first, but you've put your mom's happiness first, and that makes me proud."

"If you'd asked me growing up or even a couple of years ago if she was happy, I would've said definitely. But I realize now, after seeing her with Seamus, that she was content, which is an entirely different thing."

"Yes, it is, as we both know all too well."

Joe put his arm around his lovely wife and nuzzled her soft blonde hair. He gazed down at the baby asleep in her arms and knew a moment of pure happiness—and contentment. Bringing their son into the world had been a traumatic ordeal for both of them, one they were still recovering from in many ways. But the only thing that mattered to Joe was that they were both healthy and safe.

"Joe?"

"Yeah?"

"I think I might be ready to, you know, get back to normal."

For a second, Joe's brain totally froze. "By normal, do you mean…"

She nodded.

They hadn't made love since before the baby was born, although Janey's doctor in Providence had cleared her to resume normal activity two weeks ago. Joe had sensed she wasn't ready yet, so he had made a conscious effort not to push her or give her any indication he was dying for her, which he was. That was nothing new. Since they'd gotten together two years ago, he always wanted her.

"How soon can we leave?" Joe asked.

Janey laughed, and the sound of it warmed his heart. He was so damned grateful that she'd survived their baby's traumatic arrival. As long as he lived, he'd never forget the overwhelming fear of that day. "It's your mother's wedding. We should be the last to go."

"Maybe P.J. will act up and get us out of here earlier."

"We can only hope."

"Janey, I want you to know… There's no rush on my part. I don't want you to feel obligated or—" He completely forgot what he was going to say when her hand landed on his thigh and traveled upward to cup him intimately under the table.

"Any questions?" she asked with a coy, calculating smile that made his blood pump faster through his veins, all of it seeming to land in his groin.

"Just one. When is he going to wake up and give us an excuse to escape?"

"Soon. Very soon."

"Good."

*

Grace, Laura and Abby planned their attack stealthily. They waited until Charlie and Sarah walked away to get fresh drinks before they pounced on Stephanie, who'd been standing with her dad and Sarah for quite some time. Grace and Laura each linked an arm through Stephanie's and walked away from the group as Abby followed.

Laura had to talk Abby into joining them. Since she opened Abby's Attic in the Sand & Surf Hotel where Stephanie's Bistro was also located, the women had spent a lot of time together. They'd long ago gotten past the fact that Abby used to date Grant and had become close friends. Laura enjoyed their company around the hotel and had enjoyed watching the two of them get closer over the course of the busy summer season.

"What're you guys up to?" Stephanie asked her friends.

"This is an intervention," Abby said.

"An intervention? What the hell?"

"We want to talk to you," Grace said kindly.

"About?"

"Grant."

"What about him?" Stephanie asked, a mulish expression occupying her face.

"Don't shoot the messengers," Laura said, "and he'd probably never admit it, but you kind of hurt him back there with how you brushed him off."

"How did I brush him off?"

"By getting up and walking away when he tried to get you to talk about your wedding."

"I didn't do that."

"Um, yeah, you did," Grace said. "Is something wrong, Steph? You know you can talk to us if you need to, right?"

"I can make myself scarce if you'd rather not talk about Grant in front of me," Abby said.

"I don't care about any of that," Stephanie said. "It's ancient history, and you're happy with Adam."

"I'm *so* happy with Adam," Abby said with a goofy grin that made the other women laugh.

"Are you going to tell us what's going on, Steph?" Laura asked. "Is something wrong between you and Grant?"

"No, nothing is wrong. Did he tell you to ask me that?"

Laura shook her head, concerned by Stephanie's obvious torment. "Whatever it is, you'll feel better if you air it out with your best pals."

"There's nothing wrong," Stephanie insisted.

"Then why don't you want to talk about getting married when you've been engaged to the man you love for almost a year?" Grace asked.

"I don't know." Stephanie's shoulders drooped with defeat that tugged at Laura's heart. "I just don't know why I don't want to talk about it. I love him. You guys know I do."

"Anyone can see that," Abby said.

"Everything is fine the way it is. What difference will it make if we're married?"

"I don't pretend to speak for him, but I think it'll make a difference to Grant," Laura said. "He wants kids someday, and he's already thirty-six. That's probably part of the reason he'd like to get married and get on with having a family."

"I don't know if that's what I want."

"You don't want a family?" Abby asked.

Stephanie shrugged. When her eyes filled with tears, she closed them and seemed determined to will away the tears.

Grace put an arm around her, and Steph dropped her head onto Grace's shoulder.

"I'd probably be an awful mother," Stephanie said softly, so softly Laura almost didn't hear her.

And then suddenly, she understood. "No," Laura said emphatically. "You'd be a wonderful mother."

"How can you say that?" Stephanie asked. "My own mother was a horror show. I have no idea how to take care of a kid who deserves someone who knows exactly what to do."

"You're nothing like her, Steph," Grace said. "Look at all you've done and accomplished by getting Charlie out of jail and opening your own business, all while having the most wonderful relationship with Grant and the rest of us. How can you say you wouldn't know what to do?"

Weeping openly now, Stephanie shook her head. "That's really nice of you to say, but there's no way to know whether or not I'd mess it up until it happens, and I can't take that risk. It wouldn't be fair to the kid or to Grant. He deserves better. He deserves so much better than me."

"God, Steph," Laura said. "You have no idea how much he loves you if you can say something like that."

Stephanie wiped the tears off her cheeks. "I know you guys mean well—"

"Ladies," a deep male voice said behind them. "If you don't mind, I'll take it from here."

They spun around to find Grant standing there.

Laura looked to Stephanie to see what she wanted them to do.

"It's okay, you guys. This conversation is probably long overdue anyway."

Each of them hugged and kissed Stephanie before they walked away to leave them to work it out. Laura squeezed her cousin's arm as she walked by, afraid of what might become of him if he lost the woman he loved.

*

A knot of fear settled in her gut as Stephanie eyed her fiancé's unreadable expression. "How much did you hear?"

He kept his hands in the pockets of the plaid shorts she'd bought him for his birthday earlier in the summer. She'd had to talk him into wearing them, and now he loved them. "Enough."

"I'm sorry. I shouldn't have shared with them something I've been unable to share with you."

"Why is that? Why have you been unable to share it with me?"

"Because I'm afraid."

He took a step closer to her. "Of what, honey?"

"Of losing you." Despite her effort to contain the emotional wallop of exposing her deepest fears, a sob escaped from her tightly clenched lips.

Grant closed the distance between them and put his arms around her, drawing her into his familiar and comforting embrace. "That's not going to happen. There's nothing you could say or do that would keep me from wanting you or loving you. I thought you knew that."

Sometimes she still felt like she didn't deserve this amazing man. "I don't know if I want kids." Saying the words out loud filled her with an unreasonable level of fear that she'd kept locked inside for months as she dodged his efforts to pin her down on a wedding date.

"Why do you say that?"

"Because! After the way I grew up, I have no business taking that kind of chance with an innocent kid who deserves better than a mother who doesn't know what the hell she's doing."

His soft chuckle surprised and infuriated her.

"Are you *laughing* at me?"

"No, babe. I'm not laughing at you. I'm laughing at the notion that anyone knows what they're doing when they bring a child into this world. Look at Joe since P.J. arrived. He hasn't got the first clue of what to do with a baby, yet he's figuring it out. And he lost his dad when he was seven. Sure, he had my dad to show him how fatherhood is done, but he probably felt no more prepared to be a father than you do to be a mother. And what about Laura? Her mother died when she was nine. No one is showing her how to do it, but would anyone deny that she's a wonderful mother to Holden?"

"No," Stephanie said in a small voice.

"Look at what she's going through to bring the twins into the world. She got pregnant again knowing that pregnancy doesn't agree with her, and she did it anyway."

"I think that might've been an accident," Stephanie said, desperately seeking some levity in the midst of her emotional firestorm.

"At their age, there're no accidents." He drew back from her, but only enough so he could see her face. "I believe in my heart that you would be an amazing mother. I believe that you would take one look at a child of ours and decide you'd do anything for that baby. I believe you'd give your own life to keep a child of ours safe. I believe all these things because I know you, Stephanie. I know *you*, the real you. I know your heart, and I know what it's like to be loved by you. Nothing you can say would ever convince me that you won't love our child the same way you love me—with all you've got to give."

Sobs hiccupped through her as he held her close and rubbed her back. "It's not fair."

"What isn't?"

"Someone ought to warn a girl that when she gets involved with a writer, she's going to be powerless when he unleashes his words on her."

"You're not powerless, babe. You've got all the power here. You've ruined me for all other women, so if you don't marry me, you're dooming me to living like a monk for the rest of my life, a lonely, worthless shell of the guy I might've been with you as my wife."

She laughed despite the tears that continued to flow freely. "See what I mean? What am I supposed to say to that?"

"You could say, 'Why, yes, Grant, as usual, you're right about everything. And it's all going to be okay. As long as the two of us are together, we can get through anything, including parenthood.' You could say, 'I love you and only you, and I want to marry you as much as you want to marry me.' You could also say—"

She reached for him, wrapping her arms around his neck and holding on to him for dear life. "What you said," she whispered against his lips. "All of it."

"Really? You mean it?"

Nodding, she kissed him again. "I'm sorry I didn't talk to you about this sooner. I should've known you'd know just what to say to talk me down off the ledge."

"I never want you out on that ledge by yourself. You're not alone anymore, Steph. There's no need to do this to yourself."

"I'm still getting used to that. I was alone for so long that sometimes I forget everything is different now, and I don't have to keep it all inside anymore."

He held her for a long time, giving her exactly what she needed the way he always did. "You know what the best thing about growing up here was?"

Surprised by the change in topic, she said, "No, what?"

"I know every path and where it leads. That one there," he said, nodding to a spot on her right, "leads around the neighbor's house and back to the road where we parked."

Stephanie smiled up at him as his plan filled her with joy and excitement and relief to have finally shared her deepest fears with him. When he held out his hand to her, she happily gave him hers and let him lead her down the path that would take them home.

*

Standing with her dad and Betsy, Laura kept an eye on Stephanie and Grant, who seemed to be working things out if the hugging and kissing were any indication. That was a relief. She loved the two of them and loved them together. Her cousin had never been as mellow and happy as he'd been since he met and fell for Stephanie. Laura admired Steph tremendously for the battle she'd waged to free Charlie from jail while working multiple jobs to support herself and pay for lawyers.

Until Grant introduced her to his friend Dan Torrington, none of those lawyers had succeeded in doing what Dan had accomplished with a couple of well-placed phone calls. Speaking of Dan, he walked over to them with his fiancée, Kara Ballard.

"I think you're the last ones we need to invite," Dan said.

"To what?" Laura asked.

"My parents are coming to the island tonight," Kara said, "and they're hosting a dinner for us tomorrow night at the Summer House. I know it's short notice, but they wanted to do an engagement party. Personally, I think engagement parties are stupid, but you can't tell my mother that."

"I have to check with Owen to make sure he doesn't have plans or a gig, but we should be able to come," Laura said.

"Please feel free to bring the baby," Kara said.

"Your Honor," Dan said, "hope you can make it, too."

"I'm Frank, Dan, and yes, we'd love to," he said with a glance at Betsy, who nodded in agreement.

"You'll have to give me some time to get used to calling you by your first name," Dan said. "I'm not conditioned to be so casual with judges."

"I'm retired now."

"Once a judge, always a judge."

Laura could tell that Dan's comments pleased her dad, who was making a smooth transition to retirement. She loved having him living close enough to see him every day. He'd been a huge help to her with Holden, too.

Evan came over and asked to speak to her.

"Excuse me," she said to the others. "What's up?" she asked her cousin, who was Owen's closest friend.

"Is he okay?" Evan asked.

She didn't have to ask whom he was talking about. "I don't know," she said with a sigh. "He says he's fine, but the closer we get to leaving, the more withdrawn he gets. I think he's terrified of seeing his father again after all this time and of having to testify. But more than that, he's terrified that no matter what he says or does, it won't be enough to put the guy away for a good long time."

"I really wish he and Sarah didn't have to go through this. Especially now, right before your wedding."

"Believe me, I wish the same thing."

"I was worried because we got asked to play a couple of gigs in the last week or so, and he declined, which is unusual."

"Especially when he gets to play with you. Those are his favorite gigs."

Evan smiled at that. "I'm going to Virginia with you."

"Evan... You don't have to. I'll be there, and so will Blaine, David, Slim, my dad, Sarah. He'll be well protected."

"He's my best friend, Laura. I can't let him go through this without me there with him."

She curled her hands around his arm and rested her head on his shoulder. "I feel the same way, so I can't blame you for wanting to come. I'm sure he'll appreciate it."

"I'm worried about him," Evan said, his gaze fixed on Owen across the yard. He was with his mom and Charlie as well as Shane, who was holding Holden, although anyone who knew Owen well could see he was smiling and nodding, but the smile wasn't his real smile. It wasn't the one that lit up his face and made his eyes crinkle at the corners.

"I am, too," she said.

CHAPTER 8

"My mom told me she's staying at Charlie's tonight," Owen said after they were home and had gotten Holden into bed.

"Really? Wow. Good for her—and him. Do you think they'll, you know…"

"I'm trying very hard not to think about that."

Laura laughed at the face he made. "My dad and Betsy were holding hands today."

"I saw that."

"Seems like things are moving forward for everyone."

"Mom said Charlie is coming to Virginia with us. Slim will need to lease a bigger plane." Because so many of them were going, Laura's dad had worked with Slim to arrange for a private plane out of Greene Airport in Warwick.

"I'm glad your mom finally told Charlie what's going on so he can support her through all of this."

"I'm glad she told him, too."

"Evan is planning to come with us."

The news seemed to catch Owen off guard. "Why? He's got too much going on with the studio to be away."

"He wants to be there for you."

Owen shook his head. "That's not necessary."

"It is to him." Laura approached him cautiously. For the first time, she wasn't sure she'd be welcome. "You don't understand how hard it is for the people who love you to watch you suffer."

He let her put her arms around him, but he seemed to be merely tolerating her, which was also a first. "And you all don't understand how embarrassing and humiliating this entire thing is for me."

"Why, Owen?"

Staring down at her, mouth agape, he said, "Because! He's my father! How would you or Evan begin to understand where I come from with Frank and Mac McCarthy as your fathers?"

The pain that echoed through his every word sliced her like a knife, making her bleed for him. She'd heard it was possible to feel the pain of others almost as acutely as they were feeling it themselves, but she'd never experienced it so profoundly until now. "Your father is no reflection on you, Owen. You had no control over who you were born to, just like Evan and I had no control over who we were born to. We got lucky. You didn't. That doesn't make us look at you any differently because something you couldn't control happened to you. If anything, it makes us admire you more than we already do, because you survived it when it might've broken a lesser person."

"How can you be so sure it didn't break me?"

"Look at you. You're strong and capable and trustworthy and loyal and loving and gentle—so gentle with me and Holden and your mother and all the other people you love. You're *nothing* like him, Owen. No one thinks you are, except for maybe you."

His cheek twitched with tension as he fixated on a spot over her shoulder. "I feel like he's in there, lying dormant, waiting to lash out when he has the right provocation."

"So if I piss you off someday, you're going to hit me?" With her hands flat against his chest, she gave him a little push.

Since he wasn't expecting it, he stumbled slightly. "What're you doing?"

"Proving a point." She raised her hand and laid it gently against his cheek. "If I slap your face, will you slap me back?"

He turned away from her hand. "No. Stop it. Why are you doing this?"

She rolled her other hand into a fist that she pressed to his abdomen. "If I punch you in the stomach, will you punch me back?"

"Laura…"

"You'd never lay a hand on me, no matter what I did to you. Never. I haven't the slightest doubt about that. I could say anything, do anything, and you'd never touch me with anything other than love."

"Stop this."

"Not until I hear you say you're nothing like him." With her hands once again on his chest, she raised a challenging brow. "Do I need to push you around a little more to make you understand what I already know?" The notion that she could physically make him do anything he didn't want to do was ridiculous, and they both knew it. "Do I?"

"No," he said with a sigh as he curled his hands around her wrists and lifted them from his chest. He kissed one of her palms and then the other. "I'd rather die than do anything to hurt you."

"And that, right there, is why you'll never be your father's son. Don't you see, Owen? That's not how he feels. He'd rather die than admit how weak and inadequate he is or how little control he has over his rage. You would rather die than hurt me or anyone else you love. Can't you see the difference?"

"I'm beginning to, but I still worry that he'll rear his ugly head in me someday."

"So when Holden is five and sitting at the table playing with his food rather than eating it, will you suddenly hit him so hard across his little face that he can't go to school for a week out of fear that someone might see the bruises?" She'd purposely used the first time his father had hit him as an example.

"No," he said, blinking furiously.

Laura framed his face with both her hands. "You would never, could never. You love Holden more than you love yourself. You love me more than you love yourself. That's why you'll never behave the way your father did. He loves no one more than he loves himself."

He slid his arms around her, letting his head drop to her shoulder.

"I want you to say it."

"Say what?"

"I'm nothing like my father. Say it."

"Laura..."

She curled her hand around his nape, cradling him against her. "Say it."

"I'm nothing like my father."

"Say it again."

He released a deep, rattling breath. "I'm nothing like my father."

"One more time."

"I'm nothing like my father."

"We'll keep working on this until it gets easier to say and believe."

"I still don't want you guys to come to Virginia."

"Too bad." Pressing her lips to his temple, she said, "Oh damn. Does it piss you off when I talk to you that way? Do you feel compelled to show me the back of your hand to keep me in line?"

He pulled her in closer. "Actually, it kind of turns me on when you talk back to me."

Laura laughed. "That's good to know."

"Thank you."

Her eyes filled, and she closed them, determined to stay strong for him when she wanted to weep. "Please don't thank me for helping you to see that you're a good man, Owen. One of the best men I've ever known. And I don't expect my opinion of you to ever change."

"It would kill me if I did something to lose your respect."

"There again you prove my point. Do you think your father ever said anything like that to your mother?"

"I doubt he did."

"I'm going to keep reminding you of all the differences between you and him."

"Okay."

"Come to bed with me, Owen. I need you."

"You need me… Seems like the other way around tonight."

"We need each other, like we have from the very beginning."

He bent his head to kiss her, lingering for a long moment. "I don't know how I ever lived without you."

"I feel exactly the same way." She went up on tiptoes to kiss him. "We're going to get you through the trial, and then we'll have the rest of our lives together."

Running his hands down her back, he cupped her bottom and lifted her.

Laura clung to him as he walked them across the room to their bed. He undressed her and then himself, all the while gazing down at her with love in his eyes. Leaning over her, he left a circle of kisses on the slight bump on her abdomen.

"I can't wait to meet these guys."

"Neither can I."

"I can't wait until they stop making you sick every day."

She slid her fingers through his always unruly blond hair. "Neither can I."

Chuckling, he kissed his way up the front of her. "Let's cover you up so you don't get cold." He lifted her effortlessly, arranged her on the pillows and covered her before he slid in next to her.

Laura turned on her side and reached for him. "This is the best part of the day. The very end, when I get to be alone with you."

He worked his leg between hers and put his arms around her. "It's my favorite time of day, too."

Despite the desire she always felt for him, especially when they were naked in bed together, her eyes refused to stay open any longer. "I can't stay awake."

"You don't have to, honey."

"Don't you want to…"

"Always, but you need to sleep."

"I'll make it up to you in the morning."

"You don't have to. You give me everything I could ever want and then some. You don't owe me anything."

"I owe you everything," she whispered. "I was wrecked, and you put me back together."

"Best project I ever worked on."

With her face tucked against his chest, she smiled, content and happy. No matter what went on around them, they'd always have this. She took that thought with her as she drifted off to sleep.

*

For a long time after Laura fell asleep, Owen was awake, listening to the South Harbor foghorn and the crash of the waves hitting the breakwater. The sounds were among his favorite from a childhood short on happy memories. He and his six siblings had spent their summers here with their grandparents, which, other than their father's deployments, was the only break they ever got from their violent upbringing.

Thinking about those long-ago summers also brought back memories of the warnings their father had given them about sharing their family's business with anyone, even the grandparents who'd doted on them. Mark Lawry's children had lived in fear of him all the time, even when they were hundreds of miles away.

Owen had spent a lot of time as an adult wondering why his twelve- or thirteen-year-old self had never confided in the grandparents who would've moved heaven and earth to rescue them from the hell they lived in. With the perspective of age and maturity, he knew he'd been governed by fear, but he wished so fervently that he'd had the courage to speak up, to say something, even if the consequences had been dire.

He'd never forget the way his strong, formidable grandmother had wept upon hearing the full truth of what her beloved grandchildren had endured at the hands of their father. It had taken a suicide attempt by his youngest brother, Jeff, to blow the lid off the entire mess. Jeff had gone to live with their grandparents in Florida and was now in college and thriving.

What might've been different for Jeff, for all of them, if Owen had only said something during one of those idyllic summers with their grandparents? Intellectually, he knew he was minimizing the overwhelming fear his twelve-year-old self had lived with when his thirty-four-year-old self still quaked at the thought of having to see his father in a few days.

He hated himself for that. Why should he feel fearful when he was bigger and stronger than the bully who'd raised him had ever been? How was it possible that his father still had the power to make him quake when he hadn't even seen him in more than ten years?

Owen would give anything for a magic wand that he could wave to fast-forward their lives to after the trial, when his father was safely convicted and headed for prison, where he would finally pay for the vicious way he'd treated his wife and children for decades.

In the absence of magic, he had no choice but to summon the resolve to power through the ordeal and get to the other side of it, where he could move forward with Laura and the life they had planned. There was no place for his father in that life, and after trial, he would never have to see him again. That day couldn't come soon enough for Owen.

He smoothed his hand over the silky length of Laura's hair, taking comfort from her presence even when she was asleep. What she'd said about him not being anything like his father had struck a chord with him. He wanted so badly to believe she was right about that, but he'd always been aware of a simmering core of rage that lived within him. While he couldn't imagine ever striking out at the people closest to him, the rage was part of him nonetheless.

Perhaps he would never find a need to tap that hidden resource, and he could only hope it would remain dormant and not rear its ugly head to cause him trouble. Staring up at the ceiling in the dark of night with the love of his life asleep in his arms, Owen made a silent vow never to allow rage to dictate his reactions to Laura or his children. He loved them too much to ever let that happen.

He was not his father's son. He would never be his father's son. Owen finally fell asleep, taking those thoughts with him into slumber.

*

This was a huge mistake, Sarah thought as she changed out of the outfit she'd worn to the clambake into the summer-weight nightgown she'd brought with her to sleep in. Earlier in the day, when she'd packed a bag to spend the night with Charlie, she'd been excited and filled with anticipation of spending hours alone with him.

Now that those hours were upon her, however, she was as nervous as a virgin on her wedding night. She felt ridiculous for allowing nerves to derail her determination to move forward with a man who'd been an amazing friend to her for nearly a year now. He'd been patient and kind and gentle with her from the very beginning. He'd shown her how a real man treats the woman he cares for, and now she wanted to show him how much she cared for him.

Except, she wasn't sure she could. It had been so long since she'd experienced the kind of feelings Charlie aroused in her just by looking at her across the table with that sly smile and those piercing blue eyes. He never had a whole lot to say, but he managed to convey his affection for her with his actions, which spoke far louder than the loudest of words ever had.

She brushed her hair and teeth and summoned the fortitude to leave the bathroom, to get into bed with him, to hold him and touch him and kiss him. He'd told her he didn't expect anything from her that she wasn't ready to give, and she appreciated that he'd known those words would matter to her. But the nerves were present nonetheless.

Taking a deep breath, she put her folded clothes into her bag and stashed it in a corner of the bathroom. Rubbing her damp palms over the soft cotton of her gown, she emerged from the bathroom to find Charlie already in bed. He was propped up against several pillows, his chest bare and the covers pulled up to his waist. She knew a moment of complete panic when she wondered if he was naked under there.

The thought caused a nervous giggle to escape from her tightly clenched lips.

"What's so funny?" he asked in the gruff tone that might've sounded harsh to someone who didn't know him as well as she did. Despite the extreme injustice he'd endured during fourteen years in prison, there was nothing harsh about her Charlie.

Her Charlie. How long had she thought of him as *her Charlie*? For quite some time now, if she were being honest with herself.

He folded the bed covers back and patted the mattress next to him. "Are you going to tell me?"

"This whole thing is funny," Sarah said as she slid into bed next to him while willing her hammering heart to settle down before she hyperventilated or did something equally embarrassing.

He turned to face her, propping himself on an upturned hand. "You wanna let me in on the joke?"

She fixated on his muscular chest, the intricate tattoo that encircled his bicep, and the mat of dark chest hair that had begun to go gray in places. He was a finely built man, and she suddenly wanted to touch him, to feel his soft skin under her hands, to examine every hill and valley of the muscles that had fascinated her for months. "I'm nervous," she said, keeping her gaze fixed on his chest rather than looking at his face.

"It's just me, Sarah. Your friend Charlie."

"Who's now in bed with me and at least half naked."

"Only half," he said with a gruff chuckle.

"Are you nervous, too?"

"Hell yes, I'm nervous."

"Why?"

"Because you're here, finally, and I don't want to do the wrong thing or scare you off."

"You could never do the wrong thing."

"Don't be too sure. It's been a long time since I was in bed with a woman. A long time."

"So you haven't, with anyone... Since you got out of prison?"

"Nope."

"Oh."

"Yeah, so I've got my own set of worries, especially knowing what that bastard you were married to put you through. I want to give you everything you deserve, everything you should've had all along, but I don't want to rush you—"

Sarah caressed the face that had become so dear to her. "Kiss me, Charlie."

He put his arm across her middle and tugged her closer. "Is this okay?"

She nodded.

Leaning over her, he studied her for a long, breathless instant before he lowered his face to hers, his lips soft but persuasive. "This is all we have to do. It would be more than enough to have you sleep in my arms."

"Why don't we see what transpires and try not to worry too much about anything?"

"That sounds like a good plan to me." He kissed her again, more insistently this time, his tongue seeking hers in deep thrusts that made her want so much more of him.

She took advantage of the opportunity to touch him, to learn the planes and textures of his muscular chest and arms.

Her touch seemed to inflame him, and he ended up on top of her as one kiss became two and then three. She couldn't get close enough to him, even with her arms and legs around him, her fingers pressing into the muscles of his back as his lips and tongue continued to devour her. His arousal pulsed against her, hard and insistent, a reminder of where their heated kisses could be leading if she wanted to go that far.

It had been so long, so very, very long, since she'd wanted anything the way she wanted this man. With desire strumming through her entire body, setting her on fire with an almost painful need for more, she moaned against his lips.

He gasped as he broke the kiss. "I'm sorry. I didn't mean to lose control. It's too much."

"It's not enough."

Looking down at her, he appeared stunned by what she'd said. "Sarah…"

"I need you. I need more."

"Are you sure?"

"Yes, Charlie. Yes, I'm sure."

CHAPTER 9

After sneaking away from Carolina and Seamus's wedding, Grant and Stephanie went home to their cozy cottage on Shore Point Road and talked for hours about all the things that had been on Stephanie's mind for months now. With the floodgates open at last, the words poured out of her in a steady stream of worries and fears that she'd kept from him for so long that she was afraid he'd be hurt by her reluctance to share them with him.

"I can't tell you how badly I wish you'd let me go through this with you, rather than feeling like you had to keep it from me," he said when she finally ran out of things to say. They were curled up together on the sofa with lit candles on the coffee table casting a warm glow over the small room.

"You've had your own stuff to deal with, after the accident and everything. You were so undone by what happened that day, how you couldn't save Dan and Steve, too, all while you were trying to finish the screenplay. I didn't want to add to your burden."

"You're never a burden to me."

"I was afraid it would change how you felt about me to hear I was having doubts about being a wife and mother."

"Steph… God, how could you be afraid of that? Don't you know how essential you are to me? Everything that happens, from the minute I get up until the minute I go to bed with you, I want to share with you. A thousand times a day I wonder what you're doing, what you would say about whatever I'm doing, things I need to tell you… Your voice is in my head—always. There's nothing you could say or do or feel that would make me want anyone else's voice in my head. When are you going to realize that?"

She blinked back the tears she'd worked so hard to keep at bay while she bared her soul to him. But, as always, his words had incredible power over her. The things he said to her… "Deep inside, I knew it was wrong of me not to share my worries with you. I also knew that you'd want to fix what was wrong, because that's what you always do. From the very beginning, you've wanted to fix what was wrong for me."

Because she couldn't resist touching him when he was lying so close to her, she unbuttoned his shirt and laid her hand on his chest. The steady beat of his heart under her palm calmed her like nothing else could. "Charlie took Sarah home with him tonight."

His hand covered hers. "Really? Good for them."

"He has this amazing second chance because of you."

"I just made a phone call. Dan gets the credit for freeing him."

"You get half the credit, because without that phone call, there would've been no Dan Torrington to the rescue."

"We're both glad we were able to right a terrible wrong—for Charlie and for you."

"I don't want to be afraid anymore, Grant, but it's almost like I don't know how *not* to be. I've spent most of my life afraid of one thing or another. It's a hard habit to break."

"I have every confidence that you're capable of anything you set your mind to doing. If you decide that fear isn't going to run your life anymore, then I have no doubt you'll make that happen. You're the strongest person I've ever met."

"No, I'm not."

"Yes, you are. You have no idea how much everyone admires you for what you've been able to accomplish all on your own."

"You admire me," she said with a laugh. "Who's the one with the Academy Award?"

"That's nothing compared to the huge accomplishment of fighting to overturn a conviction that never should've happened in the first place."

"At which I was hugely unsuccessful until you came along and made that phone call."

"Steph… Come on. Why can everyone see this but you? You're the hero of this story, not me. Not Dan. You. If you hadn't kept fighting, I would've never known about Charlie or his situation. If you hadn't cared about him more than you cared about yourself, he'd still be sitting in that prison. You need to take most of the credit for freeing him, and you need to free yourself by letting go of the past and embracing the future."

"I'm trying. You have no idea how hard I'm trying."

"I know you are. When you and I are together, there's nothing we can't handle."

"I was on my way to believing that when the accident happened, and I had a whole day to contemplate how I'd ever manage to live without you."

"Ah Christ," he said with a sigh. "And then I came back a total wreck, and all the focus was on me when you were dying inside. I'm sorry, honey. I should've paid more attention to how traumatizing it was for you."

"It was way worse for you."

"That's not necessarily true." He pulled her in closer to him, his lips pressed to her forehead. "God, I love you so much. I had no idea it was possible to love anyone as much as I love you. And the thought of you worried or afraid for all this time, and me not even knowing it… I feel like a selfish bastard."

"You're not. It's not your fault. I went out of my way to hide my worries from everyone. No one knew until today."

"Will you promise me you won't suffer in silence anymore?"

She nodded.

"Say it. I want to hear the words."

"I promise I won't suffer in silence anymore."

"And do you promise to remember every day that I love you more than I love myself and all that matters to me is that you're safe and happy?"

"If you promise to remember I feel the same exact way about you."

His smile filled her with giddy joy. It was okay. He knew all her darkest worries and loved her anyway. "Promise."

"Me, too." She drew him into a soft, sweet kiss. "Let's go to bed."

"Not before we set a wedding date."

"Oh, I thought you'd forgotten about that," she said with a coy smile to let him know she was kidding.

"I haven't forgotten and neither have you." As he spoke, he pulled her top up and over her head, released her bra and removed it. "What's it going to be?"

"Whatever you want is fine with me."

Nuzzling her breasts, he said, "How about next weekend, then?"

Her mouth fell open in shock, and she tugged at his hair to get his attention, which was fully on her breasts. "What? Next weekend?"

He looked at her briefly before stroking her nipple with his tongue. "Why not?"

Stephanie squirmed as desire shot through her, hot and insistent, until she throbbed from wanting him. "We can't get married next weekend."

"How come?" he asked as he sucked her nipple into his mouth.

She gasped and squiggled, forcing him to release her. "First of all, that's right before Laura and Owen's wedding, and I don't want to upstage them. Second of all, it's still high season at the restaurant, and it took a lot of juggling to get today off. I don't want to be worried about work when I should be focused on you. Third of all… I can't think of a third reason, but the first two are enough."

He cupped both her breasts and ran his thumbs over her nipples until they were hard and tingling. "Okay, then Labor Day. We'll get married on the last day of the official summer season when everyone will be headed home and we get the island back—for the most part." The season lingered these days until Columbus Day, but things definitely quieted down on Labor Day.

"Fine. We'll get married on Labor Day."

"Where?" he asked as he unbuttoned her shorts and slid his hand down the front of her until he was cupping her sex.

"On the beach."

His fingers pressed and probed until they encountered the well of moisture that awaited him. "And then what?"

"We'll have a party at the restaurant."

"Good. It's a plan." He sat up suddenly, pulling her shorts and panties off her in almost frantic motions that indicated how badly he wanted her. After removing his own clothes, she expected him to help her up and lead her to bed. But he came down on top of her, apparently in too much of a rush to change locations.

"I love you, too, you know. Unreasonably."

"There's not one thing about it that's unreasonable," he said, kissing and touching and caressing her until she was on the verge of begging him to take her.

"You're often extremely unreasonable, but I love you anyway."

His huff of laughter preceded the press of his erection against her sensitive opening.

Stephanie raised her hips, needing to get closer, to take him in, to show him what he meant to her. She wanted to give him everything, including the family he wanted so much. If it meant making him happy, she would swallow all her remaining fears and have faith that the future he promised would be as bright and as glorious as he said it would be. As long as she had him, she couldn't imagine her life playing out any other way.

With a hard thrust, he entered her fully, and every thought that didn't involve the exquisite pleasure they found together was pushed from her mind, swept away on a waves of desire that required her full attention.

"Nothing has ever been like this, Steph," he whispered against her ear as he pushed deep into her before withdrawing and doing it again. "You're the best thing to ever happen to me."

Listening to him, feeling him, surrounded by him, Stephanie finally was able to let go of the past, of the fears that had ruled her, and embrace the future that would revolve around him and the love they'd found together.

"You can't ever leave me," he said. "You'd ruin me."

"Where would I go when the only thing I need is right here?"

Her words seemed to light a fire in him that had him picking up the pace, until they both cried out from the power of what they'd created. She clung to him, her anchor in the storm, and took everything he had to give until he was spent and lax in her arms, his heart beating fast and his breathing rapid.

"So Labor Day it is?" he asked after a long period of silence.

"Labor Day it is."

*

Mac and Maddie arrived home from the day's festivities to find a party going on at their house. Daisy and David, who'd been babysitting for them while they attended what they thought would be a clambake, were entertaining Jenny Wilks and her fiancé, Alex Martinez, as well as Jared James and his new wife, Lizzie. With them was another woman Maddie didn't know.

"Hey," Daisy said when they came in through the sliding door. "Mom and Dad are home, and we're in so much trouble for having a party."

"Oh stop it," Maddie said to her friend. "As long as no one was drinking, there's no trouble." The kitchen table was littered with beer bottles, wineglasses and snacks.

"Um, well," Alex said, trying to hide his beer bottle.

Mac laughed at his lame effort. "Are there more of those somewhere?"

"In the fridge," David said. "Help yourself."

"Don't mind if I do," Mac said.

"It is your house after all," David replied.

"Do you want us to go?" Daisy asked Maddie when she pulled up a chair to the table.

"No need to break up the party," Maddie said, even though she was beyond exhausted. Since discovering her third child was on the way, exhaustion had been her closest friend. She'd never been this tired with Thomas or Hailey. "How were they?"

"Thomas didn't want to go to bed, as usual, but he's out cold now."

"He didn't give you a hard time, did he?"

"Nothing like that. He and Uncle David were having fun with the trucks, and he didn't want to stop playing."

"I can picture that. We have the same issue with Daddy most nights. How was Hailey?"

"An angel, as always."

"That's good to hear. She is a nice, easy baby." Maddie rested her hand on her belly, which was just starting to expand. "I hope this one is, too."

"Maddie and Mac," Jenny said, "this is my friend Erin Barton. She's interviewing with the town council Monday to take my place at the lighthouse."

Erin had long, light brown hair that she wore in a ponytail that made her look younger than her age, which Maddie estimated to be in her mid-thirties. "So nice to meet you, Erin," Maddie said.

"My dad is on the council," Mac said. "I'll tell him to be nice to you."

"He's nice to everyone," Jenny said.

"That he is," Mac said with a smile for Erin. "I'm sure if Jenny is recommending you, you're a shoo-in."

"I'm still not a hundred percent sold on this change Jenny insists I need," Erin said, "but she can be hard to resist when she gets something in her head."

"Don't I know it," Alex said drolly, winking at his fiancée.

"You love when I get something in my head," Jenny said with a meaningful smile that made everyone laugh.

"TMI," Erin said, covering her ears.

"I'm sorry," Jenny said with a somberness that took Maddie by surprise. Jenny had obviously been joking around. Why would she feel the need to apologize to her friend?

Sensing Maddie's confusion, Erin said, "I'm Toby's twin sister. The original fiancé."

"Oh," Maddie said as the import settled in on her. Toby had been killed on 9/11. "I'm so sorry for your loss."

"That's very kind of you. It was a long time ago, and no one is more thrilled for Jenny than I am. Truly."

Jenny gave her friend a one-armed hug. "Thanks."

"I might be happier for Jenny than you are," Alex said, which had them all laughing again.

"I like him," Erin said.

"So do I," Jenny replied. "And the best part? He has a brother who's almost as handsome as he is."

"He is nowhere near as handsome as I am," Alex said. To Erin, he added, "I'd hate to see you get your hopes up only to have them dashed."

"Oh my God," Jenny said. "You're insufferable. Paul is every bit as gorgeous as you are, isn't he, ladies?"

"Absolutely," Lizzie said.

Her new husband glared at her playfully.

"What? He is. Just because I'm married now doesn't mean I'm suddenly blind."

Maddie giggled behind her hand.

"What's so funny over there, Mrs. McCarthy?" her husband asked.

"That you all think we get hysterical blindness or something once you put a ring on our fingers. My eyes still work just fine, and Paul Martinez is hot."

Alex cringed as Mac glowered.

"You'll pay for that later," Mac said.

"I'm not afraid of you. I have things that you want."

"Damn straight you do."

"And that," Jared said, "is our cue to move along, people."

They got up and gathered the empty bottles and glasses.

"Was it something I said?" Mac asked.

"You know it was." Maddie rolled her eyes at her husband, who was never shy about his desire to spend time alone with her. She loved that about him, not that she'd ever tell him that.

They said good night and thank you to Daisy and David for babysitting and saw them out the door.

Mac locked up and turned off the outside lights once they were safely in their cars.

"You didn't have to run them off," Maddie said as they went upstairs together.

"I can tell you're about to fall over, but you'd never say so."

"Don't act like you know me so well."

"I know you better than anyone, and I also know this pregnancy is kicking your ass big-time."

"Yes," she said with a sigh, "it is. I've never been so tired in my entire life. I can't figure out why this time is so different than the last two times."

"Um, maybe the fact that you have two other kids to contend with while you're pregnant might have something to do with it?"

"Could be."

"I need to be doing a better job of helping you out around here."

"This is your busy season at the marina. You're doing what you can."

"I could spend more time at home. We're not that busy, and I have partners who can help me so I can help you."

"You don't have to do that, Mac. So I'm a little tired. I'll get through it. Taking care of the kids and the house is my job."

He came to her and put his hands on her shoulders. "It's *our* job, and I don't mind taking on more around here while you're busy growing Malcolm the third in there."

She raised a brow. "Malcolm the third? First of all, how do you know it's a *boy*, and second of all, *Malcolm*? *Really*?"

"Is this your way of saying you don't like my name?"

"I like Mac a lot better than Malcolm."

"So do I. So we'll call him Mac."

"There're already too many Macs in this family, and Janey still wants to name a kid McCarthy and call him Mac. That'll be mayhem."

"Then we'll call him M.J."

"Along with P.J?" she asked, reminding him of his new nephew.

"We have to come up with something. I grew up hating my name, but now that I'm older, I love that I was named after my dad. I love being the oldest son and the one who got to carry on the tradition. I want the same for this guy, even if he's not my oldest son."

"You have no idea what it does to me when you talk about Thomas that way."

"How else would I talk about him? He is my son. He's been my son since the day I met the two of you."

She bit her lip and shook her head.

"What?"

"I should be used to it by now."

His brows knitted with confusion. "Used to what?"

"You and the amazing way you love us. Almost two years married, and you're still taking my breath away."

He put his arms around her. "You do the same to me. Every damned day."

She slipped her arms around his waist and held on tight to him.

"Let's get you in bed."

Determined to fight through the powerful exhaustion so she could spend some more time with her husband, Maddie changed into one of the silky nightgowns he loved, brushed her hair and teeth and got into bed with him.

"Come here," he said, reaching for her.

She curled up to him and relaxed into his embrace. "I can't remember what it was like to sleep alone."

"Neither can I, but I suspect it was kind of boring and lonely."

"Compared to this, anything else would be."

"Mmm, so true." He rubbed her back in small circles. "Go to sleep, honey."

"You don't want to…"

"Not tonight. You need the sleep more than you need me."

"That is never true."

"Shh. Go to sleep. We've got millions of nights when we can do all sorts of naughty things."

"Like what? Tell me about them."

"Well, first…"

Maddie fell asleep to the familiar, comforting sound of his voice.

Chapter 10

"A bride should not ever, ever, *ever* do dishes on her wedding night," Seamus declared as he came into the house after seeing off the last of their guests. He shut the door, locked it, turned off the outside lights and then leaned against the door.

Tomorrow, they would face a frightful mess in the yard, and Carolina had decided to try to make a dent on the equally frightful mess in the kitchen sink, but apparently her new husband wasn't having it.

Husband… She hadn't had one of those in more than thirty years. How odd it was to use that word again so long after her dear husband Pete had been killed in an accident. Carolina dried her hands on a dishtowel and turned to him. "Where did you hear of this rule?"

"It's in the marriage bible under part B subsection two point two: a bride should never, ever, ever do dishes on her wedding night. Rather, it reads, she should service her husband in any way he sees fit and show him how truly grateful she is to have had the good fortune to marry him."

If they each lived to be a hundred years old—of course she'd get there way before he did—he'd probably never stop making her laugh. "You just made that up."

"I had to do something. I thought you were in here making yourself ready for me, and I find you doing the dishes. This called for drastic measures and rulebooks."

"How were you expecting me to 'make myself ready' for you?"

"By getting naked, for one thing."

"So you expected me to be standing naked in the kitchen, waiting for you to tell me how best I can service you?"

"That would've been an excellent way to begin our marriage."

"Let me know when you wake up from this dream you're having and are ready for a dose of reality."

"I never want to wake up from this dream I've been having, even when you don't honor and obey me with your nakedness in the kitchen."

"Has anyone ever told you that you're incorrigible and delusional?"

He pushed off the door and started toward her, his green-eyed gaze fixed on her. "You have. Many times."

Carolina felt like prey caught in the crosshairs. "And yet you still come back for more."

He stopped when he was merely an inch away from her. "I'm a glutton for punishment."

"Today you signed on for a lifetime's worth of punishment."

"Yes, and thank Christ for that." Wrapping his arms around her neck, he kissed her as if he'd been dying to for days, weeks, months, a lifetime, completely losing himself in the kiss.

Surrounded by him, Carolina could only hold on and go along for the ride the way she had since the last of her defenses had fallen, allowing him into her heart and soul where he was now so firmly entrenched she couldn't picture a day without him at the center of it.

Carolina had no idea how much time had passed when he finally withdrew from the kiss in small increments, keeping his lips touching hers as he gazed into her eyes. "God, I've needed that since Judge McCarthy said I could kiss my bride."

"You behaved very admirably all afternoon."

"Which means I should be rewarded for my good behavior." He slid his hands from her shoulders to her hands and tugged her along behind him as he left the kitchen and headed for their bedroom. "We should've gone somewhere tonight. Somewhere special."

"This is somewhere special. It's our home, and it's become much more special to me since you moved in."

He stopped, dropped her hands and turned to face her. "Do you really mean that?"

"Yes," she said with exasperation. "Of course I mean it." He was much better at speaking about his feelings, which was something she needed to work on if he was honestly asking if she meant what she'd said. "I was thinking earlier today that I had no idea how lonely or bereft my adequate existence was until you came along and showed me."

"Carolina…"

"I don't know if I've said it often enough or shown you…"

"Shown me what?"

"How much I love you."

"God, yes, I know, love. I know. How could I not know?"

"Maybe because half the time, including during our wedding, I'm threatening to murder you."

His loud bark of laughter made her laugh, too.

"Sorry about that today. I wasn't planning to include that in the vows."

"I loved that you included it. I drive you to it, love. I know I do. And I do it on purpose because I love the way you look at me when I vex you."

"You vex me, all right. But now that I know you're doing it on purpose…"

"You have to still give me that look." As he spoke, he worked on buttons and snaps and hooks. When he had fully revealed her, he stared at her, his gaze hungry and heated. "You're so very lovely. I look at you," he said, with his lips close to her ear, "and I want. I want you, Caro, and I'm so bloody grateful you agreed to marry me."

"You didn't give me much choice," she said, filled with pleasure at knowing he was so happy.

"Aye, I didn't. Left to your own devices, you'd still be deciding to let me back into your bed after you kicked me out the first time."

"What you didn't know then, and I probably shouldn't tell you now, is all you had to do is talk to me in that insanely sexy Irish accent, and I would've given you anything you wanted."

"Now you tell me! This is grounds for an annulment!"

"Shut up about annulments and make love to your wife, will you please?"

"Gladly, my love." He removed his clothes as if the hounds of hell were chasing him and dragged her into bed with him.

"Finesse. Where's the finesse?"

"I ain't got none tonight. I'm like a randy goat on the prowl."

Carolina cracked up laughing and couldn't stop no matter how hard he tried to distract her—and he tried very hard to distract her before dropping his head to her chest in utter defeat.

"All this laughter isn't good for a man's fragile ego."

"You're not a man. You're a randy goat, remember?"

"Poor choice of words. Are you done laughing at me now?"

"I might be until you say something equally hilarious."

"I love to listen to you laugh, especially when I make it happen."

"Which is *all* the time. You have no idea how funny you are."

"I'm funny because I like to make you laugh. I've never been funny before you."

"I find that very hard to believe."

"'Tis true. My life was hardly anything much to laugh about until I found you. Losing my brothers the way I did... There was a lot of sadness. You make me want to laugh again, Caro."

Touched to hear him speak of losses he rarely mentioned, she combed her fingers through his thick auburn hair, hoping to provide comfort. "We've both had more than our share of sadness."

"Indeed, which is why we're now due a lifetime's worth of happiness."

"I'm down for that."

He kissed a path from her throat to her chest and belly. "You know what I'm down for?"

"I'm starting to get an idea."

The deep rumble of his laughter made her skin tingle with goose bumps. She had learned over the last year not to fight him when he set out to overwhelm her senses, which was exactly what he was doing right now. As he made love to her with his mouth and tongue, Carolina tried to remember who she'd been before this sexy, charming, larger-than-life Irishman came bombing into her life and turned her entire world upside down.

"I want to do this every single day of our lives," he said as he kissed her inner thigh and pushed his fingers into her. "It's my favorite thing to do in the whole world."

"Is it better than when I do that to you?"

"Well, now… It might be tied for first place with that."

"Thought you might say that."

How was it possible that he amused her even when he was doing *that* to her? "Seamus…"

"Yes, love?"

"Let's change places."

"Not tonight. I'd never last. I want to make love to my wife, and it's been a very, *very* long day. I bet the person who decided there ought to be a huge party after the wedding wasn't a guy." This was said as he thrust his fingers into her again and made her gasp from the pleasure that shot through her.

"Please. Come up here. I need you."

Those words always worked with him, and tonight was no different. Keeping his fingers tucked deep inside her, he used his other arm to move up the bed so he was lying next to her. "What do you need?"

She laid her hand on his face. "You."

He kissed her with lips and a tongue that tasted of her, which didn't surprise her. He was an earthy, erotic lover with an endlessly creative imagination. Carolina had done things with him that she wouldn't have thought possible before him.

Tonight, however, he didn't seem interested in showing her how creative he could be. Rather, he was all about the love as he looked down at her.

"Tell me I didn't dream this day," he said in a gruff whisper as he withdrew his fingers and replaced them with his cock.

"It wasn't a dream."

He pressed against her, entering her in small increments before retreating to do it again. "I keep feeling like it has to be, because nothing that's real could ever feel this good."

"It's real, and it's good, and it's going to stay that way." He was driving her crazy, but that was nothing new. In bed or out, he took an almost perverse pleasure in testing her limits.

But she'd learned a few things in the time she'd spent with him and knew how to mess with his plans. So the next time he pushed into her, she clamped down on him, making him gasp. At the same time, she gripped his ass and pulled, taking him deeper.

"Holy Christ, woman! Are you trying to give me a heart attack?"

"Not at all," she said with an innocent smile. "Just trying to move things along a bit."

"You almost moved things right past the finish line with that maneuver."

Carolina laughed at his indignant expression. Her laughter—and the squeeze of internal muscles that went with it—made him groan.

"Ahhh, love, you'd try the patience of a saint."

"Good thing you're the exact opposite of a saint."

"Good thing indeed." He began to move faster. "Is this what my demanding wife wants?"

"Yes," she said with a satisfied sigh. "It's exactly what she wants."

*

"I don't know what's wrong," Joe said, clearly despondent by his body's failure to understand his pressing need to make love to his wife.

"Nothing is wrong," Janey said. She laid her hand flat against his stomach, thrilled to be close to him even if things weren't going according to plan.

"I don't get it. This has never happened. Ever."

"It's no big deal, babe. Just relax. We can try again tomorrow."

"I don't want to try again tomorrow, and don't tell me to relax. If your equipment wasn't working right, would you be able to relax?"

It took everything she had, along with a reserve pool of strength she didn't know she possessed, to refrain from laughing at the expression on his face.

"If you laugh, I'll divorce you."

"I wouldn't dream of laughing. It's not funny."

"No, it isn't. Something is wrong with me. How can I be naked in a bed with you and not be hard as a freaking rock?"

Janey knew she needed to be very, very careful about what she said. "Um, I don't know? Would it help if I, you know, gave him some special attention?"

"It might."

"You aren't doing this on purpose to get me to do that, are you?"

"Have I ever needed to resort to tricks to get what I want from you?"

"No, but we've never had postpartum sex before either. You—and he—might be afraid I'm going to turn into one of those wives who forgets all about her poor husband after she gives birth."

The look he gave her was positively hilarious, but again, she didn't dare laugh. "Are you?"

"Am I what?"

"One of those wives who forgets all about her husband after she gives birth?"

"How could I ever forget about you?" She coaxed him onto his back and began with a light massage of his chest and the six-pack of muscles that rippled under her touch. "You're supposed to be relaxing."

"I am."

"Close your eyes. Don't think. Just feel." Janey continued the massage, adding a string of kisses across his lower abdomen. When that didn't work to arouse him, she lowered herself until she was on top of him, with his penis cradled in the valley between her breasts.

He pulled in a deep breath and held it.

"Relax."

"I can't relax when you're doing that."

"Yes, you can." She continued to kiss him, adding some tongue action that usually made him crazy, but not tonight. Nothing was working.

"It's broken. That's got to be it."

"You're thinking, and you're not relaxing. How can I be expected to work under these conditions?"

"Come up here, will you?"

"I'm not finished here. I haven't even gotten to the good stuff yet."

"Please?" He held out his arms to her.

The pleading tone of his voice had her giving in to what he wanted. She crawled toward him and loved the feel of his strong arms encircling her. She always felt so safe—and so desired—in his arms. That there could be something actually wrong between them was so unimaginable, she couldn't bear to even think about it.

"I'm sorry," he said grimly.

"Please don't be. We've had so much going on, it's a wonder we aren't both drooling by now."

"I hope you know it's not because I don't want you. I've been dying for you."

"I do know that, it's just… Never mind. It doesn't matter."

"Don't do that. Whatever you're thinking, just say it."

Janey propped her chin on her hands and studied his face, which was tight with the kind of tension she hadn't seen since the day their son was born under dramatic and frightening circumstances. "The way everything happened with P.J. It's got to be on your mind that it all began right here with you and me in a bed together, making love. And I'm just wondering, if it's possible, that you're so afraid of getting me pregnant again that it might be messing with the equipment."

Joe began to protest but stopped himself, sighing and closing his eyes. "Yeah, it's possible."

"Do you know that in all the weeks since P.J. was born, you've never told me what that day was like for you?"

"Because that doesn't matter now. You're both safe, it's in the past, and there's no need to relive it. Once was more than enough."

Janey wished he could see how tormented he looked at the reminder of what had to be one of the worst and best days of his life all rolled into one unforgettable twenty-four-hour period. "I think you relive it every day and suffer in silence over it because all the focus has been on me and the baby—"

"Which is exactly where it should be. You're the one who went through the trauma of emergency surgery."

"I had it easy, Joe. I was unconscious and had no idea what was happening until it was all over and everything was fine. That's not how it was for you, is it?"

His jaw pulsed and clenched as he struggled to retain his composure. "I don't want to talk about this. Why are we rehashing the past when it doesn't matter now?"

"It does matter if it's still weighing on you so heavily." She moved farther up to kiss his unresponsive lips. "Joe, honey, talk to me. Tell me what you went through so we can get past it and move on. Don't keep it all bottled up inside."

He turned them so she was on her back and got out of bed, pulling on a pair of shorts with hasty, jerky movements. "I don't want to talk about it. I don't want to relive it, and if you'd been awake, you wouldn't want to either."

Janey held out a hand to him. "Come back."

"I don't want to talk about it."

"I heard you."

He took her hand and reluctantly allowed her to guide him back to bed. "I'm sorry. I don't mean to bite your head off."

"It's okay. I get it. But I have all these blanks, you know? One minute I was napping in Mac's guest room, and the next I'm in Providence with a new baby and a traumatized family all around me."

"It's better that you don't remember it. Trust me on that."

"I do trust you. I wish you would trust me enough to talk to me about how it was for you."

"Don't make this about trust, Janey. That's not fair. I trust you more than I trust anyone."

"I know you do, so trust me to help you get past this by talking to me about it."

He raised both his hands to his head, running his fingers through his hair repeatedly until the short strands stood straight up. "You're really going to make me do this?"

"Afraid so."

"Fine. Don't say I didn't warn you."

"I won't."

He was quiet for a long time, so long she wondered if he'd changed his mind, and then he began to speak in a dull, flat tone that was nothing like his usual animated speech. "The one image I'll never get out of my head was how much blood there was. I went up to wake you because Blaine and Tiffany were on their way over after their wedding at the lighthouse, and I thought you'd want to be there when they arrived. I couldn't get you to wake up. I thought you were just really asleep, but then I touched you… You were really cold, and for a minute, I thought…" His voice caught and his eyes filled. He covered them with his hands as if to hide his anguish from her.

With her heart breaking for him, Janey wanted so badly to hold him, but she didn't dare touch him.

"I pulled back the covers, and there was just so much blood. I almost passed out at the sight of it, but I forced myself to move, to scream, to call for David. Thank God he was there. I'd spent so much time—years—hating him for what he'd put you through and then to have him right there when this happened... There's nothing I wouldn't do for him after what he did for you, for me, for P.J.

He was… He was incredible." Speaking in a whisper, he added, "I've never been so scared in my entire life, Janey." Tears rolled down his face, but he made no move to deal with them as he stared up at the ceiling. "Not even when my father died."

She went to him then, putting her arm around him and laying her face on his chest.

His arm locked around her. "It was a fucking nightmare, from the second I saw the blood until you woke up in Providence four hours later. The whole time, I thought I was going to lose you—and the baby. David and Victoria operated right there in the clinic, and even though I was completely panic-stricken, I knew they couldn't possibly be equipped for an emergency of this magnitude. And it turns out, they weren't, but they made do with what they had because they didn't have any choice. From all accounts, David was fucking amazing during a surgery he'd never done by himself before. Victoria and Mason both made a point of telling me that later. Without him…" He released a deep breath. "We were *so lucky* he was dating Daisy, and she brought him to Mac's, otherwise he never would've been there. I would've lost you because we wouldn't have had time to track him down, to get you help. That's the part that haunts me, how your life—and our son's life—came down to shit luck. The randomness of it all is hard to live with."

"We were very lucky that day," Janey said softly. "But we've *been* very lucky for a long time when you think about it. We were lucky to be born to great parents who loved us, to have an amazing life on this island we love so much, to have wonderful friends and families who love us. We've always been surrounded by good luck, so it stands to reason that our luck would hold when we needed it most."

"I suppose."

"I'm really proud of the way you held up during all of it. From what I heard, David wasn't the only one who was amazing. You were, too."

"No, I wasn't."

"How can you say that? You got me help when I needed it and stayed strong during a crisis. You've been my rock through it all."

"You wouldn't say that if you knew everything."

"What don't I know?"

Joe rubbed at the late-day stubble on his jaw. "When David was taking you into surgery… I told him… I said…"

"What did you say, Joe?"

"That if it came down to a choice—you or the baby—I wanted him to save you. And now I look at our beautiful son, and I remember how easily I chose you over him, and I hate myself for that."

"Joe, God, I would've done the same thing. You hadn't even met him yet, and you've loved me for years. Anyone would've done the same thing."

"Still… It makes me sick to think about it now that I can hold him and touch him. Now that I love him, too."

She put her hand on his face and turned him to look at her, brushing away his tears as she kissed him. "I love you so much. I love the all-consuming way you love me. I'll never forget that day on your deck when you told me you'd been in love with me for years. I was shocked and not shocked at the same time. With hindsight, I think I'd known all along that you loved me like that. To hear that in the midst of the biggest crisis of your life you picked me above everything else only makes me love you more than I already do. It doesn't mean we don't love P.J. with all our hearts. It only means that he got lucky to be born to parents who love each other so much."

He hugged her tightly as the tears continued to roll down his cheeks. "I don't think I can do it again, Janey."

"Do what?"

"Have another baby after what happened this time. To spend almost ten months living with that kind of fear… It would kill me."

"Then we won't have another one. We'll be very thankful for the wonderful son we have and be grateful for all our many blessings."

"You've said you don't want him to be an only child."

"I wouldn't have chosen that for him, but he'll be surrounded by cousins who'll be like siblings to him. That'll have to be enough for him."

"Do you mean it? You'd really be okay with just having him?"

"I'd be okay with it. If we're being entirely honest, the whole episode scared the hell out of me, too, and I only heard about it after the crisis had passed. If we're just going to have P.J., maybe next year I could go back to school and finish my degree. I doubt I'd ever get around to finishing if we decided to have more kids."

"I'd love to see you finish school. I'd be all for that."

"Do you feel better at all after sharing it with me?"

"A little. You might've been right about something..."

"Just one thing?"

His laugh let her know he was really okay. "Subconsciously, me and my boys might've been worried about getting you pregnant again."

"I'll talk to Vic about getting on something to keep that from happening. In the meantime..."

"I'll buy some condoms."

"I should get Mac to buy them for us. He owes me from when he was dating Maddie and made me get them for him so no one would know they were sleeping together."

"That would be funny, but I'd rather not have your brother in our business, if it's just the same to you."

"So I can't torture him even a little bit?"

"Oh, all right, have your fun, but leave me out of it."

"I will. Let's meet right back here tomorrow night and see how things go."

"It's a date."

Relieved, Janey closed her eyes and held on tight to him, thankful that he had shared his pain with her.

"Janey?"

"Yeah?"

"Thanks for not dying on me. I never would've been able to live without you."

"I'd like to say no problem, but that doesn't seem appropriate since it was apparently a huge problem for you and David and many others."

"They would all agree with me that you and our beautiful son were well worth it."

Chapter 11

Owen was being hunted. Pursued. Chased. His father was home and looking for him, and there was nowhere to hide from his wrath. He'd done something to make him mad again, and there'd be hell to pay. He made himself as small as he could get and hid behind the bunk beds in the room his sisters shared. They weren't home, so maybe his dad wouldn't look for him there.

In the distance, he could hear his mother screaming and crying, telling her husband to leave Owen alone. It hadn't been his fault that the window got broken. All the kids in the neighborhood had been playing basketball in the driveway when one of them hit the window.

The crack of flesh on flesh ended his mother's cries and forced Owen to hold back one of his own so he wouldn't be found. He'd hit her. Again. Every time she tried to defend him or his siblings against his father's rage, he'd strike out first against her. Even knowing what was coming, she still tried to stop him. But nothing could stop Mark Lawry when he was in one of his rages.

"A man comes home from work and wants to relax a little, and what does he find? A broken window *he has to deal with* because his goddamned kid can't control his friends. Well, I don't think I should have to deal with it when I wasn't even here when it happened."

"I'll get someone out to fix it," Sarah said in a small voice. "You don't have to worry about it."

"And who's going to pay for that?"

"It's glass, Mark. Glass breaks. Things happen."

"Shut up! Just shut up!"

Owen began to cry, silently pleading with his mother to do as his father told her and shut up. All her begging wouldn't change the inevitable and would only get her another slap or punch. Mark Lawry was enraged, and someone had to pay. Owen would rather it be him than one of his younger siblings or his mother.

Someday, he'd be bigger and stronger than his father and be able to fight back. He lived for that day. He dreamed about being able to flatten his father with one punch. In gym class, he took every chance he could get to lift weights so he'd get bigger and stronger faster. He lifted rocks in the backyard and concrete cinder blocks that sat outside his friend Jimmy's house.

"Where is he?" Mark asked in the rage-fueled tone that had Owen shrinking back against the wall, wishing it would open up and swallow him.

"I don't know."

"He'd better show his face, or I'll go looking for one of his brothers. How do I know it wasn't one of them who broke the window?"

"They weren't even here!" Sarah cried. "Leave them alone. Leave them all alone."

"Don't tell me what to do, you useless, worthless bitch. If you had the first idea of how to discipline them, I wouldn't have to do it."

"I hate you."

"*What did you say?*"

Owen bolted from his hiding place and ran for his mother. "Get off her, you miserable bastard!"

He woke up, gasping and sweating and crying. Jesus. His heart was beating so fast, he feared he might be having a heart attack. Thankfully, he was alone in bed, so he had a minute to collect himself. Where in the name of hell had that come from? He hadn't thought about the broken window in years or the hellish beating he and his mother had both withstood that day.

The goddamned trial was dredging up all sorts of shit Owen had thought he'd buried a long time ago.

He ran his hands over his face and took a series of shuddering breaths, trying to calm himself before he got up to find Laura. A sound from the bathroom had him sitting up and getting out of bed. He pulled on a pair of boxer shorts and headed for the bathroom. Tapping lightly on the door, he opened it a crack. "Princess?"

"I'm okay. Go back to sleep."

Owen went into the bathroom and closed the door behind him so they wouldn't wake Holden.

"You're not going back to bed," she said weakly as she rested against the wall between bouts of vomiting. She took a closer look at him. "What's wrong?"

"Nothing." He sat next to her and took her hand. "It started early today."

She leaned her head against his shoulder. "It never really ended yesterday."

"I don't mean to beat a dead horse or anything, but how are you planning to manage feeling this way while we're in Virginia? It's bad enough when we're home."

"Don't you worry about that. I'll manage it. Somehow."

"Laura…"

"*Owen…*"

"How did I end up shackled to the most stubborn woman in the history of the universe?"

"You fell in love with me."

"Yes, I did." He released her hand so he could put his arm around her. "Best mistake I ever made."

"This is where I fell in love with you. Right here on the floor of this bathroom, when I was so sick with Holden."

"That'll be a story to tell the grandkids someday."

"I'll tell them their grandpa was the nicest man I'd ever met. That when I was pregnant with another man's child, he took care of me like I was the most precious thing in his world and he barely knew me."

Moved by her, as he was so often, he slid his lips over the fine silk of her hair.

"He knew you. He knew you from that first day standing in the rain outside this place."

"I'll tell them how he held my hair back when I was sick, bathed my face with cool cloths afterward and how he brushed my teeth for me when I was too weak to do it myself. We'll talk about how he waited so long for me to be free to love him the way I wanted to, and in all that time, he was nothing but patient and kind to me, the best friend I'd ever had long before there was anything else between us. And I'll end my story by telling them that the greatest thrill of my life was the first time he told me he loved me."

Owen could barely breathe, let alone speak as he stroked her arm. He cleared his throat. "Will you tell them how he knocked you up with twins and made you even sicker than you were with Holden?"

Her gentle laugh was a balm on his wounded soul. "I'll find some better words to use for that part of the story."

"Is it over for now?"

"Might be."

Owen got up and held out a hand to help her up. He kept his hands on her hips while she brushed her teeth and then scooped her up the way he had from the beginning and carried her back to bed, tucking her in under the covers before going around to his side. Lying on his side, facing her, he noticed how pale she was with deep, dark circles under her eyes that were new since the last time he looked closely.

He wanted to ask her once again to stay home, but by now he knew the argument was pointless, and he ran the risk of making her think he didn't want her around, which couldn't be further from the truth.

"Are you going to tell me what's wrong?"

"Nothing's wrong."

"I could tell with one look at you when you came into the bathroom that something happened. I wish you'd tell me so I don't have to wonder."

"I had a dream. No biggie."

"What was it about?"

"I don't remember."

"I don't believe you."

He smiled at her saucy reply. He expected nothing less from her. "It was about something that happened a long time ago, something I'd forgotten about."

"With your dad?"

"Yeah." Resigned now to having to tell her about it, he looked at the wall behind her so he wouldn't have to see the sympathy on her face. "My friends and I broke a window playing basketball, and he flipped out about it when he got home. My mom and I got into it with him. It was ugly. I haven't thought about it in years."

"How old were you?"

"Ten or around there."

"The trial has you thinking about stuff you'd sooner forget."

He appreciated that she didn't offer platitudes or sympathy he didn't want. "I guess."

"It'll be over soon."

"Will it? Will it ever really be over?"

"Yes, it will. It's all resurfacing now because you know you have to see him in a couple of days and testify and hear your mother testify. Before all this, you'd managed to put a lot of distance between yourself and your past."

"Not as much as I thought I had if I'm this easily undone by the thought of seeing him again."

"Owen, he terrorized you for years. You'd have to be superhuman not to be undone by the thought of seeing him again. Please don't put yourself through the added hell of wondering why you're undone. Anyone would be."

"I don't want to be. I want to look right through him so he'll know he doesn't matter to me anymore."

"He'll know. When he sees us together and how happy we are, he'll see that he didn't win. That's the second reason I want to be there. I want him to see that he didn't win. *You* did. He's going to jail, and you're going back to your happy life full of love and joy and all the things he denied himself because he couldn't control his rage."

"What if he doesn't go to jail? What if he gets off and never has to pay for what he did?"

"I've been thinking a lot about that possibility and worrying about what it'll do to you and your mother if that happens."

"And?"

"I've decided you'll both be fine. He's out of your lives. That's the most important thing. And a tiger doesn't change his stripes. He'll find someone else to bully, and maybe the next time, the law will catch up to him."

"I don't want him to be able to do what he did to us to anyone else."

"Then let's hope for the best and prepare for the worst. You'll have to find a way to live with it if it doesn't go your way. You've lived with it this long and have made a good life for yourself. Stay focused on that, and you'll get through it. I'll be right here with you the whole way."

Of all the incredible things she'd said to him, that last one touched him the most. "I'm sorry we have to deal with this."

"I'm not. If it means your father has his day of reckoning for what he did to you, then it's well worth whatever else has to happen. At the very least, from everything you've told me about him, the public aspect of the trial will be extremely humiliating to him, which is the least of what he deserves."

"Yeah," Owen said with a grunt of laughter, "you're right about that. It gives me a perverse amount of pleasure to imagine him squirming in court while my mother and I air out the family's dirty laundry. He'll hate every minute of that."

"And you should enjoy every minute. If that's the only justice you ever get, find a way to make it good enough."

"I will." He reached out to touch her face, amazed as always by how soft her skin was. "I've gone from not wanting you to come with me to wondering how I ever thought I could do it without you."

Her satisfied little smile drew one from him, too.

"Which was your goal all along," he said with a laugh.

"That sounds so calculating."

"I love you. I can't wait until this is over and we can focus exclusively on our wedding with nothing standing in the way."

"I don't want to add to your worries or anything, but there is one teeny tiny other thing still standing in our way."

Alarmed to hear that, Owen said, "What?"

"I haven't gotten my final divorce papers yet."

The reminder that she was still legally married to someone else hit him like a fist to the chest, stealing the breath from his lungs. "Have you talked to Dan? What did he say?"

"He assures me it's all on schedule and we should be getting the papers any day now."

"What if they don't come in time for the wedding?"

"They will."

"Laura..."

She propped herself up and leaned over to kiss him. "I shouldn't have said anything. I'm sorry."

"Of course you should tell me that. We're calling Dan at one minute after nine today to make sure he's all over it."

"If you insist."

He pulled her closer to continue the kiss she'd started. "I insist."

*

Mac was on his way to work when he took a call from his sister. "What's up, brat?"

"How old do I have to be before I don't have to put up with that nickname anymore?"

"Sixty? Ish?"

"Very funny. Speaking of very funny and how life comes around full circle, I need you to do something for me."

As always Mac was prepared to give her a hard time, but since they'd nearly lost her the day P.J. was born, he found that more difficult to do than it had ever been before. Usually, giving Janey a hard time was as easy as breathing to him. He couldn't allow himself to think about how very close they'd come to losing her without being reduced to tears. Not that he'd ever tell her that... "What do you need?"

"Condoms."

Okay, he might've guessed diapers. He hadn't seen that one coming. "What? What the hell?"

"Joe and I need condoms, and I've decided you're going to get them for us."

"You've decided? What the hell is wrong with him that he can't do it?"

"Absolutely nothing is wrong with him, but I want *you* to do it."

Recalling the time he'd sent her to get them for him and Maddie when they were first dating and didn't want the whole island talking about them sleeping together, he had to concede he owed her one—and she knew it. "You think you're pretty funny, don't you?"

"I do. In fact, I think I'm downright hilarious. Just make sure you get them to me before bedtime. Joe's feeling a bit...*cooped up* and ready to get back to normal. You wouldn't want me to get pregnant again after what happened with P.J., now would you?"

"This is like a form of emotional blackmail. Right? You know I'm totally over all the train-wreck deliveries around here, so you're blackmailing me into doing dirty work your husband ought to be doing for you, right?"

"Oh, it's going to be dirty, all right. The dirtier the better."

"Janey! *Come on!* Spare me the gory details, will ya?"

"I'm counting on you, big brother. Don't let me down."

"I hate you right now."

"No, you don't. You love me, and you know it. Oh, and Mac?"

"Yeah?"

"Get the extra-large ones, will you?" She hung up laughing before he could begin to fashion a reply to that. Disgusted, he tossed his phone onto the seat and grunted out a laugh. He had to give his baby sister credit for a game well played. As the younger sister of four older brothers, Janey had learned to fight dirty from an early age. He could only imagine her plotting out this scheme with Joe and the two of them having a good laugh at his expense.

He'd once done the same exact thing to her, right down to the extra-large comment, so he probably had this coming.

It would be just what they deserved if he poked holes in all the condoms he bought for them. Not that he'd actually do that, because he truly didn't want Janey having any more kids after what'd happened with P.J. That had been one of the scariest days of his life, and he had absolutely no desire to relive it.

And, as Maddie often told him, it really was all about him.

Now he just had to think of some way to get Janey back for this...

CHAPTER 12

Sunday mornings in early August were among Big Mac McCarthy's favorite days at the marina he'd owned and operated for forty summers now. Many of the boaters left early to head for home, and after they'd seen off the others, he and his boys had time to sit around and shoot the shit.

This year had been the best of times because his brother Frank had joined the morning crew after his retirement in June, and having Frankie back in his everyday life made Big Mac almost as happy as having his four sons living home again on the island. His oldest son, Mac, now a partner with him in the marina, was an everyday regular, and his other three boys made occasional appearances at the morning "meeting," at which Big Mac and his band of buddies attempted to solve the world's problems.

His longtime best friend, Ned Saunders, was the first to arrive that Sunday morning, and he grunted out a good morning on his way inside to get a coffee and some sugar doughnuts.

Thinking about the early days here, after he'd persuaded Linda to leave her life in Providence to marry him and come live with him on his island, made Big Mac feel sentimental. She'd taken to the place like the proverbial fish to water, making the restaurant her own with her special brand of class and charm that his customers had responded to instantly. The doughnuts had been an inspired idea that had become part of the magic of the place.

And it was magic. What other word could you use to describe the view he had every day of the Salt Pond and all her many personalities? Some days she was so bright blue it hurt his eyes to look at her. Other days, she was gray and angry and frothy and just as beautiful as every other day. Big Mac appreciated all her many moods.

He loved the boats, the people, the smell of diesel fuel mixing with sand and seaweed. He loved the seagulls that stalked the docks looking for anything edible. He adored the kids who dropped their crabbers into the water off his floating docks, using hot dogs for bait, until they filled a bucket with the slimy creatures. He enjoyed the "crab races" down the ramp off the main dock where the captured crustaceans escaped back into the water unharmed, but leaving behind priceless childhood memories.

Big Mac needed to invite his grandson Thomas down to do some crabbing one of these days. Thomas was old enough this summer to appreciate something his father had once loved. They'd invite Ashleigh, Thomas's cousin and constant companion, too.

Ned came out to the table and dropped a box of doughnuts in the middle as he took a seat.

"What's got you so cranky this morning?"

"I ain't cranky."

"Tell that to someone who hasn't seen you every morning for going on forty years." Ned had been Big Mac's first friend on the island. Their bond had been immediate and enduring. Now that Big Mac's other lifelong best friend, his brother Frank, was on the island, Big Mac had gone out of his way to make sure he still had plenty of time for Ned. "What gives?"

"Seamus and Carolina," Ned said, taking a drink of his coffee.

"What about them?"

"They stole our idea."

"What idea?"

"Have a cookout and git married."

"Oh! When was this going to happen?"

"Coupla weeks. After Laura's. You got any idea how hard it is to find a time around here to git married without steppin' on someone else's toes these days? Now I don't know when we're gonna do it."

"Do what?" Big Mac's son Mac asked as he joined them.

"Git married."

"Who's getting married?" Mac asked.

"Everyone but me," Ned replied glumly. "Waited a long time fer this. I'm ready. She's ready. Now we gotta come up with another idea cuz Seamus and Caro stole ours."

"So wait," Mac said, "you guys were going to do a surprise wedding, too?"

"Was gonna. Didn't want all the fuss and bother. Now? Who knows?"

"As the son-in-law of the future Mrs. Saunders, I'd be happy to offer up my house, my yard, anything you need to make it happen," Mac said. "You just say the word, and we'll get it done."

At that, Ned visibly brightened, and Big Mac looked upon his oldest son with an unreasonable amount of pride. He knew it wasn't always cool for a man to love his kids the way Big Mac loved his, but when you had five kids as amazing as his, it was damned hard not to be talking all the time about how great they were. At times like this, they did the talking for him.

"That's a great idea, son," Big Mac said. "What do you think, Ned?"

"I'll talk ta Francine bout it. 'Tis all up to her."

"You'll be a fine husband if you already realize that," Big Mac said.

"Ya think I will? Really?"

"I'm sure you will," Mac said. "You love her and her girls like they're your own. Maddie says all the time that she and Tiffany had no idea what it was like to have a father until you came into their lives. And the kids adore their grandpop. You're going to be great at it."

With his chin propped on his hand, Ned blinked a few times.

For a second, Big Mac wondered if his old pal would hang on to his composure in the face of such a ringing endorsement.

"Thank you," Ned said softly. "Means a lot coming from ya."

Luke Harris joined them, along with some of the other daily regulars who came by for coffee, doughnuts and bullshit every morning.

"So hey, before the day gets away from us," Mac said, leaning in so his father and Luke could hear him. "I need to start spending a little more time at home. This pregnancy is kicking Maddie's ass, and she needs some help with the kids."

"No problem," Big Mac said. "Do what you've got to do."

"I'll cover for you," Luke said. "Maybe someday you'll get to return the favor."

"I really hope so," Mac said.

"You know we don't want to pry," Big Mac said tentatively, aware that Luke and his wife, Sydney, were trying to have a baby after she'd had a tubal ligation reversal.

"Yes, you do," Luke said, laughing. "Nothing yet, but we're having lots of fun trying."

Big Mac had loved Luke Harris like a son since the fatherless boy showed up at the docks when he was fourteen and asked for a job. He'd been working there ever since. Best thing Big Mac had ever done was make him a partner in the business a couple of summers ago. Luke and Mac were doing a brilliant job of running the place so he could spend more of his time doing what he did best—passing the bull with his friends.

Grant came along a short time later, taking a seat at the table with a coffee in hand. "I have news from the trenches," Grant said with a triumphant smile that had everyone's immediate attention.

"Spill it," Mac said.

"Steph and I are getting married on Labor Day!"

"Oh for shit's sake," Ned muttered as the others congratulated Grant.

"What's wrong with him?" Grant asked, using his thumb to point to Ned.

"He's having a little trouble fitting his wedding in among all the others," Mac told his brother. "But I'm happy for you and Steph. That's great news."

"Yes, it is," Big Mac said to his second son, who had found the perfect partner in Stephanie. Big Mac and Linda wholeheartedly approved of the delightful young woman who'd overcome a hardscrabble upbringing to become someone anyone would be proud to welcome into their family. "This is very good news indeed."

"Happy fer ya, too," Ned said gruffly. "Don't think I ain't. We all got a soft spot for that gal."

"Thanks," Grant said. "We're excited."

"Ah, here comes our newest Romeo," Big Mac said, making room at the table for his brother.

"Oh shut up."

"Holding hands, Uncle Frank," Mac said. "Looks like someone's got himself a *girlfriend*."

"So what about it?" Frank asked testily as he helped himself to one of the doughnuts.

"He's not even denying it," Mac said. "It's worse than we thought."

"You all need to get busy minding your own business rather than everyone else's."

"That ain't never gonna happen," Ned said to laughter from the others.

"What the hell fun would that be?" Big Mac asked. "So… You and Betsy. Going steady. This is very exciting."

"You're a jackass, you know that?"

"Um, excuse me, but who was up in my grille every time I brought a new girl home? I never got the chance to do that to you because you were with Joann since eighth grade. Now it's my turn, and revenge is sweet." Big Mac wasn't sure if he'd done the right thing mentioning the wife Frank had lost to cancer so young, but Frank just smiled at him, full of the good humor Big Mac expected from his older brother.

"Have your fun, pal. I'm happy to take your abuse, because she's worth it."

"Oh, wow," Mac said. "This is *way* more serious than we thought."

"I don't know if serious is the word I would use," Frank said. "At least not yet, but it does have potential."

"Good fer ya," Ned said. "Been a long time comin'."

"Indeed it has," Frank said.

"Pardon me," a female voice said. All eyes turned to a striking, dark-haired woman. She was tall with brown eyes and a cautious manner.

"Help you with something?" Mac asked her.

"I'm looking for Mac McCarthy?"

"That'd be me," father and son said together, as they usually did.

She looked from Big Mac to his son and then back to him. "Senior," she said.

"What can I do for you?" Big Mac asked.

"Could I have a moment of your time, please? In private."

"Uh-oh, Dad," Mac said. "What did you do now?"

The young woman gave his son a curious look before returning her attention to him. He had no idea who she was, but since she'd asked so politely… "Sure thing. Right this way."

He led her down the main dock to the very end, where the Salt Pond stretched out before them.

"I'm sorry to drag you away from your friends."

"That's all right."

"I'm Mallory." She swallowed hard as if she were nervous. "Mallory Vaughn."

"It's nice to meet you, Mallory."

"It's nice to meet you, too. Does the name Vaughn mean anything to you?"

"I can't say that it does. Should it?"

She withdrew a crumpled piece of paper from her pocket and handed it to him. "You should read this."

Holding her earnest gaze, Big Mac took it from her with a sinking feeling in the pit of his stomach. What was this about? Turning his attention to the paper, he began to read handwriting that obviously belonged to a woman.

My dear Mallory,

Now that I am gone, I feel it is only fair to share the one piece of information I was too fearful to give you in life. You have asked me for years about who your father is, and I had good intentions of telling you when the time was right. Then I got sick, and time became our most precious commodity. I had other things I wanted to do besides revisit my painful past.

Your father is a good man; at least he was during the short time that I knew him. He had an opportunity to start a business on Gansett Island, and since I was tied to my home and family here, there was no future for us. So I let him go to pursue his dream and stayed here to pursue mine. A short time later, I discovered I was expecting you.

"Oh my God," Big Mac whispered as the dock beneath his feet seemed to move as his entire existence shifted. "Your mother was Diana Vaughn."

"Yes."

"So that makes you…"

"Your daughter, apparently."

Big Mac couldn't seem to breathe as he stared at the young woman before him and tried to make sense of what she was saying.

She gently removed the letter from his hand and read the rest to him. "'Your father owns a marina called McCarthy's Gansett Island Marina. His name is Mac McCarthy, and he will be surprised to know you exist because I never told him I was expecting you. By the time I learned you were on the way, he and I had ended our relationship, and a short time later, I heard he was engaged to someone else.

"'I harbored an irrational fear that he might try to take you away from me if he knew about you, and I couldn't let that happen. I wish I had been a stronger person for both your sakes, and I'm sorry for what I've denied you both through my silence. I hope you can find it in your heart to forgive me and perhaps find him now that you are alone in the world. You should also know I named you Mallory because his real name is Malcolm. I thought you might someday appreciate that connection, however tentative, to the man who fathered you. I love you with all my heart. Mom.'"

Mallory folded the letter and returned it to her pocket. "I'm sorry to shock you this way. I don't want anything from you. I just wanted to meet you, to fill in the blanks. I'll go now. It was really nice to finally meet you. This is a beautiful place you've got here."

As she turned to leave, something in him rose up, forcing him to react before she got away. "Wait. Don't go yet."

She stopped and turned to him. "Honestly, I meant it when I said I don't want anything from you. I'm perfectly fine. You have your life, and I have mine. I just wanted to put a face to the name. That's all."

"You can't just walk away after telling me you're my kid," he said, stammering over the words. He couldn't recall ever being quite so rattled by anything.

"Why not?" she asked with an amused little smile that reminded him in some small way of Janey.

He couldn't begin to fathom how this was going to affect his life, his family or his marriage, but he knew he'd never forgive himself if he let her walk away. "Because that's not how I roll."

"Excuse me?"

"If you think a kid of mine is going to be out there in the world for all this time without me knowing about her and then walk out of my life as casually as all that, well, that isn't going to happen. You may not want anything from me, but I want something from you."

"And that is?"

"I want to know you. I want you to know me. If what your mother says is true, you have five half siblings. Wouldn't you like to know them?"

"Are you doubting the truth of what my mother said?"

"I don't want to, but I'd be a fool to accept the word of someone I haven't seen in more than…"

"Thirty-eight years," she said tightly. "I'll be thirty-nine on Wednesday."

"I have a lot at stake here."

"I told you. I want nothing from you."

"Dad?" Mac asked as he approached them. He took a long measuring look at Mallory. "What's going on?"

"Give me just a minute, son, will you please?"

"Um, sure." Hesitantly, Mac turned and walked away.

"That's your son."

"My oldest, Mac Junior."

"How old is he?"

"Thirty-seven."

"How old are your other kids?"

The question was asked in a cool, relaxed tone, but he could see how hungry she was for information about his family. "Grant is thirty-six, Adam is thirty-four, Evan is thirty-two and my baby, Janey, just turned thirty."

"Four boys and a girl," she said softly. "I wondered if I might have siblings."

"You don't have any others?"

She shook her head. "My mom never married. I was her only child."

"As I recall, she had a big family."

"Who didn't approve of her decision to have a baby on her own." Mallory shrugged. "We didn't need them. We had each other."

"So now you're alone in the world."

"Not entirely. I have fantastic friends and a career I'm proud of."

"What do you do?"

"I'm an emergency room nurse in Providence."

"That's very impressive."

"You really think so?" she asked wistfully, clearly hungry for more than just information.

"I really do." He cleared his throat and tried to think of what his next move should be. "I need to talk to my wife. Her name is Linda, and she's the center of my life. She has been since shortly after your mom and I broke up. Do you have a phone number or some way I can reach you?"

She shook her head. "I can see that you're a nice man. You're the good guy my mother said you were, but I just wanted to meet you, not turn your entire life upside down. There's no need to explain me to your family or your wife. That's not why I came. I got what I needed, and I appreciate your time. I won't take any more of it."

"So you're not one bit curious about your five siblings? How about your cousins? There're quite a few of them. Laura and Shane both live here on the island. They're my brother Frank's kids. He's up there at the table. He's a retired Superior Court judge. My brother Kevin is a doctor—a psychiatrist, actually. He's got two sons—Riley and Finn. They'll be here in a couple of weeks for Laura's wedding. She's marrying Owen Lawry, who's my son Evan's best friend. If I were you, someone who doesn't have much family to call my own, I'd at least want to meet everyone before I decided I didn't want anything to do with them."

"And how do you plan to introduce me into this lovely family of yours?"

"As the daughter I never knew I had?"

She folded her arms and looked down at the wooden dock. "I don't know what to say. I didn't plan for anything beyond introducing myself."

"Do you have a place to stay?"

"No, I was going to take the ferry back tonight."

"You should stay. Spend a little time here. See what you think of the place." He was about to offer up one of the empty bedrooms at his house when he stopped himself, knowing he couldn't do that until he talked to Linda. "We own that place up there on the hill." He pointed to the hotel that sat just outside the entrance to the marina. "Go on up there, tell them I sent you and to bill me for your stay."

"I couldn't do that."

"Why not?"

"I wouldn't feel right."

"I'm inviting you to be my guest, but if you'd rather not stay, I understand. I would like your phone number, though."

She seemed to be engaged in an argument with herself as she weighed what he'd said. "I'll stay for tonight."

"Good," he said with a smile. "See that house up there on the hill? The white one?"

"Yes."

"That's my place. Come for dinner tonight."

"You can't just invite me without talking to your wife first."

"Funny, you've never met my wife and yet you seem to already have her figured out."

"I'm a woman, Mr. McCarthy. It doesn't take a degree in rocket science to predict that this news might take her by surprise." She withdrew a card from her purse and handed it to him. "My cell number is on there. Call me later after you talk to her, and you won't hurt my feelings if you tell me I'm not welcome there."

"Don't call me Mr. McCarthy. At the very least, call me Big Mac. That's what everyone calls me."

"Big Mac," she said, trying it on for size. "I will. Thank you. You've been really nice about all of this, when I wouldn't have blamed you if you told me to take a hike."

"I'm not going to do that. I wonder, though, if I could borrow that letter from your mom. I'd like to show it to my wife."

She pulled the letter from her pocket and handed it to him. "You'll understand that it's precious to me—"

"I'll make sure you get it back."

"Thank you."

"I'll call you."

"Okay." The smile she left him with reminded him, in a way, of his mother. And then he remembered the photo of his mother that he kept in a frame in his study and realized Mallory was the image of her as a younger woman. After she walked away, he watched her until she was past the table full of men, who eyed her with curiosity. She didn't stop to speak with them but rather kept walking toward the hotel. Big Mac's mind raced with thoughts and memories and fear over what this news might do to his family—and his marriage.

As Mac and Frank approached him, clearly looking for information about what'd just happened, Big Mac knew he couldn't tell anyone about Mallory until he'd told Linda. With that in mind, he walked purposely toward the parking lot.

As he approached his son and brother, Mac tried to stop him. "Dad?"

"Hold down the fort. I'll be back."

"Is everything all right?" Frank asked.

"Yeah. Nothing to worry about." As he said the words, Big Mac hoped and prayed they were true.

CHAPTER 13

At the first sounds of chatter from the crib in the next room, Owen was up and out of bed, hoping Laura would sleep for a while longer. He changed the baby's heavy overnight diaper, washed him up and left him in only a new diaper to feed him his cereal and applesauce for breakfast, knowing he'd probably need a full bath after he ate.

Holden was getting better all the time at eating from a spoon, but mealtime was messy nonetheless. After he'd devoured the runny cereal and a jar of applesauce, Owen rewarded him with a scattering of Cheerios on the table of his high chair. Watching the baby's fat fingers pick up the Cheerios and get them to his mouth was one of Owen's favorite things. With every new day, Holden learned how to do something else, and being part of that was nothing short of miraculous.

At times like this, when he got to spend time alone with Holden, he felt a little sorry for Laura's ex-husband, who'd never know how much he was missing with the son he saw only sporadically, whenever he could manage a day trip to the island. Laura had been married to Justin for a couple of months when she discovered he'd never disabled his online dating profile and was still arranging meetings with other women.

Imagine being married to a woman as amazing as Laura and not being satisfied. Owen couldn't conceive of such a thing, because being with her—and her son—was the greatest honor of his life. Since Justin had agreed to sign the divorce papers shortly after Holden was born, Owen bore the guy no ill will. He'd done the right thing and set her free. He wouldn't be entirely satisfied until her divorce was officially final, though, and worrying about when that would happen had him placing a call to Dan Torrington.

"Morning," Dan said in a mumble that had Owen checking the clock and then wincing.

"Sorry. I had no idea it was still so early. We're on baby time over here."

"No problem. What's up?"

"Laura's divorce is what's up. What're you hearing?"

"Should have the final decree any day now."

"Will it be in time for the wedding?"

"You've got plenty of time, Owen. Try not to worry. I'm keeping a close eye on it, and we'll get it done."

"Okay," Owen said, even though Dan's assurances didn't completely address his anxiety, which was all over the place lately.

"How you holding up?"

Owen grunted out a laugh. "Fantastic. Never been better."

"I don't want to fill you with platitudes, but it'll all be over soon, and you can move on."

"That's what everyone is telling me."

"If there's anything I can do for you or your mother, you only have to ask."

"Thanks, Dan. It makes us both feel better that you'll be with us in Virginia."

"I'm glad to be going. The greatest satisfaction I get out of my career is seeing justice done—no matter what form it takes."

"I just hope we get justice."

"You have a good case. Is it a slam dunk? No, but I think it'll go your way in the end."

Dan's assurances helped address some of Owen's greatest fears. "I'll see you Tuesday morning."

"I'll be there."

*

After he ended the call with Owen, Dan returned the phone to the bedside table. He'd tried to get up when the phone woke him out of a sound sleep, but Kara's arm around him had kept him in bed while he talked to Owen.

"Sorry about that," he said as he turned toward her.

"It's okay." By now she was certainly used to the phone calls he received at every hour of the day and night. While working on his memoir about his quest to free wrongfully convicted people, Dan continued to oversee the team of lawyers who worked on his innocence projects. They worked out of his Los Angeles office while he was on the other side of the country becoming more entwined every day in his life on a tiny island that had begun to feel like home, especially since he met and fell in love with Kara.

"Go back to sleep for a while," he said as he kissed her shoulder. "It's early yet."

"Mmm." Her smooth leg slid between his, coming to rest just below his groin.

Dan's hand, which had been caressing her back, moved down to cup her bottom, bringing her in even closer to him.

"Looks like one of us is wide awake."

"He can't help himself when you're all naked and soft and warm."

Her hand on his stomach did nothing to help the growing problem below.

"Today is going to be a very long day," she said with a sigh. Her parents had come to visit so they could meet him and had insisted on throwing them an engagement party so they could meet the rest of Kara's friends. Dan knew she'd rather skip the entire thing but was humoring her parents, with whom she'd had a difficult relationship over the last couple of years.

"At least they didn't put up a fuss when you told them we want to get married here." They'd booked The Chesterfield for the following June.

"They know better than to put up any kind of fuss where I'm concerned.

They're probably relieved that I'm engaged so they can stop feeling guilty for supporting my sister when she made off with my boyfriend."

"*Ex*-boyfriend."

Her soft giggle made him smile. "Extremely ex. So ex he barely warrants a mention."

"That's right, and don't forget it. Your fiancé is the jealous type who doesn't want you pining after old loves."

"My fiancé has nothing to worry about, and he knows it. I was never really in love until I met him."

"Kara…" He held her even closer, if that was possible. "You don't know what it does to me when you say stuff like that. How anyone could ever be stupid enough to let you go is beyond me."

"You'd better never let me go."

"No worries there, babe." He kissed the top of her head and breathed in the arresting scent of her hair. "You going to be okay at this party today?"

"Of course I am. My parents want to celebrate our engagement. I'm all for that. It's just hard sometimes to forget the way they acted when Kelly and Matt got together. It was like they forgot all about me, and now that I'm marrying Mr. Famous Celebrity Lawyer, suddenly they're all excited about me again. It feels sort of… I don't know…"

"Hypocritical."

"Yeah."

"I hate the way they hurt you, baby. I never want you to feel that way again."

"I love you for that. I really do, and for putting up with this party idea of theirs when I'm sure you have a few things you'd like to say to them."

"I'd never do that to you. They probably know how we both feel, and this is their way of trying to bridge the gap."

"Maybe. I thought they'd flip out when I told them I don't want to get married in Bar Harbor, but they didn't say a word."

"They knew better. You might not see it, but you've changed a lot since you've been here. You're much more assertive than you used to be."

"I've had to become more assertive dealing with you," she said dryly.

"Exactly, and that's carried over into all areas of your life. No doubt they see it, too."

"Thank you for that," she said, propping her chin on his chest. "I needed to learn how to stand up for myself, and you showed me how."

He gathered her long hair into a ponytail that he let slide through his fingers in silky waves. "Nah. You had it all along. I just helped you find it."

She left a trail of kisses from his chest to his chin and moved along his jaw until her teeth found his earlobe. The painful clamp sent a jolt of heat all the way through him, which only made him harder. He loved playful, lighthearted Kara so much. It had taken him months to find her underneath the wounded veneer she'd hidden behind when he first knew her.

Over time, though, she'd begun to recover from the awful betrayal at the hands of her sister and ex-boyfriend. The showdown she'd had with Kelly earlier in the summer had gone a long way toward helping Kara put the past to bed once and for all.

"You're awfully frisky this morning, my love," Dan said as he arranged her on top of him, aligning his hardness with her heat. "Have I also succeeded in turning you into a morning person?"

She snorted with laughter. "That's one thing I'll never be." As she came down on him, taking him into her tight heat, she said, "Consider this a very rare exception."

"I'm considering this the perfect start to a day that'll already be perfect because I get to spend just about every minute of it with you."

Her smile made her golden-brown eyes twinkle. "All that money your mother spent on charm school was a very worthwhile investment." She swiveled her hips and made him groan.

"No charm school, babe. It's all in the wiring."

"It's good wiring. Really good wiring."

He grasped her hips, intending to turn her over and take control.

"Don't even think about it. This one's all mine."

"I love when you get bossy with me."

"I can tell," she said, gritting her teeth as she accommodated his expanding length.

Dan laughed and drew her down to him so he could kiss her. The taste of her lips and the press of her breasts against his chest were nearly enough to finish him off. "I can't believe we get to do this any time we want to for the rest of our lives."

Her mane of light brown hair came down around him like a silky curtain that closed them off from the rest of the world. "Not *any* time."

He squeezed her bottom with both hands. "Just about any time."

"I'll give you that—and this." She moved in sexy, teasing circles on top of him.

"I see, so you're looking for a quickie, then."

She smiled and kissed him, lingering for a full minute before she sat up and got really serious about finishing him off.

*

After seeing Laura through another round of grueling morning sickness, Owen left her to sleep and took Holden with him when he drove out to Evan's studio. He hadn't been there in a while and was surprised to see the driveway had been landscaped. In the foyer, he made use of a window into the studios to make sure no one was recording before continuing inside with Holden in his arms.

"Ev? Are you here?"

"Back here," Evan called out. "In the office."

Owen walked through the studio space to Evan's office in the back of the cavernous building. "Not recording today?"

"This afternoon," Evan said. "Sunday mornings are for paperwork. I like to get it out of the way so I can enjoy the rest of the week." He held out his arms for Holden. "Come see Uncle Evan, big guy."

Holden squealed with delight when Owen transferred him to Evan's arms. The baby loved to listen to the two of them play their guitars.

"God, he's bigger than he was when I saw him last week."

"I know. It's crazy." Owen removed a stack of mail off one of the chairs and took a seat, handing the envelopes over to Evan.

"It never ends," Evan said with a scowl as he tossed the envelopes into the pile on his desk. "I wasn't meant to sit at a desk."

"I suppose the upside of too much paperwork is that you're busy."

"True." Evan gave Holden a light-up pen to play with. Like everything else he came into contact with, the pen went right into the baby's mouth.

"Is that clean?" Owen asked.

"It's not filthy."

"Don't tell Laura I let him play with it."

"I won't if you won't."

"Deal."

"What brings you out this morning?"

"I heard you're planning to come to Virginia."

"What about it?"

"I wish you wouldn't. It's not that I don't appreciate the sentiment or the gesture."

"It's not a gesture, O. If I were looking to make a gesture, I could pat you on the back and tell you I'm pulling for you and your mom as I send you on your way."

"I know you mean well and that you care, but there's really no need for you to leave your work and your home and Grace. I'll have lots of people with me—"

"So it shouldn't be that big of a deal to have one more."

"Evan, please… You don't understand."

"Then make me."

"It's embarrassing that the people I care about are going to hear the dirty details of how I grew up. I'd rather you didn't know."

"I already know. You've told me." He handed a ball of rubber bands to Holden when he'd tired of the pen.

"You don't know the half of it, and I'd like to keep it that way."

"What would you do if I was about to go through something like this?"

"Luckily, that's a rhetorical question because you'll never have to go through something like this."

"Humor me. Put the shoe on the other foot. I have to go through something awful and difficult and embarrassing and terribly upsetting. Where would you be if that was happening to me?"

Because Owen couldn't argue with Evan's point, he didn't try. He wished everyone would try to understand that he wanted to spare them. Laura's words from the night before were a reminder that he didn't have to protect those he loved, but that was a hard habit to break.

"You'd be there for me, O. Don't ask me to do less for you than what you'd do for me. You asked me to stand up for you at your wedding, and that's such an honor, you know?"

"Who else would I ask?" Owen said with a small smile.

"You and me—we're not just about the good times and the music. At least I didn't think we were."

"We're not. You've been my best friend for as long as I can remember."

"Then let me do what any best friend would do in this situation." As they talked, Evan rocked the baby in his office chair, patting his back until Holden was out cold for his morning nap.

"You're good with him."

Evan looked down, seeming surprised to find Holden asleep. "Check me out."

"You're going to be a great dad someday."

"I'm kinda looking forward to that day."

"What the hell's happened to the two of us?"

"The best possible thing," Evan said.

"You said it."

"So we're cool about me coming on Tuesday?"

"Yeah, we're cool. Thanks, Ev."

Evan waved off the gratitude as if it was no big deal to put his life on hold to be there to support Owen at the trial.

"While I have you," Owen said, anxious to change the subject, "I've figured out what song I want you to play when Laura and I have our first dance at the wedding."

"Lay it on me, brother."

CHAPTER 14

After Owen left with Holden, Laura tried to go back to sleep for a while. The vomiting always took a harsh toll on her, but with so much to be done before their trip, she couldn't seem to turn off the busy brain that refused to get onboard with the fact that the rest of her was a hot mess in need of more sleep.

She reached for her cell phone on the bedside table and made an appointment to see Victoria Stevens, the local midwife-nurse practitioner before the trip on Tuesday. Luckily, the clinic was open seven days a week in the summer, and she was able to book an appointment with Vic late tomorrow afternoon. Laura had resisted Victoria's suggestion that she take something for the nausea, because she was convinced she could power through it the way she had with Holden. She also hated the idea of taking something that had even a small chance of harming her unborn children.

But there was no way she could "power through it" and accompany Owen to Virginia, too. Desperate times indeed called for desperate measures. She got out of bed and took a shower, hoping her stomach would calm down enough to allow her to be productive. She thanked God every day for the fact that Sarah was with them and could manage the hotel as efficiently as she could herself, but Laura still felt guilty about deferring so much of the responsibility to Owen's mother when she was collecting a paycheck from his grandparents.

She forced herself to consume a handful of saltine crackers and some weak tea before heading downstairs, where the smells of breakfast coming from the dining room had her heading directly for the ladies' room, where the crackers and tea came right back up.

Afterward, she sat on the floor of the lobby bathroom and tried to collect herself. She was so damned sick of being sick. At times she wondered what Owen saw in her when she'd been in this condition for much of the time they'd spent together.

A light tap on the door had her standing and rinsing her mouth. She opened the door to find Sarah outside.

"Are you okay, honey?"

"I've been better. It's been going on since about four o'clock this morning."

Sarah winced and slid an arm around Laura's shoulders. "Come with me." She led her around the reception desk past the front door just as Abby came in.

"Morning!" Abby said.

"Morning," Laura said.

"Ugh, not feeling good again?" Abby asked.

"Another day, another battle," Laura said with a weak smile.

"I'm getting her away from the smell of breakfast," Sarah said. "We'll be in the sitting room if you need us."

"Go ahead. I'll keep an eye on the front desk for you."

"Thanks, Abby." She ran the gift shop, Abby's Attic 2, in the lobby of the Surf, so watching the front desk certainly wasn't her job, but like everyone else around her, Abby had stepped up to help more than once this summer.

"No problem at all. Hope you feel better."

"So do I. Thanks again." Laura went with Sarah to the sitting room, where they'd spent a lot of family time over the last year. During the winter, they'd passed many a cold, stormy night in front of the fire while Owen played for them and Holden slept in his mother's arms.

"Stretch out on the sofa and get comfortable," Sarah said, fluffing pillows and tossing a light throw over Laura.

"This is ridiculous. I'm supposed to be working and packing and getting ready to leave the hotel for a week or more, and what am I doing?"

Sarah ran a gentle hand over Laura's hair. "You're taking a few minutes to yourself while you can. Relax. I'll be right back."

Laura forced herself to follow Sarah's orders. From her vantage point on the sofa she could see the ferries coming and going from the harbor and the sparkle of the sun on blue water as another summer day on Gansett began in earnest. Outside the front side of the hotel, voices and cars and mopeds blended into a cacophony of noise from town that had become as familiar to her as the crash of the ocean on the breakwater out back.

"Here, honey," Sarah said when she returned with a steaming mug. "Try this."

"What is it?"

"Mint tea. It worked for me when I was pregnant."

"You've suggested that before, and I've been meaning to try it."

"As I recall, you said mint flavor isn't your favorite thing."

"It isn't, but at this point, I'm willing to try anything." She sat up and took a tentative sip of the brew. When it went down easy and stayed down, she took another. "Thank you."

"I'm sorry you're feeling so poorly."

"I keep waiting for Owen to say enough already with the hot mess he's shackled himself to."

"That's not going to happen, and you know it. He's crazy about you."

"I'm still trying to figure out why when all he's seen me do is breed and puke since we've been together."

Sarah's silent laughter brought tears to the older woman's eyes. "I'd venture to say he's probably seen a few other things in you besides those two endearing qualities."

"You are far too kind," Laura said with a smile for the woman who would be her mother-in-law before too much longer. "Enough about me. How was your night with Charlie?"

Sarah's cheeks flamed with color.

"That good, huh?"

"I had no idea," she said softly. "All this time… I didn't know."

"I'm so happy for you, Sarah, and for Charlie, too," Laura said. "You so deserve this amazing second chance."

"When I think about how I could've lived my whole life without knowing *that* was possible…"

"So you…" Laura rolled her hand, hoping Sarah would dish the details.

"Not everything, but what we did was incredible. And," Sarah said, lowering her voice to a whisper, "he said he loves me."

"Why are you even here this morning? You should be with him!"

"Because I knew you'd need me, and being here for you is also important to me."

"Sarah! For crying out loud, go back to him."

Sarah laughed at Laura's outrage. "It's fine, honey. I'll see him again later."

Laura's eyes filled with tears, and before she knew it, they were sliding down her cheeks.

"What's wrong?" Sarah asked, alarmed by Laura's sudden breakdown.

"Nothing." Laura swiped at the stupid tears that were almost as annoying as the nausea. Both were a byproduct of pregnancy that she would rather live without. "I'm so happy for you. I can't even begin to tell you… Having you here with us, helping me through this first year with Holden and taking care of all of us and teaching me so much about the hotel… It means the world to me. I feel like I have a mother again for the first time since I was nine."

"Oh, Laura…" Sarah brushed at her own tears as she took the mug of tea from Laura so she could hug her. "That's about the sweetest thing anyone has ever said to me. It's such an honor to know you think of me that way. Thank you, honey." She drew back so she could see Laura's face. "Being here with you and Owen and Holden truly saved my life, and I've loved every minute I've gotten to spend with you."

She tucked a strand of Laura's hair behind her ear. "For the longest time, I worried that Owen would never take a chance on love or have a family of his own. He'd given up so much of his childhood to help raise his siblings and seemed content with his footloose existence. But the minute I saw him with you, I knew. I just knew you were the one for him, and I was so very thankful that he'd found you."

"I'm thankful, too. When I think about the condition I was in when we first met… And the beautiful friendship I found with him before anything else ever happened between us. He's an amazing man, Sarah."

"I know he is, and I couldn't be prouder of him."

"I'm worried about what the trial and the worries about seeing his father are doing to him, though." She eyed the guitar that sat in a stand on the other side of the room. "I haven't heard him play or sing in days. Evan told me yesterday that Owen turned down a couple of gigs this week, which isn't like him. He loves having the chance to play with Evan, which doesn't happen as often these days because Ev is so busy with the studio."

"That is worrisome," Sarah said. "I think we just need to have faith that once the trial is over, the Owen we know and love will be back with us."

"I hope you're right," Laura said. "More tea, please."

Smiling, Sarah handed her the mug.

"Now let's talk about this amazing night you had with Charlie."

Once again, Sarah blushed furiously. "Girls my age don't share the dirty details."

"So the details are dirty?" Laura asked with a coy grin.

"I don't kiss and tell," Sarah said primly.

"Oh come on! You know you want to."

Sarah laughed and the sound filled Laura's heart to overflowing with love for the woman who'd come to mean so much to her. "I really do want to."

"Spill it, sister."

*

Returning to the hotel after his visit with Evan, Owen carried the sleeping Holden and followed the sound of laughter into the sitting room to find his mother and Laura gabbing on the sofa. He immediately noticed Laura's pallor and the cup of tea she held in her hand. She'd been sick again.

"What's going on around here?" Owen asked them. Was it his imagination or did his mother look mortified to see him standing there?

"You didn't hear any of that, did you?" she asked.

"Any of what?"

The question set off another wave of laughter between the two women, giving him a warm feeling of homecoming that had been so rare in his life before the last year. While this hotel had been the only true home he'd ever had during a childhood marked by frequent moves and the strife of his violent family life, it was even more so now that he and Laura were living here together. Having his mother with them only made it that much better.

"Why do I feel like I'm missing the punch line to a joke—or maybe I am the joke?"

His question set them off again. Seeing them both laughing so hard was good for what ailed him, and he couldn't help but smile at their glee.

"Trust me when I tell you," Laura said, wiping tears from her eyes, "you do not want to know what we were talking about."

Eyeing them with trepidation, Owen said, "I take it you had a good night with Charlie, Mom?"

Sarah gasped and looked to Laura for help. "Make him stop. I'm not talking about that with him."

"I don't want any details, and I mean that with every fiber of my being. I was simply asking if you had a nice time."

"Um, yes," Sarah said. "Yes, I did."

Her demure reply made Laura snort inelegantly.

Sarah slipped a hand over Laura's mouth. "Stop it. This instant."

"Can't," Laura said feebly.

"I'm going back to work," Sarah said. "Try to behave yourself."

"I'll do my best."

"See you two later." Sarah scurried out of the room, and Owen moved to take her place next to Laura on the sofa.

"What was that all about?"

"You'll never get it out of me. Girl talk."

"She's okay, though? You'd tell me if she wasn't, right?"

Laura took his hand and leaned in to press a kiss to the chubby cheek of her sleeping son. "Owen, honey, she is far more than okay. She is *divine*."

"Eww. Gross."

"Not gross at all. Very, *very* lovely. She's extremely happy this morning."

"Although I'll beg of you not to share *any* details, I'm glad to hear that."

Laura dissolved into giggles that made him smile at her delight despite the dark mood he'd been in for days now.

"Has it been a rough morning around here?"

"Rougher than usual."

"I shouldn't have left."

"I was fine, and you can't be with me all the time."

"I'd like to be."

"I know. Did you have any luck talking Evan out of coming with us?"

Stunned by the question, he stared at her. "How'd you know that was where I was going?"

She rolled her eyes. "I've got you figured out, Lawry."

"You're kind of scaring me right now."

"So, what did he say?"

"He's almost as bullheaded as you are," Owen said with a sigh.

"Sucks having all these people around who love you, doesn't it?"

He reached for her hand and linked their fingers. "It doesn't suck nearly as bad as being all alone did. That was worse."

Laura rested her head on his shoulder. "So Evan is coming with us?"

"Yeah, he's coming."

"Good."

"Are we going to Dan and Kara's engagement party later? The party is at two. Appetizers and drinks."

"I suppose we can go for a little while if you want to."

"You sure you feel up to it?"

"Anything is better than trying to find a way to think about something else."

She turned toward him, putting an arm around him and Holden. "I can't wait for this to be over," she said.

"I can't either."

*

For the first time in longer than she could remember, Stephanie woke up feeling unburdened. She'd spent years frantically trying to free Charlie from prison, and then after that had finally happened, she'd trapped herself in a cage of her own making.

It had been foolish, she now knew, to worry that Grant wouldn't understand her fears or want to help her manage them the way he had for as long as she'd known him. Even after all this time with him, she'd still been waiting for the bottom to fall out the way it had so many times before. After last night, though, she'd finally begun to believe it wasn't going to happen this time.

Grant wasn't going anywhere. He'd convinced her of that as he once again showed her how very much he truly loved her. With the memories of their incredible night together fresh in her mind, she was eager to share their good news with the person she loved second best.

Despite her assurances, she could tell that Grant was still concerned about her. She'd insisted he go share their news with his father, even though he'd offered to stay home with her. She was determined to move forward with their plans and try to enjoy her life in a way she'd never been able to before. After a shower, she got dressed in a tank and shorts and headed out.

The bright sunny day that greeted her made her grateful to live in such a beautiful place. After she decided to stay permanently on Gansett, she'd worried about being bored. However, she'd been anything but bored. With Grant's big family nearby and their wide circle of friends, there was always something going on, even in the winter when the tourists had gone home.

She'd loved her first full winter on the island, during which she'd kept the restaurant open only on the weekends and had spent the rest of the time hunkered down with Grant while he worked on the screenplay about her efforts to get Charlie freed from jail. For months, she'd cautiously avoided his frequent attempts to pin her down on a wedding date by changing the subject or evading the questions. He'd never pushed her, but she could tell that her refusal to discuss it had hurt him on more than one occasion.

It was such a relief to know she no longer had to dodge the issue. They'd talked through all of her fears and set a date. She was going to marry Grant in a few short weeks. The thought set off a wave of giddy laughter as she pulled into her stepfather's driveway, where he was cutting the grass. As he was wearing only a pair of shorts, his impressive physique was on full display. He had muscles on top of muscles, which came from the time he'd spent in prison with nothing to do but work out for several hours a day.

Seeing her there, he turned off the mower and used a bandanna to wipe the sweat from his face. He bent to pick up the T-shirt he'd tossed on the grass and put it back on. "Hey there. What brings you out so early?"

"I wanted to see my dad. Is that allowed?"

"Always. I could use a cold one. Join me?"

"Lead the way." She followed him into the small house he rented from Ned Saunders. He'd intended the rental to be temporary until he figured out a plan for life after prison. Like so many others who'd come to Gansett, that life had found him, and she was thrilled to have him close by. The first thing she noticed inside the house was the vase of artfully arranged flowers on his kitchen table. "Nice flowers."

"Oh, thanks. Sarah picked them from the garden."

"How is Sarah?"

"Good, as you know. You saw her yesterday."

Stephanie smiled at him as she accepted the glass of lemonade he'd poured for her.

"I'm actually glad you came by," he said. "I was going to call you today to tell you I'll be off the island for the next week or so."

"Where're you going?"

"To Virginia with Sarah and Owen. Her ex-husband is going on trial for beating her up last fall."

"*What*?" Stephanie asked with a gasp as she sat down hard on a chair at the table.

Charlie brought his drink to the table to join her.

Her mind whirled as she tried to absorb that the woman she'd come to know so well through her dad and working close to her at the hotel had been abused. "Did you know?"

"Not until the other day. I suspected, though. She's always so timid and skittish. I hated to think that was the reason."

"I had no idea."

"It's not something she or Owen speak freely about. I guess it was pretty bad when he and his siblings were growing up."

"God, poor Owen—and Sarah. He seems like such a happy, laid-back kind of guy. I never would've guessed. And I never heard a word about Sarah either."

"They've been private about it, for obvious reasons, and they're doing well now. We just have to get them through this next week or so, and then they can get on with their lives."

"I'm glad you're going with her."

"So am I. I'm glad she told me about it and is letting me be there for her."

"So things are good with you guys?"

"You could say that. She stayed here last night."

Stephanie's mouth fell open before she quickly closed it. "Really? Do tell."

"That's all you're getting."

"Oh come on!"

"End it," he said with a playful scowl. "What brings you over here, and don't tell me you missed me. You just saw me."

"Don't be so saucy," Stephanie said, amused by his gruffness. "I came to share some good news with you. Grant and I have set a wedding date. Labor Day."

"This year?"

"Yep."

"Good for you, honey. I'm happy for you. I was wondering when he was going to get around to making a real commitment to you."

"He wasn't the holdup. I was. He's been wanting to set a date for almost as long as we've been engaged." She slid a finger up and down the side of the glass, moving the condensation around. "I've wasted a lot of that time worrying that I might turn out to be more like my mother—"

"*Whoa*! Wait, what did you just say?"

"That I might turn out to be like her, which had me worried about having kids of my own."

"You are *nothing* like her. Nothing. If I hadn't seen pictures of her holding you as a newborn, I'd never have believed you were really hers—and I thought that from the time I first met you two. She was always a bit of a mess, and you… Even as a little kid, you were so incredibly smart and capable. There's no comparison, Steph. None."

Stunned by the emphatic, impassioned speech that was wildly out of character for her quiet stepfather, Stephanie slumped in her chair. "I let the fear get the better of me, and it feels sort of silly now that I finally aired it all out with Grant last night."

"He was good to you, I hope?"

"Yeah," Stephanie said softly. "He's always good to me. It's been hard, though, you know... To give him everything."

"You were holding something back, protecting yourself in case it fell apart, right?"

She could hardly be surprised that he understood so well after what he'd endured at the hands of her mother. "Yes."

"Classic defense mechanism. I know it well."

"You would, wouldn't you?"

"Look, we're both conditioned to expect it all to go to shit because that's what's always happened in the past. I'm choosing to believe that's not going to happen this time with Sarah. You should do the same with Grant. Despite the absolutely amazing thing he did to help me, I'll admit I wasn't a hundred percent sold on him for you when I first met him. He seemed kind of... I don't know... Fancy, I guess. I wondered if a guy like him could be happy with the simple life you need."

"You never told me any of this."

"You were ass over teakettle for the guy. Would it have mattered?"

"Yes! It would've mattered! You have no idea, do you?"

Charlie's brows knitted with confusion. "About what?"

"The whole time you were locked up, your voice was in my head. You were always my compass, even when I couldn't see you any time I wanted to. It would've mattered to me that you didn't think he was right for me."

"I never said he wasn't right for you. I said I wasn't sure at the beginning, but I trusted you to know your own heart, and over time I've come to see he's perfect for you in all the ways that matter most. The two of you... You complement each other." Charlie took her hand. "He comes from good people. That matters, too."

"They're very good people. I love them almost as much as I love him."

"You need to allow yourself to be happy, honey."

"I'm learning how to do that."

"Won't happen overnight, but we both deserve it, wouldn't you say?"

"Absolutely." Feeling suddenly shy, she glanced at him. "You'll give me away on Labor Day, won't you?"

"I'd be so very honored. Come here and give your old man a hug."

She went to him and let him wrap his strong arms around her, surrounding her with the unconditional love he'd given her long before he'd made the huge mistake of marrying her mother. "Love you, Charlie bear," she whispered, using her childhood nickname for him. She was so damned grateful to be able to hug him any time she wanted or needed to.

"Love you, too, Stephie Lou."

CHAPTER 15

Charlie walked Stephanie out to her car and gave her another hug before he sent her on her way with a wave. He was so damned proud of her. She'd been a bright, happy, joyful kid growing up in the midst of a nightmare with an abusive, neglectful, drug-addicted mother. After her mother had accused him of kidnapping and abusing her, they'd walked together through the fires of hell and made it through to the other side, somehow still whole and healthy despite their ordeal.

He hadn't thought about Renee in a long time. In fact, he went out of his way to never think about the day he'd walked in on her beating the hell out of the girl he'd come to love as a daughter. He'd done what anyone would do in that situation—he'd gotten Stephanie out of there and had paid for that decision with fourteen years of his life behind bars. Seeing her now, grown up, beautiful, glowing with happiness and in love with a great guy, Charlie knew he'd do it all over again if he had to. She was worth every minute he'd spent locked up.

As he was about to resume his yard work, another car pulled into the driveway, this one a low-slung black Porsche that made Charlie want to drool with envy every time he laid eyes on it. He'd always appreciated cars, and Dan Torrington's car was one of his favorites. It suited the LA lawyer to a T.

Charlie had learned the hard way to be wary and cautious around lawyers, who were often out to protect their own interests over those of their clients. Dan was a notable exception. Charlie owed him everything. With one phone call from the notoriously successful attorney, Charlie had suddenly been granted the hearing he'd been denied for years, at which Dan had successfully argued for his release.

"Hey, Charlie," Dan said when he unfolded himself from the car. He'd once told Charlie the car had originally belonged to his brother Dylan, who'd been killed in Afghanistan. Charlie had seen the depths of Dan's grief and the pain of his loss that day when he talked about his only brother.

Charlie shook the hand he offered. "Counselor. What brings you out this way?"

"A rather intriguing phone call from a friend of mine in the state attorney general's office."

"On a Sunday? You all never take a day off, huh?"

Dan was another one Charlie had found to be a bit fancy, until he got to know him better and came to appreciate the man beneath the urbane veneer. "We're both off today, but he wanted to give me a heads-up that the state is preparing to offer a settlement in your unlawful imprisonment claim."

Charlie had resisted filing that claim until Dan, Stephanie and even Grant had compelled him to consider it. After all, the original proceedings had completely disregarded the testimony of the girl he'd supposedly abused, who'd pleaded with someone, anyone, to hear her assertions that he'd actually saved her, that her mother had been the abuser, not her stepfather.

Renee had died a short time after he was charged without ever admitting she'd lied about what happened that day in their home. She'd condemned him to hell without an ounce of remorse, as if she'd never professed to love him when she was clean and sober.

"What kind of offer?" Charlie asked hesitantly. He'd told himself over and over that it didn't matter if anyone ever paid for what he'd been forced to endure. He had his freedom and his daughter was back in his everyday life. What else mattered?

"This is strictly off the record because it's not an official offer yet, but he heard they're going to come back with half a million for every year you spent in jail."

Seven million. Holy shit.

"I still think we could get more," Dan said. "This is just their preliminary offer, and they'll expect us to come back with a higher number."

"No," Charlie said.

"Um, no? What do you mean?"

"No higher numbers. That's more than enough. How much of that do you get?"

"None of it. I don't want it, and I don't need it."

"I don't get you. Why aren't you like all the other hucksters out there who'd have their hands so deep into a settlement like this, I'd be lucky to be able to buy a hamburger when they were done?"

Dan tipped his head back and laughed. "Don't think too much of my profession, do you?"

"Can you blame me?"

"Not one bit. You and most of the people I work with these days have seen the worst of us. I like to show you the best. I made a fortune as a corporate lawyer before I started the innocence project. I'm not in it for the money, but if you want to donate to the project so we can help others who've been unjustly convicted, I won't say no to that."

"Done."

"I wish all my clients were as easy to please as you are, Charlie."

"It doesn't take much to make me happy these days."

"I bet it doesn't. I'm happy for you. A thousand times more wouldn't fully compensate you for what was lost."

"Maybe not, but seven million will keep me pretty well for the rest of my life and give me something to leave my daughter someday, too."

"Good enough. I'll let you know when I receive the official offer."

"You're going to Virginia with Sarah and Owen, right?"

"I am. Are you?"

"Yes."

"I'll see you Tuesday morning, then."

"I'll be there. You'll be looking out for her, won't you?" Judging by the fierce expression on Dan's face, Charlie didn't need to elaborate any further.

"You bet your ass I will. That's why I'm going. I've been overseeing the divorce, and that husband of hers is a real piece of work. I'm not taking any chances that he's going to pull anything on her. I'll be right there the whole time."

"Makes me feel better to know you're on her side."

"Always." Dan offered his hand again.

Charlie grasped it with both hands. "I'll never be able to properly thank you for all you've done for me—and for Stephanie. We'll always be grateful."

"Believe me when I tell you, Charlie, it was indeed my pleasure. See you at the party later?"

"We'll be there. Wouldn't miss it."

Charlie waved to Dan when he drove off, leaving a cloud of dust in his wake.

Seven million dollars.

While part of him wanted to say fuck them and their money, the other part of him—the part that had once been an intellectual, a teacher and a fairly decent human being before life ripped the rug out from under him—would never say that. He could do a lot of good with that kind of money, for himself and the people he loved.

He could buy Sarah any house she wanted, he thought with a smile, imagining her reaction to hearing that she could have her pick of anything she'd ever wanted. That thought brought a smile to his face and had him once again thinking about the night they'd spent together.

She'd surprised the hell out of him when she asked him for more, and though he burned with the desire to do everything with her, he hadn't given in completely to those desires, as he was still afraid of scaring her or moving too fast after all she'd been through.

They'd still managed to have one hell of a good time together, and sleeping with her in his arms had been one of the best experiences of his life—even if they hadn't actually had sex. They'd come awfully close to that, and he had every reason to believe it would happen soon. At least he hoped so.

As much as he'd once loved Renee, this was different. With her, the slope had always been slippery. Even before he discovered her addiction issues, she'd been unpredictable, prone to irrational bouts of anger that kept him—and Stephanie—constantly off balance, waiting for the next explosion.

Sarah had her own experiences with waiting for the anger and living on the edge. Other than an occasional flinch when she was touched, you'd never know it to be around her. She was serene and peaceful and delighted with the simple things in life. Like him, she was grateful to be free of a past that had kept her every bit as imprisoned as he had once been.

Now that he'd been able to tell her—and show her—how much he loved her, he was hoping they'd get to spend the rest of their lives together. Once she got past the trial and her divorce was final, it would be time to make some plans. Charlie couldn't wait for that day. It was nice to have something to look forward to again.

*

After sending his wife a text asking her to meet him at home, Big Mac went to the house to wait for her. His mind raced with questions and implications and worries. He was deeply concerned about how Linda would react to hearing he'd fathered a child with another woman. Granted, it had happened before he met her, but still… He knew his wife and was worried the news would upset her.

Though it was only ten thirty, he thought about having a drink to calm his nerves but decided against it. He wanted to be at his best for this conversation. His thoughts kept wandering back to the beautiful young woman who'd appeared out of nowhere bearing life-changing news for him and everyone he loved. Had he been foolish not to agree to her wishes to let her go without anyone the wiser that she even existed?

"No," he said out loud. He'd never have a minute's peace if a child of his were walking around alone in the world when she could've been part of his large and loving family. Blowing out a deep breath, he ran his fingers through thick, wiry gray hair as he thought about the time he'd spent with her mother.

Theirs had been a brief fling, spanning most of the winter before he met Linda. That was before he owned a home on the island, so he'd gone to stay with Frank in Providence after the season ended. Neither he nor Diana had taken their relationship all that seriously, and when it came time to move on, they'd done so with no ill will or hard feelings.

He recalled Diana as a dark-haired, vivacious beauty with a zest for life and a yearning for adventure. She'd talked about the traveling she wanted to do and the places she hoped to see. None of her plans had fit with his goal of building his ramshackle marina on Gansett Island into a flourishing business. In fact, she'd teased him that he would lose his mind on the isolated island. But he'd been determined to pursue his dreams, as had she, so they'd gone their separate ways when it became obvious that their divergent dreams would never jell.

He'd liked her a lot, but he hadn't loved her. Probably because he'd always suspected theirs was a temporary relationship at best. When he met Linda, he'd immediately seen the potential for much more than he'd ever had with Diana or anyone else for that matter. Following his instincts where Linda was concerned had resulted in the kind of love most people could only dream about. And here they were, going strong thirty-nine years later, and he'd never had a single regret where she was concerned.

Despite their fleeting relationship, it saddened him to hear that Diana had died. In her letter, she'd told Mallory that she'd been tied to her home and her family, which was why she'd been unable to pursue a relationship with him. There'd been no mention of travel or adventure. He wondered if she'd gotten to do any of those things she'd wanted so badly or if taking care of their child had derailed all her hopes and plans. The thought of that possibility pained him greatly.

The screen door slapping against the doorframe, a sound as familiar to him as anything in his life, indicated Linda's arrival.

"Honestly, Mac. I was right in the middle of coffee with Doro when I got your text. I'm enjoying our summer of love as much as you are, but I do have commitments, you know." She stopped short in front of him and looked up, expectantly. "Well? I'm here." She ran her finger down the center of his chest and then hooked it into the waistband of his shorts. "You said it was urgent."

She was so damned beautiful, and when she looked at him that way, he would give her anything. He had to force himself to say the words. "I need to talk to you."

Before his eyes, she took a closer look and registered something amiss. "What's wrong?"

"Something happened today."

"The kids?"

"Are all fine. It was something else, something completely unexpected and out of the blue."

"Okay..."

"The winter before I met you, I dated a woman named Diana Vaughn for a couple of months."

He watched her guard go up against whatever she was about to hear. "That name doesn't ring a bell with me."

"I probably never mentioned her. It was short-lived. We had different paths in life, and it wasn't meant to be. By the time I met you, it'd been over for a while."

"So why bring it up now?"

"Because her daughter came to find me today."

Linda's blue eyes widened with surprise. "What did her daughter want with you?"

He forced himself to meet her gaze when he said, "It seems I'm her father."

Her mouth moved with words that didn't materialize. She shook her head. "That can't be right. How is that even possible? I mean, I know it's possible, but you've never been irresponsible about those things. And why did she keep her from you for all this time?" His heart broke when he realized she was on the brink of tears. "I don't understand."

"I was never irresponsible. I swear to you about that. But nothing is a hundred percent foolproof." Big Mac withdrew Diana's letter from his pocket and handed it to her. "This might help to explain why Diana kept her from me."

Warily, Linda took the letter from him and began to read it, her eyes flying over the page. Shaking her head, she covered her mouth with her hand, her shock palpable.

"Lin, listen to me. I had no idea. I swear to you. I didn't know."

"Of course you didn't. If you had, you would've done something."

"Yes," he said, relieved but still worried nonetheless. "I definitely would have."

"What is she like? Mallory?"

"She's gorgeous. She has dark hair and eyes. She's an emergency room nurse in Providence."

"So she looks like her mother?"

"Yes, I guess she does, but I could see Janey in her, and my mother. The picture I have of my mother as a young woman—Mallory is her all over again."

Linda swallowed hard and looked up at him with tearful eyes. "Did you love her? Diana?"

"No, I liked her. A lot. But I didn't love her. The only woman I've ever loved is the one I married, and you know that." He reached for her and was thankful when she came willingly into his arms, wrapping hers around him. "I haven't told anyone else. Mac was there, and Frankie… I could tell they wanted to know what was going on, but I came right to you."

"Thank you for that."

"What're we going to do about this, Lin?"

"I'd like to meet her. Is that possible?"

"I hoped you'd say that, so I talked her into staying at the hotel for the night."

"Invite her for dinner."

"I was hoping you'd say that, too." He held on tight to her. "What do we tell the kids?"

"Nothing for now. Let's talk to her and figure things out between the three of us before we involve them."

"Mac will be wondering what's going on. He saw me talking to her."

"He can wait. It won't kill him."

"It might. You know how he is."

The small gurgle of laughter that came from her told him it was going to be okay. They were going to be okay. "What's he going to say when he discovers he's not the oldest anymore?"

He drew back to look down at her. "Oh Jesus. And when Janey hears she's not my only daughter…"

Her smile faded as the implications for their children set in. "Janey has nothing to worry about where you're concerned."

"No, she doesn't, but still… It'll be a shock to her. To all of them."

"No more than it was for you."

"This isn't going to cause trouble between you and me, is it? Tell me it isn't, because I couldn't bear that. I'm floored by this entire thing, but even knowing she's alone in the world, if it meant trouble with you, I'd let her walk away. I hope you know that."

"I'd never ask that of you. It would kill you to do that to a child of yours, even one you didn't know you had."

"I know you've heard this before, but I've never meant it more than I do right now. The luckiest day of my life was the day I walked into that party with Frankie and found you there."

"That was a pretty good day for me, too."

He forced a smile for her sake. "Only pretty good?"

"It's right up there among the best days of my life, as *you* well know." She laid her head against his chest, seeming content to stay there for as long as he'd have her, which was forever. "Will you call her now and invite her?"

"If you're sure that's what you want."

"It is."

Though he was reluctant to let her go, he did as she asked, withdrawing his phone and Mallory's card from his pocket. His fingers felt clunky and awkward as he dialed the number. While he waited for her to answer, he put his free arm around his wife.

"Hello?"

"Hi, Mallory. It's Mac McCarthy."

"Hi."

"I take it you're settled at the hotel?"

"Yes, they were very nice, but then I did drop the owner's name."

"Never hurts anything." He cleared his throat, astounded by the unusual bout of nerves. "I spoke with my wife, Linda. We'd like to invite you to join us at the house for dinner, if that's all right with you."

"That would be very nice. Can I bring anything?"

Linda shook her head.

"Just yourself. You remember which house it is, right?"

"I do. What time would be good?"

"Six," Linda whispered.

"Six o'clock?"

"I'll see you then, and thank you. For the invitation."

"Sure thing. See you then." He ended the call and met his wife's gaze, uncertain of what he'd find there. But as always, she looked at him with love and compassion and understanding. "Thank you for this, Lin," he said gruffly.

"You're welcome."

CHAPTER 16

"This whole thing is so freaking pretentious," Kara said to Dan when they arrived at the Summer House, where her mother was supervising the staff with all the authority of a drill sergeant. "I hate it."

He slipped an arm around her and brought her in tight against him, kissing the top of her head. "Your folks wanted to do something nice for you, hon. It's really the least they can do."

"I know, but I still hate it."

"I don't hate getting to see you in that dress." He stepped back a bit to take a perusing look at her, spending extra time admiring the tanned legs that were on full display. "Mmm, mmm, *mmm.*"

A bolt of heat lit up her face whenever he looked at her that way, which of course he knew. "Knock it off," she said in a low growl.

"Just trying to get your mind off how pretentious this party is," he said with a wink that made her laugh. Dan took in the tables laden with crystal, china and silver as well as artful centerpieces made up of hydrangeas, roses and snapdragons. "My own mother would be right at home at this shindig."

"Speaking of your mother—and your father," Kara said, "when do I get to meet them?"

"I've been thinking about that and getting quite a bit of pressure from the home front. How about a trip to LA after your season ends in October? I could use a little time in the home office, and my folks are dying to meet the woman who finally got me to commit."

"*I* got *you* to commit?"

"That's exactly how I remember it."

She reached up to twist the bow tie he'd spent half an hour trying to tie just right. "You're full of shit, you know that?"

Scowling at her even though he loved her best when she was feisty, he rescued his poor bow tie. "I'm almost positive that word is not allowed inside this building."

In a flurry of movement and still barking out orders to the wait staff that looked ready to have her killed, Kara's mother came over to them bringing a cloud of expensive perfume with her. She was tall and lean and tanned with every blonde hair perfectly in place. To look at her, you'd never guess she was the mother of eleven children. Rather, you'd picture a life of leisure on the tennis courts at the country club.

Kara had told him they'd had nannies to help out growing up, and that her mother had, in fact, taken a lot of time for herself away from her children. The pampering was evident as Judith air-kissed her daughter.

"You look lovely, honey," she said with obvious approval for the dress Kara had bought at Tiffany's store. Dan would bet a million bucks that if she'd known it came from a place called Naughty & Nice, she wouldn't have been so appreciative.

She turned her attention to Dan, her scrutiny nearly making him squirm. "Love the bow tie. It works on you."

"Thank you." He'd decided to give Judith and Chuck Ballard the benefit of the doubt. They were going to be his in-laws, after all. But he would never, ever forget or forgive them for the way they'd treated Kara after the debacle with Kelly and Matt. That didn't mean he couldn't be cordial, however.

Kara had told him they'd been impressed by him after they met over dinner the night before. As soon as her sister, Kelly, had gone home to Bar Harbor to report that Kara was engaged to a celebrity lawyer, her parents had suddenly taken all new interest in their daughter's life on Gansett, much to Kara's dismay.

Leaving Bar Harbor and all the family drama behind had been the best thing she'd ever done for herself, and it had brought her to him, which was the best thing that'd ever happened to him. He'd be damned if he'd ever let these people or anyone else hurt her again.

That was why he stayed close to her as their guests began to arrive. Surrounded by their friends, all of whom had dressed up for the occasion, Dan felt Kara begin to relax. This was their new family, the one they had cultivated together, and being around their friends always made them happy.

He had to give her parents credit, they stayed right by their sides, meeting all their friends and exchanging pleasantries with each of them. Chuck Ballard was tall with white hair, a deep tan and a friendly, engaging manner. A "guy's guy," Dan had thought upon their initial meeting, the kind of man others gravitated to. At the moment, he was talking about marinas and the boating business with Big Mac and Linda McCarthy.

Dan had to admit that with the liquor flowing, the endless supply of tasty appetizers, his girl at his side and his friends all around him, this party didn't totally suck the way Kara had told him it would.

"How ya doing?" he whispered in her ear when they got a break from the socializing.

"Not bad."

"It's actually kind of nice."

"I'll remember you said that later when you want sex. You're either with them or you're with me. You can't have it both ways."

He burst out laughing, which earned him a glower from his beloved. "I love you so much, Kara Ballard. You'll never know how much."

She crooked her finger at him.

Tipping his head in close to her, he held his breath when she whispered in his ear.

"Knowing that makes all of this bearable." She curled her hand around his arm and gave a possessive squeeze that made him want to drag her out of there in search of a coatroom. Certainly a place like this had a goddamned coatroom, didn't it? Probably not, since most of the venues on the island catered to a summer crowd that didn't wear coats. But it was a hotel, too… The idea had his wheels turning. "Would you excuse me for one minute, hon?"

"One minute and one minute only," she said.

"I'll be right back." He left her with a kiss on the cheek and headed for the registration desk, delighted with his plan to surprise her after the party.

*

Watching Dan walk with purpose out of the room, Kara wanted to chase after him, but he was probably going to the men's room or something.

"What a great party," Abby Callahan said as she gave Kara a hug.

"I can't take any of the credit," Kara said, introducing Abby and her boyfriend, Adam, to her parents.

"There're a lot of McCarthys on this island," Judith said when she shook hands with Adam.

He laughed and nodded in agreement. "Five in my family, then there're my cousins Laura and Shane, and their dad, my Uncle Frank. My Uncle Kevin and his family are coming over soon for Laura's wedding. He's got two sons."

"I suppose we're hardly ones to talk," Chuck said with a laugh. "We've got eleven kids, including Kara."

"The thought of that makes me feel faint," Abby said.

"I was pregnant for *years*," Judith said.

Kara was well aware of exactly how many months her mother had spent pregnant, because she'd heard the number ninety-nine all her life.

"It's nice to meet you both," Adam said. "We love Kara."

At that moment, Kara loved him right back.

"She's a wonderful daughter," Chuck said with an affectionate squeeze for Kara.

It took everything she had not to push him away like she had for the last two years after he and her mother threw a fancy wedding for Kelly and Matt, as if their relationship hadn't left Kara completely flattened. Her dad was trying. She'd give him that much, but not much more. Where the hell was Dan?

"So are you guys going to be next?" Kara asked Adam and Abby.

Abby blushed while Adam stammered. "Um, well, not really quite there yet, are we, babe?"

"Not yet," Abby replied with a smile for him.

"Sorry," Kara said. "Didn't mean to put you on the spot." She wondered if Adam had noticed the same flash of pain in Abby's eyes that she had seen. If Kara wasn't mistaken, Adam was the only one who "wasn't there yet."

"This is a great party," Adam said, seeming eager to change the subject.

"Thanks," Kara said. "Typical Judith Ballard production. Nothing but the best."

Dan returned in time to shake hands with Adam and kiss Abby on the cheek. "Glad you guys could come on short notice."

"A McCarthy never misses a chance for free booze," Adam said.

"I've heard Grant say that very thing a hundred times," Dan said.

Jenny Wilks and Alex Martinez walked over with Alex's brother, Paul, and another woman.

"Congratulations, guys," Jenny said with kisses for Dan and Kara. "What a great party!"

"Thank you," Kara said, leaning in. "Secretly, I think engagement parties are kind of stupid. They're like pre-weddings. Same people, different day."

"See?" Alex said. "That's what I say, too. I'm glad you agree, Kara."

"You don't need to tell her that engagement parties are stupid when you're *at* hers," Jenny said, making Paul laugh at his brother's distress.

"She started it," Alex said with a cheeky grin.

"This is Hope Russell," Paul said. "She's come to save our lives by helping out with our mom. Hope, this is Kara Ballard and Dan Torrington, the happy couple suffering through this stupidly awesome party."

"Nice to meet you both," Hope said. "I was assured that crashers were welcome."

"Always," Dan said. "The more, the merrier around here."

"Totally," Kara said. "We're glad you could join us. How are you liking island life so far?"

"I love it," Hope said. "My son does, too, which is the best part."

"Make sure you all get something to eat, or my mother will consider herself a complete failure," Kara said.

"You don't have to tell me twice," Alex said.

They headed for the buffet table while Kara and Dan introduced Blaine and Tiffany Taylor to her parents.

"Blaine is the island's police chief," Dan added.

"That must be a nice quiet job in a place like this," Judith said to laughter from Blaine and Tiffany.

"In the winter it is," she said. "In the summer, I hardly see him."

"And what do you do?" Judith asked Tiffany.

Kara choked on her champagne as Dan nudged her.

"I own a lingerie store in town," Tiffany said. "Naughty & Nice. In fact, that beautiful dress of Kara's came from my store."

"The naughty side," Dan added.

He would pay for that later, Kara thought, not daring to make eye contact with her mother.

"I'll have to stop in to see your place," Judith said.

"Any time," Tiffany said, giving Kara a saucy wink.

"I'd like to be there for that," Kara said.

"Me, too," Dan added, making everyone laugh except for Judith, who didn't get the joke.

"She sells more than lingerie and party dresses there, Mom," Kara said.

For a moment, Judith seemed stumped, and then she said, "Oh. *Oh.*" Color flooded her cheeks.

"It's a long, cold winter out here, Mrs. Ballard," Tiffany said. "We have to find a way to stay busy."

"Well, yes, I'm sure it is. I'm going to see where your father has gone off to." Judith scurried away.

"That was awesome," Kara said as she shook with laughter. "You're the best."

"Happy to be of assistance," Tiffany said.

"You're just a walking, talking scandal, my love," Blaine said with a grin for his wife.

"Thank you," Tiffany said. "I do what I can for the people."

The sound of silverware striking crystal caught their attention.

"If everyone could find a seat, please," Chuck said as his wife stood next to him, beaming.

"Oh God," Kara said under her breath. "What's this all about?"

"Kara? Dan? Could you join us up here?"

"Whatever it is, let's get it over with so we can get to my surprise for later," Dan said as he took her hand and led her to the front of the room.

"What surprise?"

"Be a good girl in front of our guests, and I'll tell you."

"I don't want to be good."

"Remember that later."

As they took their positions with her parents, Kara felt the eyes of everyone on her and wanted to die of embarrassment. She hated being the center of attention and always had, which her parents certainly knew. That had never stopped them from forcing her out of her comfort zone whenever they felt the need to. Today was no exception.

"Thank you so much for joining us today to celebrate the engagement of our daughter Kara to Dan Torrington," Chuck said after Judith had ensured everyone had champagne. "Kara is the sixth of our eleven children and has always had the strong independent streak that led her here to Gansett to start the launch service in your Salt Pond. We were thrilled to hear of her engagement to Dan Torrington, a man who was certainly no stranger to us. Dan, we've admired your work for years, and we look forward to welcoming you into our family."

As everyone clapped and raised their glasses, Kara went along with it because she was expected to. But part of her wanted to stop everything and ask her parents if they were happy for her for the right reasons. Was it because she'd found the perfect man for her? Was it because he was rich and successful? Or was it because knowing she was happy with him made them feel a little less guilty about the way they'd treated her?

Dan leaned in to kiss her cheek. "Smile," he whispered. "You're supposed to be happy today."

She thought about the way he'd proposed to her, after her sister tried to ambush her earlier in the summer with an unexpected and unwelcome visit. Dan had literally run for her when he discovered Kelly was on the island with her husband and new baby and intended to take Kara by surprise, forcing a confrontation he knew Kara didn't want.

Thinking about the day they'd spent hiding out from the rest of the world and his adorable, romantic proposal, suddenly it didn't matter anymore why her parents were happy for her. It didn't matter that her sister had stolen her boyfriend and the rest of the family had acted like that was no big deal. Nothing mattered but the man who stood beside her, wanting to spend the rest of his life with her.

Kelly and Matt had actually done her a favor. If they hadn't betrayed her, she never would've felt the need to leave Bar Harbor. She wouldn't have come to Gansett or met Dan, and that would've been truly tragic. She'd loved Matt, but not the way she loved Dan. Nothing could compare to that.

Kara could tell she surprised her fiancé when she turned to him, gave him a big, warm smile and then leaned in to kiss him right there in front of everyone. As their friends whooped it up around them, she curled her hand around his neck and slipped him a hint of tongue. When she ended the kiss, he stared at her, confounded, as if trying to decide what had come over her.

Happiness had come over her, pure and simple.

She laughed at his befuddlement and then hugged him, loving the way his body fit against hers, as well as the scent of his cologne and the rough scrape of his whiskers against her face.

"You never fail to amaze me, babe," he said close to her ear, sending a shiver all the way through her body.

"I love you."

"I love you, too."

The clatter of smashing glassware interrupted the moment as everyone turned to see what all the noise was about. Beside her, Dan gasped at the sight of Jim Sturgil, Tiffany's ex-husband, as he pushed past a waiter carrying a tray of champagne glasses and knocked the tray out of the waiter's hand, sending more glass smashing to the floor.

"What the hell?" Dan said.

Out of the corner of her eye, Kara saw Blaine get up from the table where he'd been sitting with Tiffany, her sister Maddie, Maddie's husband, Mac, and Mac's parents. Tiffany stared at Jim, her eyes big and her face suddenly pale.

"Is everyone having *a good time*?" Sturgil asked, his voice slurring. His eyes were wild looking, and his white shirt was dirty and hanging untucked over torn pants. He looked like he'd been on a multiday bender. "Is everyone celebrating the man who's *ruined* my life? You ruined my life, Torrington! Everything was fine until you showed up here with all your money and connections, and now everyone wants the big celebrity to be their lawyer, and no one wants me! I am this island's lawyer. *Not you*! You need to go back to your fancy life in LA and leave us alone. No one wants you here." From the table where a man in a chef's coat and hat had been carving tenderloin, Jim picked up a large knife and began swinging it around.

"Don't take another step," Blaine said in a tone Kara had never heard from him before.

"You! *You stole my wife and kid*! My own kid likes you better than she likes me!" He swung the knife in Blaine's direction. "I ought to gut you the way you've gutted me."

"You did this to yourself, Sturgil," Blaine said calmly but firmly. "You can toss all the accusations around that you want, but you have only yourself to blame for your problems."

Jim lunged at him with the knife, but Blaine jumped out of the way.

Dan dropped his arm from around Kara's shoulders and moved across the room to help Blaine.

"Dan!" Kara screamed after him, afraid he would get hurt again after only recently recovering from the injuries incurred in the sailboat accident.

Everyone was on their feet, and Evan and Mac went to help Dan and Blaine, who were confronting Jim. He waved the big knife around in front of him, daring anyone to get close to him.

"Someone should call the police," Judith said nervously.

"Blaine *is* the police," Kara said. "Give him a minute. He'll take care of it."

"Jim," Tiffany said as she walked toward her ex-husband. "What the hell are you doing? Think about your daughter. Put down that knife and quit acting like a jackass."

"Tiffany, step back," Blaine said without taking his eyes off Jim or the knife. "Right now."

"You think *I'm* a jackass?" Jim screamed at her. "*You did this to me, you stupid bitch*!"

Blaine roared and pounced on Jim, his arm tight around Jim's neck as Dan went for the knife.

"Dan!" Kara screamed, feeling as if her worst nightmare was unfolding right in front of her. "*No*!"

Cornered, Jim slashed at Dan, who grunted when the knife made contact with him before clattering to the floor.

Kara ran for her fiancé, who was bent in half, while Blaine dragged Jim kicking and screaming from the room. "Dan! *Dan*! What's wrong? Are you hurt?"

He looked up at her, grimacing in pain. "Just a scratch."

That's when she noticed the pool of blood forming on the floor in front of him.

"Someone call for rescue," Mac said behind her. "Come on, Dan, have a seat." After getting Dan into a chair, Mac grabbed a napkin that he wrapped around Dan's right hand. The napkin quickly soaked through, and Mac calmly swapped it out for another one.

"Sorry 'bout this," Dan said.

Kara cradled his head against her chest. "It's not your fault. You weren't the one with the knife."

"What've you done now, Torrington?" his close friend Grant McCarthy asked as he squatted in front of Dan.

"I was safer in LA than I am here," he said, forcing a smile for Kara's benefit. "Might be time to go home."

Kara knew he was joking, but the comment scared her nonetheless. Gansett was their home, or at least she thought it was.

The EMTs arrived a minute later, and Kara stepped back from Dan to make room for them to tend him.

Her mother's arm encircled her waist. "Are you all right, honey?"

"I will be when I know he is."

"He did a brave thing rushing at that man with the knife. Who is that guy?"

"Jim Sturgil. He used to be married to Blaine's wife, Tiffany, and people don't like him because of the way he treated her when they got divorced." As she filled in her mother, Kara never took her eyes off Dan. "When Dan came to the island to write his book, people started seeking out his legal advice, and now they prefer him to Jim."

"So Dan is actually practicing law here?"

"Has been for a while now. He didn't intend to, but that's how it worked out."

The lead EMT signaled to Kara to come with them.

"I'll call you later, Mom. Sorry about all this."

"I just hope he's okay."

"So do I." Kara ran after the stretcher that Dan was strapped to.

"Much ado about nothing," he said to her when she caught up to him. Despite his assurances, his face was pale and his eyes were glassy with shock, which reminded her of the aftermath of the boating accident—a time she'd much rather forget than relive. "Do you like how I got you out of the stupid party?"

"Don't make jokes." The instant the words cleared her lips, she regretted sounding so snappish. It wasn't his fault he'd gotten hurt.

"I'm okay, babe. I swear. It's just a cut. They'll stitch me up, and I'll be good as new."

Kara forced herself to breathe through the need to cry with relief that he was okay. When she thought about what might've happened, she shuddered.

In the ambulance, Dan held out his good hand to her, and she took it, holding on tight to the man she loved with all her heart.

CHAPTER 17

"What. The. Hell." Maddie stood with Tiffany, watching the EMTs take Dan Torrington away from his engagement party on a stretcher.

"Goddamned Jim," Tiffany muttered, mortified and humiliated by her ex-husband's tirade. At times like this, she had no idea how she ever could've loved him. "What was he hoping to prove by pulling a stunt like this?"

"He looked like he'd been drinking for days."

"I wondered why he hadn't called to see Ashleigh in a while. For all his faults, that's not like him."

Maddie's arm came around her. "Are you okay?"

"Yeah, I guess. Just kind of shocked to see him lose it that way. I had no idea his business was in such bad shape." Suddenly chilled to the bone despite the warm summer day, Tiffany wrapped her arms around herself protectively. "You don't suppose Blaine will kill him, do you?"

"I'm sure he'd like to rough him up a bit, but he'd never do that to you or Ashleigh. He'll go totally by the book on this one because of who Jim is to you.

"He's nothing to me," Tiffany said forcefully.

"You know what I mean. He's still Ashleigh's father."

Tiffany knew her sister was right, even though Blaine was already more of a father to Ashleigh than Jim had ever been. Speaking of her husband… He came back into the room, his face stony with anger. When the brown eyes that normally looked at her with nothing but love and lust and tenderness connected with hers, she realized he was incredibly angry. At her.

Tiffany's stomach ached with apprehension, a feeling that reminded her all too well of her unhappy years with Jim.

"Uh-oh," Maddie muttered as Blaine crossed the room to them.

"Where is he?" Tiffany asked. "What happened?"

"I turned him over to my people." His words were clipped and economical, nothing extra offered to calm or soothe her the way he normally did. "He's on his way to jail, where he belongs. Let's go."

With a grimace for her sister, she let her husband lead her from the room. He held the passenger door to his department-issued SUV for her and waited for her to get settled before he slammed it closed. As he stalked around the front of the truck, Tiffany's nerves skyrocketed into all-too-familiar terrain. She'd spent years with a man whose mercurial temper left her in a constant state of dread over when the next blowup might occur. If a blow up with her new husband were imminent, at least Ashleigh wouldn't witness it. She was spending the afternoon with Jim's parents.

Blaine got in the truck and slammed his own door as hard as he'd slammed hers. He pulled out of the parking lot, leaving a cloud of dirt in their wake, and drove to their house in total silence.

She noticed his knuckles were white as he gripped the wheel with all his considerable strength. Swallowing hard, she finally worked up the courage to poke the tiger. "What's wrong?"

He looked over at her, seeming incredulous, before returning his attention to the road.

"So you're just not going to tell me? It's not my fault Jim did that! I hadn't seen him in weeks."

No reply. Fantastic.

She crossed her arms to contain her own fury, which was mounting by the second.

He pulled into the long driveway that led to their home a few minutes later, the truck swerving as he braked abruptly, threw the truck into Park and got out. Opening her door, he said, "Come."

"I don't want to. You're acting like a madman."

"I'm acting like a madman?"

"Yes! What the hell has gotten into you?"

"You want to know what's gotten into me?"

"Stop answering my questions with questions!"

"Then how about you tell me *what the hell you were thinking* confronting a man *who has professed his hatred for you to anyone who will listen* when he's wielding *a fucking butcher knife*?"

All of a sudden, she got why he was so upset. She'd scared him. She released her seat belt and turned to him, still sitting in the SUV while he stood outside. "Blaine..."

"Don't do that. Don't go all soft like that and think you're going to get out of this by sweet-talking me. He could've killed you!"

Despite his reluctance, she put her hands on his face and forced him to look at her. "You were right there, and you never would've let that happen."

"What were you thinking confronting him like that? He was clearly over the edge and looking for vengeance. You nearly made it easy for him."

"I wasn't thinking about anything other than trying to make him stop before things got even worse. I knew you were right there and would protect me if it went bad." She leaned in to kiss him. "I knew you were right there."

"Baby," he said with a tortured moan as he hugged her so tightly she couldn't breathe, "don't ever do anything like that again. Do you hear me?"

"Yes, I hear you."

"You have to promise me. I think my heart stopped for a second there when I saw you approach him. I need you to promise."

"I promise."

He scooped her right up and out of the truck and carried her to the house, kicking the door open and then kicking it closed behind them.

Tiffany wrapped her arms around his neck and kissed him with all the love and desire he aroused in her every time he touched her. "You scared me, too, you know."

"When? When did I scare you?"

He sat her on the counter in the kitchen, right where their first significant encounter had occurred. "When you were angry with me. It reminded me too much…of him. Of how it always was with him when I spent most of my time waiting for him to lose it with me over every little thing."

"This wasn't a little thing, but I'm sorry I made you feel that way. I never want to make you feel the way you did with him."

"I know."

"So we scared each other." He ran his hands up her legs and under her skirt until they were cupped around her bottom. "It's only because I love you so fucking much that I nearly lost my mind when you confronted him. The thought of you in any kind of danger, no matter how fleeting, makes me want to lose my shit."

"I'm okay." She caressed his face and smoothed his hair, which had gotten mussed in the altercation with Jim.

"I should be at the station dealing with him, but I need to be inside you right now more than I need my next breath. I need you, Tiff."

She unbuttoned and unzipped the dress pants she'd had to talk him into wearing to the party. "Take me. I'm all yours."

He growled as he ripped the lace panties off her body in a move that sent her own need into the red zone. With his hands under her skirt gripping her ass, he pulled her toward him and impaled her on his hard cock, drawing a gasp from both of them. "Shit," he whispered as he froze. "Sorry."

"For what?"

"That was rough."

"I loved it, and I love you."

Her words sent a tremble rippling through his muscular body as he took her on a wild ride. She hooked her arm around his neck and urged him into a frantic, passionate kiss.

He made an inarticulate sound as he pulled at the bodice of her dress, tugging until her breast popped free of her bra. Squeezing and kneading, he pinched her nipple between his fingers until she cried out from the orgasm that ripped through her, sending waves of heat and sensation from her core to every part of her body.

"Fuck, you're so hot," he said on a groan as he pushed hard into her again stayed there this time as he rode the waves of her climax into his own. Sweating and panting in the aftermath, he let out a gruff laugh. "I need to get mad at you more often. That was incredible."

"Please don't get mad at me more often. I couldn't take that."

"You have absolutely nothing to fear from me—ever. I'm your slave. I'm completely and totally under your spell."

Charmed and moved by his heartfelt words, she tightened her legs around his hips and pushed against the cock that was still hard inside her despite his orgasm. His stamina never failed to amaze and exhaust her. "Look at where we are."

He seemed to snap out of the sex-fueled daze to realize he'd taken her right on the kitchen counter where he'd once given her the orgasm that changed both their lives. "I do some of my best work right here," he said with a proud grin that made her laugh.

With his hands still wrapped firmly around her buttocks, he lifted her off the counter without losing their connection and carried her to the sofa in the living room, where he came down on top of her. Lifting her skirt, he eased the dress up and over her head, leaving her only in the bra that had matched the now-shredded thong. He released the clasp on her bra and disposed of it with expertise that never failed to amuse her.

"I know, I know," he said before she could. "I'm good at that." He nuzzled her bare breasts, teasing her nipples with his tongue and the rough brush of his late-day whiskers against sensitive skin. "It's because I have the best possible reason to get rid of your bras with all due haste."

She grasped a handful of his hair and directed him to focus on her nipple. Her husband knew how to take direction and had her twisting and gasping and straining against him within minutes. "Blaine..."

"What, baby?"

"I want you to know..."

"What do you want me to know?" He never stopped kissing or sucking or teasing as he spoke, and the wash of his hot breath over her wet nipple was nearly enough on its own to make her come again.

"I told you that when you were angry with me, it reminded me of him. But you're nothing like him, and our marriage... It's nothing like that one was. It's so, so much better. It's more than I ever dreamed possible."

His forehead dropped to her chest. "You kill me, baby. The stuff you say to me... You're so damned sweet, and I'm so sorry you went through everything you did with him, but I'm so, *so* glad it led you to me." He raised his head to meet her gaze. "I never felt like I belonged anywhere until I belonged to you."

"I know exactly what you mean. I feel the same way."

"Love you," he whispered as he began to move again, making slow, sweet love to her this time.

"I love you, too."

"And you'll never do anything like you did today again, right?"

"Yes," she said with a sigh.

"Promise?"

"I promise, Blaine."

"In that case, I'll let you come again."

Laughing, she closed her eyes and held on tight to him and the love he'd brought into her life. "You are just *too* good to me, Chief Taylor."

*

The engagement party broke up shortly after the guests of honor left in an ambulance. Kara's parents had tried in vain to salvage the festivities but gave up when it became clear the party was over. After saying good-bye to their family and friends, Adam extended his hand to Abby to walk the short distance to the house they rented from Janey.

"That, right there, is why we should never have an engagement party," Adam said as they navigated the crowded downtown, which was overrun with tourists late on that sunny Sunday afternoon.

Abby had no idea what to say to his joking comment. She'd had reason to wonder if they'd ever have an engagement, let alone a party. At times, she feared she'd made another mistake by moving in with him before they were married. Since she was right there, at his disposal, what reason did he have to want to move things forward? If her father said one more word about cows and milk in regard to her and Adam, she'd never speak to him again.

The sad part, if you wanted to call it sad, was that she'd never been happier in her life. Adam was everything she'd ever wanted—and their relationship was light years better than the ones she'd had with his brother Grant and her ex-fiancé, Cal. Adam understood her on a deep, intense level that had created an indelible bond between them.

And the sex continued to be a revelation. All of which had her wondering whether he had any plans at all to take the next step with her.

"Hello? Anyone in there?"

Abby realized she'd zoned out on him. "Sorry. What were you saying?"

"I was making jokes about why we'll never have an engagement party."

She glanced over at him, slayed as always by the wavy dark hair, the glasses that made him look like a smart, sexy nerd, the sardonic little smile and the light dusting of stubble on his cheeks that made for one incredibly sexy package.

He bumped her hip with his. "What's the matter?"

"Nothing. Just thinking."

"About?"

"Dan and Kara, and Jim with the knife, and how I hope Dan's okay. He's just finally back to normal after what happened on the sailboat, and now this."

"Is that all you were thinking about?"

"Yeah, I guess."

"You guess. So you don't really know what you were thinking about?"

His persistence had her looking over at him again. "Why do you want to know so badly?"

He surprised her when he led her across the street to a bench that overlooked the ferry landing below. "Sit."

"Okay…"

Adam sat next to her, turning to face her. "Talk."

"What do you want me to say?"

"I want you to tell me why you went all quiet on me when I made a joke about our engagement party."

"You need me to tell you why? Really?" The comment was testier than she'd intended, but honestly, how obtuse could he be?

"Yeah, I guess I do."

"For someone so smart, you can be rather dense at times."

"What's that supposed to mean?"

"Nothing. Never mind."

"Abby… Come on. This isn't how we roll. We air it out. Don't we?"

She wanted to be cool and calm and collected, but this was too important, and she'd already been burned twice before by long romances that didn't work out in the end. If that happened this time…

"Baby, why are you crying?"

Abby hated herself for the tears that came despite her ardent desire to be unemotional and pragmatic about broaching this subject with him. She forced herself to look at the face she loved above all others. "I want to get married, Adam," she said softly, "and we never, ever talk about that. Which leads me to wonder if that's what you want, too."

"It is what I want."

"Then what're we waiting for?"

"The right moment."

"For what?"

"For this." Before she knew it, he was on his knees in front of her. "Abigail Callahan, I love you more than anything in this world. You've changed my life in every possible way, and I want to be with you forever. Will you do me the great honor of becoming my wife?"

She was crying so hard that she could barely hear him over the sound of her own sobs, but his words registered just the same, as did the slide of the ring over the third finger on her left hand.

"Where… What… How long…"

"On the mainland, two carats and about three months ago now. Any other questions before you answer mine?"

She gazed down at him and then at the exquisite ring and shook her head.

"You aren't saying no, are you?"

"I'm not saying no." She cupped his cheek and leaned in to kiss him. "I'm definitely not saying no."

"A double negative is hardly what a guy is looking for when he asks the most important question of his life."

"How about a triple positive, then? Yes." She kissed him. "*Yes.*" She kissed him again. "*Yes.*" She kissed him a third time and stayed there when his arm encircled her neck, keeping her trapped against him.

"I like triple positives," he said, coming up for air after kids walking by on the street yelled at them to get a room.

"Did you say that about engagement parties on purpose?"

"Maybe. I've been waiting for an opening."

"I've always been open to this conversation. Since the day you told me you were moving back here permanently." She paused, needing to ask him something but unsure of how she should put it. "Adam?"

He rejoined her on the bench. "Yes?"

"We're going to actually *get married*, right?"

"Of course we are," he said, laughing. "Why would you ask me that?"

"I don't have the best track record when it comes to making the close."

He waggled his brows. "You have a very good track record for making the close with me."

"I'm not talking about sex."

"I know you're not, honey, and I'm well aware of what you've been through in the past. And you know what's happened to me. I think it's safe to say we both want to see this through to the finish line. I know I do."

"So do I. I can't wait to be married to you."

He propped his sexy glasses on the top of his head and leaned in to kiss her again.

"Don't you guys have your own house?" a female voice behind them asked.

Abby looked up to see Owen and Laura walking toward them, holding hands. Abby held up her left hand. "Big news, and you're the first to know!"

Laura let out a shriek and came over for a closer look at Abby's ring. "It's gorgeous! Congratulations, you guys." She hugged Abby and then her cousin. "Nice job on the ring, Adam."

"Why, thank you."

Owen shook Adam's hand. "Congrats, man. Happy for you."

"Thanks."

"We'll leave you to celebrate in private," Laura said, taking Owen's hand and giving a gentle tug. But before she walked away, she gave Abby one more squeeze. "So happy for you. I know you really wanted this."

"Thanks, Laura."

"We're going to be cousins!"

Abby laughed at Laura's delight and waved as they headed off toward the Surf.

"What do you say we go home and celebrate this momentous occasion?"

"I would like to celebrate, but not the way you have in mind. Until later, anyway," she said with a giggle at his distressed expression.

"What do you have in mind?"

She took his hand and turned it so the palm was faceup, drawing a line across the inside of his wrist. "I would like for both of us to get today's date tattooed right here, so we'll never forget it. And then when we get married, we'll put our wedding date on the other wrist."

His smile stretched across his face as he shook his head.

"No?" she asked shyly, uncertain of what he was thinking.

"I love the idea, and I love that my sweet, gentle girl has an inner wild child. I want to see plenty of her after we're married, okay?"

"Okay." When he leaned in to kiss her, she met him halfway. "So that's yes to the tattoos?"

"That's yes to the tattoos. It's yes to everything."

CHAPTER 18

"I'm so happy for Adam and Abby!" Laura said as she walked along the sidewalk with Owen's arm draped across her shoulders. His mother had chosen to sit out the engagement party, preferring to stay home with Holden so they could have some time to themselves.

"They're great together. I'm happy for them, too."

"She's been really wanting this. She's never actually said so, but I can just tell by the look on her face when everyone is talking about weddings and husbands and babies that she wanted in on it all."

"It's nice to see good people get what they want."

"Yes, it is."

Though he was participating in the conversation and had done the same with their friends at the party, he was distracted and distant and not fully present. "Want to take a walk on the beach? I'm sure your mom won't mind a little more time with Holden."

"If you want."

She stopped walking and turned to him. "I'm asking if *you* want to."

"I'd rather take a nap than a walk."

Now *that* sounded like the Owen she knew and loved. "Is that so?" she asked, smiling up at him.

His gaze took a greedy, hungry journey over her face as he nodded.

Holding his hand, Laura went up the stairs and into the lobby, where they greeted the young woman working at the reception desk on the way upstairs to their apartment. She released him only so he could use his key in the door. Inside, they found a note from Sarah that said she and Charlie had taken Holden to Charlie's house for a couple of hours and would be back after dinner.

"Have I mentioned how much I adore your mother?" Laura asked.

"A few times."

"Never more so than right now."

"Is that right?"

"Uh-huh." She unbuttoned the dress shirt he'd worn in deference to the location of the party at one of the fancier venues on the island. Pulling the shirttails from the waistband of his khakis, she pushed it over his broad shoulders and tugged it down his arms until it was on the floor behind him. Next, she unbuckled his belt and unbuttoned his pants.

The whole time, he kept his hands by his sides, waiting and watching her undress him.

"What's on your mind, love?" she asked.

"Not a single thing besides wondering what Laura is up to."

She laughed softly, charmed by his reply and the effort he was making to connect with her despite the burden of his thoughts and worries. She peppered his belly with kisses, nuzzling the trail of golden-blond hair that led into his pants. Unzipping him, she worked slowly and carefully around the huge bulge. He held his breath, waiting to see what she would do next.

Working her hands into the back of his pants, she pushed them down over his hips and then rubbed her nose and lips over his cock through the soft cotton of his boxer briefs.

He gasped and clutched handfuls of her hair. "Laura… Come here."

"Not yet."

Still on her knees in front of him, she eased his underwear slowly over the straining tip of his cock, letting the elastic rest halfway down his shaft. Then she ran her tongue over the area she'd exposed while cupping his balls through the cloth.

His breathing became choppy and erratic as she teased him with her tongue and lips, focusing only on the wide head.

"Babe," he said on a gasp. "Are you trying to make me lose my mind here?"

Knowing he was now thinking only of the pleasure and not of the many other things that had been weighing so heavily on him for the last few weeks, she kept up the erotic torture. Sliding her free hand around him, she cupped one of his tight, round cheeks and squeezed.

"God, Laura," he moaned. "You're killing me."

"Relax and enjoy."

"Right… Relax? Not bloody likely. Enjoy? Hell yes."

Smiling, she pulled his underwear the rest of the way down and wrapped her hand around the base as she sealed her lips over the tip and sucked. She dipped her tongue into the slit at the top and ran it back and forth while stroking with her hand. He was far too big for her to take more than a few inches into her mouth, so she did what she could while continuing to knead his backside.

"Feels so good," he whispered.

She looked up to find him gazing down at her, his eyes heated with desire and passion. In them she saw none of the torture that had been so prevalent over the last few difficult weeks. She saw only the pleasure.

"Come here, Princess. Let's do this together."

Without releasing him, she shook her head. Though her own sex tingled with need, she loved knowing she was thoroughly distracting him. His thighs tightened and quivered, and his cock got even larger in her mouth, stretching her lips to their limit. When she pulled back to readjust, he pounced, lifting her from the floor into his strong arms, devouring her mouth with his lips and tongue. They landed on the bed in a tangle of arms and legs without losing the kiss.

He was careful, as always, not to put too much weight on her abdomen, but his hands were all over her, lifting her dress and breaking the kiss only to pull it over her head. Her bra was next, followed by the matching panties, a set she'd bought from Tiffany.

"You are so beautiful," he whispered as he tongued her nipple until it was standing up tall. "Sometimes I still can't believe that I can hold you and touch you this way any time I want to."

"Any time, Owen. I always want you."

With his hand on her face, he brushed back her hair and kissed her again, softer this time but with no less urgency. He broke the kiss and raised himself up so he was above her, kissing a fiery path down the front of her. "You know what they say about payback, don't you?"

Laura let her nervous laugh speak for her as he propped her legs on his wide shoulders and used his fingers to open her to his tongue. She was so ready, so primed, that all it took was a few concentrated strokes of his tongue to trigger her orgasm. He extended it by sliding two fingers into her, connecting with the place inside that set off another wave of intense pleasure.

Before she could come down from the incredible high, he aligned his cock with her entrance and pushed into her, moving slowly, giving her time to adjust and accommodate him. She liked to tease him about getting more than his share, but she loved the way he felt inside her.

"Easy, babe," he whispered as he rocked against her. "Nice and easy. You can do it. You can take me." Bending his head, he laved her nipple, sending a bolt of heat to where they were joined. "That's it. Let me in so I can love you."

His words were almost as potent as the tight squeeze of his hard flesh, and then he added the press of his thumb against her clit, and Laura came again, drawing a deep groan from him as she clutched him from within.

"Christ," he whispered on a gasp as he surged into her, riding the waves of her release to gain entry. Once he was fully seated, he stayed still, letting her catch her breath. "Every damned time."

"What?" she asked when she could speak.

Holding himself up on his elbows, he cupped her shoulders and held her as close to him as he could get her without squeezing the part of her where their babies rested. "You freaking ruin me every damned time."

She pushed the shaggy blond hair back from his forehead. "*I* ruin *you*? Let's talk about what you do to me."

"Tell me what I do to you."

"First of all, you make it so I can't walk properly for days afterward."

"That's not true." He raised her legs one at a time until they were wrapped around his hips. When he had her arranged the way he wanted her, he retreated slightly before advancing again, drawing a keening moan from her as she arched into him.

"It is true, but I love it. I love that I can feel you inside me long after we make love."

"You can? Really?"

She nodded.

"You've never told me that before."

"Hours later, I can still feel you, and everything is still pulsing and quivering." As if to make her point, she contracted around him, making him groan. "It feels like mini-orgasms that go on and on."

"God, I love it when you talk dirty to me. Tell me more."

She laughed at his playful commentary, thrilled and relieved to see him relaxed and fully involved in what they were doing. "I love how big you are."

He snorted with laughter. "Now you're just lying to me."

"No, I'm not. I do love it. I don't love that it takes me forever to let you in, but I love the way you feel when we get there and I'm totally impaled by you."

He growled against her neck, nibbling and sucking on her skin as he rocked deeper into her. "You're going to make me come just from listening to you."

"I love the way you hold me and kiss me. I love the way you smell and the way your cute butt flexes when you make love to me." She sent her hands down his back to squeeze his cheeks, which sent him surging into her. "And I absolutely love when you lose control and really let go."

"I'm always afraid to do that. I don't want to hurt you."

"You won't. You couldn't."

"But the babies…"

"Are fine." She lifted her hips, daring him to give her what she most wanted. "Please, Owen…"

"Tell me what you want."

"You know!"

"Say it."

"I want you to make love to me."

"Oh so polite, Princess. Say what you really want."

Her entire body was on fire for him, with every pressure point throbbing and tingling. "I can't."

"Then I'm afraid I can't help you."

"Owen!"

His soft chuckle made her smile, but her smile quickly faded when she realized he was withdrawing from her.

"No!" She grasped his ass and pulled him back. "I want you to fuck me."

"There we go," he said with a satisfied grin that had her averting her eyes in mortification.

"I've never said that in my life."

"I love that you said it to me. I fucking love it." He curled his hands around hers. "Hold on tight, babe." He squeezed her hands. "Ready?"

"*Yes.*"

He started slowly, looking down at her and watching her closely to make sure she was with him before he picked up the pace, driving into her with deep strokes that made her scream from the full-body pleasure that overtook her. "Good?"

"Mmm, more. Faster. *Harder.*"

He released her hands to put one of his under her, lifting her to him as he possessed her. There was simply no other word for it. She was possessed by him, owned by him and captivated by him in every possible way. Their bodies were slick with sweat as they moved together, breathing hard and racing toward the finish line.

"Come for me," he said pleadingly. "*Laura…*" He stroked into her and triggered another release, this one bigger and stronger than the other two put together, taking him with her this time.

Sagging against her, he continued to protect her abdomen until his arms began to tremble from the effort. He rolled to his side, bringing her with him, still embedded in her. "I love you. That was… I don't even have the words."

"Astonishing."

"Yes. Yes, it was. You are astonishing."

"You're pretty damned astonishing yourself, and I love you, too."

"When I'm making love with you, there's no way I can think about anything but you and me and what we have together."

"I'll keep that in mind over the next few days. I see a *lot* of sex in your future."

"I like the sound of that."

She rested her hand on his face and smiled at him. "Anything I can do to help the cause."

*

On the way home from the eventful engagement party, Mac and Maddie rode with the windows down in her SUV, letting in the warm summer breeze. "What a crazy-ass stunt on Jim's part," Mac said, disgusted by the asshole who'd once been his brother-in-law. "He's all but ruined any chance he ever had to practice law on this island again."

"I know. I'm so glad Tiffany isn't with him anymore, but I hate that he did this to Ashleigh."

"He never has had the proper respect for either of them, if you ask me."

"He's no Mac McCarthy, that's for sure."

He reached for her hand and gave it a squeeze. "That's nice of you to say, and really, when you think about it, who is?"

Maddie groaned. "I'm not going to dignify that with a response." She looked over at him and then leaned across the center console to kiss his cheek. "Seriously, though, I mean it. Every day I feel like I hit the jackpot with you, but never more so than when I'm reminded of how awful my sister's first marriage was."

"I'm the one who hit the jackpot, babe, and as for Tiffany, at least she's happy now with Blaine."

"That she is, although he didn't look too happy when he came back in for her."

"I'm sure he's pissed that she tried to confront Jim, and I don't blame him. I would be, too, if you ever put yourself in that kind of danger."

"I don't blame her for what she did. She wanted him to stop before things got out of control."

"Things were out of control the minute he walked in there and started knocking stuff over."

"True. What do you suppose will happen to him now?"

"He's going to face charges for sure. If he hadn't grabbed the knife, it might've been a misdemeanor, but waving a knife around in front of a cop probably qualifies as a felony, and he actually stabbed Dan."

"Jeez."

"If he's convicted, he could get disbarred, too."

"I'll never understand what's wrong with him. He had everything and threw it all away."

"His loss."

"Definitely. Did you ever talk to your dad about the woman who came to the marina today?"

"I didn't get a chance to with so many people around. I'll ask him about it in the morning. I'm sure it's nothing, or he would've told me." He glanced over at her. "So I had this absolutely brilliant beyond brilliant idea today that I wanted to run by you."

"I can hardly wait to hear this."

"Ned was grousing this morning about how Seamus and Carolina stole their idea."

"Stole their idea?"

"Apparently, he and your mom were planning to pull off a secret wedding disguised as a cookout."

"Seriously? They were going to do that, too?"

"Yep, and he's all bummed out because he really wants to be married to your mother, and it's almost impossible to find a time when there isn't something else going on. Then Grant showed up and announced that he and Steph are getting married on Labor Day. That really set Ned off."

"I'm so glad Grant and Steph finally set a date. I was starting to worry about that."

"So was he."

"So what's your brilliant idea?"

"Let's give *them* a surprise wedding."

"You want to surprise them with a wedding."

"Yes."

"Mac, when we got married, what exactly did you do to help plan the wedding?"

He thought about that for a moment. "I bought the house where we had the wedding."

"*And*?"

"And I um... Well... I ah... I got married?"

"Exactly," she said with a laugh. "You don't have the first clue as to what it takes to plan a wedding, which is why you think this is such a brilliant idea."

"How hard can it be? We can do it at our place. We need food and flowers and music. We invite everyone over for a party, and Uncle Frank marries them. Voilà. Done."

"What about a license and rings?"

"Huh... Um, we can do that for them, can't we?"

"As I recall, there're signatures involved."

"Come on, Maddie. There's got to be a way. I'll talk to Uncle Frank about how we get around the license thing. Will you talk to Tiffany to see if she approves of this and if she'll help us? You two know what your mother would like. Let's just do it."

"It's a nice idea. I'll give you that."

"It's a *brilliant* idea."

"Whatever you say, dear."

Mac pulled into Grace's pharmacy and turned off the truck.

"What do we need here?"

"I'll tell you after I get it." He left her with a kiss. "Be right back." Mac went into the store and straight to the condom aisle in the back, which had been in the same place since he was a horny teenager on Gansett. Back then, the Golds had owned the store that now belonged to his future sister-in-law, Grace, who was fortunately not working tonight. In fact, he didn't see anyone he knew. Thank God for small favors.

Grimacing, he grabbed an economy box of the extra-large ones, and then, laughing to himself, he got a box of the small ones, too, and went up to pay for them. "Could I get two bags please?"

"Sure," the teenage girl at the register said, blushing to the roots of her hair when she realized what he was buying.

Even as a married man of thirty-seven with two kids and a third on the way, this transaction never got any less embarrassing. "Thanks."

He walked out of the store with his bags and got back in the truck.

"What'd you get?" Maddie reached for the bags before he could explain. "Something you want to tell me?" she asked with that arched brow of hers.

"They're for Janey. And Joe."

"Huh?"

"She's getting me back for what I did to her when we were dating."

That set Maddie off into fits of giggles that had him laughing at her delight. "Oh my God, I love that! Good for her!"

"Good for her? You can't be on her side and be married to me, too."

"What're you going to do? Divorce me?"

"I just might."

"Oh hush. You couldn't live without me. Why two bags?"

"Look at the sizes."

Maddie examined the boxes and then burst out laughing again. "What're you up to?"

"She told me to get the extra-large ones. You'll see."

CHAPTER 19

Mac drove to his sister's house, which was located close to theirs. P.J. had been fussy earlier, so they'd decided to skip the party. Since Mac had texted Janey to tell her they were on the way over, the outside lights were on for them. At the front door, Mac knocked quietly, not wanting to wake a sleeping baby.

"Funny how you never would've thought to knock softly a few years ago," Maddie said.

"I'm fully domesticated now."

"Not fully, but I haven't given up yet."

"You're full of beans tonight, Mrs. McCarthy. You'll be made to pay for that later."

"Oh I do so love your threats, Mac," she said, patting his backside. "You know I do."

"Keep that up and this is going to be a very quick visit."

"Based on what you're bringing them, I think they have other plans for tonight anyway."

"Ewww. Don't remind me." He opened the front door and poked his head in. "Brat," he said in a loud whisper.

"Just go in."

"No way. Not when there's a chance they're in there 'getting back to normal.'"

"For crying out loud." Maddie pushed past him and walked straight into his sister's house.

Hesitant to stumble upon anything that would leave permanent scars on his psyche, he followed behind her, taking the coward's way out. He was fine with that. They found Joe and Janey in the screened-in porch, where they spent most of their time since they bought the house in the spring. P.J. was asleep in a rolling bassinette next to the sofa.

"There you are!" Janey said, getting up to grab the bag from him as her pets circled around their feet, wanting in on the excitement. "I thought you'd never get here."

"Don't look at me," Joe said with a grin. "This was all her idea."

"I have no doubt about that," Mac said to his oldest and closest friend, who was now his brother-in-law. He liked how that had worked out, except for times like this, when he was reminded that his oldest and best friend was now legally allowed to have *sex* with Mac's baby sister. Ugh.

"Look at him," Joe said, laughing at Mac. "He's all in a tizzy."

"You would be, too, if you got called in on a mission like this one."

"Turnabout is fair play." Janey looked into the bag and then at him. "You only got the small box of *three*? That's barely enough for tonight."

Joe took the box from her. "Extra small? Seriously?"

"That's what she told me to get," Mac said.

"I did not! I said extra *large*, you ass hat."

Behind her hand, Maddie snorted inelegantly.

"So you're saying those won't work?" Mac asked, enjoying this far more than he'd expected to.

"They definitely won't fit," Joe said with predictable male ego.

Mac pulled the second bag from behind his back and tossed it at them.

Joe caught it in the air and peered inside. "Ahhh, much better. Extra large and lots of them. Too bad you've got to go now, Mac."

"Yeah, you're welcome. No problem. Anything else I can do for you? Wait.

Never mind. Forget I asked that." He'd learned not to challenge Janey when she was feeling vindictive.

"You think you're pretty damned funny, don't you?" Janey asked. "Bringing extra smalls."

"Those are for P.J.'s sock drawer," Mac said. "Never too early to be prepared."

"Get out," Janey said with a growl. "*Now.*"

He kissed her cheek. "Love you, too, brat. Go easy on poor Joe. He's out of practice. Things might happen *quickly.*"

Joe took him by the arm and escorted him to the front door. "Sorry to throw you out of my house, Maddie, but that's what you get for marrying him."

"I understand," Maddie said dramatically. "I want to throw him out of my house sometimes, too."

"You do not," Mac said. "You're always like, '*More*, Mac, *harder*, Mac, no, *there*, Mac…'"

"I'm going to kill you when I get you home."

"She doesn't mean that," he said over his shoulder to Joe and Janey, who were laughing in the doorway.

"Yes, she does!" Maddie said. "You call her brat, but no one is a bigger brat than you are."

He held the car door for her and then leaned in to kiss her. "You love me. Admit it."

"Yes, Mac," she said with a long-suffering sigh. "I do love you."

"And the extra-small thing was pretty funny. Admit it."

"I'll do no such thing. I refuse to encourage you."

"You'll be encouraging me, all right. In about thirty minutes if it takes that long. '*Harder, Mac, oh thereeeeee.*'" The kids were spending the night with Ned and Francine, and he had big plans for his wife tonight.

She pulled his hair. "Shut up and drive before you find yourself sleeping alone on the deck tonight."

He grinned at her and stole another kiss before he walked around the truck, whistling as he went. "You're only mad because you know I'm right," he said as they pulled out of Janey's driveway.

"Mac, I swear to God, if you don't stop talking and drive this car, I'm not going to be responsible for my actions."

Thrilled with her and everything about their life together, he did as she directed. But he'd have her screaming his name in thirty minutes flat or his name wasn't Malcolm John McCarthy Junior.

*

"Upstairs," Joe said to his wife the second he closed the door behind Mac and Maddie.

"It's only five thirty," Janey reminded him.

"So?"

She crossed her arms as she took a long look at him. "Do I have time to retrieve my baby from the patio before you drag me upstairs?"

Joe held up his hand to tell her to stay put and went to get the baby. "I've got to say," he said as he carried the bassinette upstairs, his eyes trained to the gentle sway of his wife's rear end as she went up ahead of him. Their pets followed dutifully behind and took to their beds, seeming to know what was about to happen and taking shelter. "I honestly didn't think Mac would do it."

"I knew he would. I gave him no choice in the matter."

"You're a rare and special woman, Janey Cantrell."

"And don't you forget it."

"As if I ever could." Joe put the bassinette down in the corner of the bedroom, not next to the bed where Janey preferred it.

"That's too far away."

"No, it isn't."

"Joe..."

"Shhhh." He put his arms around her and quieted her with a kiss. "All day, you've been walking around with those yoga pants on, flaunting your cute little ass, bending over to tend to the baby, taunting me..." He cupped her buttocks and squeezed for emphasis. "I can't wait any longer to have you, Janey."

She looked up at him with the bottomless blue eyes he adored. "Is everything in working order?"

"Why don't you check for yourself?" After last night's disaster, he'd been a walking, talking hard-on all day.

"Oh my," she whispered, giving him a thorough examination that had his head rolling back on his shoulders. "That feels like it might hurt."

"It aches. For you." The time for fooling around was over. The time for action was right now. He all but ripped the tank top off her body, leaving her naked from the waist up.

"Wait! I need a shower! I smell like sour milk and baby puke."

"No shower. No delays. Only this." He ground his hard cock against her belly, needing relief and needing it right now.

"Joe... Seriously."

"I'm dead serious. Right now, Janey." He cupped her breasts and bent his head to tongue her nipple.

"Um, you might not want to do that..."

"You love when I do that."

"Normally, yes, but they don't belong just to us right now. I might leak, and that'll be kind of gross."

"You think I'd find that gross? No way. I think it's incredible."

"You won't think so when it's all over you."

"I don't care about that, Janey."

"I do," she said, sounding miserable, and he couldn't have that.

He laid her back on the bed. "Don't worry about anything. Just let me love you. I'm dying for you."

Sighing, she stretched her arms over her head, which made her breasts thrust upward. Everything she did turned him on, and that was no exception. He kissed her everywhere, giving special attention to the stretch marks that marred her otherwise flawless skin. "Don't look at them."

"Hush. Close your eyes and relax. Let me have my fun." As he spoke, he removed her yoga pants and panties and then quickly shed his own clothes.

"You have an odd sense of fun."

"Any time I get to touch any part of you, I'm happy."

"My body is different than it was."

"It's better. You're a goddess." His words were whispered in a husky voice as he nibbled her hipbone and gently kissed the pink line of her cesarean scar, making her squirm beneath him. "My goddess. This body gave me my son, and it'll never be anything other than perfect to me."

She reached for him, pulling at him to come up to her.

"I wasn't done down there," he said, smiling at her.

"I need you. Now."

"What'd you do with those condoms your brother was good enough to get for us?"

"Bedside table. Hurry."

Joe moved quickly to suit up and returned to her, loving the way she wrapped her arms and legs around him. "Tell me if anything hurts?"

"Nothing hurts, I promise."

He entered her slowly, watching her closely for any sign of distress, but all he saw was the smile that occupied her lips.

"Feels so amazing," she whispered. "I've missed you—and this."

"Me, too, honey. You have no idea…"

"I think I have a teeny tiny idea." She combed her fingers through his hair and met his every stroke with the upward thrust of her hips. "Let's turn over."

"Not this time. That's too much for you."

"No, it's not. Please? I know how much you love that."

He could deny her nothing when she asked him that way, so he grasped her bottom and turned them so she was on top. "I wish you could see what I see when

I look at you." Her hair had gotten long—so long it nearly covered her breasts. Her nipples peeked out from between the strands, and her kiss-swollen lips were pouty as she rode him slowly but intently. "So hot, Janey."

She started to say something, but her face twisted in distress. "Oh crap."

"What? Does it hurt?"

"No… My breasts are tingling—and not in a good way, at least not for this."

"Any way is a good way." He reached up to cup breasts that were much bigger than usual, running his thumbs over the moisture that gathered at the tips. If the clamp of her internal muscles around his cock was any indication, it turned her on when he did that. So he did it again.

Her head fell back as she groaned and picked up the pace of her hips.

Joe pinched her nipples between his fingers, making her cry out.

"Shhh, don't wake him up."

"You made me forget he was here," she said with a choppy, breathless laugh. "I didn't think that was possible."

Knowing they were on borrowed time where P.J. was concerned, Joe decided to move things along. He banded an arm around her waist and turned them over, taking control once again.

"Speaking of hot," she said breathlessly.

"You liked that, huh?"

"I like it all, Joe. Any time we get to be together like this…"

"I love you so much," he whispered against her lips as he reached between them to coax her. It didn't take much to get her there, and he'd been primed all day. They came together, clinging to each other, and he drowned out her cries with hot, openmouthed kisses that had him ready for round two before round one was even over.

Despite their efforts to be quiet, they'd failed miserably, so Joe wasn't surprised when P.J. woke with a squawk of protest at having been so rudely disturbed. Joe laughed even as he continued to pulse with aftershocks.

"Game off," Janey said.

Joe withdrew from her to let her up. "At least our boy has good timing."

"I hope we didn't permanently traumatize him."

"Nah." Joe lay on his side, his head propped on his upturned hand, enjoying the sight of her walking across the room naked to bend over P.J.'s bassinette.

"Are you hungry, my love?" she asked the baby as she picked him up and carried him to the bed. It had taken weeks for her to recover to the point where she was allowed to pick him up, and now she did it every chance she got. She sat against a pile of pillows on the bed and guided the baby to her breast.

Joe watched her every move, consumed with love for her and the son she'd given him.

"What?" she asked when she caught him staring at her.

"You… You're just…" There were, he discovered, no words adequate enough to describe this kind of love. "Mine. All mine. And nothing has ever made me happier."

She smiled at him, her eyes bright with emotion. "Me, too, Joseph."

*

"He's so perfect, isn't he?" Sarah asked Charlie as they watched Holden sleep on the sofa next to them.

"He's beautiful, all right."

"It's funny… Of course I know Owen isn't his biological father, but that doesn't make me feel any less like a grandmother than I would if he had fathered him. That's weird, right?" Sarah had loved watching Charlie play with the baby earlier. He'd been right down on the floor with Holden and his toys until the baby began fussing and rubbing his eyes.

"Nah. I get it. I'm not Steph's real father, but I'm the only one she's ever had and she's the only kid I've ever had. Biology doesn't matter when you love someone." He brought her hand to his lips and kissed a line across her knuckles. "She asked me to give her away at her wedding."

"Oh, Charlie. That's wonderful! I'm so happy for you—for both of you."

"You know," he said tentatively, "after all this business with the trial is over and your divorce is final… I mean, it's probably way too soon and all, but really, when you think about it, we've been together a while now. Ah geez, I'm making a mess out of this."

She turned to face him, surprised to see his normally relaxed expression twisted with unusual tension. "Making a mess out of what?"

"Afterward, when you're free… I hope you might consider… Well, I'd like to marry you, Sarah. I'd like to live with you and wake up with you every day. I'd like for your family to be my family and for my daughter to be your daughter. Would you, I mean, down the road when you're ready… Do you think you might want to—"

Laughing and crying, she kissed him. "Yes, Charlie, I will want all of that."

"You would? Really?"

"Yes, of course I would. The time I've spent with you has been the happiest time I've ever spent with a man. Until I met you, I didn't even know there were men like you out there. I was so accustomed to a whole other kind of man."

"You'll never have to worry about anything like that again. Not as long as I'm still drawing a breath."

His fierce assurances were nearly as endearing as his bumbling proposal. "Does this mean we're engaged?"

"This means we're pre-engaged," Sarah said. "Let me get past the trial and get the divorce finalized. Then we can talk about it again."

He put his arm around her and drew her into another kiss.

Sarah was amazed by how quickly she'd gotten over her hesitancy to be touched by him. In only a few days, she'd become addicted to his kisses and the way he held her. He made her feel safe and protected and desired and loved, all things that were so new to her. Her only other romantic relationship had been violent and unpredictable, so being with Charlie was a revelation in every possible way.

When he began to pull back from her, she curled her hand around his nape, keeping him from getting away. He looked at her for a moment before he continued the kiss, this time running his tongue over her lower lip.

Her mouth opened to his tongue, and Sarah pressed against him shamelessly as the need took over and every thought fled her mind except for one—she wanted him. Their kisses had become more heated over the last few days, and the desire had grown to the point where it couldn't be denied any longer. In bed the night before, they'd kissed until her lips were numb and swollen, but he hadn't pushed her for anything more.

Sarah didn't know if she could handle another night that began and ended with kissing, but she lacked the ability to come right out and tell him what she wanted. She knew he was being careful with her because of her past, and she loved him for that, but she wanted much more of the edgy, needy way he made her feel.

"Charlie," she gasped as she broke the kiss.

"What, honey?"

"We shouldn't do this in front of the baby."

Laughing, he nuzzled her neck, firing her senses with kisses and nibbles to the sensitive skin there. "He's asleep, and I doubt he'd remember even if he was awake."

"Still…"

Sighing, Charlie withdrew from her, holding up his hands in surrender.

Sarah rested her head on the back of the sofa and took a good long look at the man she loved. His cheekbones were slashed with color, and his eyes were heavy with arousal and desire. The lips she loved to kiss were slightly swollen and still damp. Sarah zeroed in on his mouth and licked her lips.

"Sarah," he said with a groan. "Don't look at me that way if you're going to tell me I can't kiss you in front of the baby."

"What way am I looking at you?"

"Like you want to have your wicked way with me."

Though she was embarrassed to realize she was so transparent, she summoned the courage to tell him the truth. "I do want that."

He seemed to stop breathing for a second. "What? What do you want?"

"You, Charlie. I want you. I want more than just kissing. I want everything."

Releasing a deep breath, he studied her in that thoughtful, intense way of his.

"Say something, will you? Don't leave me hanging out here all by myself."

"You are certainly not out there all by yourself, but you need to be sure you're ready, honey. You've been through a lot, and I'd hate to do anything to set you back or upset you."

"You wouldn't. You couldn't. Everything about this, about us, is different. I'm not afraid of you, Charlie, and you don't need to worry about me. I'm okay. I really am. Except for the fact that all I can think about is you and kissing you and touching you…"

His groan echoed through his chest as he put his head back against the sofa and closed his eyes. "That's all I've thought about for months—kissing you and touching you. I was so hoping you'd let me someday."

Sarah's cellphone chimed with a text from Owen. *Back from the party. Want us to come pick up Holden?* "Owen and Laura are offering to come pick him up," Sarah said.

"Why don't you let them come get him, and then you can stay here with me? If you want to, that is."

"I want to." She replied to Owen, letting him know it would be fine if they wanted to come get Holden.

Be there shortly, Owen replied. *Thanks again for watching him.*

Loved every minute of it.

"They'll be here soon," Sarah said, resting her head on Charlie's shoulder.

"And then what?"

"Then we'll have all night to spend together, if that's okay."

"Yes, Sarah," Charlie said with a laugh, "that's more than okay."

CHAPTER 20

As the clock ticked closer to six, Linda's nerves became more frayed. How did one greet the child of one's husband? The child neither of them had known about until a few hours ago? What would she say to her? How would her presence threaten the family Linda treasured above all else? Not to mention the marriage that was the center of her life.

Her husband was everything to her, and she'd always tried to give him the support and encouragement he deserved. From the very beginning of their relationship, she'd embraced his desire to build a business and a life on the remote island they called home. And it had been a good life, the very best life she could've ever hoped for. She would do anything to hold on to that, which was why she'd encouraged him to invite Mallory to dinner.

Even knowing she'd done the right thing for her husband, that didn't mean she wasn't nervous and worried about what would happen when their children found out they had another sister. She couldn't begin to guess how they might react. She suspected Mac would be put out to learn he was no longer the oldest, and Janey might have something to say about another girl in the family.

Her husband came into the kitchen, looking handsome in the clothes he'd worn to the engagement party. "Can I do anything to help?"

"You never help in the kitchen."

"That doesn't mean I'm not willing to, especially tonight."

He was hard to resist most of the time, but never more so than when he was being sweet. "I'm nervous, Mac. I don't want to be, but I can't help it. It scares me to think of someone coming into our family and changing things. I hate myself for even saying that—"

"Shh, honey." His arms encircled her from behind, and his lips brushed against her neck. "It's okay to be nervous. I am, too. But she's really nice and made a point of telling me she's not looking for anything from me—or us. She just wanted to meet me. Anything else that happens from this point on is up to us, and we'll decide the next steps together. Okay?"

She relaxed against him, buffeted by his assurances as well as the way he wrapped her up in his love. Turning, she looked up at the face she'd loved for so long, she could no longer remember her life before Mac McCarthy had changed everything. As always, he looked down at her with love in his eyes.

"You have nothing at all to worry about. This doesn't change anything between us. It doesn't change anything that really matters. Perhaps, maybe... It might give us one more person to love in this world. And that wouldn't be so bad, would it?"

When he put it like that, it wasn't so bad at all. "No, it wouldn't."

"All I'm asking is that you meet her and make her feel welcome here."

"I can do that."

"I know you can, honey. And I want you to know I appreciate it. I appreciate the way you reacted earlier and that you invited her into our home. You're doing that for me, and don't think I can't see that."

"I'd do anything for you, Mac. You know that."

"And vice versa. That's what's made us work so well for so long. But I'm asking a lot of you this time." When his phone rang, he checked the caller ID and saw it was Adam. He put the call on speaker so Linda could hear, too. "Hey, bud. What's up?"

"I have some news for you. Is Mom around?"

"We're both here, and the phone is on speaker."

"Hi, honey," Linda said.

"Hey, Mom."

"What's your news?"

"Since I'd never want to be accused of pulling a Grant, I wanted you to be the first to know that Abby and I are engaged."

"Oh, Adam!" Linda said. "That's wonderful! Congratulations to both of you."

"Thanks, we're excited."

"When did this happen? We just saw you a little while ago."

"I popped the question on the way home."

"So it was totally spontaneous?" Mac asked with a smile for her. She knew he was just as thrilled as she was to see their kids settling down with mates who were perfect for each of them. Not that long ago, Linda had worried that none of their sons would ever marry, and now one was married and three were engaged.

"Not totally. I've had the ring for a while and was waiting for the right moment."

"Abby must've been thrilled."

"She cried, so I guess that's a good thing."

Linda rested her hand on her heart, moved at the thought of the young woman she adored crying over her son. "I'm so happy for you both, Adam. Thanks for calling us."

"Make sure you tell Grant that you were the first to know."

"I'll do that," Linda said with a laugh. Her kids were incredibly close but still enjoyed one-upping each other every chance they got.

"Congrats, pal," Mac said. "We love you both and can't wait to dance at the wedding."

"We can't wait either. Love you guys, and I'll talk to you tomorrow."

"Bye, honey." To her husband, Linda said, "What wonderful news!"

"The best news. They're great together."

"I was afraid they'd never get around to getting married since they moved in together."

"He told me a while ago that he'd been thinking about it."

"And you never said a word to me?"

"Private conversation with my son, babe."

"Private..." She attempted a scowl that probably failed because she was too happy with Adam's news to be mad. "You still should've told me."

The doorbell rang, and they both went still, looking to each other for reassurance. He bent his head to kiss her. "I love you. Everything is fine. All right?"

"Yes. I love you, too."

With his hand on her lower back, they walked to the entryway to welcome their guest.

Mallory wore a pretty summer dress and carried a bottle of wine. As Mac had said, she was tall and striking with dark hair that fell in curls to her shoulders and pretty brown eyes. Though their coloring was completely opposite, Linda saw a hint of Janey in her and could see the distinctive resemblance to her late mother-in-law that Mac had mentioned.

"Come in," Mac said. "This is my wife, Linda. Linda, Mallory Vaughn."

"It's nice to meet you," Mallory said, extending her hand to Linda.

"Yes, nice to meet you, too."

"It's okay if you don't really mean that."

The humorous comment, delivered with a warm smile, had Linda thinking of her own kids, who might've said something similar. "I do mean it," Linda said, earning a pat on the back from her husband. "We're happy to have you. Come in."

Mac led the way to the kitchen with Mallory following him and Linda bringing up the rear. Passing the framed photos of their five children on the wall, Mallory stopped.

"These are your kids."

"Yes," Linda said. "That's Mac, Grant, Adam, Evan and Janey. And that's everyone—with one husband, one wife, three fiancées—as of today—and three grandchildren."

"You have a beautiful family," Mallory said wistfully.

"Thank you. Our family is growing in leaps and bounds. Adam and Abby just told us they're engaged."

"Congratulations."

"Would you like to see some other pictures?"

"I'd love to."

While the lasagna she'd taken from the freezer finished baking, Mac opened the bottle of wine Mallory had brought and poured glasses for both women and got a beer for himself. In the family room, Linda pulled out recent albums to show Mallory pictures of Mac, Maddie, Thomas and Hailey as well as Janey, Joe and P.J., Evan and Grace, Adam and Abby and Grant and Stephanie.

"They're all coupled up."

"They are—finally. For the longest time, I thought none of them would ever settle down and get married, and now all of them are. Grant and Steph told us earlier today that they're getting married on Labor Day."

"That's very exciting."

"Are you married?" Linda asked and then regretted the question as possibly too personal."

"Not anymore."

"Oh, I'm sorry."

"I'm better off. Believe me."

Though she'd love to know what that meant, Linda didn't want to pry. "Well, you must be hungry."

"Linda... I just want to say... Thank you for having me here and for being so nice to me. I know this had to come as a shock to both of you, and I have no desire to mess up anything for you or your family." She glanced at Mac. "I just wanted to meet you."

"I'm very glad you came," he said. "I'm only sorry your mother didn't tell me about you sooner. I would've liked to have known you."

"I hope you aren't angry about what she did, although I suppose you have every right to be."

"I don't want to be angry with her," Mac said thoughtfully. "But I'm disappointed she didn't come to me when she found out she was expecting you. I would've liked to be part of your life, and I never would've tried to take you away from her. I wish she'd trusted me a little more."

"I do, too. I've spent most of my life wondering about you."

"Did she ever talk to you about him?" Linda asked.

Mallory shook her head. "She was very vague on the subject of my father even after I was an adult and there was no chance I could be taken from her. That's why it was such a surprise to find the letter about you among her things after she died."

"We can't make up for the time we've lost," Mac said, "but I sure hope you'll let me be a part of your life going forward. I'd really like to be."

"Oh… You would?"

He nodded. "I absolutely would."

"I expected you to ask me for proof, and I wouldn't be opposed… If, you know, you wanted…"

"I don't need proof." Mac got up and went to his study off the den, returning a minute later with a framed photograph. Linda knew exactly which one it was. "This was my mother as a young woman." He handed the frame to Mallory, who gasped and then covered her mouth as tears filled her eyes.

"Oh my God."

"I know," Mac said, "right? The proof is in the DNA."

Mallory ran her finger over the image of her grandmother. "This is unbelievable. I always thought I looked like my mother."

"You do. I can definitely see her in you."

"This is so amazing," Mallory said, still staring at the photo. "To fill in these blanks… It's so priceless to me."

"I'm glad we were able to do that for you," Mac said. "We'll fill in a few more when you meet the rest of the family."

"What do you think they'll say when they hear they have a half sister?"

Mac looked to Linda to answer for him. "If I had to guess," Linda said, "they'll be surprised, of course, but Mac will be rattled to hear he's not the oldest, and

Janey will be a little disturbed to learn she's not the only girl. If I know my kids, though, they'll be welcoming and friendly, if a little hesitant at first."

"Which is certainly understandable."

"I'd like for you to meet them while you're here," Mac said. "We don't keep secrets from them, so I'd rather do it sooner than later. Mac is already aware that something's up. He knows me very well and could tell I was rattled after we spoke this morning. Would you be willing to meet them before you head home tomorrow?"

"Sure. I'd like that."

"Okay, then," Mac said. "We'll tell them to come by at ten. Perhaps you could come a little later so we have a chance to speak to them first?"

"Of course."

"Great," Mac said with a big smile for both women. "Now that we've got all the business out of the way, I'm ready for lasagna. Wait until you taste Linda's lasagna."

"I'm looking forward to it," Mallory said.

As she realized that Mallory was a nice person who wasn't out to destroy her family, Linda felt herself relax. Tomorrow they would tell their children about Mallory and then figure out their next steps as a family. Though slightly apprehensive about how the kids might take the news, she decided not to get too far ahead of herself. They'd find out soon enough.

*

David finished stitching up the gash in Dan's palm and applied a bandage that covered most of his hand. "Keep it clean and dry for the next couple of days," he said. "I'll write you a script for pain meds."

"No need," Dan said. "I've got stuff left over from the earlier disaster."

"Come back on Friday to get the stitches out."

"Got it. Can I go?"

"What's the status of your tetanus shot?"

"I've had one."

"How long ago?"

"I don't know."

"Since we have no idea what was on that knife or how clean it was, I recommend a tetanus shot and a dose of antibiotic, too."

"Fine, whatever you say, Doc. Let's just get it over with."

"You're in an awful rush, Counselor. You're giving me a complex."

"Nothing personal, but I've got plans with my lady. And besides, I'm sure you've got better things to be doing on a Sunday afternoon than stitching me up."

"Not to worry," David said. "Part of the job. Be right back."

Kara came into the cubicle with a can of Coke that she handed over to him. He'd sent her to get it so she wouldn't be in the room while David stitched him up. She was upset enough without having to see that.

"Come hold my hand while David sticks more needles in me." The shots to numb his palm had been so painful he'd nearly passed out. The thought of more shots made him queasy and sweaty.

Kara came to sit next to him on the hospital bed, reaching for his uninjured hand.

David returned with two syringes and administered two more shots that burned like a bastard on the way in. "There you go," he said, adding for Kara's sake, "Keep it clean and dry."

"We hate it clean and dry," Dan said, earning an embarrassed scowl from his fiancée.

"Yeah, he's fine," David said with a laugh. "Get out of here so I can go home."

"Thanks again, David."

"No problem. Let me know if you have any problems or if it gets especially red or swollen."

"Will do."

As they left the clinic, Dan dropped his arm over Kara's shoulders. "Do you have my keys?"

"Yes."

"Can I have them?"

"You're not driving."

"Yes, I am."

"No, you're not."

"Baby, I'm fine. I swear."

"You just had thirty stitches in the palm of your right hand. How do you propose to drive a stick shift?"

"My fingers are still working fine," he said, waggling his brows as he demonstrated his manual dexterity.

"Everything is a joke to you, isn't it?"

Seeing that she was on the verge of tears, he stopped walking and turned to her. "Not everything. I got us a room at the Summer House. I was going to surprise you after the party."

She leaned her head against his chest.

He ran the fingers on his uninjured hand through her silky hair.

"I hate that you got hurt again."

"I'm really fine. I promise." He caressed the nape of her neck, one of his favorite places to kiss. "Will you come with me to the Summer House and spend the night with me so we can celebrate our engagement properly?"

"Haven't we already done that at least a hundred times since we got engaged?"

He laughed at her reply. He loved her saucy mouth. "Baby, I've only begun to celebrate our engagement. I plan to celebrate it as much and as often as I can for the rest of our lives." With his fingers under her chin, he urged her to look at him. "Are we good?"

"We're great."

"Then will you please take me to the Summer House and have your wicked way with me?"

"Since you asked so nicely, yes, I will."

"Excellent."

CHAPTER 21

Adam had forgotten the hideous pain of getting a tattoo. The first time, he'd had an image of Gansett inked onto his bicep and had nearly cried like a baby from the pain. Like then, Abby sat in the next chair looking blissed out as her favorite tattoo guy, Jeff, inked their engagement date onto her inner wrist while Duke did the same to him.

"You're looking a little pasty, dude," Duke said. "You're not gonna puke or anything, are you?"

"No," Adam said through gritted teeth, "I'm not going to puke."

"Are you okay?" Abby asked him.

"I'm fine." He'd be even better when Duke finished torturing him and he could get the fuck out of there. And then it occurred to him that he'd already agreed to undergo this torture again when they added their wedding date to the other arm. *Ugh.*

Forty-five minutes later, they emerged into twilight as the horn of a departing ferry pierced the peaceful evening.

"I love Sunday nights when all the weekend people are gone," Abby said, "and things calm down for a brief moment before it all starts up again tomorrow."

He took hold of her hand as they walked along the sidewalk, and he tried to ignore the throbbing pain coming from his left wrist. "My dad has always loved

Sundays at the marina for that same reason. People leave on Sunday, the place clears out, and he gets it back for a short time before another influx arrives."

"Thanks for doing that just now," she said with a sweet smile that made all the pain worthwhile. "I know you don't enjoy it as much as I do, so I appreciate it."

"I enjoy watching you get all blissed out. Reminds me of when you—"

Her face turned beet red, which he loved. "Don't say it. Not out here where anyone can hear."

He dropped her hand and put his arm around her. Leaning in close to her, he pressed his lips to her ear and said, "It's just like when you come."

"Adam… Stop it."

"Why? We're engaged now. I should be able to speak freely about these things."

"What does being engaged have to do with it? You've always spoken freely about 'these things.'"

"Don't pretend you don't love it when I talk dirty to you."

"I don't love it when we're in public."

"So you do love it in private. Good to know."

Abby elbowed him in the ribs, making him grunt and then laugh. His girl was such a lady most of the time, but he particularly loved when she let loose with a four-letter word or got bossy with him in bed. He knew he was provoking her, but that usually led to good things with Abby.

His phone buzzed with a text from his mother. *Please come by tomorrow around ten. Your father and I would like to speak to you all about something—nothing bad, so don't worry. Please come by yourselves, if you don't mind. See you then!*

Adam shared the text with Abby. "What do you suppose that's about?"

"I have no idea, but I'm glad she said it was nothing bad."

"Me, too."

"I guess you'll find out in the morning."

They arrived home a short time later at the house they rented from his sister. Predictably, Abby tugged a house key from her bra, also known as her storage bin. How she managed to fit anything else in there around her perfectly awesome breasts was beyond him, but he'd learned not to ask questions where the bra was concerned.

She turned to say something to him, and he pounced. He'd been dying to touch her and kiss her since the second she said yes to his proposal. He'd sat through the torture of the tattoo, all the while biding his time until he could get her alone. With his hands on her hips and his mouth devouring hers, he walked her backward to their bedroom. When the backs of her legs connected with the mattress, he gave her a nudge, propelling her onto the bed. He came down on top of her without missing a beat in the kiss.

Her arms wrapped around his neck, and her legs parted to make room for him. Both these things happened so organically, so naturally that he knew a moment of pure contentment at having found the woman he was meant to be with. He only broke the kiss when he needed to breathe. "Are you really going to marry me?"

"I really am. Are you really going to marry me?"

"You bet your life I am. Who else would have me?"

"That is true…" Her smile lit up her eyes, and a surge of love left him breathless. She reached up with both hands to touch his face, and he turned his lips to kiss her left palm, just above her new tattoo. "What're you thinking?"

"That I can't believe how lucky I was to end up on the ferry with you when you were ranting about how sick of men you were."

"Don't mention that. It still embarrasses me to think about how out of control I was that day."

"How can I not mention it when you being out of control brought us together? Besides," he said, kissing her again, "I love you best when you're out of control."

"You're a very bad influence on me."

"Now that is just not true." With dexterity that she often teased him about, he divested her of the dress she'd worn to the party, quickly followed by her bra.

"You must've had a lot of practice to be so good at that," she said as she always did.

"Shut up and kiss me."

She did as he requested, her sweetness and enthusiasm sending his need into the red zone after about thirty seconds of slick lips sliding over his while her tongue teased and tempted. "Adam?" she asked after long moments of silence.

"Hmm?" He was now focused on her neck.

"I want to get married soon. I don't want a long engagement."

He raised his head to look into her eyes. "That's fine. Whatever you want." He was on his way back to her neck when her fingers on his chin stopped him.

"I want something else, too."

"What do you want, honey? I'd give you anything. You know that."

"A baby," she said softly. "I want so badly to be a mother."

"Then we'll have a baby," he said as if it wasn't the biggest thing he'd ever committed to in his life. Committing to having a child with her didn't feel like the overwhelming notion it might've been with anyone else.

"Really? You mean it?"

"Yes, I mean it. I want kids, too. You know I do."

"But do you want them now?"

"I want what you want. Now, later… Doesn't matter to me, as long as you're happy." When her eyes filled with tears, he leaned in to kiss her tears away. "Why the tears?"

"I'm so happy. This is what I've wanted all along, and as hard as I tried, I just couldn't seem to find *this.*"

"That's because you weren't looking for it with me."

"Please tell me you're not going to suddenly go crazy and lose your mind and tell me this isn't what you want after all. Because I don't think I'd ever get over it if that happened with you."

"I'm not going to do that, Abs. How could I when I can't possibly live without you?" As he spoke, he began to press against her, letting her know what he wanted so badly he burned with it. Thankfully, she got the message and began tugging on his button and zipper.

Sliding her hands into the back of his pants, she pushed them down and over his hips, her obvious haste fueling his desire. He loved how much she always wanted him and how she responded to him the way she never had to anyone else.

Adam left her only long enough to shed his clothes and remove the tiny scrap of fabric she called panties. He absolutely adored her sexy-underwear fetish and encouraged it with frequent gift certificates to Tiffany's shop that she put to good use. But he liked her best in nothing at all, like now when she was spread out before him like an erotic buffet.

With her, he'd found a partner who understood him better than anyone ever had. In turn, he'd helped to unlock the secrets to her sensuality, and he reaped the benefits of that effort every day.

"Adam… I want you. Right now."

They'd come a long way from the days when she'd required a lot of foreplay to get to the finish line. As much as he loved every second of that foreplay, he was in just as much of a rush tonight. Since he was dying to be inside her, he took what she offered so freely, sliding into her in one deep thrust that nearly finished him right off. He was still for a moment, trying to regain control as she tightened around him and her breasts brushed against his chest.

"What's wrong?" she asked, unaccustomed to his unusual restraint.

"Nothing." He trembled from the effort to hold back the orgasm that wanted out right now.

"Adam…" She put her arms around him and brought him down into her embrace, her legs encircling his hips at the same time. Completely surrounded by her softness, her alluring scent and the tight heat of her wrapped around his cock, he gave up the fight and let go, feeling like a teenager who was getting laid for the first time.

"Sorry," he muttered.

"For what?"

"That was over fast. You didn't get there."

"So what? I owe you about five hundred orgasms."

He laughed. "I didn't know we were keeping score."

"We're not. That's why it doesn't matter."

"Yes, it does matter. You went without for too long. There's no way you're leaving this bed until you've had at least two."

"That's really not necessary, Adam. This was more than enough for me."

"It wasn't enough for me. I'm left unfulfilled by your unfulfillment."

"That isn't a word."

"It is now." He withdrew from her and began to kiss his way down the front of her, hitting all the places that made her crazy. "Now be quiet and let me have my fun."

"If you insist," she said with a sigh of pleasure.

"I do. I most definitely insist."

*

After receiving the cryptic message from his mother, Mac had slept like shit. He'd known something was up since the day before, when that woman showed up at the docks and said something that left his father upset. Between his dad disappearing from the marina right after the woman left and the engagement party for Dan and Kara, Mac hadn't had a chance to corner his dad for answers.

He'd driven Maddie crazy speculating as to what was going on and why his parents wanted to speak with him and his siblings without their partners present.

"They said it was nothing bad," Maddie had said between yawns as midnight became one a.m. "You should try to relax and not worry."

Right. Relax and not worry. Too bad he wasn't wired that way, which his wife knew all too well. In the last couple of years, his dad had suffered a terrible head injury, Maddie had delivered their daughter at home during a tropical storm, he and two of his brothers had nearly been killed in a boating accident, and then came the latest disaster with Janey's near-fatal delivery of P.J. And Maddie wondered why he was on edge?

He felt like he was constantly waiting for the next shoe to drop and send his life spinning out of control again. And now this… His mother had said it was nothing to worry about, but he couldn't recall the last time she'd summoned all five of them—by themselves—to talk about something.

The next morning, Janey pulled up to the house as he got out of his truck, so he waited for her.

"Hey, brat."

"What's this all about?"

"Your guess is as good as mine."

"Are you worried about whatever it is?"

"Hell yes. They don't just summon us like this unless it's something big."

"She said it was nothing to worry about."

"I worried anyway."

"Yeah," Janey said, "me, too. I'm kind of afraid to go in there. Part of me doesn't want to hear whatever it is."

"I agree." He unlatched the gate and held it for his sister as she went ahead of him. The scent of his mother's roses filled the air as he followed Janey into the house, where they were greeted by the smell of coffee and something cooking.

"She's making food," Janey said. "This is a big deal."

"Why do you say that?"

"She always cooks when she's worked up about something."

"You don't think they're splitting up, do you?" Mac asked.

"That would count as something bad, and they said it wasn't bad." She gave him a little shove to move him toward the kitchen.

"Hey, guys," Linda said when she saw them coming. "Coffee?"

"I'll have some," Mac said.

"None for me," Janey said. "I'm avoiding caffeine while I'm breastfeeding."

"Don't say breastfeeding around me," Mac said. "I can't take it."

"I have extra-big breasts right now," Janey said, "and I use them to feed the baby I had after lots and *lots* of sex with your best friend."

"I hate you."

"You do not."

"No, I actually do hate you."

"Why does Mac hate Janey now?" Grant asked as he came in with Evan.

"She's talking about her big breasts," Linda said.

"And all the sex she had with my best friend before she got pregnant," Mac added.

"I hate her, too," Grant said.

"Me three," Evan said.

Janey beamed with pleasure. "I've got them all hating me before noon. It's just like old times, Mom."

"Are we hating on Janey?" Adam asked as he came in and went straight for the coffee. "What's the occasion?"

"She's talking about her breasts and her sex life," Grant informed his brother.

"Count me in on the hate," Adam said, guzzling black coffee.

"Rough night?" Evan asked him.

"Great night. Abby and I got engaged."

"That's fantastic news," Mac said. "Congrats."

Janey kissed Adam's cheek. "I love when my brothers marry my best friends. Thank you for that."

"Anything for you, brat," Adam said.

"*Cuz it's all about Janey*," the four brothers said as one.

"Awww, you guys..." Janey dabbed at her eyes dramatically. "I'm just feeling the love today."

"When's the big day?" Grant asked between bites of the banana bread Linda had set out for them.

She stood over a pan full of scrambled eggs and another with fried potatoes. Mac's grumbling stomach reminded him he'd been too wound up to eat earlier.

"And don't say Labor Day," Grant added, "because I'm getting married then."

"You guys set a date?" Janey asked. "Finally!"

"Yes, we set a date, and don't make a thing over how long it took. Steph was dealing with some crap from her childhood. We talked it out and set a date."

"I'm glad for you," Evan said. "I know you were wondering what was up with her not wanting to talk about the wedding."

"Speaking of weddings," Mac said, "Maddie and I want to throw a surprise wedding for Ned and Francine."

"A surprise wedding?" Linda asked. "How exactly does that work?"

Mac outlined his plan to help their dear friend Ned and Maddie's mother get their happy ending.

"That's an amazing idea," Janey said. "I love it."

"They will, too," Linda said with a smile for her oldest child. "Francine said something to me recently about dreading all the planning that comes with a wedding. When are you thinking about doing it?"

"Maybe the weekend after Laura's wedding? I wanted to check with all of you to make sure you're available. Ned would want us there."

"That works for me," Janey said.

The others agreed.

"Great, I'll keep you posted," Mac said.

"And let us know how we can help," Linda said.

"We will."

Footsteps on the stairs preceded their father into the kitchen. "Good," Big Mac said. "You're all here."

"Now maybe you can tell us what this is about," Adam said. "You said it was nothing to worry about, but I worried anyway."

"Me, too," Mac said.

"You worry about everything," Evan said teasingly.

"The burden of being the oldest is a heavy one," Mac said in an intentionally grave tone. "You wouldn't get it."

"Oh shut up," Grant said with a groan. "Do you ever get tired of listening to yourself?"

"No," Mac said. "Not really."

"So listen up," Big Mac said. His serious tone put Mac immediately on edge. "I have something I want to tell you, and I want you to listen to the whole thing before you say anything."

"You're not sick, are you, Dad?" Janey asked in a small voice, airing Mac's greatest fear.

"No, sweetheart, nothing like that. I promise. Mac and Grant, you were at the marina yesterday when a woman came to see me."

"What woman came to see you?" Adam asked.

Big Mac looked at Linda, who seemed to nod in encouragement. "It turns out the woman who came to see me is my daughter, Mallory."

His words were met by stunned silence as a thousand thoughts cycled through Mac's mind in the span of a few seconds.

"*Your daughter?*" Evan asked. "You have another daughter? Where's she been all this time?"

"In Providence with her mother, who recently passed away and finally told her who her father is. Mallory came here to meet me with no intention of disrupting my life. If you know me at all, and the five of you know me as well as anyone does, you'll understand there was no way I was going to let her walk away like I'd never met her."

Grant held up a hand to stop his father. "Start at the beginning. Who's her mother? And I assume you knew her *before* you met Mom?"

Big Mac's brows narrowed at the implication he might've been unfaithful to their mother. "Yes, son. I dated her before l met Mom."

"Sorry," Grant muttered.

"I dated her mother for a few months the winter before I met Mom. Her name was Diana Vaughn. She died recently and left a letter for Mallory, giving her my name and where she could find me."

"So up until then, she had no idea who her father was?" Adam asked.

"No. Neither of us knew."

"Wow," Grant said. "That must've been shocking."

"To say the least," Big Mac said. "And I'm fully aware that it's shocking for all of you to hear you have a half sister you never knew about, but I'm asking you to meet her, to give her a chance—"

"*Meet* her?" Janey asked, seeming panicked by the thought. "When?"

"She'll be here in a few minutes."

"I'm out," Janey said, her chin quivering. "I'm sorry, Dad, but I can't do this right now." She rushed out of the room, and the screen door slammed behind her.

"Brat," Mac called after her. "Wait."

"Let her go, son," Big Mac said. "I'll talk to her later." He looked at each of his sons, who were unusually somber in light of the bomb that had been dropped on them. "Does anyone else wish to leave before she gets here?"

Mac wanted to go. He had no desire to meet the sister he'd never known he had. He liked his life—and his family—exactly the way it was. However, the thought of disappointing his father in any way had him holding his tongue and remaining seated on a barstool when he really wanted to bolt the way Janey had.

One by one, his brothers demurred when their dad asked if they wanted to leave. When Big Mac's gaze landed on him, Mac shook his head.

"I appreciate this." His father made eye contact with each of his sons. "More than you know."

CHAPTER 22

Linda served up eggs, potatoes and toast, which Mac ate because he was hungry, but every bite required effort to get the food past the lump in his throat. How could he feel so threatened by someone he didn't even know? Under normal circumstances, any time he and his three brothers were in the same place at the same time, the insults would be flying, the laughter loud and raucous.

Today the four of them ate in silence as their mother stood watch over them and their father paced nervously.

"She doesn't have anyone," Linda said softly. "Her mother was her only family."

"Is Dad going to require proof?" Mac asked. "He has assets to protect."

"I don't need proof," Big Mac said.

"Dad, seriously," Mac said, "I know you think everyone is as upstanding as you are, but that's just not the case."

"First of all," Big Mac said, "I appreciate your concern, but I don't require proof."

"Dad, come on," Grant said. "Anyone in this situation would be a bit skeptical."

"I understand, but when you meet her, you'll see why I don't need proof. I also knew her mother quite well and have no reason to believe she'd lie about such a monumental thing."

"People lie all the time about monumental things," Evan said tentatively.

"Indeed they do," Big Mac said. "I don't believe this is one of those times."

"Boys, follow your father's lead on this," Linda said. "I promise you no one is more skeptical than I was, but when you meet Mallory, you'll see what we saw."

Big Mac sent his wife a grateful smile.

"So you're okay with this, Mom?" Adam asked.

"Okay with it?" Linda asked with a laugh. "What do you expect me to say to that? We were both surprised—shocked—to hear your father had a daughter he never knew about. But I don't blame him, if that's what you're asking. He didn't know. If anyone is to blame, if that's the word you want to use, it's Mallory's mother, who made the choice to keep your father's daughter from him for nearly forty years. She's gone now, though, so there's no point tossing blame around. All we can do is manage the situation we're in."

"That's very Zen of you," Evan said. "I wouldn't have expected you to be so chill about finding out Dad has another kid."

"I'm sorry if I've disappointed you by not flipping out," Linda said with a grin for her youngest son. "One thing I've learned is that life tosses you challenges you never see coming. The only thing you can control is how you react to those challenges. I choose not to make the sudden appearance of a daughter your father never knew he had into a marriage crisis."

"You see why I love her?" Big Mac said.

Mac was slightly relieved to hear that Mallory's appearance wasn't going to cause a rift between his parents, who'd always been solid as a rock.

The doorbell rang, ending the moment of levity.

"I'll get it," Big Mac said.

They heard him exchanging greetings with her and inviting her in. Though he'd seen her yesterday, everything was different now, so Mac held his breath as anxiety flooded his entire body. This sister he'd never known he had was older than he was. If his parents planned to open their arms and welcome her into their family, as it seemed they were going to do, he would no longer be the oldest sibling. He loved being the oldest and had always embraced the responsibility he felt toward his younger siblings, even if they chafed against his need to be the boss.

Would the arrival of this woman change the entire dynamic of his family? That thought caused the kind of panic he hadn't felt since the sailboat accident.

Their father came into the kitchen with a dark-haired woman. Knowing what he knew now, Mac took a much closer look at her than he had the day before. And then he saw it—the shocking resemblance to the picture his father kept on his desk of their grandmother as a young woman. No wonder why he hadn't required proof.

"This is Grant, Adam, Evan and Mac," Big Mac said. "Boys, this is Mallory Vaughn."

Each of them shook her hand as they tried to pretend they weren't staring at her.

"Janey couldn't be here this morning," Big Mac said. "You can meet her another time."

"It's so nice to meet all of you." Mallory seemed to be battling her emotions. "I know this must be so weird for you, and I'm sorry about that."

"You look just like our grandmother," Evan said.

"I wondered if you all would see it, too," Big Mac said.

"I saw her picture yesterday," Mallory said. "It was... Well, you can imagine it was rather overwhelming. I've wondered for so long about my father and his family, and to see that I so closely resemble his mother..." She wiped at a tear. "Sorry. I was quite determined to get through this without getting emotional, but it's not every day a girl meets four brothers she didn't know she had."

Mac didn't want to like her. He *really* did *not* want to like her. As he had that thought, he could hear Maddie's voice in his head telling him to grow up and get over himself.

"Once you get to know us," Grant said dryly, "you may wish you'd never met us."

The comment made everyone laugh, and Mac felt himself relax ever so slightly. Maybe this wouldn't be the cataclysmic event he'd imagined before she arrived.

"This is very true," Linda said. "One minute they're all standing around talking, and the next minute they're on the floor wrestling like ten-year-olds."

"Um, that's Adam and Evan," Grant said. "Not us." He gestured between himself and Mac.

"We're far too mature for that," Mac said, trying to rise to the occasion for his father's sake. There was nothing, absolutely nothing, he wouldn't do for his dad, and if that meant welcoming a sister he hadn't known he had into the family, Mac would find a way to do it.

"He likes to boss everyone around." Adam gestured to Mac with his thumb. "Just ignore him. That's what we do."

Mallory seemed to hang on their every word, making no effort to hide her fascination and curiosity.

"Despite their often poor behavior," Linda said, "we're proud of them."

"I feel like a crazy voyeur," Mallory said with a nervous laugh. "I have so many questions."

"Pull up a seat," Evan said, giving up his barstool for her to take his place.

"Are you hungry, Mallory?" Linda asked.

"No, thank you. I was a nervous wreck before I came over, so I didn't dare eat."

"How about coffee?"

"That would be great. Thank you."

Linda put a mug in front of her along with a creamer, sugar bowl and spoon.

Mac watched with fascination as Mallory put just a dash of cream in her coffee before adding two healthy spoonfuls of sugar—exactly the way he took his coffee. It was a coincidence, he told himself.

They waited on her, giving her time to collect her thoughts as she took a couple of sips of her coffee. "I'm an emergency room nurse. What do you guys do?"

The question seemed to break what remained of the ice, and the conversation flowed freely from there. Mac watched his father visibly relax when he realized his sons planned to make an effort where Mallory was concerned. If he could actually control the world, Mac wouldn't have chosen for this to happen, but it had happened, and he'd do what he could to make it easy for his dad.

"I run the marina with Dad, and I have a construction company on the island, too," Mac said when it was his turn. "I'm married to Maddie, and we have two kids, Thomas and Hailey, with a third on the way."

Seeming to sense he was the toughest nut in the bunch, Mallory smiled warmly at him. "I can't wait to meet them."

*

Somehow Janey managed to get herself home, where she found Joe and P.J. in the sunroom together, the baby asleep in his father's arms. The sight of them was all it took to trigger the tsunami of tears she'd managed to contain so she could get herself home.

"Janey, honey, what is it? Is something wrong with your parents?"

She dropped onto the sofa and curled up to him.

He wrapped his free arm around her and held her close.

Janey breathed in his familiar scent and that of her son, who'd had a bath in her absence.

"Baby, you're scaring me. What's wrong?"

"My dad has another daughter," she said between sobs.

Her dog Riley scooted across the floor, dragging his hind end behind him until he was close enough to nuzzle her.

"*What?*"

Janey patted Riley's head. "She showed up yesterday, out of the blue, claiming to be his daughter. And he's *happy* about it."

"Wait... Back up... She showed up from where?"

"Providence, I guess. Her mother just died and left a letter telling her who her father was. She came out yesterday to find him, and... And... I don't *want* him to have another daughter. *I'm* his daughter. He doesn't need her. And believe me, I know I'm being a total jerk, and I hate myself right now. But I can't help it." Sobs hiccupped through her, making her feel sick and stupid for being so emotional.

"Holy shit," Joe whispered. "What did your mother say?"

"She was all calm about it because Dad didn't know, and it happened before they met, so really, how could she be mad with him?"

"Still… They must've been totally shocked."

"They were, but they've had some time to get past that. They found out yesterday."

Joe kissed the top of her head and ran his hand up and down her arm. "I'm sorry you're upset about it. Did you get to meet her?"

"I left before she came. I just couldn't do it, and I feel so bad because I could tell Dad was disappointed when I left, but…I couldn't."

"Honey, listen to me. You just had a baby under extremely traumatic circumstances. Your emotions are all over the place. Your dad knows that. Don't be too hard on yourself. There's nothing you could do that he wouldn't forgive. You're his little girl."

Hearing that set her off again. "I won't be his only little girl anymore if he has another daughter, and yes, I do hear myself acting like an ass, but I can't seem to stop feeling this way. I had a violently negative reaction to hearing about her. I don't want her. I don't want a sister. I've got my brothers and Laura… I don't need her."

"You're shocked, and it's perfectly natural for you to feel threatened by something—or someone—who has the power to change your whole life."

"I don't want my life changed. I like it the way it is."

"I'm afraid you don't have much choice in the matter, honey, if your dad has decided to accept her into his life."

"He has! All she had to do is show up and stake her claim, and he's all excited to have another daughter. Like the one he had wasn't enough for him."

"Janey," he said, shaking silently.

"Are you *laughing* at me?"

"Of course I'm not."

"Yes, you are! There's nothing funny about this!"

"When you've had a little time to get your mind around it, you might feel differently."

"How do I get my mind around a *sister* I never knew I had?"

"What did your brothers say about it? I'm trying to picture Mac finding out he's not the oldest anymore."

"I don't know. I didn't stick around long enough to hear what they had to say."

"What's her name? This sister you didn't know you had."

"Mallory."

"That's a nice name."

"I guess." Janey reached for the baby that Joe transferred to her arms. "There's my little boy," she whispered, running her lips over his soft head and breathing in the baby-fresh scent. "I wish I hadn't run out of there the way I did."

"You can always tell your dad that when you see him."

"What if he's mad at me?"

"He won't be, Janey."

"I didn't know what to expect when they asked us to come over, but it certainly wasn't this." Her phone buzzed with a text message. "Can you get it out of my back pocket?" she asked, raising herself up.

"With pleasure."

His predictable comment made her laugh. "What does it say?"

"From Mac. 'Are you okay, brat?' Want me to write back to him?"

"Just say I'm fine, and I'll talk to him later."

Joe sent the text and put her phone on the table. "You know your dad is going to be over here wanting to talk to you. If he's not on his way already, he will be soon."

"I don't know what to say to him. I feel like a jerk for leaving the way I did."

"Maybe just tell him that. He'll understand, babe."

"I'm going to have to meet this person, aren't I?"

"The sister you never knew you had?" he asked with a teasing smile. "Yeah, you are."

*

Though he'd planned to go to the marina after the meeting at his parents' house, Mac found himself driving home instead. He needed to see Maddie. After two years of marriage, his need for her only seemed to grow exponentially every day, and he'd learned not to question it anymore. It just was. She'd know what to say to set him straight again.

He pulled into the driveway at the home he'd once surprised her with. Thinking about that day brought a smile to his face. After a brief time apart that damn near killed him, he'd gotten her back that day, and they'd been together ever since. Bounding up the stairs, he opened the sliding door and came to a stop when he saw her on the sofa holding Hailey as she slept.

Maddie gave him a quizzical look full of questions about what he was doing home early on a workday.

He went to her, took their sleeping daughter from her and walked his baby girl upstairs to her crib, where he tucked her in with a kiss. When he turned to leave Hailey's room, Maddie was waiting for him in the hallway.

Mac took her hand, led her to their bedroom and shut the door. "Where's Thomas?"

"At the beach with Tiffany and Ashleigh."

Mac put his arms around his wife and hugged her.

"What's wrong? You're freaking me out."

"Sorry," he murmured, his lips finding her neck. As he breathed in the scent of summer flowers, a sense of calm came over him. No matter what happened, he would always have her, and she was all he needed.

"Mac? Honey, what is it?"

"My dad has another kid."

Her entire body went rigid. "What?"

"Well, I guess she's not a kid anymore at thirty-nine."

"Start from the beginning. Don't leave anything out."

Mac told her about the woman who'd come to the marina the day before seeking his father and how she was actually Big Mac's daughter Mallory.

"Wow," Maddie said, exhaling a deep breath as she sat on the bed. "So you met her?"

"The boys and I did." Mac sat next to her on the bed. "Janey left before Mallory got there. She was upset."

"She loves being your dad's only daughter. Almost as much," Maddie said, glancing at him tentatively, "as you love being the oldest."

"Yes."

"Are you okay?"

"I guess. I mean there're certainly worse things they could've told us."

"Still… That must've been pretty shocking to hear." She took his hand and held it between both of hers. "So what's she like?"

"She's actually really nice. She's an emergency room nurse in Providence, and she looks just like my father's mother as a younger woman."

"So he's not going to make her prove it, then?"

"There's really no need to. The proof is in the picture. But you'll be glad to know I asked the same question."

Maddie leaned her head against his shoulder. "It's okay to tell me this upsets you. I'd totally understand."

"I know you would, and that's why I came to you when I should've gone to work."

"I'm glad you came to me. I'd always want you to do that."

"How're you feeling?"

"Pretty good today, actually."

"Is that so? And is it possible that we find ourselves completely alone in the middle of the day with a bed right here for anything that might come to mind?"

Maddie giggled softly. "What comes to mind?"

Always a believer in showing rather than telling, Mac guided her hand to the evidence of what he had in mind.

"I thought you were upset."

"I was, until I came home to you. Now it seems I have other issues on my mind that you could help me with."

"Was this all a ploy to gain my sympathies so you could ravish me in the middle of the day?"

The word "ravish" coming from her sent a bolt of lust to his already painfully hard cock. "That makes me sound so devious," he said while nuzzling her neck and ear. He tugged on the formfitting tank top that molded to her incredible breasts. She hated them. He loved them. They'd agreed to disagree on the matter. "What do you say? Wouldn't we be foolish not to take advantage of this nearly unprecedented opportunity?"

"What about work?" she asked, tipping her head to give him better access to her neck.

"Luke is there."

"Does he know where you are?"

"No, but he wouldn't mind." He eased her top up and over her head. "How long has Hailey been asleep?"

"Not long."

"Oh boy." Mac dragged his finger from her neck to the deep valley between her breasts, making her shiver. He loved that his touch did that to her. "That means we have hours." He kissed her. "And hours."

"Mac," she said with a nervous laugh, "I did have a few things I planned to get done today."

"Is it anything that won't keep until later?"

"No," she said with a sigh that sounded an awful lot like surrender to him. "It'll keep."

CHAPTER 23

Laura sat on the exam table, fidgeting as she waited for Victoria. She could hear her talking to other patients, her infectious laughter echoing in the hallway. While she waited, Laura became more and more anxious about the trip tomorrow, about Owen's withdrawal as the departure drew closer and about what would become of him—of them—if his father somehow walked away without being convicted.

The thought of that last possibility made her shudder with fear.

Since Owen had decided to go surfing, she'd left Holden with Sarah while she was at the clinic. Laura glanced at her watch to see that Victoria was running thirty minutes late, and with everything Laura still had to do to get ready to leave for a week, she hoped it wouldn't be much longer.

As she waited, the anxiety that had been with her for days now seemed to peak in a maelstrom of worries that involved her health, that of her unborn babies, Owen's well-being, the pending trial and the impact it might have on him and his mother, leaving the hotel in the hands of Shane and the summer staff as well as Stephanie and Abby, who'd offered to help while they were away, the dreadful way she felt most of the day and how would she ever get through the traveling, let alone the strain of the trial, without adding to Owen's worries?

By the time a tap on the door preceded Victoria into the room, Laura was about to spontaneously combust. "Hey, there! Sorry to keep you waiting. Things are crazy today." Victoria took a closer look at Laura. "Feeling okay?"

"Nauseated twenty-four-seven, but other than that, not so bad."

"Ugh," Victoria said. "All day every day?"

"Pretty much so in the last week, and we're leaving tomorrow for Virginia, and I need something to make it stop, if only for the week that we're gone."

"I thought you were dead set against medication for the nausea?"

"I was. I am. But there's no way I can go with Owen on this trip feeling the way I do now, and not going isn't an option. Desperate times..."

"Gotcha. I'd like to do a quick exam first, just to make sure everything is okay with the babies, and then we can talk about your options for combatting the nausea."

"Why did I know you were going to say that?" Laura asked as Victoria handed her a gown.

"I'm nothing if not thorough. Since you're wearing a dress, everything off but the bra."

When Laura stood up to comply with Victoria's instructions, the entire room seemed to swim before her eyes. She reached for the exam table to keep from falling.

"Whoa," Victoria said, taking hold of Laura's arm. "Has that happened before?"

"A few times."

"What's the urine output like? Normal or less than usual?"

"Probably a little less."

"And is it darker in color?"

"Maybe a little."

"Hmm," Victoria said. "Would you mind if I helped you get changed?"

"I don't mind."

With Victoria's help, Laura removed her dress and put on the gown. Once she was covered, she removed her panties as well. Victoria helped her onto the table and made her comfortable with a pillow and light blanket.

Victoria consulted Laura's chart. "You've lost weight since the last time I saw you and your BP is low. Have you been eating?"

"When I can, which isn't often. Everything makes me sick. Even the smells make me sick."

"I hate to say it, but I suspect you're a bit dehydrated. I'd like to consult with David and perhaps start an IV to get some fluids into you."

"How long will that take?" Laura asked, alarmed by the prospect of being sidelined when she had so much to get done.

"A couple of hours."

"I can't be here that long!"

"It's either that or I'm going to recommend you stay home when Owen leaves tomorrow."

"That's not an option." The thought of not being able to go with Owen had her eyes filling with tears that flowed down her cheeks. "I have to be with him, Victoria. I can't let him go through this alone."

With a hand on Laura's shoulder, Victoria said, "Let's get you fixed up so you can go, but you need to take it easy."

"I will. I promise. I'll do whatever I have to do to be able to go with him."

"Try to relax. I'm going to talk to David, and we'll be back to see you in a few minutes."

"I'll try. Would you mind handing me my phone from my purse so I can let Sarah know I'm going to be here a while? She has Holden."

"Of course. Here you go. I'll be right back."

She typed the text to Sarah: *Apparently, I'm dehydrated, so they're going to put me on an IV. I'll be here a couple of hours. Are you okay with the baby? I can try to find Owen if you have somewhere to be.*

So sorry to hear that! Holden and I are fine. Take your time.

Okay, thanks. Don't tell Owen I'm here. He has enough on his mind. I'll be fine once I get some fluid.

Please don't ask me not to tell him, honey. He'd never forgive me.

Hopefully I'll be back before he gets home.

Call if you need a ride home.

I will. Thanks.

Left alone with her thoughts, Laura couldn't seem to stop the tears from flowing freely. With her hormones all out of whack, the tears had been almost as annoying as the nausea. Dehydration was the last thing they needed with so many other worries to contend with, but she couldn't deny that she felt awful. Hopefully, Victoria and David could get her patched up enough to travel.

Whatever it took to be able to go with Owen. Staying home was not an option.

*

In need of some peace and looking for something else to think about besides the trial, Owen had taken to the waves. His grandfather had taught him to surf when he was eleven, and it was something the two of them had done together for years until his grandfather reached the point where the risk of injury was no longer worth the thrill of the ride.

Surfing with his grandfather had been among the highlights of a childhood short on happy memories. He and his siblings had lived for their summers on Gansett, the only time all year they were able to escape the horror of their home life. So many times he'd been tempted to tell his grandfather the truth about his father, but he'd always feared what would become of his mother, who had no annual vacation from her hellish marriage. Worries about her safety coupled with his father's threats of what would happen if they blabbed about their family's "personal business" to anyone resulted in Owen keeping his mouth shut.

With hindsight, he regretted that now. If only he'd trusted his grandparents, how different everything might've been for all of them. Of course he had no way to know if that was actually true, but he liked to think he might've changed the outcome somehow.

Watching the horizon, he gauged the swells and bided his time, waiting for the perfect curl. His grandfather had taught him how to tell the difference between a wave that would break too soon and one that would carry him all the way to the beach. With his eye on one such wave, he waited patiently, holding his position as the wave grew and gathered steam.

He paddled into position to grab the wave as it crested exactly where he expected it to, sending him on a wild ride to the beach that ended only when he bailed out. With adrenaline zipping through his veins, Owen reveled in the rush that was second only to the thrill of making love to Laura. Nothing was better than that.

Standing, he pushed his wet hair back from his face and saw Evan standing on the beach, gesturing to him. Carrying his board under his arm, Owen walked out of the water and onto the beach. “Hey, man. What’s up? Can you surf?”

“Not today.”

“What’re you doing here then?”

“Your mom called me.”

Something about the way Evan said that had Owen immediately on edge. What now? “What’s wrong?”

“Everything is fine, so don’t worry, but Laura is at the clinic and they’re putting her on an IV because she’s dehydrated. Your mom thought you’d want to know, and she thought I might know where to find you.”

Owen grabbed his T-shirt and towel from where he’d left them on the beach and put the shirt on without taking the time to dry off. He jammed his feet into flip-flops. “Thanks for coming to find me.”

“Let me take you.”

“I’m fine.”

Evan took hold of his arm. “Owen…”

Owen shook him off. “Let me go. I need to get to her.”

“I’m going with you whether you let me drive you or not, so you may as well let me drive.”

Owen grabbed his board and headed for the stairs that led to the parking lot where he’d left his Volkswagen Vanagon. “On that deathtrap motorcycle of yours? I don’t think so. I’ve got three kids to think about.”

“We’ll take your luxury vehicle. I’ll leave my bike here and get it later.”

“You don’t have to do that.”

"I'm doing it, so stop being such a pain in the ass. Were you always this much of a pain and I didn't notice, or is that just a recent development?"

"Recent."

Evan took the keys from Owen. "I'm looking forward to getting back to normal."

"Believe me, so am I." The bickering with Evan helped to take his mind off the unreasonable fear that had assailed him when he heard Laura was at the clinic. What if something was really wrong with her besides the relentless nausea? What if the babies were in jeopardy? What if he had to leave her behind feeling unwell while he went to Virginia? How would he ever do that?

"Stop thinking the worst," Evan said as he navigated the twisting, turning roads that led back to town. "She's going to be fine."

"How do you know that? Do you have psychic powers now?"

"First of all, she's a McCarthy, and we're a hardy people. Second of all, she's in very good hands with David and Victoria. Remember David? You know, the guy who saved my sister's life when she would've bled to death without him?"

"Yeah, I remember." It did make Owen feel better to be reminded of how highly skilled David Lawrence was, and he knew that Laura had nothing but the utmost faith in Victoria, too. The nurse practitioner-midwife had already seen Laura successfully through one difficult pregnancy. Surely, she'd get her through this one, too.

"I've got some news that'll take your mind off your own troubles," Evan said.

"What's that?"

"Apparently, I have an older sister no one knew about until yesterday."

"You wanna run that by me one more time?"

"My dad has a daughter he didn't know existed until she showed up at the marina yesterday with a letter from her recently deceased mother naming my dad as her father."

"Holy. Shit. What did your mom say? What did your dad say?"

"I guess my mom has been pretty cool about it. I mean, what could she say?

It's not like my dad had an affair and fathered a kid while he was married to her. He was with this woman before he ever met my mom."

"So she's older than you guys? The sister."

"Yeah, she's thirty-nine. Her name is Mallory, and get this—she looks just like my father's mother did as a young woman. It's uncanny."

"Wow, that's amazing. Are you like…weirded out to find out you have another sister?"

"Just a bit. Wasn't what I expected to hear, that's for sure."

"How did the others take it?"

"Pretty good, overall. Except for Janey. She left before Mallory showed up. She said she couldn't deal with it."

"She's had a lot going on lately. She's probably on overload."

"Definitely. But she also loves being the only girl in our family and plays the part to the hilt. If Mallory is going to stick around, it'll be a big adjustment for her. For all of us, really."

"Is she going to stick around?"

"I don't know what her plans are. She's a nurse in Providence, so I'm sure she has to get back to work at some point."

"But she'll be back?"

"I guess. You know my dad. He's going to want her around. He probably feels guilty that he didn't know about her before now."

"That's not his fault."

"Still…"

"Imagine having a kid walking around out in the world for almost forty years, and you don't know about her. It's got to be pretty crazy to find out about her after all this time."

"Yeah."

"You were right," Owen said.

"About?"

"This took my mind off everything for a few minutes, and I would've said that wasn't possible. Thanks."

"The sister I didn't know I had and I are happy to help." Evan pulled into the parking lot and cut the engine. "I know you've got a lot of heavy shit going on right now, but you're not alone with it, O. I hope you know that."

"Thanks for the reminder."

Evan handed him his keys. "I'll come in to see how my cousin is, and then I'll leave you alone."

With Evan following close behind, Owen went into the clinic and asked for Laura.

"I'll wait out here," Evan said to Owen as the receptionist led him back to her cubicle.

The first thing Owen noticed was how pale her face was. How could he have failed to notice that before now? Was he so wrapped up in his own issues that he hadn't noticed such an important thing?

She held out her hand to him. "Did your mother call you?"

He moved to the side of the bed and took her hand. "She might've, but I left my phone in the van. She called Evan. He came to find me."

"I didn't want to interrupt your surfing time. I know how much you enjoy it."

"Don't be silly. I don't want to be anywhere as much as I want to be wherever you are."

She blinked furiously but couldn't contain a flood of tears. "Damn it! Every freaking thing makes me cry, especially you when you're so sweet."

Leaning over the bed, he kissed away her tears. "I'll try to be mean and nasty going forward, then."

Laura reached up to try to bring some order to his hair. "You don't have it in you, and you're all sandy."

"Sorry." He tried to pull back from her, but she stopped him. "I came right from the beach."

"I don't care. I'm glad you're here."

"What're they saying?"

She gestured to the IV that was releasing a steady drip to a needle in her hand. "They're rehydrating me, and she's going to give me something for the nausea."

"That's exactly right," Victoria said as she joined them. "We're going to get her all fixed up for the trip."

"Are you sure it's safe for her to go?"

"As long as she takes it as easy as possible, she'll be just fine," Victoria said. "Once we get the nausea under control, she should start to feel a lot better."

"I thought you didn't want to take anything," Owen said.

"I didn't," Laura said, "until it got worse."

"I'd be recommending it at this juncture even if she wasn't asking for it," Victoria said. "The complications from dehydration can be far more dangerous for mom and babies than the meds will ever be. You have two options when it comes to meds. One is pretty reasonable. The other will run you about five hundred bucks."

"Which is better?" Laura asked.

"The more expensive one, of course."

"Then we'll take that one," Owen said. "Whatever she needs."

"Owen—"

"It's fine, honey. Don't worry about it." To Victoria, he said, "How soon can we get her on that?"

"The pharmacy would probably have to special order it, so we'll give her a shot before she leaves today and write her a script to fill when you get to the mainland tomorrow."

"Thanks, Vic," Laura said.

"No problem. We'll get you feeling much better soon. I'll be back to check on you soon."

"Shots and pelvic exams and IVs… Not what I expected today."

Owen winced. "You got the full deal, huh?"

"They're nothing if not thorough around here."

"I'm glad you got checked out before we left and that you're getting something for the nausea. I don't know how much more of that I could've handled, so I can't imagine how you must feel."

"Life with me has been a real thrill ride, nothing but nonstop puking, breeding and breastfeeding."

"That's not what I meant," he said with a chuckle as he kissed her. "I couldn't bear to see you go through that, and PS, life with you is indeed a thrill ride. Every single day."

"Sure it is."

"Are you for real right now? Do you have any idea how thrilling it is for me to be able to look at that gorgeous face every day? To know this incredibly strong and resilient woman loves me enough to go through this to give me not just one baby but three? It's a thrill ride, all right. The best ride I've ever been on in my life."

Once again, she blinked furiously but couldn't stop the tears.

He laughed as he brushed them away and then kissed her, consumed as always by the sweet taste of her lips. "Do you want me to call your dad and Shane?"

"No need for them to worry when you're here with me."

"I'm here, and I'm not going anywhere without you. Evan's here, too, along with some extremely interesting family news that you'll want to hear. Want me to get him?"

"Um, *yeah*. And hurry up about it."

Cheered by her saucy reply, Owen left her to go get Evan. As long as she was okay, he was, too.

CHAPTER 24

All day, as Janey took care of the baby and tended to a few chores around the house, she'd waited for him. During dinner with Joe, she'd expected to hear the doorbell followed by his booming voice calling her name. He would come. If she was certain of anything in her life, she knew he would come.

"You should call him," Joe said quietly after they'd bathed P.J. and put him down for the night.

"I don't have to."

"You're the one who left, Janey."

"It doesn't matter. He'll come to me. I know he will."

As she washed a few dishes, Joe put his arm around her. "I can do that. Why don't you get off your feet?"

"I'm fine. It helps to keep busy."

"You're not fine. You don't have to pretend with me."

"What difference does it make if I admit I'm upset? Will that change anything? Will it make my dad less disappointed in me than he already is?"

"I'm sure he's not disappointed. He's probably worried, but never disappointed."

"I acted like a twelve-year-old having a snit because her daddy gave someone else attention he should've been giving her."

"You were shocked. He's going to understand that. Don't you think he's shocked, too?"

A light tap on the door was followed by her dad's loud whisper. "Princess?"

Janey choked up at the sound of the familiar nickname. He'd called her that all her life until she turned nineteen and begged him to come up with something else.

"Go ahead, honey," Joe said as he kissed her forehead. "Go make things right with him."

Janey nodded, dried her hands and went to the foyer, where her dad was standing with unusual awkwardness, as if trying to gauge whether or not he was welcome here.

Her menagerie of special-needs dogs and cats surrounded her father, who gave each of them one of the treats he kept in his truck for them. Then Joe whistled and opened the back door, which had them all scurrying toward the fenced-in yard.

Janey walked straight into her father's outstretched arms, where the familiar scent of the aftershave he'd worn all her life nearly broke her. "I'm sorry. I don't know what's wrong with me. I shouldn't have left, and I should've called and... I'm sorry."

"Shhh. No apologies necessary."

"I acted like a jerk."

"No, you didn't. I sprang something extremely unexpected on you, and you weren't prepared to deal with it in that moment. Doesn't mean you never will be."

"I don't know if I'll ever be ready to share you with another daughter. That might be too much to ask of me."

"Janey, sweetheart... There'll *never* be another daughter for me like the daughter I've had for the last thirty years. Through no fault of Mallory's or mine, I was never able to hold her as a baby or feed her or change her diapers or brush her hair into pigtails or take her to dance class or watch her grow up and graduate from high school and college and walk her down the aisle or see her become an incredible wife and mother. I'll never get to do *all* of that with any other daughter but you."

"You're going to make me cry if you don't stop it."

"I'll never stop it. You know how I am."

Janey laughed even though a huge lump settled in her throat. "I acted badly today. I should've been more supportive of you."

"Today's a memory. You'll have other opportunities to meet Mallory, and I know she'd love to meet you. Your brothers seemed to like her well enough. Truly, there's nothing not to like about her. She's a nice person."

"I wouldn't expect anything else. She is your daughter, after all. Nice is in your DNA, but not mine, apparently."

"That's not true, Princess. You're one of the nicest people I know. Who was bringing home injured squirrels to nurse them back to health from the time she was the tiniest little thing? Who rescued a motley brood of pets that no one else wanted because they weren't perfect? Who's been taking care of her older brothers all their lives without them even knowing she was doing it?"

Despite her best efforts to control her emotions, a tear rolled down her cheek. She swiped it away.

"Who was the first to welcome Maddie into our family when people who should've been much wiser than you were still wondering if she was worthy of Mac? Who gave up her dreams to allow the man she loved to follow his?"

Laughing, Janey held up her hands. "Waving the white flag. I'm no match for you."

"I hope you see what I see when you look at yourself."

"I've made this all about me, and I'm sorry for that, too." She took him by the hand and led him to a sofa in the living room. "How about you? You must be reeling."

"A little bit. It's a shock for sure, but that's life. Shit happens, and we have to play the hand we're dealt. That's all we can do. I'm already blessed beyond all measure by the family I have, and now, to think… There could be more. That's how I'm choosing to look at it, and I hope maybe you can, too."

"I'll reach out to her. I'll do that for you. I'd do anything for you."

"I know, sweetheart, and I appreciate that."

"So you forgive me?"

"Nothing to forgive."

"What did you tell her about me?"

"That you have a new baby at home and couldn't make it this morning."

"Which was more than I deserved."

"Don't be too hard on yourself. You've had a lot going on. I don't blame you for being overwhelmed by one more thing. So don't blame yourself."

"Love you."

"Love you, too."

"We're good?"

"We're always good. Now, where's my grandson?"

"Sleeping like the angel he is."

"Can I see him?"

"Sure you can. Come on."

Taking his hand, she took him upstairs to the baby's room. They tiptoed inside to look down upon the sleeping baby. His bum was in the air under the blanket.

Big Mac raised a hand, silently asking if he could touch him.

Janey nodded.

Big Mac ran his hand over the baby's head and then smiled at her before they left the room. "That," he said in a whisper that was too loud to count as a whisper, "right there, made my day."

"He has that effect on people."

"Thank you for him, Princess." Her dad kissed her forehead. "I'll see you tomorrow?"

"Absolutely."

He went downstairs, and she heard him talking to Joe on the way out. Then Joe whistled for the dogs, who came in from the backyard and headed straight upstairs to their beds. Janey took the time to give each of them some attention as they went into the room they all shared.

Joe brought up the rear. "Everything all right?"

"It's better now."

"What'd your dad have to say?"

"All the right things. As always." She took a deep breath. "I've got a sister, Joe."

"So I've heard. What do you think of that?"

"I haven't the first clue what to think of that. He said my brothers liked her. That counts for something."

"Sure does. Maybe you will, too. Have you considered that possibility?"

"It's beginning to occur to me."

"How about you sleep on it and see how you feel tomorrow?"

She closed the small distance between them and put her arms around him. "Do I get to sleep just like this? With your arms around me?"

He hugged her tightly. "Every night for the rest of your life."

The baby monitor crackled to life as P.J. let out a wail. "Duty calls."

He kissed her. "I'll get him and change him."

"I'll be waiting for you." She took advantage of the opportunity to change into a nightgown and prepare the bassinette for the baby. They were slowly introducing the crib for naps, but he still slept close to them at night. For the first month, he'd had wicked day-night confusion that had him up all night and wanting to sleep all day.

Thank goodness that stage was over, and they were sleeping at least part of the night, even with at least one middle-of-the-night feeding. Joe was always willing to help with anything he could do. By the time he delivered the baby to her a few minutes later, P.J. had worked himself into a full-on rage that immediately subsided when she guided him to her breast.

"Mommy has magic boobies, buddy. I've been telling her that for years now."

Janey laughed, which dislodged the baby from her nipple. "Don't make me laugh. It makes him mad."

Joe ran a finger over the baby's cheek. "Imagine having a child out there in the world that you didn't even know existed."

"I can't. My dad has to be so spun up inside over everything he missed."

"Yet he still made time to come here and make things right with you."

"That's because he's the best daddy ever."

"And he always will be. That's one thing you can count on in this world."

"That's not the only thing." She nodded at him, asking him to come closer so she could kiss him.

"Oh no?"

"I can count on you, too, to keep me sane when I'm losing my mind over something ridiculous."

"This wasn't ridiculous."

"In the grand scheme of things, it was pretty ridiculous. After everything that happened when P.J. was born, I prefer to focus on my many blessings rather than obsessing about things that don't really matter."

"That's a nice goal, but you're still human, Janey, and something like this is going to throw you no matter how badly you'd like to think otherwise."

"I love you, Joseph. Thanks for always having my back."

"I love you, too, Jane Elizabeth. And your back is my favorite back in the whole world."

Wrapped in her husband's arms with her baby at her breast, Janey was at peace.

*

A somber group gathered at the ferry landing the next morning for the trip to the mainland. Laura's mind raced with all the details involved with leaving the hotel for a week or more. Shane had assured her she had nothing to worry about. Even though his construction season was short, he was taking a week off from the affordable-housing project to oversee the hotel in their absence. Stephanie and Abby would be helping, as would the eager group of young summer staffers.

Though she knew her brother was more than capable, Laura was still nervous about leaving the hotel in the midst of the busy summer season. However, she was determined to put those worries aside so she could focus exclusively on Owen, who seemed to be focused exclusively on her.

"How do you feel?"

"Fantastic," she said truthfully. Though neither of them had slept well the night before, she'd woken for the first time in months without the nausea and with more energy than she'd had in ages. "I feel like a new woman."

"I'm so glad." He eyed the open water outside the breakwater with trepidation. "Looks a little choppy out there. I hope you don't get sick."

"I won't," she said with more conviction than she actually felt. She'd been a victim of seasickness on nearly every crossing to the island for as long as she could remember. But the sickness had always been worth the payoff of seeing her beloved aunt, uncle and cousins. "Maybe the stuff Victoria gave me works for seasickness, too."

"Let's hope so."

"What's this? I thought you found puking women attractive?"

"Only one puking woman is attractive to me, and I think she's had enough with the puking for now."

"Yes, she has."

David arrived with Daisy, who had come to drop him off at the ferry. She approached Sarah and gave her a hug. "I'll be hoping and praying for a successful outcome," Daisy said.

"Thank you, honey," Sarah said.

The two women had bonded over their unfortunate histories with violent men.

"I wish I could come to support you," Daisy said. "But we're so crazy busy at work right now."

"Not to worry. I'll be well taken care of with this group."

Daisy hugged Sarah again and whispered something in her ear that made the older woman tear up as she nodded. Then Daisy hugged and kissed David and left them with a wave.

Frank handed ferry tickets to Laura and Owen, Sarah and Charlie, Blaine, David, Dan, Evan and Slim.

"Before we go," Sarah said, "I just want to thank you all for putting your lives on hold to help us. It means a lot to me and to Owen that we have such amazing friends and family to rely on."

Charlie put his arm around her and squeezed her shoulder. Seeing them together filled Laura with happiness for her future mother-in-law.

"We're happy to do it, Sarah," Blaine said. "I think I speak for all of us when I say we want the bastard thrown in jail."

"You definitely speak for me," Owen said.

"Who's covering for you this week?" Laura asked David as they walked onto the boat behind Owen, who pushed Holden in the stroller.

"One of my former colleagues from Boston came out for the week. He sees it as a vacation. We'll see what he says after a week at the clinic."

Holden kept everyone entertained on the ferry, and the conversation flowed among the group as if they were going somewhere fun rather than to a trial for a man who'd beaten his wife and children.

"How you feeling, hon?" Owen asked as the ferry dipped and rolled.

"Remarkably fine. It's so weird to not feel nauseated."

"We probably should've done this a long time ago."

"Probably," she said with a sigh. "I just hate to take anything when I'm pregnant. You never know if you'll have a bad reaction or, God forbid, the babies do."

"So far, so good. I hope it continues to work. I've hated watching you suffer."

"Right back atcha. How're you doing?"

"Good. Better now that we're on the way. The thinking about it has been brutal the last few weeks. I just want to get it over with, and it feels like we're doing that now."

"What happens once we get there?"

"My mom and I have a meeting with the prosecutors at two o'clock today. Dan and your dad are going to come with us. It's just procedural stuff, so no need for you to be there."

"Your father won't be there, will he?"

"No." His tight-lipped expression told her a lot about how much he was dreading the inevitable confrontation with his father.

Curling her hands around his arm, she rested her head on his shoulder and watched his mother and Charlie play with Holden on the bench across from theirs. Holden laughed at everything Charlie did, which made Laura smile. He was going to be an incredible grandfather to their children.

"For what it's worth," Laura said, "I have a good feeling about all of this."

"I'm glad you do."

"My dad brought me up to believe that while our justice system is flawed, most of the time it works exactly the way it's supposed to. You and your mom have a strong case and a good team backing you. It's going to be okay."

"Keep telling me that, will you?"

"Any time you need to hear it."

Chapter 25

At one thirty that afternoon, Owen, Sarah, Frank and Dan took a cab from the hotel to the downtown Richmond office of the Commonwealth's Attorney. Tom Corcoran, the assistant commonwealth attorney who was prosecuting the case, met them in the reception area and welcomed them into a conference room.

Here we go, Owen thought, girding himself for battle.

Tom's warm personality and helpful attitude had been a source of comfort to Owen and his mother over the last year as they prepared for this day. They introduced him to Frank and Dan, and took seats around a big table.

Sitting at the head of the table next to a stack of file folders, Tom asked about their trip and made a big deal out of meeting Dan Torrington, whose reputation preceded him.

"A few developments since the last time we spoke," Tom told them after all the pleasantries had been dispensed with. "Chief among them is General Lawry's willingness to entertain a plea deal."

Owen felt like he'd been electrocuted. Was it really going to be that easy?

"What kind of a plea deal?" Sarah asked hesitantly.

"He's willing to consider pleading no contest to one felony count of domestic assault and battery in exchange for us dropping the other charges," Tom said.

"What does that mean?" Sarah asked, looking to Frank and Dan for an explanation.

"It means," Frank said, "he's not admitting guilt or claiming innocence. Basically he's entertaining the option as a way of avoiding the trial."

"Would there be jail time?"

"We'd ask for seven years and probably get five with three to serve and at least two years' probation after he's released."

Owen knew a moment of pure relief at hearing his father would definitely spend time in jail. That was all he'd wanted from the outset. "What do you think, Mom?"

"So," Sarah said carefully, "he wouldn't plead guilty, but he'd still go to jail?"

"That's right," Tom said. "Here's the thing, Sarah. We all know what happened that night. You know it, he knows it and the witnesses who've come to testify know it. But we have no way to prove that Mark Lawry was the one who actually beat you that night. We have your son's testimony detailing years of abuse at the hands of his father, but we also have no proof of that. No police reports or anything to back up his claims. It becomes a matter of your word and Owen's against Mark's. As I've mentioned before, Mark's standing in the community is also working against us. No one wants to believe a high-ranking air force officer is capable of this."

"You're recommending we take the plea, then?" Owen asked.

"If Sarah were my mother, I'd encourage her to take the deal to avoid the strain of the trial," Tom said.

"Frank? Dan? What do you think?" Owen asked.

"It puts him in jail for years," Frank said, "which has always been the goal."

"I agree," Dan said. "It's not a perfect deal, but it includes prison time, so I'd advise a client to consider it very seriously."

"Mom?"

After a long period of silence, Sarah said, "I appreciate what all of you are saying, and I see the benefit of accepting the plea deal. But I want to hear him say he did it. I want him to admit, in public, that he beat me and our children while the rest of the world was holding him up as a hero. I want him to say the word *guilty*. If he's unwilling to do that, no deal."

"He's indicated he's unwilling to plead guilty."

"Then I guess there's no deal," Sarah said.

"You understand we have no guarantee of a guilty verdict, right?" Tom asked.

"I understand."

"He could walk free, Mom. Are you prepared for that possibility?"

"He may walk free, but everyone will know what he did, and that would be punishment enough for me."

"Then we're going to trial," Tom said.

*

"You should've seen her," Owen said to Laura that night in bed. "She was so strong and resolute. I was so proud of her."

"I don't blame her for wanting him to have to say the words in public. Do you?"

"No, I don't, but I sort of wish we could've taken the plea and made it all go away. We could've chosen not to be in court when he entered the plea and left without even having to see him."

"That might've been easier for both of you, but I'm sort of secretly glad that Sarah is sticking it to him. It's the least of what he deserves."

"I have an awful confession to make."

"What?"

"When I was a kid and everything was happening with my dad, I used to sort of secretly hate her a little bit. That she could stand by and let that happen to us. I blamed her, you know?"

"You were a child, Owen. How could you be expected to understand all the deeper issues that kept her tied to him?"

"I couldn't understand. I know that now. But then, I hated her. I hated her later for not leaving him when there was no reason to stay anymore. I thought she was weak and spineless and all sorts of other unflattering things."

"She might've been all those things when she was with him, because that's how she was able to survive. But since she left him, I've seen her strength and her resolve and her determination. All those qualities were in her all along. She just needed the opportunity to let them out."

"You're right about that. Today was the first time I truly understood just how strong she's always been, and I feel so bad for the way I used to feel about her."

"She wouldn't want you to feel bad. She'd tell you to put those unproductive emotions where they belong—in the past. She'd tell you all of it was your father's fault, not yours and not hers. She'd tell you she loves you more than just about anyone else in the world for what you helped her to endure. And I know all this because she's told me so, many times."

"I love how close the two of you have gotten."

"She's like my second mother, and I love her very much."

"She loves you, too."

Laura raised herself up and propped her chin on his chest, looking him in the eye. "No matter what happens at this trial, neither of you ever has to see him again, so you've already won."

"That's true."

"Take comfort in knowing that in all the ways that truly matter, this nightmare is already over for both of you. He's out of your lives, and he's going to stay out of your lives. When you see him tomorrow, remember that."

"I'll try to," Owen said, dreading the showdown that had been ten years in the making.

"And in the meantime," Laura said, straddling him and then leaning over to kiss him, "you really ought to take advantage of your fiancée's newfound burst of energy."

"Is that right?" he asked, thrilled to see her looking so well again.

She sank down on him, forcing every thought from his head that didn't involve her and the exquisite pleasure they found together. "Yes," she said with a sigh. "That's exactly right."

*

Mark Lawry was a lot smaller than Owen remembered. Or maybe Owen was just a lot bigger. Either way, the startling realization that he was now substantially taller and broader than his father provided a measure of calm that he hadn't expected to feel the first time he laid eyes on him again. The mean sneer was exactly as he recalled it, though, and was directed at him and his mother as they took seats in the courtroom.

He kept telling himself that his father couldn't touch him—in any way—unless he let him, and he had no plans to let him.

Owen wasn't at all surprised to see his father in full uniform, as if he wanted to remind the judge of who he was and how honorably he'd served his country. The judge would be hearing and deciding the case, as Mark had waived his right to a jury trial, putting all his eggs in the judge's basket.

Over breakfast, Dan had shown them the in-depth Associated Press story the *Richmond Times-Dispatch* had run that morning about the decorated air force general who would stand trial for domestic assault and battery. Dan had pointed out that because an Associated Press reporter had written the story, it would be picked up all over the state and possibly beyond. Any time a high-ranking military officer got into trouble of any sort, it was big news.

Owen pondered his father's likely reaction to the press coverage the trial was generating. He would be enraged and looking to blame everyone but himself for the mess he found himself in. Once upon a time, Owen, his mother and siblings would've paid the price for that.

His mother reached for his hand and held on tight, while Laura held his other hand. They held on through opening statements that detailed the charges against his father.

"You will hear from Mark Lawry's oldest child, who will tell you about a childhood marred by abuse and violence," Tom said. "The defense will portray Mark Lawry as an all-American hero, but Sarah and Owen Lawry will tell a different story. They'll tell you about a man who beat his wife nearly to death over undercooked chicken. You'll hear about a man who once broke his young son's arm in a fit of rage and then later had that same son arrested for assault when he dared to defend himself against his father's fists. They'll tell the truth as they lived it. Mark Lawry is a violent, vicious predator who belongs in jail, Your Honor. To allow him to walk free, wearing the uniform of the United States Air Force, is a travesty to everyone who has or is serving our country honorably."

Whoa, Owen thought. *Impugning his honorable service to the air force will make the old man mad as hell.* Sure enough, he caught a glimpse of his father's face and saw it was red and flushed. Good thing he and Tom weren't squaring off in a bar rather than a courtroom. Otherwise, Tom might get an actual demonstration of what Mark Lawry was capable of after that statement.

Sarah squeezed his hand, letting him know she was thinking the same thing. Her comical grimace nearly made Owen laugh out loud. He certainly hadn't expected to laugh this morning, but he had to admit it felt pretty damned good to have most of the power for a change. He and his mother had the truth on their side, and there was comfort in that.

Over the course of the morning, Tom called Slim, David and Blaine to the witness stand to testify to Sarah's condition the night she arrived on Gansett Island bruised and battered.

"Did Mrs. Lawry tell you how she came to be so egregiously injured?" Tom asked Blaine, who was the last to testify.

"Yes, she said her husband beat her after she served undercooked chicken for dinner." Blaine had worn his dress uniform to testify. "From what she said, a verbal altercation escalated into a physical confrontation that left Mrs. Lawry severely injured."

"The defense will ask how a woman so badly injured could've managed to travel hundreds of miles," Tom said.

"We all wondered that, too," Blaine replied. "Personally, I think she was fueled by fear and a desire to get to her son, where she knew she'd be safe."

"Objection," the defense attorney said. "Speculation."

"Withdrawn," the prosecutor said. "Nothing further."

Blaine held up well under questioning from the defense attorney before he was dismissed from the witness stand. The judge then called a recess for lunch.

As he watched the proceedings all morning, Owen's nerves had been stretched nearly to the breaking point. Laura had held his hand the whole time, her support never wavering.

"That went well," Dan said of the morning's testimony. "Slim, David and Blaine were very credible and held up well under cross."

Tom agreed when he joined them. "I'm feeling good about this. With Sarah's testimony and Owen's, we paint a pretty good picture of what went on."

"We still don't have anyone outside of our family who was aware that this had been happening for years," Owen said.

"I wish we did," Tom said frankly. "It would definitely cement our case. But I think we'll be okay without it."

The words "I think" didn't do much for Owen's nerves. He turned to leave the courtroom and thought he was seeing things when his grandparents appeared in the doorway. "Mom. Look." He directed Sarah's attention to the older couple waiting for them.

Adele wore her white hair in a stylish bob and was dressed to the nines in a red suit and heels. Her husband was tanned from spending his days on the golf course in Florida, but his twinkling blue eyes lit up with delight at the sight of his eldest grandchild.

"Oh... Oh wow."

"Who is it?" Laura asked.

"Adele and Russ." After working for them for close to a year, Laura certainly recognized those names.

"Did you know they were coming?"

"I had no idea, and neither did my mother."

Sarah was in tears as she hugged her parents. "What're you doing here? You didn't say you were coming."

"Of course we're here," Adele said. "We wouldn't be anywhere else." She hugged Owen tightly, surrounding him with the scent of Chanel No. 5 that took him right back to childhood summers on Gansett.

They all moved into the corridor, where Owen had the pleasure of introducing his grandparents to Laura.

"It's so lovely to finally meet you in person," Adele said as she hugged Laura.

"I'm so happy to meet you, too," Laura said.

While she chatted with his grandparents, Owen shook hands with David and Blaine, who were leaving to go home. "Thank you again for this. I'll never be able to tell you how much it means to us that you came."

"We'll be hoping for a positive outcome," David said.

"Keep us posted," Blaine added.

"I will."

"Hopefully, you'll be on your way home very soon," David said.

"Let's hope so."

They said good-bye to Sarah and left for the airport, where they would catch a commercial flight back to Rhode Island.

Frank came in pushing Holden's stroller and met Owen's grandparents, who made a huge fuss over the baby they'd heard so much about.

"There's a great diner across the street," Frank said. "Holden and I had some coffee there earlier."

"I'm starving," Sarah announced.

Owen was glad to hear she felt hungry, because all he felt was sick. Then his father emerged from the courtroom, coming to a halt when he encountered the gathering in the hallway. The look he gave Sarah had her shrinking right before Owen's eyes. Old habits died hard.

"Move along," Owen said to his father.

"Watch yourself, boy."

"In case you haven't noticed, I'm not a boy anymore, so you'd be wise to watch *yourself* and the way you talk to my mother."

"Still playing the role of the hero, huh?"

"Still playing the role of the dickhead, huh?"

"Move along, Mr. Lawry," Tom said. "You're under a restraining order that prevents you from contacting your ex-wife. This counts as contact."

"I'll move along, but you should've taken the deal, Sarah. You've got nothing against me."

"Move," Charlie said in a tone that forced Mark to take notice.

"What's it to you?"

"Keep talking, and you'll find out."

Sarah took Charlie by the hand. "Don't bother, Charlie. He's not worth it. Let's go have lunch." Sarah led him and her mother to the door.

As Laura and the others followed Sarah, Owen hung back. "Go away and leave us alone," he said to his father when the others were out of earshot. "You're nothing to us, and we like it that way."

"Your mother will come around," Mark said confidently. "She always does."

The statement had Owen laughing out loud. "Keep telling yourself that."

Laura came back to look for him. "Are you coming?" she asked.

"Yeah, I'm coming." As he walked away from his father, he felt the weight of the world lift from his shoulders. Mark Lawry no longer had any power over him, his mother or his siblings. No matter how the trial worked out, he couldn't hurt them anymore.

He took Laura's hand and smiled at her, feeling more like himself than he had in weeks.

"Is everything okay?" she asked, her expression filled with concern.

"Everything is just fine. It's absolutely fine."

CHAPTER 26

They returned from lunch to another surprise. His mother's old friend Eva Lewis was waiting for them.

"Eva?" Sarah let out a cry of surprise and delight as she hugged the other woman. "What're you doing here?"

"I read the story in the paper this morning. I told Bill I had to come."

"It's so good to see you! How long has it been?"

"At least five years, maybe more."

"You remember Owen, of course. This is his fiancée, Laura, and their son, Holden."

"Nice to see you again, Mrs. Lewis," Owen said.

"Look at you all grown up and so handsome."

"He is that," Sarah said with a proud smile for her son.

"I had to come," Eva said. "I read the story this morning, and the defense attorney said you didn't have anyone to testify that this had been going on for a long time. I can do that. I always knew. Bill knew, too. Everyone knew, Sarah."

Owen's heart ached as his mother looked down at the floor, her face flooding with shame.

"I've never had more arguments with my husband over anything than I did over what Mark was doing to you—and the kids. I wanted to report him, but Bill feared for his career. He regrets that now, and I wish I'd stood up to him and done the right thing. Let me do the right thing now. Please."

Sarah looked up at Owen, who felt a profound sense of relief at knowing the one thing they needed to shore up their case had just appeared in the form of his mother's old friend.

"I would appreciate that, Eva," Sarah said.

They introduced Eva to Tom, whose eyes lit up with pleasure at the news that Eva was willing to testify. "You're certain about this, Mrs. Lewis?"

"I'm absolutely positive."

"All right, then. Let's see what the judge has to say."

Court reconvened a short time later, and Tom asked for permission to approach the bench. The defense attorney accompanied him, and the three men conferred in whispers for several minutes.

The burger Owen had forced himself to eat at lunch sat in his stomach like a cinder block while he waited to hear what would happen. After what felt like an hour, the defense attorney returned to his seat to confer with Mark, who spun around to look at the gallery. When his gaze settled on Eva, he scowled, shook his head and said something else to his lawyer. Owen wished he could read lips. His father's shoulders slowly but surely lost the stiffness Owen had always associated with his military bearing. He seemed to sag in on himself as the attorney watched and waited.

The courtroom was completely silent. In the hallway, Owen heard the unmistakable sound of Holden's laughter. The joyful noise was a balm on the ache inside him as he waited to see what would happen.

After a fierce argument with his lawyer followed by an interminable period of silence, Mark nodded.

His attorney stood. "Your Honor, my client wishes to change his plea."

"Approach," the judge said.

Both attorneys walked to the bench to confer again with the judge.

Owen couldn't seem to breathe.

Laura gripped his hand.

After the attorneys stepped back from the bench, the judge cleared his throat. "The defendant has agreed to plead guilty to all charges."

The group around Owen erupted into cheers as the judge banged his gavel and called for order.

"The defendant will please rise." One by one, he read the charges, and one by one, Mark pleaded guilty to each of them. The judge set sentencing for one month from today and advised Mark Lawry to use that time to get his affairs in order.

His father had admitted his guilt and was going to jail. Owen leaned forward, his elbows on his knees. He couldn't move. He couldn't seem to breathe. He couldn't make himself believe it was actually over and neither he nor his mother had had to testify.

"O?" Laura said, her hand on his back. "Are you okay?"

He nodded because that was all he was capable of at the moment.

She gave him a little tug, encouraging him to lean on her, which he gladly did.

"I don't understand," she said softly. "Why would he plead guilty?"

"Because he'd rather go to jail than have the dirty laundry aired out in the press," he said haltingly. "Eva Lewis cemented our case. We've known the Lewises for years. Her husband was one of my father's subordinates."

"I'm so happy for you and your mom."

"So am I. I'm happy for all of us."

"Owen?" Sarah said.

He raised his head to look at her.

"Come here, son." She held out her arms to him, and he rose to hug her. "I can't believe this."

Owen didn't think he'd ever heard her sound so euphoric. She hadn't had much reason for euphoria during her dreadful marriage. As he held his mother, he locked eyes with his father, who watched them with a look of such abject hatred that Owen's blood went cold. "Let's get out of here, Mom. It's time to go home."

*

They were back on the island by sunset. While Laura took a shower, Owen brought Holden down to his favorite spot on the porch and chose a rocking chair that was separated from a livelier group at the other end of the porch. As he rocked the baby, he continued to process what had happened. His father had pleaded guilty. He'd been forced to take responsibility for the nightmare he'd inflicted upon his wife and children.

Owen would never see him again. Of that he was certain. They wouldn't attend the sentencing hearing because neither he nor his mother felt the need to be there when Mark learned his fate. He was going to prison. That was all that mattered to them.

Holden snuggled in closer to Owen, his sweet breath warm against Owen's neck. He and Laura could never believe how much heat that little body generated when he was sleeping. Owen rubbed Holden's back as they rocked, and a feeling of peace and contentment unlike anything he'd ever experienced came over him as he looked out over the town he now called home while holding the baby he loved more than life itself.

His emotions were raw and close to the surface tonight, threatening to spill over at any second. He'd managed to hold it together during the flight home during which everyone had been in high spirits—no one more so than Sarah. Owen had never seen his mother so happy.

"There you are," his grandmother said when she came onto the porch. She and her husband had hitched a ride home to Gansett with them and planned to stay until the wedding.

"Hey," Owen said. "Sorry. Were you looking for me?"

"All over the place."

"If I'm not upstairs with Laura, you can usually find me and my little buddy right here."

"You always loved this porch," Adele said as she took the chair next to his.

"What's not to love?"

"Indeed. I hadn't realized how much I'd missed it until we arrived earlier. And what you and Laura have done with the place! The pictures simply didn't do it justice."

"I'm glad you're happy with it. Laura must've asked me a thousand times during the renovation if Adele would be pleased with whatever decision we were making at the moment."

"Adele is very, *very* pleased—and not just with the hotel, which is spectacular. I'm also extremely thrilled to see you so happy and in love with such a wonderful young woman."

"She's quite something, isn't she?"

"Oh, Owen… She's incredible. I already loved her from all our phone conversations, but to spend time with her and to see how much she loves you…" Adele smiled and shook her head. "It does your old granny's heart good to know you have that in your life—to know you allowed yourself to have it."

"I didn't have much choice. She bowled me over from the first time I met her."

"I can see why."

"And PS, there's nothing old about my granny."

She laughed at that. "Whatever you say, you charmer." Adele zeroed in on the movement of his hand on Holden's back. "He's a sweetheart."

"He really is."

"I'm so glad you and Laura can focus on your wedding now and all the exciting things to come. The past is now officially where it belongs. Finally."

"It's such a relief, but it's also surreal. I never thought it would be resolved so easily."

"I'm not as surprised as I probably should be. Mark's ego is as healthy as it ever was, and there was no way he was going to let you, your mother *and* Eva drag him through the mud in public."

"Thank God she showed up when she did."

"He could've fought back against the two of you, and I bet that was his intention. But he couldn't do a thing about her, and he knew it. His goose was cooked the minute she walked into the courtroom."

"It's amazing when you think about it. All those years, I thought no one knew. I thought people were oblivious."

"They weren't oblivious. They were as intimidated by your father as all of you were. He was a powerful man with a powerful temper. No one wanted to cross him." She reached over to rest her hand on his arm. "I'm only sorry it took this long for someone to come forward on your behalf. It should've happened a long time ago."

"It doesn't matter now. All that matters is that it happened when it needed to, and now it's over."

Sarah came out to join them on the porch. She wore a pretty dress and had obviously spent time on her hair and makeup.

"Going out, Mom?"

"Charlie is taking me to dinner to celebrate."

"He's a nice man, Sarah," her mother said.

"Yes, he is."

"Will we be seeing you in the morning, then?" Owen asked.

Sarah blushed to the roots of her hair. "Honestly, Owen. Not in front of my mother."

Adele burst into laughter. "Oh for goodness sakes, Sarah. You're almost sixty years old and have seven grown children and a grandchild. Go have some fun while you're still young."

"In that case," Sarah said with a saucy grin, "don't wait up." She leaned over to kiss Holden's cheek and Owen's forehead and then kissed her mother.

Charlie arrived a few minutes later to pick up Sarah. They walked off arm in arm, his head tipped toward hers so he could hear what she was saying.

"Well," Adele said as she and Owen watched them walk away, "isn't that a sight for sore eyes?"

"You know it. They're great together."

"Do you think they'll get married?"

"Eventually. Once her divorce is final."

"And you'd be okay with that?"

"I'd be thrilled for them both. They've been to hell and back and made it through intact."

"As have you, my love. And now it's time to leave hell behind and wallow in the joy."

Since that sounded like a fine idea, Owen decided to take his grandmother's advice. It was definitely time for some joy around here.

*

The next two weeks flew by in a flurry of last-minute wedding details, while the bride and groom tried not to think about the fact that they'd yet to receive her divorce papers.

"What'll we do if they aren't here in time?" Laura asked Owen three days before the wedding.

"We'll go forward like everything is okay, and we'll do it again later, by ourselves, to make it official. No one, other than your dad, would need to know it wasn't entirely legit."

"Evan and Grace will need to know why we need them to sign something later as our witnesses."

"Then we'll tell them and no one else." Owen kissed her. "Try not to worry. It's all going to be fine. I promise." It wasn't an ideal solution, but neither of them wished to postpone the wedding.

The next night, Evan threw a bachelor party at the marina restaurant that turned into an all-nighter.

As he and Evan walked back to town early the next morning, Owen was still buzzed from the evening with most of his favorite men and an endless flow of liquor.

"What a fantastic time," he said again as they crested the top of the hill near Evan's parents' house and headed down the sidewalk that led to home.

"Glad you enjoyed it," Evan said. His voice was husky from smoking cigars and singing all night. His dark hair stood stiffly on end, the result of a beer shampoo compliments of his brother Mac.

"We kinda stink," Owen said.

"That means the party was a success."

"I can't believe I'm actually getting married *tomorrow.*" Later today, his sisters Katie and Julia would arrive, followed tomorrow morning by his brothers Jeff and Josh and his other sister Cindy. Only his brother John wouldn't make the wedding because he'd been unable to get out of work.

Though they kept in close touch, especially lately, Owen hadn't seen his siblings in a couple of years and was looking forward to their arrival.

"You ready?" Evan asked.

"To get married? Hell yeah, but only because I get to marry Laura. If it was anyone else, I wouldn't be so ready."

"If it was anyone else, you wouldn't be getting married."

"Well, duh. How about you? Ready to get married?"

"Absolutely. I hate that we decided to wait until January. That was a huge mistake in hindsight. I want to be married now."

"I hate that we're probably going to miss it since Laura will be too pregnant to fly by then."

"I know," Evan said with a groan. "I can't imagine getting married without you there with me."

"She wants me to go without her, but I don't think I can do that. You'll understand, won't you?"

"Of course I will, but I'll miss you. I wanted you to be my best man. You know that, right?"

"You have three brothers, Ev."

"So do you, and you still picked me to be yours."

"That's because..." Owen blamed the liquor for the surge of emotion, but in truth, he'd been an emotional mess for weeks now, ever since that day in the courtroom when he'd been officially set free from the past. "You didn't know it then, Ev, but the time we spent together in the summers, our friendship… It meant so much to me. It still does, but back then… There was no one else I would've asked."

"Aw jeez, man. You're gonna make me bawl like a girl."

The comment made them both laugh, which eased the knot of emotion that had settled in Owen's chest. He'd wanted to tell Evan that for some time now, and it felt good to have it out there. It was important to him that Evan know how important their friendship had been to him during an extremely difficult time in Owen's life.

"Laura wants us to play tonight at the rehearsal," Owen said. "You game for that?"

"Dude, I am *always* game for playing with you. Always."

They parted company at the pharmacy where Evan lived with Grace.

Owen shook his hand and gave him a bro hug. "Thanks for a truly memorable night."

"Entirely my pleasure."

"I'm still a little drunk and sloppy here, so you'll excuse me for what I'm about to say."

"No, I will not leave Grace for you. I told you that the last time you asked me."

"Shut up, will you?" Owen said with a laugh. "All I was going to say… Well, now it sounds doubly stupid since you want to leave Grace for me, but… I love you, man. I truly do."

Evan hugged him. "Love you, too. We all do. We're so happy to have you officially joining the McCarthy family."

He might've been drunk and sloppy, but he'd been overwhelmed with more emotion than he knew what to do with since his father's trial ended, and right now was no different. Before he made a complete fool of himself in front of Evan, he released his friend. "We must never speak of this again."

"Ever," Evan said gravely. "See you tonight."

"See you then."

"You aren't going to fall over or find some other way to injure yourself on the way home, are you?"

"Nope, I'm good. I'm really, really good."

Evan smiled and shook his head in amusement as Owen waved and headed toward the Surf and the home he'd found with Laura and Holden. A few early risers were enjoying coffee on the porch when he went up the front stairs and stepped inside. The reception desk was dark and quiet, as was Stephanie's Bistro and Abby's Attic. Both would open in a couple of hours to start another summer day on Gansett. Eager to get to his family, Owen took the stairs two at a time, stopping short when he found a large envelope outside their door.

He picked it up and brought it inside, going directly to the bathroom, closing the door so he wouldn't disturb Laura or Holden. Inside the envelope, he found a sheaf of papers and a note from Dan. "Thought this might make your wedding day a little more special. It took an act of Congress, but we got it done, and Slim flew the papers over last night. Congratulations and best wishes. Dan."

Laura's divorce papers.

Owen's knees went weak with relief and gratitude for the amazing friends who'd gone all out to make it happen in time for the wedding.

CHAPTER 27

Owen showered, shaved and brushed his teeth before sliding into bed with Laura. His intentions had been good—catch a couple hours of sleep before Holden woke them up. But then he caught the scent of her hair and felt the heat of her body, and the next thing he knew, his arm was around her, his leg was between hers and his face was buried in the silk of her hair.

"So you decided to come home," she said in a gravelly, sleepy-sounding voice that instantly turned him on.

"It was a tough call, but you know, Holden needs me, so I figured I'd better come back."

Her hand covered his, which was curved over the round bump of her belly. "I'm glad you did."

"Nowhere else on this entire planet I'd rather be."

"Mmmm," she said, her bottom snuggling back against his cock, which was suddenly and rigidly erect. "Looks like you brought me a present."

The unexpected comment made him laugh. "He shows up whenever you're close by." He kissed her cheek and every other bit of soft skin he could get to as his hand slid upward to cup her breast. Rolling her nipple between his fingers, he teased it until it was hard and tight. "Guess what was waiting outside the door when I got home?"

"What?"

"Divorce papers."

"Oh God! *Really*? They really came?"

"Thanks to Dan and Slim, who flew them over."

"Oh my God! That's the best news I've ever gotten." She let out a laugh full of happiness and relief that was infectious. Their wedding could proceed without anything standing between them and happily ever after.

He continued to tease her nipple until she strained against him.

"Owen..."

"Do you want me to leave you alone so you can go back to sleep?"

"Absolutely not."

"Have I told you yet today how much I love you and how much I can't wait to be married to you?"

"You just did."

He slid his hand down her side, over her hip and down her leg until he encountered the hem of her nightgown, which he eased up to her waist.

"Let me turn over."

"No, like this. Just like this." Owen removed her panties and tested her readiness, moaning when he found her slick and hot. "Were you thinking about me before I got home?"

"Maybe a little. I kept waking up looking for you."

Never in his wildest dreams had he ever expected to love a woman the way he loved her. And when she said things like that... "You'll never sleep without me again."

"What about tonight? We're not supposed to see each other before the wedding."

"Screw that. I'm not superstitious. Are you?"

"I have been in the past," she said. "I am Irish, after all."

"And now?"

"Screw it."

"I do love the way you think, Princess." Lifting her leg over his hip, he pressed into her slowly and carefully.

She squirmed, trying to get closer. "I'm sort of digging the way you're thinking right now, too."

He smoothed his hand down over the bump where their babies were and found the heart of her desire.

She gasped as he went deeper, and her head came back to rest against his shoulder. "Owen, God… Feels so good. So good."

"For me, too. Nothing feels better than this."

"And after tomorrow, we get to do this forever."

"And legally, too."

"Bonus." When he thrust farther into her, she groaned. "Speaking of bonus."

"Every time!" he said with a laugh.

"It's tradition now."

"All these complaints… It wears a guy down, I tell you."

"I've discovered it's almost impossible to wear you down—or out."

"Since you're going to complain no matter what, I may as well get my money's worth." Without losing their connection, he arranged her so she was on her knees, bent over a pile of pillows. Grasping her hips, he moved slowly at first, always concerned about hurting her.

"Good?"

"Mmm, yeah. So good."

"Ready for more?"

"There's *more*?"

He gave her a teasing tap on the ass that made her giggle. The sound was a balm on his wounded soul, which had finally begun to heal when she came into his life. "Such a brat."

"Soooo much more than your share."

"There it is. Now we can get really serious."

"We weren't already getting serious?"

"We were just getting started."

She laughed as she groaned, and then he showed her what he was capable of when he got really, *really* serious.

*

Lying with Owen in the aftermath of magical morning lovemaking, Laura had never felt so happy or content. He was back. Her Owen had come back to her a little at a time since the trial ended. With every passing day, he'd been less broody and withdrawn. Today, though, he'd laughed freely and loved fiercely. He'd faced his greatest fears and came out stronger on the other side. His demons had been exorcised once and for all.

"So the party was fun?"

"It was fantastic. So many laughs. Evan went all out."

"Would you expect any less?"

"Nope. He's the best."

"That's why he's the best man."

"Yep." He ran his hand up and down her arm, making her skin tingle the way it always did when he touched her.

"Do you have a little bit of gas left in the tank?"

His eyes opened. "Why? You want to do it again?"

"Not right now," she said, laughing. "I have something I want to show you before things get crazy around here."

"I've always got gas in my tank for you, Princess."

"I hope we're talking about the same kind of gas," she said dryly as she got out of bed to retrieve the photo album she'd located the night before.

"Ha-ha, very funny." He sat up against the pillows, watching her as she walked around naked.

Laura hated how ungainly she felt as her pregnancy progressed, but didn't dare move to cover herself because she knew he loved her au naturel. She brought the album back to bed and sat with him against the pillows.

"What's that?" he asked.

"The album from my first wedding."

"Oh."

"I know it may seem inappropriate to break this out the day before our wedding, but I've been thinking about something, and I wanted to share it with you." She flipped open the heavy embossed cover to a photo of her dressed for her wedding. Her hair was pulled back in an elaborate style that had taken hours to get just right. Her makeup had been professionally done and every detail seen to by a wedding planner with meticulous attention to detail.

"Wow," Owen said, gazing at the photo. "You look incredible. So beautiful."

"Thank you." Her throat tightened. "I wanted you to see this because that's not me. That's not the real me. The real me is the one you will see tomorrow. Far less perfect and far less polished, but all me."

"That's the only you I want, Laura."

"I know, and that's why there's no hair stylist or makeup artist or wedding planner this time around. There's only you and me and Holden."

"Which is all we need."

"Last time, with Justin, all of this felt necessary. I don't feel that way with you, and I wanted you to know how comforting it is that I can be completely myself with you—no pretense, no artifice, no charade. Just me."

"There's nothing you could give me that would mean more to me than that, Laura." He cupped her cheek and ran his thumb over her bottom lip.

His tenderness brought tears to her eyes.

"Could I see the rest of the pictures?"

"I didn't intend to show you the rest. I just wanted you to see that one."

"I'd like to see the others if that's okay."

She hesitated, but only for a moment, before she handed the album over to him. What did it matter now? He knew she didn't love Justin anymore—if she ever had to begin with. He knew she'd never loved Justin the way she loved him, and that was all that mattered to either of them.

Owen flipped through the pages, studying each photo with intense concentration. The wedding had been glamorous and elegant and classy—all the things she'd once thought mattered so much. Until her elegant classy marriage went up in flames a month after the "I do's."

"You're spectacularly beautiful," he said after a long period of silence. "I still can't believe you picked me to spend the rest of your life with."

"That day," Laura said haltingly, "I knew something was wrong. I didn't know what, but I knew it was wrong."

"I can see that in some of the pictures." He pointed to a photo of her with Justin. "You're glowing and radiant, but I still see the sadness in your eyes."

"I was sad, but I didn't know why then. I do now. It was because I was always meant to be with you, and I've known that for almost as long as I've known you. Please don't look at those photos and think that's what I really want. It isn't." She took his hand and brought it to her lips. "This is. You are. We are."

"I know, baby." He leaned over to kiss her. "I know that." Closing the book, he put it on the bedside table and then turned to face her, putting his arm around her. "Thanks for sharing that with me, and thanks for giving me the real you. That's always going to be exactly what I want."

"Thank you for accepting me as I am, for the incredible way you take care of me and Holden, and for giving up your carefree life to take on an insta-family."

"Best decision I ever made. I was thinking about that day recently, watching the boats leave and remembering last Columbus Day when the last boat left without me for the first time in years. I knew then that I was committing to forever with you, and I haven't regretted it for one second. I never will."

"I'm glad to hear that."

"You didn't wonder, did you?"

"Not really, but it's still nice to hear." With her hand flat on his belly, she kissed his chest. "I thought you'd be exhausted after being up all night."

"I'm too excited to sleep. My sisters get here today, the others tomorrow. We've got our rehearsal dinner tonight and the wedding tomorrow."

She was thrilled to hear him say he was excited. "And you're going to be facedown on the table tonight if you don't get some sleep."

"My little man will be awake soon."

"I'll take care of him this morning so you can sleep."

"I don't want to sleep when I can be with you guys."

"You get to be with us every day for the rest of our lives." She kissed him. "Close your eyes."

"Don't wanna."

"Owen..."

His devilish smile lit up his face. "Make me."

She lifted herself up and over him, kissing each eyelid until he closed his eyes and sighed deeply. "Now keep them closed."

He put his arms around her, bringing her down on top of him. "Stay with me. Can't sleep without you."

"Only until Holden wakes up."

"I'll take whatever I can get."

She placed soft kisses on his eyelids, his cheeks and lips, stopping only when she felt him begin to harden beneath her. "Don't even think about it."

"I don't have to think about it. Just happens."

"I'm out of here."

"No! I'll behave. I promise."

"That's an empty promise if I've ever heard one."

"Stay," he whispered.

Only because he kept his eyes closed did she rest her head on his chest, listening as his breathing deepened and his arms loosened around her. She stayed until she heard Holden stirring in his crib, and then she extricated herself from Owen's embrace, leaving him to sleep while she went to start her day.

*

"Oh my God!" Full-on panic seized Laura. "It doesn't fit!"

"Yes, it does." As Laura's maid of honor, Grace had been the epitome of calm and cool all day, and now was no exception.

"No, it doesn't! How could my belly have expanded that much in *three days*?"

"Um, you're pregnant with twins, and you've stopped puking seventeen times a day?"

"No one told me this would happen if I went on the meds!"

"Laura," Grace said with a giggle. "Are you listening to yourself? Would you honestly prefer to be puking and feeling like crap on your wedding day?"

"I would prefer that my dress actually fit."

"It doesn't fit?" Stephanie asked as she came in wearing an off-the-shoulder coral-colored dress that offset her dark red hair and deep summer tan. Along with Abby, Maddie and Janey, the girls would each wear a different style of the same color dress. Unlike the last time around, Laura had told the girls to pick whatever they felt comfortable wearing. They were gorgeous and would look beautiful no matter what dress they chose.

"It doesn't seem to want to zip," Grace said, confirming Laura's worst fears.

"What am I going to do?" she asked. "People will be here in an hour!"

In the mirror, she watched as Grace, Abby and Stephanie assessed the situation. The three of them had become Laura's closest friends in the last year, and asking them to be her attendants had been the easiest decision she'd ever made. As much as she loved the girls she'd grown up with in Providence, they were part of her old life now. She'd also asked Maddie because she'd been such a great friend and an incredible help with all of Laura's questions about Holden. Janey was the sister Laura had never had, and had been a bridesmaid last time, too.

"How would you feel about going backless?" Abby asked.

"Wouldn't that also mean going braless? That's not an option with these pregnancy boobs."

"I feel you there, sister," Maddie said, making them all laugh. Her breasts were substantial when she wasn't pregnant, and her jokes about pregnancy boobs were hilarious.

"If we cut it here," Abby said, "we can sew the excess fabric into a halter."

"And this can be done *in an hour*?" Laura couldn't believe she was actually considering this plan, but what choice did she have? The dress didn't fit. "Get Sarah. She sews! She'll know what to do."

"I'm going," Stephanie said. "Relax. It'll all be fine."

Laura laughed because what else could she do? And honestly, what did it matter? She could marry Owen in a burlap sack, and it would all be fine. The pictures would give them something to laugh about in their old age.

"You're awfully calm," Abby said. "You're not in shock or something, are you?"

"Nope. I'm good." Trying to imagine her bridesmaids taking scissors to her dress on the day of her first wedding had Laura giggling madly. She would've lost her shit if this had happened then.

"Should we call Victoria?" Grace asked, her brows furrowed with concern.

"No! I'm really fine. I'm just laughing at how ridiculous this is."

"It's going to be fine," Abby assured her.

"I know that, which is why I'm laughing. At the end of the day, I'll be married to Owen. Who cares what my dress looks like?"

"She's going into shock," Grace said.

"I'm not. I swear." Laura tried to be convincing, but she couldn't stop laughing.

Stephanie returned with Sarah, who'd brought her sewing kit and a sharp pair of scissors that Laura recognized from the kitchen.

Her stomach fell when it registered that they were actually going to *cut* the gorgeous white silk dress.

"Let me see it," Sarah said.

The other girls stepped aside to give Sarah room to work.

"What's going on?" Adele asked when she joined them.

"Dress disaster," Laura told Owen's grandmother. "Compounded by a rapidly growing set of twins."

"Oh no," Adele said.

"Not to worry," Sarah said confidently. "I know just what to do."

Since she couldn't contain her burgeoning waistline, Laura decided to have faith that her new mother-in-law would take care of it.

CHAPTER 28

With an hour to kill before his sister's wedding, Shane McCarthy decided to go for a swim. He could shower and get dressed in ten minutes, and with the hotel overrun with wedding guests and preparations, the beach was the one place he could hope to find a few minutes of peace and quiet.

He was thrilled for Laura—and Owen, a terrific guy who'd become a close friend to Shane since he'd moved out here to live with them at the hotel. However, Shane couldn't help but think about his own wedding day, three years ago now, and everything that'd happened since then.

He missed Courtney. He missed having a wife and a companion. He'd loved being married. Discovering his wife had a raging drug addiction had been the single most shocking moment of his life. Losing her and their marriage to that addiction had nearly broken him.

He still thought about Courtney every day, but he focused on the bad times so he wouldn't forget why he couldn't be with her. He rarely, if ever, thought about the good times. Floating on his back, looking up at the cloudless blue sky, he indulged in memories of better times, such as the day he'd married the woman he'd expected to spend the rest of his life with.

They'd had one great year before it all fell apart. Or at least *he'd* had one great year. All that time, she'd been battling a foe bigger than both of them. It'd begun with a routine surgery to relieve a compressed disk in her back.

He met her six months after the surgery, from which she'd fully recovered—or so she said. It had taken two years for him to discover that she was addicted to the pain medication she'd taken after the surgery. She'd kept her dependence on the meds well hidden from him, and by the time he'd uncovered the web of lies and financial ruin she'd left in her wake, he was nearly ruined, too.

His happy life blew up in his face during one twenty-four-hour period that still ranked among the worst days of his life—second only to the day his mother died when he was seven. Left shocked, despondent and nearly bankrupt, Shane had done what he could to get help for her. A year later, after months of rehab he was still paying for, she'd asked for a divorce and crushed him all over again.

What was that old expression? Fool me once, shame on you. Fool me twice? Yeah, he was an idiot, and she'd played him every way it was possible to be played by a woman. First by getting him to believe she truly loved him and then by lying to him about everything else that mattered.

So while he was truly happy for Laura and Owen, he was done with love and marriage and all that shit. He was happy to leave that to his sister and cousins, who'd fallen one right after the other in the last couple of years, leaving him and his cousins Riley and Finn still unattached. In his opinion, the three of them were the lucky ones.

He was about to swim for shore when a scream caught his attention. With the sun still high in the afternoon sky, it was difficult to see where the sound had come from. But then he heard thrashing and another cry for help coming from a distinctly female voice.

Shane swam in the direction of the cries while hoping this rescue mission wouldn't make him late for his sister's wedding. Following the sound of splashing and struggle, Shane swam faster until he reached the woman.

"Hey," he said, "relax. I'll help you."

Panicked, she latched on to him, her arms tightening around his neck as she climbed on to him.

Holy shit, Shane thought as he was sucked under water so quickly he barely had time to close his mouth before the water rushed over him. The woman had such a tight grip on him that he couldn't do a thing to help himself—or her. *Am I going to drown out here?*

They went down together, the darkness surrounding him. This could not be happening… With a sudden realization that he couldn't save himself and her, too, Shane began to fight back, pulling frantically on the arms that wrapped around his neck like a noose. His lungs began to burn for air, but he never stopped fighting until he managed to free himself.

Surging to the surface, he sucked in greedy breaths as his heart pounded and his head spun from the lack of oxygen. He looked all around him for the woman but didn't see her. Did he dare dive down for her and risk his own life again, or should he head for shore while he had the chance?

How could he leave her and live with himself if he did? His conscience won the debate, and after taking a huge breath, he dove under the water. He spotted her floating peacefully and grabbed for her, coming back with only the top of her bikini. He swam for the surface, took another breath and went back down, this time wrapping his arm around her middle and dragging her up with him.

Either all the fight had gone out of her, or she was unconscious. He suspected the latter as he dragged her with him to the shore, which now seemed like a mile away. Every muscle in his body ached from the effort to keep his head and hers above water while pressing forward against a strong current.

After what felt like an hour of epic struggle, his feet finally made contact with the sand. He shifted the woman so he had his arms under her back and legs and carried her onto the sand, where he deposited her carefully before collapsing next to her. He needed to make sure she was breathing, but he couldn't seem to catch his own breath.

Where the hell were all the people who were always on this beach? Rising to his knees, he glanced at her face, which was lost under a mask of blonde hair. His gaze traveled down to where her breasts were fully exposed. Summoning first aid training from years ago, he pushed the hair back, plugged her nose and opened her mouth to blow a steady stream of air into her lungs. He did that twice before she began to cough. He rolled her to her side when she began to vomit up saltwater.

Pushing the hair all the way back from her face, he gasped when he recognized Owen's sister Katie, whom he'd met the night before.

"Katie! Jesus! Say something. Are you all right?"

She coughed and gagged and dry-heaved. Then she began to sob uncontrollably.

Christ, what the hell should he do?

"Katie, it's Shane, Laura's brother. Can you speak?"

She kept her eyes closed but wrapped her arm around her breasts. "Lost my top."

"You almost lost your life! What were you doing so far out?"

"Riptide," she said, panting softly as tears continued to flow down her cheeks. "Thought I was going to die."

"So did I for a minute there."

"I'm sorry. Panicked."

"It's okay," he said, patting her shoulder awkwardly. "We're both okay."

"Thanks to you."

"I'm glad I heard you." Thinking of Owen losing his sister on a day that was supposed to be filled with happiness made Shane doubly grateful to have been in the right place at the right time. "Do you think you can walk?"

"I don't know. I'm shaking like a leaf, and I'm half-naked."

"Let me find my shirt. I'll be right back."

They'd landed quite a distance from where he'd started out, so he jogged down the beach on legs that trembled from the effort it had taken to swim to shore. He scooped up his shirt and towel and went back to where he'd left Katie.

"Here," he said. "Put this on."

She sat up and awkwardly worked her way into his T-shirt, which was huge on her. "You got quite an eyeful, huh?"

"I was far more worried about whether you were breathing than I was with ogling you."

She crossed her arms over her chest.

"Do you need a hand up?"

Shaking her head, she began to cry again.

Even though neither of them had the time, he sat next to her on the sand. As her shoulders heaved with sobs, he had no idea what to do. Thinking about Owen and what a great friend he'd been over the last year had Shane putting his arm around Owen's sister and offering whatever comfort he could.

"You're all right, Katie. Everything's all right."

"I almost killed us both—on the day your sister is marrying my brother," she said as sobs hiccupped through her.

"Since that would've thoroughly ruined their day, let's just be glad it didn't happen."

"I'm so sorry," she said between sobs. "I panicked. I was so scared. I've been swimming at this beach all my life and never had that happen."

"No need to be sorry. All that matters is that we're both safe. But we're going to have bigger problems if we don't get back to the hotel and get ready for the wedding."

"Oh God! What time is it?"

He checked his watch. "Twenty minutes till five."

"We have to go!"

"That's what I'm trying to tell you." He got up and extended his hand to her.

She took his hand and let him pull her up, swaying when she got her legs under her.

Shane put his arm around her shoulders to steady her. "Take a second."

She looked up at him with wet blue eyes. "You won't tell anyone about this, will you?"

He experienced a profound feeling of protectiveness for a woman he'd only known for a day. But it seemed like it had been much longer, knowing what he did about how she'd grown up. She seemed fragile standing next to him with her hair matted to her head and her eyes translucent from tears.

She was Owen's sister. Of course he felt protective toward her. He shook off the weird feelings and looked down at her. "I won't tell anyone, but we should get going."

Nodding, she began walking slowly toward the steep flight of stairs that led to the hotel. Her legs, he noticed, wobbled beneath her as she moved.

"How about a hand up the stairs?" he said.

"What do you mean?"

He turned his back to her. "Hop on."

"Oh, I couldn't. I'm fine. Honestly. I can do it."

Shane blocked the stairs so she couldn't proceed unless she let him help her.

"I said I could do it."

"And I said I wanted to help you."

"Haven't you helped enough? You saved my life after all."

"Yes, I did, so I would think that in your gratitude, you'd *allow* me to help you up the stairs. Now hop on."

"Fine, but you have to put me down right away. I don't want anyone to see me on your back."

He glanced at her over his shoulder. "Why not? I'm not exactly a convicted felon."

Her face fell, and he immediately realized what he'd said. "I'm sorry. I wasn't thinking."

"It's fine. He is a convicted felon, and he should be. It's just still kind of…new."

"I'm sorry."

She looked up at him. "Is the offer of a ride still good?"

"You bet."

"Let's do it, then."

Shane hoisted her onto his back, and even though his own legs still felt rubbery from the shock of nearly drowning, he managed to get them both up the stairs without further incident. He deposited her on the deck and waited to make sure she was steady before he let her go.

"Everything all right?" a voice inquired from one of the chairs on the deck.

They spun around to find Katie's grandmother watching them with keen interest in her wise eyes.

"Oh, Gran, you scared me. Yes, everything is fine. I fell asleep in the sun, and Shane was good enough to wake me. I'd better go hit the shower, or I'll look frightful at the wedding."

Shane wanted to tell her that there was no way she could ever look frightful, but he kept his mouth shut.

"I'll see you shortly," Katie said to both of them as she scampered inside.

Shane felt trapped by Adele's intense gaze. "I'd...ah, I'd better go get ready, too, or Laura will be looking for me." As one of Owen's groomsmen, he should've been with the groom half an hour ago.

"I saw what happened down there." She stood and came over to him. "I was about to call the rescue, but you beat me to it." She crooked her finger at him to bring him closer to her and then kissed his cheek, leaving him flabbergasted. "Thank you, Shane. I don't think this family would've survived losing our darling Katie, and I'm profoundly grateful for what you did."

"Oh, um... I just happened to be in the right place at the right time."

"Thank God for that. I won't keep you. I just wanted to say thank you from the bottom of my heart."

"You won't say anything, will you? We don't want to upset Laura and Owen. Not today."

"I won't say a word other than thank you."

"You're welcome. I'm going to hit the shower and get ready." Shane raced through the lobby and up the stairs to his room on the third floor. He shaved and showered in record time and donned the white linen shirt and khaki pants he'd been asked to wear as a member of the wedding party.

Emerging from his room ten minutes later, he encountered Katie in the hallway. Her hair had been washed and dried and hung in waves to her shoulders. She wore a floral dress that hugged all her curves and landed just above her knee, leaving her exceptional legs on full display.

"You clean up well," she said, breaking the silence.

"So do you—and you clean up quickly."

"I grew up with six siblings. I learned to be fast in the bathroom."

"You feeling okay?" he asked.

"A little shaky but otherwise okay, all things considered. You?"

"Same."

"Did I say thank you? I don't recall if I ever said that, and I should have."

"You did, and it's fine. I'm glad I was there when you needed help." He extended his arm to her. "How about we try to forget about it and have a good time at the wedding?"

"Not sure I'll ever forget it, but I'm all for having a good time at the wedding. The Lawry family is long overdue for a celebration."

"Then let's get to it."

*

Laura stood alone in her apartment, taking in her reflection in the full-length mirror Sarah had unearthed from the basement. Her future mother-in-law had produced a wedding-day miracle. She'd used material cut from the back of the dress to fashion a halter that looked like it belonged there. The designer would have a heart attack if she ever saw what they'd done to her creation.

Laura turned and took a good long look at her back on full display, covered only by the filmy headpiece Sarah had fashioned from tulle she'd found in the attic. Her mother-in-law was astonishingly resourceful, which she had credited to years of making Halloween costumes for seven children.

Laura hadn't planned to wear a headpiece, but she felt more comfortable with the tulle covering her exposed back.

A knock on the door preceded her father into the room. He stopped short at the sight of her. "Oh my goodness, love. Look at you."

"Good?" she asked with a smile for her dad.

"Exceptional. I've never seen you look more beautiful. You're positively glowing."

"Thank you so much for marrying us, Daddy. You know I wanted you last time, but Justin's mother pushed for the church."

"I know, sweetheart, and I'm much more pleased to be performing this ceremony than I would've been about that one. I love Owen. He's a man worthy of my beautiful daughter."

"Yes, he is," Laura said. "But don't make me cry. I don't want to be a mess at my own wedding."

"You couldn't possibly be a mess." With his hands on her arms, he placed a tender kiss on her forehead. "Close your eyes so you won't cry. I have something I want to tell you. Two things, actually."

"You're really going to do this to me, huh?"

"'Fraid so."

Laura smiled at him and closed her eyes as directed.

"One, I love you so very much. You and your brother are the best part of my life, and I'm incredibly proud of both of you. And two, your mother would be, too. She would've loved Owen, and she would've loved the woman you grew up to be. I wanted you to know that." The brush of his handkerchief under her eyes caught the tears that escaped despite her effort to contain them.

"Thank you for telling me that. I like to think she'd be proud of me."

"She would be, honey. Definitely. Now, are you ready to get married?"

"I'm very ready."

Frank extended his arm to her. "Then let's get to it."

CHAPTER 29

"Everybody out," Sarah said as she walked into the sitting room where Owen had gathered with his groomsmen. In addition to Evan and Shane, Adam McCarthy and Sarah's other sons, Josh and Jeff, made up the wedding party. Having all but one of her kids in the same place at the same time was a rare occurrence, and Sarah was loving every minute of it. "The mother of the groom wants a moment with her son."

Now that their father's trial was behind them, her kids had a lightness about them she'd never seen before. They laughed easier and smiled more often. It was like they finally had permission to be themselves now that Mark Lawry was out of their lives forever. She should've left him years ago, but hindsight was always twenty-twenty, and she was choosing to look forward rather than backward these days.

"You heard her," Owen said to his wedding party. "Hit the beach. I'll be right behind you."

Each of them kissed Sarah's cheek on the way out of the room. "What a handsome bunch of guys," she said to Owen when they were alone.

"I feel shaggy and overgrown next to them."

"You're neither of those things. You're gorgeous, and Laura is a lucky woman."

"I'm the lucky one, Mom."

"You both are, honey, and don't ever forget it."

"I won't. You look great. I love your dress."

"It's not too much?" she asked of the frilly, revealing lavender dress Tiffany had talked her into.

"It's perfect."

"Your father never liked it when I showed any skin." With a saucy grin and a wink, she added, "Charlie loves it."

Owen put his hands over his ears. "I can't hear you."

She laughed at the face he made.

"All kidding aside, I'm so glad you're happy with him. You deserve it more than anyone I know."

"I deserve it as much as you do, my love. What do you say we give ourselves permission to be happy from here on out?"

"I'm on board with that."

She picked up the one remaining coral rose boutonniere from the florist box on the table and held it up. "May I?"

"Please do. I had no idea what to do with that."

"That's what mothers are for."

When the rose was in place on his white linen shirt, she flattened her hands on his chest. "I love you more than you'll ever know. You and your little family and this magical hotel saved my life last year, and I'll always be grateful."

"We're equally grateful to you, Mom. You showed up just when we needed you most."

She smiled up at him. "Laura will be down any minute. How about you escort your mom to the beach."

He kissed her cheek. "It would be my pleasure."

*

The late-afternoon sun shone brightly as Owen accompanied his mother down the steep flight of stairs to the sand. Per Laura's wishes, everyone was barefoot.

Her mantra from the beginning had been to "keep it simple," which had been just fine with him.

His beloved sisters, Julia, Katie and Cindy, came down with Julia carrying Holden. Though they were twins, Julia had dark hair and Katie was blonde, but they had blue eyes in common. Cindy's hair was light brown, as were her eyes. She, Jeff and Julia favored their father's side of the family, while the rest of them were blond like their mother. His sisters smiled brightly at him as Julia handed over the baby to him. Owen kissed and hugged them. He was so damned glad to see them.

Holden wore the same white shirt and khakis as the other men in the wedding party and took in the proceedings with a curious expression on his adorable face.

Evan was doing double duty as Owen's best man while providing the music. The florist had placed two huge arrangements of tiger lilies, day lilies, daisies, roses and something Laura had told him was called "bird of paradise." Owen had wondered about Laura's decision to go with corals and oranges, but he had to admit the flowers were quite spectacular. He should've known Laura would get it just right. She always did. Their guests stood in a half circle around the flowers. Since the ceremony would be short and sweet, they'd skipped the bother of bringing chairs down to the beach.

The wedding party came down the stairs in pairs: Adam and Abby, Shane and Janey, Jeff and Stephanie, Josh and Maddie. As the maid of honor, Grace came down alone, and Owen watched Evan's face light up at the sight of her. Evan never took his eyes off his fiancée as she made her way to them in a coral dress that clung to all her curves.

And then Laura appeared at the top of the stairs, her arm tucked into her father's bent elbow, and everything else faded away. There was only her. There would only ever be her. Evan played an acoustic rendition of "Here Comes the Bride" as Laura came toward him, her gaze locked on his.

Owen couldn't seem to breathe until she smiled, and the knot of nerves in his chest became a feeling of pure joy, the likes of which he'd never experienced quite so profoundly before. His Princess... His love. His life.

The time they'd spent together ran through his mind like the best movie he'd ever seen, from the day he'd first laid eyes on her at her cousin Janey's wedding to finding her outside the Surf the next morning in the pouring rain to scooping her up off the bathroom floor when she'd been felled by morning sickness during her pregnancy with Holden. He'd been by her side when she gave birth to Holden and on the day they discovered their "surprise" pregnancy was twins. She'd stood by his side through the nightmare of his mother being beaten by his father and provided unwavering support through his father's trial.

Every minute he'd spent with her had been the best time he'd ever spent with anyone, and he couldn't wait to have forever with her. They'd already had good times and bad, sickness and health. Today they would make official what had been in their hearts for nearly a year now.

Frank extended his hand to Owen.

Owen shook hands with his new father-in-law. In the time they'd known each other, Frank McCarthy had been more of a father to Owen than Mark Lawry had ever been.

Then Frank joined Laura's and Owen's hands, kissed his daughter and stepped up to the front of the assembled group. "It is my very great pleasure to welcome you all today to witness the marriage of my gorgeous, wonderful, sensational daughter Laura to the love of her life, Owen Lawry.

"Owen, I could not have handpicked a man better suited to my daughter. You've cared for her and Holden with unwavering love and tenderness, and I thank you for that. I sleep much better at night knowing my daughter is well and truly loved by a man I admire and respect."

Frank's heartfelt words had Owen blinking back tears.

Laura squeezed his hand and smiled at him, settling his emotions as only she could.

"Owen and Laura have chosen to recite their own vows. Owen?" Frank reached for his grandson, and Owen transferred Holden into Frank's outstretched arms.

Laura handed her bouquet of orange flowers to Grace and then joined hands with Owen.

"I wasn't expecting your father to make me cry," Owen said, releasing her hand to brush at a tear on his cheek.

"He took me down earlier," Laura said.

"Glad it's not just me." Owen drew in a deep breath and gazed down at her gorgeous face. She looked up at him expectantly, waiting to hear what he had to say. He'd thought long and hard about this because he wanted to say it just right. "From the first day I met you, you've been my Princess, so beautiful and regal to look at, with a heart of pure gold under that elegant exterior. In the year we've spent together, I've known more happiness, contentment and peace than I experienced in my entire life before you. I thought I was happy until I found you and discovered I was merely existing. You taught me how to *live*, Princess, and that I get to live with you and love you every day for the rest of my life is the greatest gift I've ever been given. There's nowhere else in this world I'd rather be than right here with you. I vow to love, honor and protect you and Holden and the babies we'll have together for the rest of my life."

Holden let out a happy little squeal that made his parents laugh even as they both dealt with a flood of tears.

"Laura?" Frank said.

"I'm supposed to follow that?" She exhaled a deep breath as she looked up at Owen. "Like you, I was merely existing until I met you and found my home, my life's work and the love of my life all in one magical place. The year we've spent together has been the best of my life, too, despite the challenges we were forced to confront from the outset. You didn't care that I was expecting my ex-husband's baby. You didn't care that I was sick as a dog every day for the first six months we were together. You picked me up off the floor every morning and gave me absolutely no choice but to fall in love with you. And then you decided to stay with us, rather than go upon your merry way, living your life as the footloose and fancy-free troubadour you'd always been. You chose us, and you changed your entire life for me. For that I shall always be profoundly grateful, because, you see… I had no idea how I was going to live without you when you left. Now I don't have to. Now I get to spend every day with you for the rest of our lives, and there is truly and honestly nothing I want more than that. I vow to love, honor and protect you for as long as I live."

With his free hand, Frank mopped up tears. "I'd say you two got your revenge," he said to laughter from the equally tearful gathering. "Evan? Rings?"

"Oh crap," Evan said, sending a gasp through the group. Then he smiled widely. "Psych." He dropped the rings into Frank's outstretched hand and then took a turn with Holden.

"Not funny," Frank said to his nephew.

"Yes, it was," Evan replied with a cheeky grin.

Owen laughed at the exchange. He expected nothing less from his best friend than a joke in the midst of his wedding ceremony. Owen took Laura's ring from Frank and slid the simple platinum band she'd requested onto her finger. "With this ring, I marry you, Laura McCarthy."

She followed suit, sliding the same simple platinum band onto his finger. "With this ring, I marry you, Owen Lawry."

"By the power vested in me by the State of Rhode Island and Providence Plantations, I'm honored to pronounce you husband and wife. Owen, you may kiss my daughter, but keep it clean."

"Don't you dare," Laura said as she leaped into his arms and kissed him passionately right in front of her father, their families and friends.

What else could Owen do but kiss her back?

"That was *not* clean," Frank muttered when they finally broke apart, breathless and laughing from the sheer joy of the moment.

"It is one of the greatest honors of my life," Frank said, "to introduce for the first time, Mr. and Mrs. Owen Lawry."

Their friends and family broke into a rousing round of applause as Owen took Holden from Evan and reached for Laura's hand to walk toward the steps where they would greet their guests as they went up for the reception at the hotel.

One by one, their friends expressed their congratulations before heading up the stairs: David and Daisy, Jenny, Alex and Paul, Victoria and Shannon, Jared and Lizzie, Tiffany and Blaine, Luke and Sydney, Big Mac and Linda, Mac, Grant, Laura's Uncle Kevin and his sons, Riley and Finn, who looked a lot like Mac and Adam with their dark hair and mischievous blue eyes.

Owen had met them for the first time the night before, and though they were both still in their twenties, they fit right in with their older cousins and their group of friends. He'd heard Riley asking Janey if she still had a dog named after him, and Janey retorting that the dog had come with the name. To which Riley had barked in response. Finn planned to stick around for the rest of the summer to help Shane with the affordable-housing project he was trying to finish before the cold weather set in.

Riley and Finn hugged Laura and shook hands with Owen. "Thank you for taking her off our hands," Finn said.

Laura slugged him.

"Ow," Finn said, rubbing his arm dramatically. "That's not very bridal of you."

"She fights dirty," Owen said to high fives from his wife's younger cousins.

"I like him," Riley said.

"Normally, I do, too," Laura replied.

"We've got them fighting, bro," Riley said to Finn. "Our work here is finished."

Pleased with themselves, the brothers went up the stairs.

*

"They're too funny," Owen said to Laura's Uncle Kevin, who rolled his eyes.

"Positively hilarious." Ten years younger than Big Mac, Kevin had light brown hair and the McCarthy blue eyes. Like his older brothers, though, Kevin was funny and dedicated to his family. Owen had liked him instantly. "I can't take them anywhere. What'd they say this time?"

"Something about Owen taking me off your hands," Laura said.

"We are thankful for that," Kevin said gravely.

"Apple, meet Tree," Laura said, tipping her cheek to receive her uncle's kiss.

"Congrats, hon. So happy for you."

"Thanks, Kev. I'm thrilled you guys could be here. Where's Aunt Deb? Did she make it over this morning?"

Kevin's smile dimmed as he shook his head. "She couldn't come after all."

"Oh. Is everything okay?"

"That, my dear, is a story for another day. This is a happy day, and I'm so glad to be here with you and the rest of the family. It's been far too long."

"Yes," Laura agreed. "It has."

After Kevin had walked up the stairs, Laura said, "That doesn't sound good."

"No, it doesn't, but try not to worry about it today. Today's our day."

She leaned into his one-armed embrace. "Other than the day Holden was born, best day of my life."

"Mine, too, Princess." He kissed her forehead and then her lips. "Mine, too."

*

Kevin McCarthy trudged up the stairs, his heart heavy after his niece asked about his wife. He couldn't exactly tell her—on her wedding day—that Deb had left him for a younger guy. Yeah, he was that cliché. He couldn't tell Laura that her Aunt Deb wanted *more* than what she had with him, that she felt her life was passing her by and leaving her behind.

He'd begged her not to go, to consider counseling, to fight for their twenty-seven-year marriage. But his pleas had fallen on deaf ears, and now he was left to explain to his family why his wife had chosen to sit out their niece's wedding.

At the top of the stairs, he noticed his brother Mac waving him over to the bar, where he sat on a stool next to their oldest brother, Frank. He might've been able to dodge Laura's questions, but his brothers wouldn't be satisfied with evasions. Even knowing that, Kevin walked over to them, thrilled to see them, as always.

"Congratulations, Dad," Kevin said as he shook Frank's hand. "I think our girl got it right this time."

"I know she did. He's the best."

"I can see that," Kevin said. "Nice job on the ceremony, too."

"Best part of the job, especially when you get to marry your own kid."

"I bet."

"I have something I need to tell you, Kev," Mac said as he handed a bottle of beer to Kevin.

"That sounds sort of ominous."

"Actually, I'm choosing to look at it as good news. It seems I have another daughter."

"*What*?" Kevin's gaze shifted from Mac to Frank, who nodded.

Mac proceeded to tell him about Mallory and her mother, Diana, and how he'd found out about Mallory's existence.

"Oh my God," Kevin said. "How incredibly shocking. How are you feeling about it?"

"Don't shrink me, Kev," Mac said with a wink and a smile. His older brothers hated when he acted like a psychiatrist around them. Little did they know he could use a shrink of his own at the moment.

"I didn't mean to."

"I'm joking," Mac said. "It was shocking, at first, but I'm settling into the idea of another daughter."

"How are the kids taking it?" Kevin asked.

"Pretty well, all things considered. They know me well enough to understand that I'm not going to let her walk away and pretend like I don't know she exists. That's just not who I am."

"No, it isn't. Good for you. It's the right thing to do."

"I'm glad you agree."

"I'm looking forward to meeting my new niece."

"She'll be back in the next few weeks for a weekend. Maybe you can join us."

"I was actually planning to stick around for a while. I'm taking a little time off from work."

"Is everything okay, Kev?" Frank asked.

"It could be better."

"Are you going to tell us where Deb is?" Mac asked.

"I don't know where Deb is. She's left me for a younger guy, of all things."

"She left you," Mac said. "When did this happen?"

"Couple of weeks ago."

"And you're just telling us this now?" Frank asked.

"It's not something I really want to talk about, so I'm sorry I didn't call you to tell you my wife left me."

"I didn't mean it that way," Frank said, "and you know it. We'd want to be there for you, the way you're always there for us."

"I know," Kevin said with a sigh. He felt bad for snapping at Frank, because he knew his brothers would be concerned. "I'm all right. At least I will be. Eventually. If I'm being entirely truthful, this has been coming for a while now. I've known she was unhappy. I just didn't expect her to actually leave."

"I'm really sorry, Kev," Mac said. "How are the boys taking it?"

"We haven't told them yet. They think she's sick and sitting this one out."

"You have to tell them before they hear it from someone else," Frank said.

"I know. I will. Soon." The thought of telling his sons their mother had left him for another man made Kevin feel physically ill.

A gorgeous dark-haired woman approached them, and Frank's face lit up with a huge smile as he held out a hand to her.

"Lovely ceremony, Your Honor," she said with a warm smile for Frank.

Kevin watched in stunned amazement as Frank put his arm around the woman and she rested her arm on his shoulder. In all the years since Joann died, he'd never seen Frank with another woman.

"Thank you. Betsy, this is my baby brother, Kevin. Kevin, Betsy Jacobson."

"Nice to meet you," Kevin said, raising a brow in his brother's direction. "Speaking of holding out..."

Frank laughed and looked up at Betsy with unabashed affection. "It's a fairly recent development."

"Not so recent," Mac said with a teasing grin for the happy couple. "It's been going on for a while now."

Kevin experienced a pang of envy for the happiness his older brother had found after decades on his own. "You've got one of the good ones, Betsy."

"I know."

"Kevin just told us he's going to be sticking around for a while," Frank told Betsy.

"That's great," she said. "I look forward to getting to know you better."

"Me, too." Kevin looked forward to that and anything else that kept him away from the nightmare unfolding at home.

CHAPTER 30

After everyone had eaten the Caribbean-themed dinner that Stephanie's chef had prepared, Evan moved to the corner of the deck that had been set aside for him, his sound engineer, Josh, and two other musicians Evan had recruited to provide the music for the night's festivities. He plugged his prized Gibson Les Paul electric guitar into the small amplifier he'd brought from the studio. Behind him, the sun dipped toward the horizon in a blaze of orange and red and gold that would end in a spectacular sunset.

When he was ready, he stepped up to the microphone. "Yo, yo, yo, listen up to the best man." The spirited group fell silent and gave him their attention. "I go way back with these two. Laura, you and Shane were way more than cousins to us. You were our summer siblings when we were all little kids, and we loved spending that time with you. Owen has been my best friend since high school when we bonded over our love of music. The nights we get to play together are always my favorite. So it was a great honor when my best friend asked me to be his best man when he married my cousin. I've known you a long time, O, and I've never seen you happier than you've been since you and Laura got together. The two of you are great on your own, but you're spectacular together. I love you both, and I wish you all the best life has to offer. To Owen and Laura!"

As the guests guzzled champagne and toasted the happy couple, Evan played the opening chords of the song Owen had chosen for their first dance. "Laura left one big decision up to her groom, and that was choosing a song for them to dance to tonight. Are you two ready?"

"Here we come!" Laura looked giddy as she led her new husband to the space they'd left for dancing.

"Owen chose 'All I Want Is You' by U2 for their first dance." Evan played the chords and put everything he had into the emotion-driven song to give Owen and Laura an unforgettable moment. But the whole time, he had his eyes on Grace, hoping she knew he was singing for her, too.

*

"Perfect choice," Laura said with a happy sigh as she danced with her new husband.

"It says everything I wanted you to know today."

She looked up at him, loving him more than she ever had.

"What?" he asked, tuned in to her as always.

"Just thinking about how much I love you."

"I love you that much and more."

"I love you more."

He laughed and kissed her, which had their guests laughing and clapping as they clinked silverware against the crystal, looking for more kisses.

"How long do we have to stay?" he asked.

"It's our party. We can't just leave."

"Yes, we can."

"No, we can't."

"Yes."

"No."

"I'm the husband. What I say goes."

"And I'm the wife. If you want to get lucky later, watch your mouth, mister."

"I love when you chastise me." As he spoke, he pulled her in closer to him. "It makes me hot."

"Not now, dear. People are looking."

"Are we really married?"

"We really are."

"I want out of here. Soon."

"Another hour. Maybe two."

"I'm holding you to that, Mrs. Lawry."

*

The party was beginning to wind down when Charlie put his arms around Sarah from behind and nuzzled her neck. "Can we go?"

"I can't leave," she said as she shivered from the brush of his whiskers against her skin. "What'll my kids say?"

"They'll say, 'Look at our awesome mom going off to spend time with the guy who loves her. How lucky is she?'"

Sarah laughed at his shamelessness.

"I can't stop thinking about holding you and kissing you and touching you. I want you so badly, I'm on fire for you."

Sarah trembled from the rush of desire that accompanied his gruffly spoken words. They'd come very close to making love the other night, but she'd held back at the last minute, a decision she regretted almost as soon as she made it. All she'd thought about since then was when they might get another chance.

"Come home with me, Sarah. Please come home with me."

She took a quick look around the deck. Owen and Laura had walked down to the water to take some photos in the sunset. Holden was with Frank and Betsy. Katie, Julia and Cindy were talking to Riley, Finn and Shane. Jeff and Josh were sitting at a table with their grandparents, and her son John had called to speak to his brother earlier. He'd been heartbroken to miss the wedding and promised to come to the island for a visit soon.

Everyone she loved, present and accounted for. And the man she loved standing behind her, asking her to run away with him.

Sarah covered the hand he'd placed on her stomach and squeezed. "Let's go." She stopped only to ask Daisy to make her excuses.

Almost as if he was afraid she might change her mind, Charlie took her hand and led her through the kitchen to the parking lot in back where he'd left his truck. They drove to his house in silence, but the awareness of what they were about to do beat through her like an electric current.

Silently, he reached for her hand and linked their fingers. "I love you, Sarah."

He didn't say much, but what he said was always worth hearing. Now was no different. He'd said exactly what she needed to hear.

"I love you, too. I love how patient you've been with me, how sweet and how tender. Before you even knew why I needed it, you knew what I needed."

"You've done the same for me, you know. You make me feel hopeful again."

"That's a lovely thing to say."

They arrived at his house, and he released her hand after kissing the back of it. "Wait for me to come around."

Sarah watched him go around the front of the truck. He looked so handsome in the navy polo shirt and khaki pants he'd worn to the wedding. The door opened, and Charlie leaned across her to release the seat belt. He held out his hands to her and helped her out of the truck.

Inside, he poured her a glass of wine and told her to wait in the kitchen for just a minute.

Wondering what he was up to, she sipped her wine and tried to keep her nerves under control. Though she was several decades and seven children removed from her first time with a man, this felt like the first time all over again because it was her first time with Charlie.

He returned and extended his hand to her.

Sarah put down the wineglass and went to him.

He led her to his bedroom where he'd lit a dozen candles. "I wish it was the Ritz or something classy for you."

"I don't need that."

"I'd still like to give it to you, and soon enough I'll be able to."

"What does that mean?"

"I'm getting a settlement from the state to compensate me for the years I spent in jail."

"What kind of settlement?"

"A really, *really* big one," he said with a smile. "I'll be able to give you anything you ever wanted. You can have your choice of houses, vacations, things for your kids. Anything you want. Sky's the limit."

Sarah stared at him, wondering if she heard him correctly. "I…I don't know what to say."

"You don't have to say anything. You just have to let me spoil you because that'll make me happy. I want to give you everything you were denied for so many years. I want you to be happy and surrounded by the people you love in a home we pick out together. I want you to marry me and spend the rest of your life with me." He raised his hands to her face and kissed her softly. "Will you marry me, Sarah?"

"Yes, Charlie. Yes, I'll marry you."

"We'll go to the mainland this week to pick out a ring. Any ring you want."

"I'm not divorced yet."

"Who cares? I'm not going anywhere. Are you?"

"Where would I go when you're here?" Sarah surprised herself nearly as much as she surprised him when she tugged his shirt from his pants and lifted it up and over his head. She flattened her hands on his chest and kissed his neck.

"You looked beautiful today," he said.

"It's the dress. Tiffany talked me into it."

"The dress is gorgeous," he said as he lifted it up and over her head. "But *you* were beautiful, glowing with happiness as your son married his Laura. I loved seeing you that way."

"It was a very special day. I was glad you were there with me." Standing before him in only the bra and matching panties Tiffany had convinced her she needed, Sarah should've felt self-conscious. She wasn't young anymore and had given birth to seven children. But with Charlie gazing at her with affection and desire in his eyes, she couldn't be bothered with being self-conscious. He loved her exactly the way she was.

"Make love to me, Charlie."

He put his arms around her and held her close. "There's nothing I'd rather do."

*

"It's time to go," Owen said, his lips pressed against Laura's ear.

"Right this minute?"

"Right this *second*."

"Am I allowed to get my son?"

"Frank, Betsy and Shane are in charge of him for the night. They're upstairs as we speak, giving him a bath and putting him to bed. Shane is staying in our room with him tonight, and I set him up with a bedtime bottle and one for the middle of the night—just in case. Shane said to tell you not to worry. He's got this."

"You thought of everything."

"I wanted you all to myself tonight."

"And where are you taking me?"

"Come with me, and I'll show you."

"Shouldn't I at least kiss Holden good night?"

"Only if you want to feel bad if he cries when we leave. He's perfectly content with Uncle Shane and Grandpa."

"Don't we need to say good-bye to our guests?" Most of them were dancing up a storm to the music Evan and his friends had provided all evening.

"No, because we'll see them all tomorrow at brunch."

"There's a brunch?"

"My grandparents are hosting a brunch, and everyone is invited."

"That's nice of them."

He took her hand. "Come with me, my love?"

"Anywhere you wish to go."

Smiling, he held the door for her so she could go ahead of him into the inn. He took her hand and led her out the front door, down the stairs and across the street to the Beachcomber.

"You're taking me to the competition?" she asked playfully.

"As much as I wanted to spend tonight at our hotel, we're overrun with family there. I thought this would be better." He held the side door to the Beachcomber open for her and guided her up to the second floor, where he used a key card in a door at the end of the long hallway.

"Wait," he said when she started to go into the room.

He scooped her up and carried her across the threshold into the honeymoon suite, where hurricane lanterns provided soft light and rose petals had been sprinkled on the bed. A bottle of champagne was chilling in an ice bucket next to the bed.

"You planned ahead," Laura said, thrilled with the room and her new husband.

"Making plans still doesn't come naturally to me, but I wanted tonight to be special for both of us."

"This is perfect. Thank you."

"Now that I have you alone," he said as he removed the comb from her hair that held her veil in place, "I want a better look at this incredible dress."

"Let me tell you about this incredible dress and what it looked like before your mother took scissors to it an hour before the wedding."

"*Scissors*?"

"Yep." Laura told him the story of the dress, laughing at his reaction.

"Were you freaking out?"

"Not even kinda. All I cared about today was marrying you. The rest was just details."

"My mother really cut up your dress and made it fit an hour before the wedding?"

"She really did. Thank goodness she knew what to do." Laura patted her belly. "These two have blossomed in the last week."

"Probably because you're not sick all the time anymore."

"Probably."

"Well, I'm glad it worked out, and I never would've known the dress had been hacked up and put back together. I thought you looked incredible." With a wink, he added, "Way better than the first time around."

Laura laughed at his joke. "I hadn't planned to wear any kind of veil, but I also hadn't planned to have my back completely bare. Your mom found the tulle in the attic. She truly saved the day."

"And she snuck off with Charlie tonight."

"She did? Really? Who told you?"

"Daisy. Mom didn't want us to worry, but she also didn't want to make a big announcement about leaving."

"Good for them. She's like a teenager in the throes of first love."

"In many ways it is her first real love. What she had with my dad could hardly be called love."

"Well, she has it now, and that's what counts."

He nuzzled her neck as he wrapped his arms around her. "No more talk. I've been waiting forever to make love to my wife."

"By all means," Laura said with a bright smile. "Don't let me stop you."

He hooked an arm around her waist and lifted her into a passionate kiss.

She curled her arms around his neck and lost herself in his kiss, thrilled to have forever to spend with him.

Here Comes The Groom

A Gansett Island Short Story

"Tell me again why I gotta wear a tie ta this thing," Ned Saunders said as he tried to remember how to knot the damned thing. He hadn't worn one in years. "It's dinner at Maddie's house. Why's it gotta be fancy? I ain't fancy."

"Because Maddie said it's a dress-up dinner party, so we're getting dressed up. It won't kill you."

"Very well might," he muttered. He'd been in a foul mood for weeks now, and he was well aware that others were beginning to notice. His buddy Big Mac had called him out on it recently, asking him what had crawled up his ass and died. He was smack in the middle of an epidemic of weddings and engagements. Everyone was tying the knot except for him—and he'd waited the longest.

They'd been stymied every time they tried to set a date since Francine's divorce had been final. He'd pitched the idea of a surprise wedding to her, and she'd loved it. They'd even set a date for that, only to have Seamus and Carolina beat them to it.

Even Grant and Stephanie were finally getting married in a couple of weeks, and they'd been dragging their feet for a year now!

It wasn't fair. He'd been waiting more than thirty years to marry his gal. He was almost to the point of whisking her off to Vegas just to get it done. Except... He didn't want to do it that way. He wanted his people there with him, including her daughters, who'd become his girls since he'd been with their mom. He wanted their grandkids there and all their friends.

Tomorrow he was going to figure this out once and for all. They were going to set a damned date and stick to it. Let anyone try to stop them.

"Ready?" Francine asked.

He glanced at her and did a double take at how beautiful she looked. She'd had her hair done earlier in the day, and every one of her auburn locks was shining and gorgeous.

"What're you staring at?"

"I'm starin' at the gal I love. She takes my breath away."

"You charmer."

"I ain't feedin' ya bull, doll. I look atcha, and I get all tangled up inside."

Francine smoothed her hands over the lapels of his one good sport coat. "I feel the same way about you and our lovely life together. Every day I'm thankful you gave me another chance."

"Gave ya another chance," he said with a laugh. "As if I had a choice. Ya have my heart, doll. Ya always have."

She kissed him. "Let's go have dinner with the kids so we can come home and continue this conversation."

It still astonished him, even after more than a year of living together, that he got to come home with her every night and sleep with her in his arms after dreaming about her for lonely, empty decades.

Since they'd been forced to dress up, he broke out the vintage Cadillac he'd bought from the Chesterfield Estate for the drive to Mac and Maddie's house. They arrived to a mess of cars in the driveway, leading all the way out to Sweet Meadow Farm Road.

"I thought it was just us and the kids," Ned said glumly. He was hardly in the mood for another festive party with all the happily married couples in their lives.

"That's what I thought, too. They must've invited the whole gang."

"Great."

Ned held her elbow as they went up the stairs to the deck, where the gathered group tossed something at them and yelled, "Surprise." He held up his arm to protect his face from whatever was flying at him. Rose petals rained down upon them.

"Surprise?" Francine said. She turned to him. "It's not your birthday or mine."

Mac and Maddie approached them, holding glasses of champagne and wearing broad smiles. "It's not your birthday," Maddie said, kissing them both. "Welcome to your wedding."

Ned figured he'd heard her wrong until things began to happen all around him.

Frank McCarthy stepped forward with a marriage license for him and Francine to sign. Maddie and Tiffany signed as their witnesses.

Next came flowers for both of them, as well as Maddie and Mac and Tiffany and Blaine. Ashleigh, Thomas and Hailey finished out the wedding party he would've chosen for himself.

"I don't understand," Ned finally said when he could get a word in edgewise.

"You wanted to get married and couldn't find a date," Big Mac said, "so Mac and Maddie found one for you." Big Mac put his tree-trunk arm around Ned. "All you gotta do, old pal, is stand there and get married."

He was going to cry, goddamn it. Right in front of everyone. He was going to actually cry. Here, standing before him, ready to stand up with him and Francine, was the family he'd always wanted but never had. He spared a glance for Francine and discovered she was already crying.

To hell with it, he decided as he stopped trying to fight his way through the emotional wallop. "'Tis a heck of a thing ya've done here," he said to Mac and Maddie. "Thank you."

"So you're happy about it?" Maddie said. "I told Mac if you were mad, it was *all* his idea."

"It *was* all my idea."

Maddie patted his face indulgently. "Yes, dear."

"Well, it *was*."

"I'm very happy bout it," Ned said gruffly as he sniffed. "Never been happier bout anything."

"I *knew* you would be," Mac said with a big smirk for his wife.

Frank rubbed his hands together. "What do you say, Ned? Francine? Shall we do this? It's been a full week since I married Laura and Owen. I'm starting to get twitchy for another wedding."

"I ain't got a ring fer her," Ned said, feeling suddenly panicked. They were really going to do this. "I need a ring. She deserves a ring."

"Gotcha covered." Mac produced rings from his pocket. "We took the liberty of choosing these for you, but the store said you can return them if there's something you'd rather have."

"I don't know what ta say. Ya thought of everything. Ya even found a way ta get a tie on me."

"That was the hardest part," Maddie said, patting her new stepfather's chest.

Tiffany and Blaine hugged and kissed Ned and Francine.

"This is so exciting!" Tiffany said to her mother. "I almost told you about it five times this week!"

"I kept the secret," Ashleigh said to her grandmother.

"Yes, you did, sweetheart. I had no idea!"

"Places, everyone." Maddie clapped her hands. To Ned, she said, "You stay here with Mac and Blaine."

Ned let her position him where she wanted him. His heart was beating so fast he worried he might pass out or something equally embarrassing. But this was the moment he'd waited so long for, and nothing was going to ruin it for him or Francine. So he took a series of deep breaths, hoping to calm his racing heart.

He gestured to Big Mac. "Come ere."

Big Mac walked over to him. "I'm here."

"Stay. Need ya right here with me."

His best friend hugged him. "You got it, buddy."

Big Mac shook hands with Mac and Blaine as he joined them.

Looking around at all the faces gathered before him, Ned saw everyone he loved in this world. The five McCarthy kids, who'd grown up with him as their beloved adopted uncle, his buddies from the morning meetings at the marina and the friends like Luke Harris, who'd become family to him over the years. He wiped his eyes and tried to keep his emotions under control even as he realized he was fighting a losing battle.

Evan and Owen played gentle guitar music as Ashleigh and Thomas came outside, holding hands.

Ned loved those kids so damned much. He couldn't wait to watch them grow up and to spoil them the way any good grandfather would.

Next came Tiffany, looking gorgeous and elated as she preceded her equally beautiful sister Maddie through the door. Maddie carried Hailey in her arms, and the baby blew kisses that made his heart melt. Ned held his breath, waiting for Francine to appear, and when she did, she carried a bouquet of white flowers and wore a smile that stretched across her pretty face.

The sight of that face and that smile settled and calmed him. In a few minutes, she would be his wife, and they'd get the rest of their lives together. Nothing had ever made him happier than that did.

The rest of it was a blur. Vows were spoken, rings were exchanged, and Frank pronounced them husband and wife. Ned hugged her and kissed her—probably longer and deeper than was technically appropriate, but who the hell cared? Francine, *his Francine*, was finally his wife, and it was all because their kids had loved them enough to do this for them.

Standing hand in hand with his new wife, surrounded by the family he'd always wanted, Ned Saunders considered himself the luckiest man on earth.

ACKNOWLEDGMENTS

It takes a village to bring a book to market, and I'm so very lucky to be surrounded by a wonderful group of helpers. First and foremost on "Jack's" Team, my right-hand wing woman Julie Cupp, who runs the whole show so I can write. I have no idea how I ever did this without her. Thank you, Julie, my major domo! And to Holly Sullivan, who reads every word before anyone else does, I love you and I love working with you! My niece, Isabel Sullivan, helps me with EVERYTHING and brings her adorable "business associate," aka my grandniece Harper, over for regular visits that brighten my days. Isabel has also become a faithful reader of mine in the last few months, which makes me so happy. Love you, Bean!

Thank you to my one of my favorite BFFs, Lisa Cafferty, CPA, who has saved the day for me in every possible way since she joined our team in November. I am so relieved to have her expertise and sharp eye on the business side of the house every day. Nikki Colquhoun (Julie's BFF) takes on every task we throw her way with endless wit. I so appreciate her contributions. Another of my longtime BFFs, Cheryl Serra, has joined the team as our director of publicity. She's AWESOME and full of energy and good ideas—thank you, Cher!

Linda Ingmanson, copy editor in chief, drops everything for me any time I need her, and I so appreciate her sharp eye and her sense of humor. It's so fun to work with you, Linda, and I'm grateful for your contributions. Joyce Lamb is the last set of eyes on many of my books these days, and she is also terrific to work with. Kristina Brinton is the brilliant graphic designer who creates most of my self-published book covers, including *Gansett After Dark* as well as the three new covers we just did for *Maid for Love*, *Fool for Love* and *Ready for Love*. With that update, all the Gansett Island book covers are now Kristina's, and I'm truly thankful for her amazing work. My beta readers, Anne Woodall, Ronlyn Howe and Kara Conrad, are always happy to read for me, and I appreciate their contributions.

On the home front, my husband, Dan, does just about everything, which gives me so much more time to write, and I'm thankful to him for taking care of us so I can do my thing. My kids, Emily and Jake, are always supportive and understanding of what I've got going on, and I love the people they're growing up to be. They make me laugh every day, and I need that!

Sarah Spate Morrison, family nurse practitioner, is always willing to take a medical question—or six—and comes back with all the info I need to keep my stories as authentic as possible. I appreciate her help, and Sarah, happy birthday!

To my wonderful, amazing, incredible readers—you will never know how much I appreciate and enjoy you all. I read every one of your emails, your Facebook posts and your tweets, and you make me smile ALL THE TIME with your love for my crazy made-up worlds. You often ask me how long I'll continue to write Gansett Island books. I'll say the same thing I always do—as long as you love to read them as much as I love to write them, we're good. Love you all and thank you so much for making every dream I ever had come true.

xoxo

Marie

Other Titles by Marie Force

Contemporary Romances Available from Marie Force

The Treading Water Series

Book 1: Treading Water

Book 2: Marking Time

Book 3: Starting Over

Book 4: Coming Home

The McCarthys of Gansett Island Series

McCarthys of Gansett Island Boxed Set

Book 1: Maid for Love

Book 2: Fool for Love

Book 3: Ready for Love

Book 4: Falling for Love

Book 5: Hoping for Love

Book 6: Season for Love

Book 7: Longing for Love

Book 8: Waiting for Love

Book 9: Time for Love

Book 10: Meant for Love

Book 10.5: Chance for Love, *A Gansett Island Novella*

Book 11: Gansett After Dark

The Green Mountain Series

Book 1: All You Need Is Love

Book 2: I Want to Hold Your Hand

Book 3: I Saw Her Standing There (November 2014)

Single Titles

The Singles Titles Boxed Set

Georgia on My Mind

True North

The Fall

Everyone Loves a Hero

Love at First Flight

Line of Scrimmage

Romantic Suspense Novels Available from Marie Force

The Fatal Series

Book 1: Fatal Affair

Book 2: Fatal Justice

Book 3: Fatal Consequences

Book 3.5: Fatal Destiny, *the Wedding Novella*

Book 4: Fatal Flaw

Book 5: Fatal Deception

Book 6: Fatal Mistake

Book 7: Fatal Jeopardy

Book 8: Fatal Scandal (January 2015)

Single Title

The Wreck

Made in the USA
San Bernardino, CA
13 June 2014